The Beauty of Regret

Pamela Clark An.

First published in 2013

First edition

ISBN 978-0-9900244-0-8

Produced by Bookstore Santa Cruz
Photography by Reija Janneson Bolwell,
StudioR Santa Cruz
Printed in the United States of America

Visit our website at
www.thebeautyofregret.com

To my father –

Your footsteps led to the way ahead, but you were always a step behind for support. Thank you for dreaming my dreams with me.

Prologue
The Last Night

My blouse stiff with blood and the stitches in my shoulder screaming, I collapsed on the bed. Memories of the night he left me seven years before rushed into my mind.

We spent that night alone, speaking words that no longer mattered. The silence in between was loaded with the ticking of the clock. Our hands touched, but our fingers were already strangers, and the sticky hours melted into an unbearable thickness. At ten o'clock, we could no longer stand the waiting abyss. There was no turning back from his leaving, and I think we both wanted it over.

I will not cry, I thought. *I cannot stand this if I cry.*

But I did cry – the loss so intense and emptying that my sobs caught inside me and made no sound, not until the unwanted tears washed over my face. Will drew me tightly against him, pulling me into him and crushing me painfully until I could not breathe. His face was invisible through my tears, and I was never sure if I heard him tell me goodbye.

And then he was gone. His warmth drained from my body, and a cold eeriness crept in. I stood singly. I was one. My heart would not beat – until I remembered the winding road that would lead him away from me. I ran to the window and watched his lights disappear in the valley below, and with them the light he shed on my life. I remained there long after he vanished, listening to the weeping of my heart.

Lust is a sudden gust of wind that blows you over.

Infatuation is a flirting breeze that wraps you in its embrace.

Love is when the wind dies down.

Book One

Chapter 1

A Call to Africa – 1965

I was eighteen back then and a senior in high school when Will landed in Larkin Green. My assignment as part time Assistant Society Editor at our small town newspaper, The Herald, was to cover the travels of a British fellow named Will Kincaid. At the age of 21, he left college and Africa, took his savings and headed out to see the world. When the savings ran out, Will worked his way from country to country for three years, eventually finding his way to my seaside town. He showed up to the interview with a box of phalaenopsis orchids from the nursery where he was working. I think we were both startled when we met. He was gorgeous, older, and had a British accent, which seemed very worldly to me, and to him I must have looked like a child. The interview went well; the article went to print. That should have been the end, I guess, but it was really only the beginning.

Two weeks later, Will showed up on a Saturday night and asked me out for the following week. I was so flustered by this older man, and didn't know if my mother would approve, that I just kept changing the subject. He finally gave up and left. I felt awful. I knew I'd messed up, and I just couldn't get him out of my mind. I returned from school the next week to find my father had run into Will on a job. He recognized him from the article I'd written, called my mother and then invited him to dinner. Will showed up on our doorstep promptly at 7:00. Shortly after dessert, my mother suggested Will and I take a drive. It was a warm night, so we drove to the beach and walked out on a weathered pier to where the moonlight lit the ruffles of bay water. I remember talking a lot and laughing a lot. When we returned, Will politely thanked my parents for a lovely evening and delicious dinner, said goodnight and left.

A week and a half passed before Will called and asked me out. My mother, playing matchmaker, invited him to dinner again. Those dinners became a staple diet for Will, and there were times I wondered whether it was my sterling personality and quick wit that he sought, or my mother's wonderful cooking. After dinner, Will took me to see *The Pink Panther*. We stopped for a coke afterwards and then headed through the little valley of orchards to my home. Aware of the not-too-late hour, and suspecting my parents would still be up, Will suddenly pulled across the street and off the road beside an apple tree. He turned off the engine and, at snail's pace, leisurely put his arm behind me. It wasn't that I hadn't dated other guys, and I'd kissed my share of them, but this was seriously sensuous. At eighteen, twenty-four was pretty much uncharted territory. He leveled me with a knee-buckling stare and started inching me towards him. I was mesmerized by the slow motion of it all and must have looked like the proverbial deer in headlights. Fortunately that didn't stop Will, because when he lowered his head and placed his perfectly gorgeous, well-versed lips on mine, it was the most soul-shattering, body-melting, consciousness-draining experience I had ever had.

When the kiss ended, all I could think of to say was, "Definitely not compatible."

We were inseparable for the next seven months. Then Will's work visa expired, and he left the United States and my life to return home to Africa. We wrote to each other for three and a half years and then the letters stopped.

Chapter 2

Seven Years Later – 1972
The Letter

I smiled at the memories, and tried to focus on the presentation I was preparing. My Silicon Valley company's new technology, a state-of-the-art voice activated computer, was being presented in several key cities worldwide. As part of the systems team, I was slated to speak on the software at the upcoming rollout in Johannesburg, Africa. I wondered if I should try to find Will. It had been seven years since he left. I argued with myself for two days before finally writing him a letter. It was short and to the point; I would be in Africa for a technology conference, and if he were anywhere close by, maybe we could meet for coffee. I used his parents' address where he lived when we wrote to each other. At the last minute, after convincing myself that he had forgotten me and moved on with his life, I nearly tore up the letter. There was even some comfort in the thought that the address was no longer current and my letter might not ever reach him. I walked to the corner where a large white and blue mail box stood with its mouth closed. I hesitated, and then pulled down the defiant lip, guiding the envelope like a mother bird into the hungry orifice. I waited, but my fingers would not release the words they had written. "*No,*" a voice in my head warned. I stood staring at the gaping maw, fear and doubt nibbling at my resolve. What was I doing? Who pulled a band aid off a wound that might not be healed? I tightened my grip on the envelope, suddenly afraid the box would suck it out of my hand. Should I take the letter home and burn it, put it in my purse and think about it for a couple of days, mail it because, what the heck, why not? I supposed there was the possibility, after all, that Will might actually be happy to hear from me. I'm not sure why I finally released the letter, but I do remember listening to it slide down the metal throat and get comfy as it shuffled against the other mail down in the bowels of the box. Then I panicked. Could I fit my arm into the mail slot? How far down would I have to reach? What if I waited for the 3:30 a.m. pickup? The whole internal conversation was exhausting.

Chapter 3

The Post - Johannesburg Hospital South Africa

Will

I could feel the letter inside the large envelope underneath my mother's ornate handwriting. Probably another brochure from one of the hospitals up north peddling its state-of-the-art facilities. No surprise my mother had sent it. She was determined that I move closer to home once I completed my residency. I tossed it into my locker in the doctor's lounge on my way to the operating theatre.

The surgery lasted longer than I'd expected. It was dark out, and I was so hungry I could have eaten my scrubs. I grabbed a quick shower and dripped across the room. When I reached into my locker for a clean shirt, the envelope came with it and hit the floor. I sat down on the bench, one hand rubbing a towel over my damp hair, and stuck the envelope between my knees to rip it open. The stamps on the letter inside were strange, but the handwriting wasn't. I recognized it at about the same time my heart slammed against my chest. *Jackie.* Well, now I knew what my patients felt like when they had heart failure. It'd been a long time since I'd held one of her letters, and I sat, staring at the square whiteness, until the towel slid off my head and hit the floor. I didn't want to open the letter because it felt like once it was open, the room would fill up with a lot of feelings I'd put away for good - a long time ago.

I knew the first time I met Jackie that there was something between us. I can still see her sitting across from me in that little café booth where she interviewed me about my travels for her newspaper.

She was only eighteen. When she called to set up the interview, I could tell she was trying to sound very professional, and she blushed when I gave her the orchids I'd brought from the nursery where I worked. I liked the way she got caught up in my answers. She'd lose her nervousness and forget to take notes. When she realized it, she'd get a little flustered and sit up straighter, bite a nail and refer back to her list of questions. She asked more of her own than she had written on that list. But I wasn't about to get involved with anyone since I was heading out of town before long. My job at the nursery was only temporary. I just couldn't stop thinking about her. She must have thanked me four times for the orchids, and when she called after the interview to ask something she'd forgotten, she was kind of nervous and kind of sweet. So, after a couple of weeks, I threw caution to the wind. I drove out to her house to see if she might like to go out sometime. There were about fifty kids there partying. She seemed surprised to see me, and pretty uncomfortable, nervous I guess, with my showing up. I tried a couple of times to set something up, but she never answered. I took that as a "no" and left. Anyway, it didn't make sense to start something between us. I'd been traveling around the world for three years, and that quiet town was my last stop before heading home to Africa.

It probably would have ended that way if I hadn't run into her father two weeks later. He invited me to dinner. That was a stroke of luck – seeing Jackie again and those home-cooked meals. Jackie was easy to talk to, funny and a little standoffish, but I thought that was because she was unsure of herself. She was more naive than the other girls and women I'd met on my travels, but she had a sharp side, too. Her moral perspective about things, like how a man should treat a woman and honesty, they were important to her. It was hard for her to talk about her feelings, and she'd joke a lot whenever the conversation turned the least bit serious.

I liked her more than I wanted to admit, but after that night I didn't intend to see her again because I knew we'd get involved, not that I was much worried about myself. The other women I'd dated were more mature, more available and some prettier. None of them had been able to keep me from leaving straight away, not unless it was my idea. I'd been around a fair amount, tasted life. Jackie was innocent. I didn't see any point in complicating things for either of us. But I still couldn't get her off my mind. Two weeks later I stopped fighting the urge and asked her out. She told me on that date that she didn't think I was going to call, and for some reason I admitted that I didn't want to because I knew we'd get involved. She didn't say anything, just gazed at me for a second and then looked away. But that was Jackie, quiet about the things that counted. It took me a long time to get her to open up.

Now Jackie was coming to Africa. That's what I'd wanted, what I'd tried to convince her to do, seven years ago, but she chose college and a career instead. Yeah, she was coming, but it took a company conference to get her here. Just for a fleeting moment, I wondered if she'd had a change of heart. *Don't be daft.* She's probably married and has kids. Anyway, I don't have time or room in my life for… What was I getting all hot under the collar about? I threw the letter back into my locker fully intending to forget the whole thing. I just didn't feel hungry anymore. I spent the next two days snapping at everyone. It took a lot of energy thinking about not thinking about that letter. A week later, I wrote to Jackie.

Chapter 4

The Answer – San Francisco

Jackie

I pulled the airmail letter with its foreign-looking stamp out of my mailbox and slapped it against my chest. It took me four trembling tries to slide my key into the door's lock before dropping my purse and briefcase at the bottom of the stairs. Feeling for the first step with my hand so that I could keep vigil over the letter, I slowly lowered myself. In the upper left corner of the envelope were the printed words, *Will Kincaid.* I squinted, blinked, read the name once more to be sure, then sat staring at the envelope as if an unknown species of African fruit bat was about to fly out. At last, I released the breath caught in my lungs, and unable to stand the suspense any longer, slid my finger under the flap.

Dear Jackie,

When I saw your name and return address, I admit, I was a bit shaken. To be honest, I thought by now you'd be writing for the New York Times. But I have to say, you sound successful and happy in your computer world and your high-tech job.

My mother forwarded your letter to me here at Johannesburg Hospital. Yes, I've become a doctor - leaves me little time to socialize. We're allowed a few hours off each week, which we all use to sleep and study. It's grueling, but I lucked out and have a few days off next month and over the holidays. Depending on our schedules, maybe we can meet and catch up.

I think you'll find Africa beautiful. I remember your foggy mornings and mild weather, at least mild to me. It can get hot here, but we don't have extremes.

I've got to get back to the books now, or I'll be up most of the night, and then trying to do rounds again without much sleep.

I hope your parents are well. Please tell them hello for me.

Fondest regards,
Will

p.s. You can reach me at hospital at 7483-4472-20.

The thin paper shook as I stared at the familiar handwriting.

Chapter 5

The Contract

My flight to Johannesburg was leaving in three hours. I frowned at the expensive red shoes as I stuffed them into the corner of my overloaded suitcase. They hurt my feet. I pulled them out and dropped them on my closet floor where they landed one on top of the other. I nudged them apart with my foot. After checking for my tickets and passport, I opened the side zipper of my purse for the three snapshots of Will. There might not be a chance to show them to him, but they somehow gave me the courage I felt I would need to see him again. In the first picture we were at the beach. Will was stretched out on a colorful towel. The second photo shows him leaning against his car near a field of flowers. The last picture was taken the day before Will returned to Africa. He was teasing me, telling me that before he returned to Africa we should admit how we felt about each other, a topic that until then, we never discussed because he was leaving. I was hoping to take the picture without him being aware of it, but he looked up just as I snapped it.

"I think we s*hould* tell each other how we really feel," he'd said, insisting we write it all down in a sort of contract. In the picture, he's propped on his arm, lying on his side on a picnic blanket, a pencil in his right hand and a small square yellow piece of paper with some writing on it in his left. The camera captured an unexpected seriousness in his eyes. I love the picture because it makes me feel like I'm right back there with him. I can smell his leather jacket and feel the cool, late autumn breeze raising goose bumps on my arms. I still have the little yellow piece of paper on which he wrote -

Said morals to be specific:

> *We will not allow our emotions (meaning involvement)*
> *to overpower our terribly sane minds. (That's terrible, I*
> *refuse to that on the grounds of the fifth.)*
> *But on the fore mentioned date, to be exact, the 15 October*
> *of the year 1900 and sixty five, we will allow ourselves*
> *the small privilege of telling each other the exact extent*
> *of the fore mentioned involvement.*

He signed the tiny document and under the "X" that I put for my signature, Will printed my name. I couldn't bring myself to sign the agreement. I was so afraid of giving into my feelings. He was hours away from leaving, and I felt like the little Dutch boy with his finger in the dike. When I realized I was smiling, I shook my head, tucked the photos back into my purse, zipped it, and left for the airport.

Chapter 6

Seat Mates

The nonstop flight from San Francisco to Johannesburg took twenty-two hours. I used my mileage and sat in business class. The blonde man next to me also preferred to work or read rather than chat. We hardly spoke until the last two hours when the plane, caught in a downdraft, suddenly lost altitude. The magazine I was reading flew out of my hands. We both reached for it and bumped heads.

"I'm sorry," I said rubbing the pounding sore spot above my eye.

"I'm afraid I'm the one with the hardest head," the man laughed. "Are you alright?" I nodded and smiled. His eyes were the blue of a cloudless noon sky, and the hair that had fallen over his forehead was a tawny, but tame, lion's mane. He had a chiseled jaw, while the planes of the rest of his face were softer. "What part of South Africa are you heading for?" he asked, retrieving the magazine.

"Staying where I land - Johannesburg."

"I'm headed there, too. You wouldn't be going to the Ability Software rollout, would you?" He dipped his head apologetically toward my business card which had fallen out of my purse near my foot. "My company is interested in your voice activated software."

"We'd hoped to roll out this release two months earlier, but our systems department convinced the execs to hold off because they had a couple more bells and whistles they thought would keep us ahead of the competition." I liked the way he tilted his head and listened when I spoke. "Which company are you with?"

"Caduceus," he said, handing me his card. It was printed in bold script - Roy Lawrence, Vice President, International Communications.

"Oh! I'm familiar with your telecommunication software. It's one of the best. I'm Jacqueline Sinclair." I reached to shake hands with him. It was a little awkward after sitting next to each other and not speaking for 20 hours. We smiled and both started reading again, and then laughed.

"I'm not very good about conversations on long flights," I admitted. "I usually bury my head in a book or some work as soon as I get on the plane. It's not that I don't enjoy people, but the chance for a little peace and quiet is hard to pass up."

"I know exactly what you mean." He shook his head.

"I sat next to a man who gave me a complete medical run down on every one of his internal organs. I couldn't eat lunch afterwards," I grimaced.

"So you ran into him, too?" He smiled, and then nodded towards my hand. "I've been admiring your ring. Your husband has good taste." Roy smiled and held up his left hand. The ring he was wearing was amazingly similar to mine – a gold band with a square diamond set so that its corners were vertical, more like a diamond than a square. He assumed, as most people did, that I was married because it was on my left hand.

"No husband," I said. "It was my grandmother's." I ran my thumb over the delicate gold band with its square diamond and felt a tightening in my chest. "It was her wedding ring. She put it on my finger when she was dying, and I've never wanted to take it off." I looked out the window to hide the moistness that unexpectedly filled my eyes. It wasn't like me to show emotion, especially in a work situation. I figured I was tired from all the prep for the conference.

The stewardess came by and we ordered wine, discussed software and then returned to our reading. I woke to the sound of the seatbelt warning bell just before landing. Roy carried his luggage, so we parted after deplaning, and I headed for the baggage area and then grabbed a cab to the Carlton Hotel. Despite its state-of-the-art presence, the hallways leading to my room smelled the same as all the other hotels I' d stayed in over the last few years – stagnant and stuffy topped off with a hint of floral disinfectant. It was eleven in the morning in Johannesburg and two in the morning according to my body. I'd slept on the plane, so I opted to try to stay up until that evening and get my jet lag under control. I unpacked, took a shower, and headed to the downstairs conference room to check things out. The afternoon sped by while I worked with our systems team setting up equipment and loading software. At five o'clock, the exhaustion hit me. Hal, our hardware guru, suggested we all go out for dinner.

"I think I'm going to crash," I said.

"Oh, come on, Jackie. The evening's just getting started," he called from the doorway where he was already putting on his coat.

I smiled and shook my head. "You've been here for two days already. I'm still on California time, and unless you want a dead body at your table, I'm having dinner in my room. I'll catch up with you wild partiers tomorrow," I promised.

Back in my room, I browsed through the TV guide. Nothing looked particularly interesting, and besides, I could hardly keep my eyes open except for the nagging little voice in my head. *Call. Just call Will.* I found the worried little piece of paper with his number in my purse and dialed. The hospital receptionist answered and told me Dr. Kincaid was not available, so I left my name and number. I hadn't expected to feel quite so relieved. Two minutes later I was sound asleep, my slippers still on my feet under the covers.

A stuffy nose woke me at five in the morning. I filled a glass with water and drank it, then showered, put on jeans and a t-shirt and headed down to the systems set up room. I stopped at the reception desk to let them know where I could be reached. About an hour later, I was downloading slides for my afternoon presentation when the phone's shrill ring broke the dense quiet.

"Hello?"

"Jackie?" The familiar voice and British accent poured over me like warm honey.

"Will?"

"Sorry for the early hour. I just got off duty. Did I wake you?" he asked.

"No, I'm actually sitting in front of a pc in our systems room."

"You can't see Johannesburg from the inside of a hotel," he scolded, adding, "I thought we could grab some coffee or breakfast after my shift, but I'm knackered. I'm going to sleep for a couple of hours. I'll ring you when I wake up." I had the impression that I wasn't going to fit into his schedule. The disappointment hit me full force and left me wondering if Will was either married or not overly excited about seeing me – or both.

"Sure. That sounds fine." Now I sounded noncommittal. There was silence at the other end of the line. "You haven't gone to sleep on me, have you?"

"Almost," he sighed. Now I really was depressed, until he added, "I'd like to sound a little more coherent when I see you." Better.

"You get some sleep, and I'll finish fine-tuning my

presentation. Sweet dreams."

"Mmm...." I could hear the smile in his voice.

I hung up, signed off the pc and headed out into the still, cool morning air.

Chapter 7

Tilly

Walking through the early morning light, I listened to the occasional barking horn, and the increasing swish of traffic and quick-stepping early morning workers. In the still near empty streets, their footsteps echoed against the skyscrapers. The sun rose behind the multi-storied monoliths and coaxed their shadows down the towers they faced. I was Gulliver to their mammoth bulk. Feeling dizzy, I lowered my eyes to window level, but even then, the backdrop they created behind my reflection engulfed me. To the south, I could see above some of the lower towers to the far off, sandy hills glowing in the sunlight. I'd read about the treasure of gold mined from beneath them.

Ahead, a small café's awning rolled out above the sidewalk like a yawning tongue. Heavy yeasty bread smells wafted through the air and my stomach growled. I stopped and bought a cup of coffee and a hot cinnamon roll. The sugary taste of the steaming pastry and the heat of the coffee cup on my palm warmed me against the crisp morning air. I felt exhilarated and reckless, eager to explore and probe every corner of this city-jungle, but a few blocks later, jet lag hit. The way back turned out to be much longer than the outgoing odyssey, and I made it to my room, dragging my feet, only to fall instantly asleep on my unmade bed.

An hour later, I was awakened by the maid who was rattling around in the bathroom. Her cart was pulled half way into the room, blocking the door open. She came out of the bathroom and plugged in a vacuum, and then straightened up and started when she saw me.

"Oh...sorry. I didn't know you was here," she said, which was pretty amazing as I had fallen asleep in my clothes on top of the bed. I peered through one eye, and tried to focus on her. She was a short, slightly stout, fortyish woman wearing what looked like a man's black-framed eyeglasses. There was a pink name tag with the word 'Tilly' on it pinned to the front of her uniform. "I thought you'd be gone ta work by now," she scoffed, frowning at me as if I were a foot-dragging sloth.

"Nope, still here," I said, my mouth buried in the side of the pillow. I raised my head slightly and winced at the crick in my neck. "Could you come back later?" She stared at me for a few seconds.

"I'll be back in half an hour."

"Could you make that an hour?"

"Hmmph," she snuffed, and then turned on the vacuum. She banged the whining instrument with vengeance against the leg of my bed three or four times, intent on some object beneath it. "Got it!" she proclaimed triumphantly, and then headed for the door ignoring the cleaning supplies she'd left on the bathroom counter

"Oh!" I yawned, running a hand through my hair, "I forgot my shampoo. Could you leave some please?" Her back still towards me, she swiveled her head slowly on the small shoulders, exorcist-style, and then leveled me with a stare that could have disinfected a toilet.

Despite my fuzzy-headedness, I wasn't going back to sleep, so I sat on the edge of the bed for a while, dangling my hands between my knees. I wasn't quite ready to put my feet on the floor, at least not until I checked under the bed to see if anything live lurked down there where Tilly had made her attack.

Refreshed by a shower, I grabbed my company badge, and spent the rest of the morning in meetings. Finding my room untouched when I returned shortly after lunch, I curled up in the oversized chair by the window to go over my afternoon presentation. I checked in with headquarters on an update, and found I needed to rewrite a section of my speech. Just as I was finishing, there was one quick rap on the door. I only had time to look up before it opened. Tilly was back, standing framed in the doorway, vacuum in hand. She stared at me, her eyes little pools of black.

"I thought you was goin ta work," she scolded.

Chapter 8

So this is Where You Are

I changed into low heels for my 3:00 presentation. Usually by mid-afternoon, the attendees were tired and drained, having been fed a day's worth of facts, pamphlets and enough lunchtime carbs to create a temporary state of paralysis. It meant the odds were I'd be speaking to a group of people who were partially comatose, and I would need to dance, sing and stand on my head to keep everyone awake.

I arrived early and set up, and then I waited. At 3:15, it looked like I wouldn't be talking to anyone. I checked the name of my presentation printed in bold letters on my first overhead, 'State of the Art – The Future Generation of Ability Software." Okay, that might not stand up to what was playing at the local theater, but these people were here to find out about the software their company was, or might be, using. At 3:20, I started packing, thinking maybe they'd heard I was going to give the presentation in Latin, or maybe the afternoon snack on the second floor sounded more interesting. As I was shuffling papers into my briefcase, a low hum began to drum its way down the outside hallway. The hum turned into a soft rumble of voices and then into a solid foot stomping approach. The double doors swung open, and a crowd of suited people pushed into the room.

"So this is where you are … Somebody should have updated the schedule … Why wasn't there a sign on the original meeting room letting us know there'd been a change?" I smiled at these people, my people, come to hear the sermon I was ready to lay at their feet. The foot shuffling and chair scraping finally calmed down and the room quieted.

"And I was worried," I began, "that I wouldn't get here in time because the pilot of my plane was using his map as a lunch napkin."

Chapter 9

Great Impressions

When I returned to my room, my message light was blinking. Hoping it was Will, I hit the button, and realized my heart was pounding as the desk clerk read me the message.

'Sorry I missed you. Have a break in the morning. I'll call you."

I was disappointed, but I had a full evening and couldn't have met Will anyway. As soon as the cocktail hour, dinner and a couple of quick meetings were over, I would retreat to the sanctuary of my room and shake the last remnants of jet lag with a little more sleep. I put on an appropriate evening suit and reached for a tissue to blot my lipstick. It was the last one, and there was no shampoo, but at least Tilly had left two bottles of conditioner.

About two hundred people were already standing in small groups, milling around the hors d'oeuvre table sipping drinks when I arrived. I answered a few customer questions and then joined a group of co-workers who were discussing a system crash that happened in the middle of two demonstrations. When the doors were opened to the dining area, I followed the crowd in and scanned the room. My boss, Jay Lindstrom, was signaling to me to join him and some customers. Jay was a casual and comfortable man. Even in an expensive suit, and despite his thin frame, his shirt never seemed to stay tucked into his pants, and his tie was always listing to one side. His hair, a thick wavy brown, always looked like he had just run his fingers through it. One of the men with Jay, a tall fellow holding a bright blue cocktail, had attended my presentation and recognized me. He introduced himself and gave me a limp handshake. I sighed inwardly, thinking limp handshakes were like petticoats without starch. What's the point? Of course no one had worn a petticoat in forever, but the ones mymother had made me when I was a child took off at a ninety degree angle from my waist. I never could bend over without exposing my underwear. My memories were interrupted by the man's voice.

"Saw your talk today. I'm glad that timing bug's been fixed. I must have called customer support five times looking for a workaround. Are you sitting here?" he asked grabbing the chair next to where I was standing.

"Glad we got it fixed," I smiled. A young woman was about to take the seat next to Jay, so I touched her elbow. When she turned towards me, I introduced her to the hand shaker. Leaving them talking, I slid into the chair beside Jay.

"Very smooth," he murmured.

"I heard the witty conversation was on this side of the table." I whispered.

"Well, thanks," a familiar voice on my other side said. I turned, but it took me a second to remember where I had seen this man.

"Made a great impression, did I?" The sound of his voice and his closeness snapped into place, and I suddenly pictured the inside of an airplane.

"Unforgettable one," I told him and meant it. I introduced Roy to Jay. While they discussed Caduceus and its phenomenal growth over the last year, I took advantage of the break and ate my salad. I was just eyeing the plump chicken breast the waiter had placed in front of me when Roy turned to me.

"I would have liked to catch your presentation today, but I had a meeting," he half-smiled. He had a way of listening with his eyes. I knew as vice president he didn't attend the presentations and was being polite. I filled him in on the room snafu.

"I haven't checked tomorrow's schedule. Are you presenting again?"

"One more time," I said, thinking I had one less day to see Will.

Chapter 10

Sophie

I was showering the next morning at 6:00 when the phone rang. I shut off the water and grabbed a towel, leaving wet footprints all the way.

"Jackie here."

"You sound wide awake," Will said. My heart started thumping.

"How about you?" I asked. "Did you get any sleep?"

"About five hours – a real windfall." I waited, dreading what I thought would be another excuse for not getting together. "I can get away for a couple of hours this morning. Do you have time for breakfast?"

"Yes," I practically gasped into the phone. Will laughed.

"Maybe I should sound a little less eager," I said, glad he couldn't see the blush creeping up my cheeks.

"Eager is good. I like the sound of it. How about meeting in your hotel lobby in half an hour?"

Twenty-nine minutes later, I stood waiting, watching the front doors of the lobby. I kept trying to take a deep breath, but I couldn't seem to get the air down into the bottom of my lungs. And then I saw him pushing through the revolving lobby door. He was dressed in hospital scrubs, and hadn't changed much - the slightly tousled chocolate brown hair and the confident walk. He was thinner than I remembered. Will saw me and broke into a smile. Feeling as if my legs had developed rigor mortis, I stood rooted to the floor, not sure if a hug was appropriate. Will, however, walked right up to me and gathered me into his arms. I don't know which one of us sighed louder.

"Hello, darling girl," he said holding me at arm's length. "You look wonderful."

"And you are one gorgeous doctor," I replied. He laughed and pulled me into another bear hug.

"I wasn't sure you were going to have the time or energy to see me," I told him. He looked questioningly at me, but said nothing. "C'mon, let's get some food into you, weary doctor." We ate in the second floor restaurant where the sunrise, reflected in the windows of the city's buildings, turned the hills orange. My stomach was in a knot. I didn't feel the least bit hungry, but I ordered fruit and toast. Will had eggs, bacon, potatoes and an English muffin.

"Hey, I didn't think doctors ate bacon."

"They eat whatever keeps them on their feet. Without vending machines, I might starve."

I leaned forward over my clasped hands, "I realize I've come at a busy time for you. Just kind of dropped in out of nowhere."

"I wanted to pick you up at the airport and show you Johannesburg, but my schedule ... " he shook his head. "It's a beautiful city." He paused and looked out the window. "I've pictured you here," he said more to himself than to me. "You can come anytime you want, whether I'm busy or not."

"Tell me about you. What made you decide to become a doctor?"

He smiled and glanced back at the distant mountains. "I always knew it would be medicine. Just never talked about it. I completed some of my pre-med courses before I traveled. You don't have to look very far in Africa to see the need. Millions die needlessly every year – mostly unhealthy living conditions, disease, starvation." He winced and shook his head. "Most of the people here don't have access to preventive medicine, or nearly any medical intervention for that matter. I guess I just wanted to do something about it." Before I could respond, he leaned forward on his elbows. "What about you? What happened to your dream to work for a newspaper and write?"

"Well, I guess I didn't follow the dream, but I can't say I'm unhappy working in the world of computers. I didn't actually like it at first, but now that I'm into it, it's good."

"Good?"

"Fine, well… no, better than fine. I get to travel, meet lots of people, and *try* to keep up with new technology."

Will tilted his head and looked into my eyes. "Still feel like you need to spread your wings?" The question hit close to home. Spreading my wings was the reason I'd given him for not accepting the written marriage proposal he sent me six months after he left. "Sorry. That didn't come out right," he said, looking mildly embarrassed. When I didn't answer, he added, "Well, maybe it did."

"It's all right," I said. "But, I think you of all people would understand." He was the one who quit college and left to travel around the world.

"I know, but it wasn't what I wanted to hear." He shrugged.

We both glanced outside to the sun lit city. I hadn't thought we would talk about this, but then it might be the only time we'd be together, and maybe Will wanted to say whatever still needed saying.

"I'm so sorry," I whispered. When Will left the States there'd been no agreement between us. When his proposal came, I was stunned. I'd had no idea that he was thinking about marriage.

Will nodded and the hint of a half-smile touched his lips.

"Well, it was selfish on my part. I always knew that."

"It was wonderful and romantic… and heart-breaking too," I admitted, feeling a twinge of regret. "So, did you...marry?" I asked and held my breath. He wasn't wearing a ring.

"No. I met a few girls that I liked, one in particular, but that relationship hit a brick wall a couple of months ago, but now it's… I'll probably be an old man before I start a family," he shrugged.

Hit a brick wall, only a couple of months ago – did that mean he fell in love, might still be in love?

"How about you…?" Will asked, breaking into my thoughts.

"Jackie!" I looked up to see Jay striding towards us. He eyed Will and stuck out his hand. "Jay Lindstrom." I finished the introductions.

"Are you with a local company?" Jay asked, hearing Will's British accent.

"I'm local, but not part of your customer base I'm afraid," Will said.

"Will is a doctor at Johannesburg Hospital." Jay's eyebrows shot up in surprise.

"Long story," I mumbled before he could ask any more questions

"I really hate interrupting you both like this, but I've got John Malcolm and Steve Bronley joining me, and I was hoping to include you in the breakfast meeting, Jackie. They want to go over the Torley Brinkham account, and you're the expert. Sorry not to give you any notice, but I didn't know they were arriving until a couple of minutes ago."

There wasn't much I could do or say since the two men were already zeroing in on us from across the room. They introduced themselves, pulled up chairs and ordered breakfast. The meeting and the time sped by. The next thing I knew, Will and I were in the lobby saying goodbye. I didn't know if I would see him again, and the ferocity of that fear surprised me. When he wasn't putting in double shifts, he was sleeping or studying. I couldn't believe how painful parting from him again was, and like before, there seemed to be no choice about it. Will leaned towards me to say something when a small child, about waist high, suddenly darted around us screaming.

"I want to go! I want to go!" About twenty feet behind him, in heated pursuit, was a short, heavy woman in a dark flowered dress. She was red in the face and puffing, trying to catch her breath and the child.

"Gianni!!Gianni!! Come back here. Papa will take you tomorrow."

Trailing behind her, like ducks in a row, was another woman, taller and much thinner. The child ran toward the front door and into one of the valets. The young man tried to stop the boy but only managed to grab his arm before he wiggled free and turned back towards the lobby still screaming, "I want to go! I won't stay!" Making another sudden turn, the boy darted between Will and me, nearly knocking me off balance. Will grabbed my arm as the little fellow took off toward the escalator. Just then, the mother screamed. She had turned to follow the boy and slipped, skidding against the sharp edge of the front desk. When she came to a stop, she lie silent for a moment looking startled before pushing herself up on an elbow. She took one look at the crimson rivulet of blood running down the side of her plump thigh and soaking into her knee high nylon stockings, and screamed for her son.

"Gianni! Gianni! Come to Mama."

Her pleading wail stopped little Gianni in his tracks. Confused, he ran up and down the lobby, crying frantically, flapping his arms.

"Gianni...get Papa, get Papa," she keened over and over.

Will knelt beside the woman, pulled a pair of glasses out of his pocket and put them on. He tried to explain to the nearly hysterical woman that he was a doctor. When she finally quieted to sniffling sobs, he gently examined her leg, but she kept slapping his hand and pulling her dress over her knee. Gianni stood three feet away, jumping up and down and whimpering. The thinner woman came up and took the boy's hand. Wanting to help, I knelt beside Will and tried to distract the woman.

"Hi. I'm Jackie. Can you lie still while the doctor looks at your leg?" I smiled and reached for the hand that was keeping Will from checking her wound. I felt Will look up at me for a moment before asking the desk clerk to call for an ambulance. The woman heard the word "ambulance" and broke into fresh sobs.

"What's your name?" I had to ask her three times before she responded.

"Sophia," she gulped.

"Is this woman holding Gianni's hand someone you know, Sophia?"

"She's my sister," she whimpered.

"Is 'Papa" her husband?" I asked the sister. The thin woman nodded. "Could you find him and bring him here? And please take Gianni. I think he might feel less anxious if he's with you." She looked doubtful, but headed toward the elevators towing the crying child behind her.

"Jackie, do you think you could keep pressure on this

tourniquet?" Will asked, snuggly wrapping a yellow hair ribbon someone had given him around Sophia's thigh.

"Um, sure. Just show me how." Will placed my hands around the knot in the ribbon, and then applied pressure with his hands over mine. Sophia looked scandalized.

"About that tight. Okay?" he asked softly, looking into my eyes. Sophia was working herself into a full-fledged wail again.

"Would someone bring me a chair cushion?" Will glanced up at the crowd that was now surrounding us. The woman's leg and the floor were covered with blood. I couldn't worry about that with her thrashing around. Besides I had already kneeled in a bright red pool of it and the bottom of my skirt was stained. Even my knees were sticky with it.

A cushion appeared. "Anything I can do to help?" I felt a hand on my shoulder and looked up at the sound of the familiar voice. It was Roy.

"Ask the people to move back and give her a little more air," Will said, glancing at my shoulder. Roy spoke quietly to the crowd, and they widened their circle. Will settled Sophia's head on the cushion and swept her hair back from her face. Someone else brought a blanket and placed it over her upper body. She twisted to search the lobby, but Will turned her head so that she was looking into his eyes. "You're doing fine. I won't leave you until the ambulance arrives." The words calmed her and her wails reduced to small, rhythmic sniffling. The crowd had grown and started inching forward again. As intent as I was on keeping the tourniquet pressure just right, I felt distracted by Will kneeling beside me. I remembered the closeness and safety I used to feel when I was with him. The pain of those memories soaked into me just like Sophia's blood was soaking into my skirt.

"Get a hold of yourself, kiddo," I thought. "You'll be leaving in a couple of days, and he's not going to care."

Even though I had not increased the pressure on the tourniquet, my hands were clenched so tightly that the knuckles were white. I suddenly felt Will's eyes on me. He looked like he was about to say something.

"Too tight?" I asked. He shook his head and smiled.

Seeing that everything was under control, Roy signaled to me that he was heading upstairs. "I'll check with you later," he said, and took off toward the elevators.

A porter rushed to the side lobby door and swung it open to admit a paramedic pulling a stretcher. It rolled in on clanking wheels followed by a second paramedic. They checked vital signs, assessing the wound and hooking up oxygen. It wasn't until one of them tried to apply a professional tourniquet that I realized how tense and frozen I was. The medic had to practically pry my hands away. Sophia started to whimper again, but Will laid a hand on her arm, and she stopped. The medics put Sophia on their stretcher and pushed it towards the door.

Will watched as they wheeled her out. "I'd better go with her. The cut may have nicked a major blood vessel. Anyway, I'm due back at hospital. Thank you for the help, Jackie." He looked back at me for a long moment. "This is turning out to be more difficult than I'd imagined." His words startled me. Did that mean I wouldn't see him again? I knew the question was in my eyes, but I remained silent. Will put his hand on my arm and was about to say something else when a man in the crowd stepped closer and tilted, what I assumed was his good ear, towards us. With the main attraction removed, we were the sequel. Will and I both looked at the man, but he just leaned closer, not interested at all in our privacy. Will looked into my eyes once more, and then he was gone.

Chapter 11

Cut to the Quick

That evening, before dinner, I decided to take a swim in the hotel's nearly Olympic-sized pool. It was likely to be empty since the bars were full and most people would either be in last minute meetings or getting ready for dinner. I was relieved to see only a young couple and an older man in the pool. I eased myself in and swam towards the deep end. The water felt cool against the heat of my face. I floated for a while, then swam to the side and laid my head on my arms, gently gliding my feet back and forth through the silky water. The setting sun's rays crept onto my face, and I turned my head in the opposite direction just as a warm breeze ran its fingers across the back of my neck. I groaned with pleasure. Sometime later, the suddenly choppy water disturbed my floating thoughts, and I opened my eyes. Two men and a woman were swimming towards me.

"We thought that was you," the woman said. "We were just talking about the update. Does that include general ledger capability?"

I eyed the steps a half a pool away. "Absolutely," I answered, inwardly wishing for a few more minutes of solace. There were more questions. Two more swimmers joined us, and then suddenly, I was backed against the side of the pool, a semi-circle of bathing-suit clad customers bobbing around me. I answered questions for the next fifteen minutes, and then at a break in the conversation, I made a, hopefully graceful, exit.

"Gee! I've lost track of time," I said looking at the not waterproof watch I'd forgotten to remove. I could see a tiny mist forming inside the crystal. "Nice talking to all of you." They parted like the Red Sea, and I swam through, raising my hand in a farewell wave. Wrapping my towel around myself, I headed quickly to the hotel elevator. I glanced toward the lobby and saw Roy looking at me and chuckling. I was sure he had seen me escape the pool and was on to me. Shivering in the cold hotel hallway, I grimaced and pulled my soggy towel more snugly around myself. For once, the air conditioning in my room did not feel good. I dropped my suit and drenched towel on the bathroom floor, and then turned on the hot shower water and buried my head under it.

Chapter 12

Corporate Spies and Human Shields

After dinner, I was checking the following day's schedule with the reception desk when I saw Roy enter the hotel. He spotted me and headed over.

"Little crowded in the pool?" he asked, a boyish smile lurking at the corners of his mouth.

"Not funny," I said.

"Didn't anyone ever teach you not to back yourself into a corner?"

"The pool was empty when I went in," I offered lamely.

"Mmm hmmm," Roy said, still smiling.

"Yeah," I sighed, "it was a Bufo frog moment." Seeing Roy's confused look, I explained, "My biology professor's doctorate project. He was studying Bufo frogs, and he pinned one to a board, spread eagle, with its little heart still beating – sort of how I felt."

"Sounds painful," Roy grimaced.

"That's what I told my professor, but he just brushed it off saying frogs don't have feelings. Hard to believe, besides, the poor little thing looked frightened."

"That's one thing I can't picture you – frightened," Roy said.

"You must not have gotten a good look at me in the pool."

"Do you have time for a drink? I promise, no software questions," he said holding up his hands.

"Sure." I suddenly wondered if Roy was on a fact finding mission about the futures of Ability. My guard went up. Rolling out a state-of-the-art product meant other tech companies would be sniffing around for as much information as they could get. Roy's company was on top because they were innovative. They were usually a step ahead of the competition, and our product would complement their own technology, making it a full offering. Together, our two products could sweep the market, but alone either company could create problems for the other. We found a couch in the lobby and Roy ordered two glasses of wine.

"Offsite meeting?" I asked, referring to his entrance into the lobby a few moments before. He looked at me, but said nothing. I felt myself blush. "Oh! Sorry," I shook my head. What business of mine was it? On the other hand, maybe I was wise to assume he might be interested in picking up some under the table information about Ability.

"Lost in thought or tired?" he asked. "Hopefully not bored?"

"No, not at all." I was more likely to say what was on my mind than not, and I figured I might as well put the topic to rest. "Well, I doubt that I have the answers you're looking for." Roy looked confused for a moment, and then laughed.

"You think I'm trying to fish company secrets out of you?" When he smiled, little lines formed at the corners of his eyes. "Well, first of all, that isn't what I do, and second, I certainly wouldn't go about it by plying innocent women with wine."

"Great, so detective work isn't an optional vocation for me?"

He picked up his glass and tapped it against mine. "To new friends and faraway places."

"And espionage," I added.

"I was impressed with the way you handled yourself this morning," he said. "Most people wouldn't have done well around all that bleeding. Ever thought about getting into the medical field?"

"Right," I groaned. "I have trouble cutting my way through a crowd."

"Have you heard how the woman is doing?" he asked.

"I don't know. I thought I'd call later and check."

"It was lucky that a doctor was nearby. What are the odds?" Roy shrugged.

I must have gone into a trance again at the thought of Will. I was wondering what he was doing now - if he was the one who stitched up Sophia's leg, or if I would ever see him again.

"You do have something on your mind. Anything I can help with?" Roy asked.

"No, sorry, I was just thinking about this morning."

"I'd be happy to call the hospital and check," he offered. "Or, if you have the doctor's name, I could try reaching him if he's still there."

"He should be. He's on duty tonight."

"Do you know him?" Roy asked, surprised.

"I do," I said.

"I thought this was your first trip to South Africa."

"It is."

"I don't understand." He was like a dog with a bone.

"You weren't going to ask any questions," I reminded him.

"No software questions," he said, amused. I looked at him skeptically.

"How did you meet him, this doctor?" Roy settled back in

his chair.

"I met Will back in the states, but this is his home." Roy waited. I knew that trick. If you want more information, just remain silent, and people tend to roll out their life story. I would make this short and simple. "I used to work for a newspaper, and I was assigned to write a short biography on the doctor's world travels. Well, he wasn't a doctor back then." I added. That was all the information on this topic Roy was getting. I'd been trying all day to stuff the memories back into their little locked drawer at the back of my mind. It wasn't that I wanted to forget them. I might need them to warm up my old age someday, but right now I wanted them out of my thoughts.

"I'm willing to bet there's an interesting story behind that interview."

"I don't know that I'd call it interesting. We dated and then his visa ran out, and he had to leave." I was still talking about Will.

"And, did you make the right choice?" Roy asked.

"Right choice?"

"To let him go," he said, watching me closely.

A scream ripped through the air to my right as the cocktail waitress tripped on the corner of a rug. As her upper body flipped forward, she tried to grab the back of a chair, but missed. I only caught the blur of her arm swinging upward and out as her tray, loaded with drinks, crashed against a cocktail table. After that, my mind captured the moment in slow motion. The sliding carpet, the table careening away and the spray of glass shards that gracefully glittered and sparkled, twisted and turned as they lazily flew toward the couch and Roy and me. He jumped up, and at the same time, threw his arm in front of me. I ducked my head, but it was too late. The sharp little jewels stung as they splattered against my face. I reached to brush the pieces off, but Roy grabbed my hand and stopped me. Stepping on the broken glass, he reached for a nearby pillow and swept the shards off the couch before sitting beside me. I could feel something grating against the corner of my right eye and started to reach up again.

"Let me take a look," Roy said taking hold of my shoulders and turning me gently toward the light.

"Ow!" I yelped, sucking in a sharp breath. I gingerly touched my right shoulder and felt something thin and hard. A curved shard that looked like the lip of a glass, was lodged about two inches below my collar bone.

"Sorry," he said, glancing at my shoulder. "Try not to move." I felt a trickle of blood run between my breasts. He peered at my face. "I can see a small piece of glass near the corner of your eye. I think it's safe to remove it. Stay perfectly still Jackie, and close your eyes." I closed my eyes and swallowed hard. I heard Roy reach into his jacket and assumed he was getting glasses. The heat of him, as he moved his face within inches of mine, startled me, and I jerked when I felt a puff of breath on my face. He was trying to blow the shard out. Another trickle of blood ran down my chest. I bit my lower lip and grimaced.

"Once more," he said gently, and blew again. The prickling sensation stopped, but I was afraid to blink for fear there was glass in my eyes, too, so I closed them and felt a sharp scrape.

"I'm going to see if there's a house doctor," he said. "Stay still and keep your eyes closed."

"Okay" I murmured uneasily, hoping I didn't sound as shook up as I felt. Roy paused a moment and then squeezed my hand and asked someone to call for a doctor. I could hear the sound of fast footsteps retreating.

"You're doing fine." His voice was steady and sure. I knew he was purposely not mentioning the piece of glass sticking out from beneath my collar bone. There were several voices all talking at once and people issuing orders to get towels and make calls.

"Is she alright?" someone asked.

I wanted desperately to open my eyes. Having them closed made me feel helpless and out of control. Roy was quiet, and it suddenly occurred to me that I hadn't even asked him if he had been hit by the flying glass.

"Are you hurt?"

"No, you seem to have absorbed all the shrapnel."

"Part of the job description. But, you deserve a purple heart for flinging yourself in front of me. Thank you for that." I tried to keep everything above my lips still. "Is the cocktail waitress okay?" Even though I had seen her get up and move around, I wanted to keep talking so I wouldn't have to think about pieces of glass making themselves at home in me.

"She looks okay – maybe a few bruises."

"Hello again," Roy said, surprise in his voice. I didn't hear an acknowledgement, but Roy stood and released my hands. Someone sat down and took hold of them.

Are you in any pain, Jackie honey?" a familiar voice asked.

"N...no, not really," I said, momentarily puzzled.

"I'm just going to check for glass. Stay as still as possible." It was Will!

"Will?" I blurted out, my eyes popping open.

"Hi," he smiled, his familiarness washing over me like a warm breeze. He was wearing slacks and a cool blue shirt. I relaxed a little for the first time and took a deep, somewhat shaky breath. The splinter in my shoulder dug in, and I winced.

"She's got a piece of glass just under her collar bone." Roy pointed to my right shoulder.

Will glanced at the shard. "Mmm," was all he said, but he tucked the collar away from my neck. The coolness of the air hit my skin, and I shivered.

"I'm going to look more closely into your eyes now," Will said taking my face in his hands and tilting it to catch the lamp light. I stared at the golden flecks in his eyes. Somewhere in my brain, a door was creaking open again and letting out more memories. Please let him think I'm just nervous, I thought, knowing my racing pulse had more to do with his closeness than the accident. He pulled my hand against his chest and took my pulse. Like that helped. I blushed and felt the heat radiate from my skin. I remembered it all, the contour of his face, the full lips and the dimple in his left cheek. My reaction was as uncontrolled as my memories, and I had to stop myself from leaning into him. But he had given me no reason to believe he ever wanted to see me again, and I tried to keep my thoughts out of my eyes. It didn't matter anyway, because what I read in his eyes was purely clinical.

"Do you have pain anywhere else?" he asked. I did a quick body check and only then realized my shoulder was beginning to throb a bit. But no reason to make a big deal out of it.

"Not really." I pressed my lips together, and tried to stop the shaking. Crazy, I thought, not to admit I was in pain, but I felt so ridiculous sitting there like a porcupine with glass quills sticking out of it.

"Okay. Close your eyes, and don't touch your face."

"Why? Did you find a Johannesburg gold nugget in there?" I was trying to show some bravado. He took my hand and rubbed his thumb back and forth across the top.

"No such luck. Actually, I can't see any foreign objects, but I think it's best if we get you to the hospital and have an ophthalmologist check you out. Keep your eyes closed. He looked up at Roy who had moved to my other side and was watching us. "It's Roy, right? Would you sit with Jackie? I'll be right back." The two men switched places again. "Keep her hands away from her face," Will said. It wasn't until Roy took hold of my hands, that I realized mine were like ice.

"How're you feeling, Jackie?" Roy asked, the warmth of his hands seeping into mine. I could feel Will walking away.

"A little nervous, but I'm trying to sound tough as nails. How am I doing?"

"If it wasn't for the shaking, mountain climber grip, I'd never know," he said.

"It comes in handy dealing with corporate spies." I relaxed my bone-crushing grasp. "Where did Will go?" Pathetic, I thought, don't be so obvious.

"He's talking to someone at the front desk."

Will returned, and I heard a box open. "I think it'll be quicker if we take my car instead of waiting for an ambulance. Jackie, I'm going to bandage your eyes to make it easier for you to keep them closed. It's only a precaution, but let's not take any chances." Will wrapped what felt like gauze around my head and then put my right arm in some sort of sling. He gently lifted me to my feet, bracing me snug against him. His closeness was like a magnet.

"I've got your purse, Jackie," Roy said and followed us toWill's car where the three of us shared the front seat. It was a little crowded, so Roy put his arm on top of the seat behind me. "I have a late meeting," he said, "and I won't be able to stay with you at the hospital. I'll send the company car to take you back to the hotel."

"Don't bother. I'll make sure Jackie gets back." Will sounded angry, or maybe he felt saddled with me.

"No problem, I'll call a cab." I wasn't about to be a burden to anyone.

Chapter 13

The Hospital

Will left to take care of the paperwork.

"Hi, I'm Dr. Seit." The ophthalmologist pronounced it "sight."

"Really?" I said with a half-smile. "I'd roll my eyes, but you won't let me." He chortled, adding drops to my eyes and settling my chin into a cold metal magnifying scope.

"Well, I have mostly good news," the doctor said, slapping his knees.

"Mostly?"

"There's no damage to your eyes."

I let out a relieved sigh. "But?"

"But, there's a tiny piece of glass floating on the surface that doesn't want to wash out with the drops I put in. I need to remove it." He must have seen the terror in my eyes. "You won't feel a thing," he assured me, patting my hand.

"White coat fear," I confessed grimacing. I'd never felt comfortable in a doctor's office or a hospital. My heartbeat would race, my blood pressure would rise and my face would flush. To make it all worse, it was pretty much the same reaction I seemed to be having whenever Will was around. Dr. Seit removed the tiny particle with what looked like a straw with a tiny suction at the end. He put the glass on a piece of gauze and moved the pernicious little chunk back and forth to catch the light.

"Your eyes are dilated, so you may not be able to see this." A tiny, blurry sparkle blinked at me from the snippet of a boulder he held. And then, to my horror, he reached for a pair of those dark, plastic glasses that make even gorgeous people look weird, and put them on me. There were two quick taps on the door before it slowly opened. Will came in wearing a white lab coat, a stethoscope hung around his neck. I felt lovely in my freaky glasses and arm sling.

"How's she's doing?" he asked, smiling at me.

"All set. Just make sure you let me know right away if you have any trouble with pain or blurry vision," Dr. Seit said as Will put his arm around my waist, and lifted me carefully to my feet. The movement jarred the glass in my shoulder and my breath caught.

"Sorry," Will said frowning. He walked me down the hall to a small room with an examination bed and a covered tray table beside it. I shuddered, imagining all sorts of sharp metal instruments under the towel, and stopped at the door. Will turned and looked at me skeptically.

"I seem to remember you telling me how tough you are." He grinned.

"I didn't know then that you'd acquired a taste for sharp objects."

"I happen to be known throughout the hospital for my gentle touch." He gave the small of my back a nudge. I must not have looked overly convinced because he reached for a small vial sitting on the counter near the tray, and shook out two pills. Will filled a tiny paper cup with water. "Here, these will relax you and help with the pain."

"I don't need those," I insisted, despite the now throbbing pain in my shoulder.

Will looked at me, one eyebrow raised. Our relationship had always been something of a tug-of-war, Will asserting himself, and me challenging those assertions. The difference in our ages was a catalyst for Will to believe he "knew best." We practically always ended up compromising, but I remember a dinner party my parents gave about a week before Will returned to Africa. My father offered me an alcoholic drink, something my parents never allowed. I was dreading Will leaving and hadn't eaten much dinner. The drink went right to my head and made me dizzy. Will took one look at me and steered me outside into the cold night air, telling me to breathe deeply. I was furious and indignant with him for treating me as if I were drunk or, worse yet, a child. I went back into the house and made myself another drink. Suddenly, a hand reached around me and dumped it in the sink.

"I think you've had enough," Will said in a fatherly tone. I wasn't about to let him tell me what to do – older or not. I fixed another drink and carried it around for a good hour before pouring it out. It was a compromise.

Will was waiting patiently, the two pills in his hand. Another stab of pain shot through my shoulder.

"You're wrong if you think I'm not tough enough to handle this." My voice shook on the last word, and it came out in two syllables.

"Well," Will said, raising one eyebrow, "let's just chalk it up to doctor's orders." I'd done a great job of backing myself into this miserable corner. I mustered a tiny smile and shook my head. "Jackie... take them," Will's deep voice brooked no opposition. I didn't move. He reached to uncover his tray of cutlery. I held out my hand for the pills and took a sip of water from the small paper cup he held to my lips.

Chapter 14

Instruments of Torture

A quick rap on the door was followed by the entry of a small, brown-haired nurse. She was middle-aged and moved with brisk efficiency.

"Will you need extra sutures, Doctor?" she asked, glancing at *the tray*. I flinched.

"No, I have all I need."

She bustled around the room opening drawers and removing bandages and placing them, along with a long metal instrument in a sealed package, on a sterilized towel. Will picked up a small bottle labeled, Novocain, from the tray. I knew there was a needle the length of a football field somewhere in his artillery arsenal. I looked away. The nurse, her lips pressed into a fine line, straightened her shoulders. She removed my sling, and then draped a large paper sheet over me before unbuttoning my blouse. I winced when her hand brushed against the piece of glass embedded in my shoulder. Will glanced up and stared at her for a moment. She ignored him, and then slipped my blouse and bra off and hung them on a hook in the corner of the room.

"Thank you, Rachel. I'll let you know when I need you."

"I...." The nurse seemed about to protest, but apparently 'following doctor's orders' overrode her objections. She spun around and walked briskly out of the room, startling me when she glanced back with a glare that would have lit the hospital during a power outage. I made a mental note to introduce her to Tilly.

"I need you to lie back on the table," Will said, putting his arm behind me and lowering me gently. The sleeves of his lab coat and shirt were rolled up, and the touch of his bare skin against mine through the opening of the robe back, startled me. In an unconscious reflex, I arched my back away from the contact.

"Just relax, Jackie. I won't hurt you." For a second, there was something in his eyes that made me think he was going to kiss me, but it passed, and Will lowered me to the table. When he reached for something on the tray, his shirt brushed against my face, and the smell of him shot through me like an aching memory. I shivered, sure he must be able to see the goose bumps he was raising. He checked his weaponry, occasionally glancing at me. I was beginning to feel dizzy from the pills, but just as my eyelids started to close, Will's face was suddenly looming above mine.

"Okay, Sweetie?" He smiled in the same old wonderful way. I smiled back lazily, some little humming sound sliding out of me as I looked into the honey gold eyes I remembered so well.

"*No.*" the ever cautious internal voice warned, remembering the long ago goodbye his eyes once held. I looked down, but found myself staring at the beating pulse in the small indentation at the base of his neck. I took a quick breath and glanced to my right. A threaded, curved needle lay pristinely on the sterilized tray. My heart lurched and the added adrenaline cleared my mind a bit.

"What terrible, awful medicine was in those pills? You don't always know best," I mumbled, and then wondered what I'd just said.

"Even under sedation," Will murmured, shaking his head. "I'm going to fold the sheet down now so I can remove the glass. Let me know if you get cold."

In the seven months Will and I spent together, we had never made love. I had a more than strict upbringing, and Will respected that. Besides, he knew he would be leaving, and I think he wanted to minimize the pain and regret that making love might cause. The cool air hit my shoulders, and I glanced down at the protruding shard, and then put my hand over my heart in reaction. Will tucked my hand back under the sheet.

"I need you to lie perfectly still," he said, and then eyeing me with mock seriousness added. "Or I'll have to call back Nurse Ratched." It was a reference to the sadistic nurse in *One Flew over the Cuckoo's Nest,* a book he must have remembered gave me nightmares.

"You're the one with the instruments of torture," I reminded him.

Will put a reassuring hand on my shoulder for a moment, then took something lethal off his tray and held it behind his back. "You might feel a slight sting."

I was determined to be brave, white coat fear or not. How could I present such a courageous facade other times and feel like such a lily liver now. After all, it was just a tiny shot, with a long, sharp needle, in a very sensitive spot. I moved my lips into position for a smile, but they felt like rubber, and I suspect it turned out badly. I swallowed loudly as Will carefully placed his fingers around the shard area. When the heel of his hand touched down lightly on the sheet covering my breast, I inhaled sharply. Will stopped and looked at me. I quickly glanced at a magazine lying on a corner table, and pretended I was reading the miniature print with my bionic eyes. He knew me far too well, and despite my drug-induced, muddled state of mind, my reactions were a clear message, at least to me, that this wasn't all fear, and that I still felt something for this man from my past.

"It's a good thing Roy was with you when this happened," Will said.

"You don't have to distract me. I'm fine, really."

He shook his head. "No, just thinking it's... opportune that you could both attend the conference."

Strange remark, I thought, but chalked it up to my mental fuzziness. There was the slight sting of the shot, and then another, and then the hand above my breast moved slightly. My heart, even in its drugged state, could not resist and lazily threw itself against my chest. Will straightened up at last and put the needle back into the tray. I tried to focus, but the room seemed a little soft around the edges.

"All done. Now we'll just wait a few minutes." Will walked over to an intercom on the wall and pressed the button. "Rachel, could you come in?"

"Great," I mouthed to myself, and even though I shouldn't, I rolled my eyes and hoped the freaky froggy glasses hid it. Will was looking at me, but seemed lost in thought. I don't remember much after that, except for the sound of glass hitting the bottom of a metal bowl, and then Will was applying a bandage.

"Would you like a souvenir?" he asked, holding up the wicked shard.

"Do you gift wrap?" I managed to mumble. The sedation wearing off.

"I'll let Rachel help you get dressed," he said and left the room. The abruptness of his exit surprised and disappointed me. I didn't even have a chance to thank him.

"You'll want to keep that arm quiet," she ordered, helping me dress and putting my arm in a sling with quick, brusque movements. "It will be best if you go directly back to your hotel and go to bed."

"*Thanks, Mom,*" I thought. And suddenly, I was alone in the room. I stood up feeling a bit wobbly just as an orderly appeared with a wheelchair.

"No thanks," I protested before he could bring it into the room. This was one battle I intended to win. I smiled before squeezing around him and through the door. Running my hand along the wall to steady myself, I headed for the nurses' station where Rachel was talking to another nurse. "Could you tell me where I can find a phone? I need to call a cab." Two hands gently took hold of my arms from behind and turned me around.

"I'm taking you back to your hotel," Will said, nodding at Rachel who was already holding the receiver. She pursed her lips and hung up the phone.

"You don't have to go to all this trouble, Will. A cab will be fine." Will's eyes followed a click behind me at the nurses' station. I turned to see Rachel holding up the phone receiver again and looking at Will with raised eyebrows. He glanced sharply at her. The receiver snapped sharply back into its cradle.

"My car's out back," he said and tucked my arm through his, pulling it against his side. I could hear grumbling coming from the nurses' station as we headed for the parking lot.

"Front parking space, nice," I said, and stumbled, probably on an air pocket the way the night was going. Will put his arm around my waist and fitted me more securely against his side. My body was doing the white coat fear thing again.

"You're still difficult to help," he said settling me in his car.

"What does that mean?" I asked a little miffed.

"You don't remember how you fought me every time I wanted to do something for you? You're still fighting that battle."

"Battle? There's no battle. I'm a joy to be around, except, of course, when I'm using my body as a human shield for flying glass."

"Yeah, It's alright if you don't do that again," he said and shut my door. His reference to the way we were seven years before was bringing up far more than I wanted to deal with. On the way back, I suddenly realized how strange it was that he happened to be in the lobby of the hotel when both accidents happened.

"You wouldn't be the on-call doctor for the hotel, would you?"

"I was at the desk trying to locate you."

"Locate me? But, I thought after the other day, you didn't..." Once again my thoughts poured out of my mouth.

"I didn't what?" Will asked, glancing at me over the dark rims of his glasses. "You think I didn't want to see you again." It was a statement, not a question. "Why would you think that?" Not wanting to answer, I reached up to rub my forehead. "Try not to do that," he said in doctor talk. "It's better if you don't disturb your eyes for a day or two."

"That would mean not making myself presentable. It's against company policy to scare customers." Will glared at me. "I'll be careful," I assured him, and got a sarcastic huff in return.

"Battles." Will shook his head. "And I'll expect an answer to that question when you're feeling up to it," he warned me.

When it was time to discuss something, Will always came at me with both barrels loaded. I never could get away with hiding my feelings or keeping things light. It was as if he could strip away all my defenses and lay me bare. I was the Bufo frog again.

Chapter 15

Sad Farewells

Will took hold of my good arm and helped me into the lobby. "Should we call Roy?" he asked.

"No, no point in bothering him. Anyway, it's late, and I'm just going to crawl into bed."

"Come on," Will said. He seemed angry. "Let's get you to your room." It was clear I had been enough trouble for one night, or one lifetime.

"It's alright. I'm fine. You've done too much already." I gently pulled my arm away from his, wincing slightly as the pain in my shoulder began to take hold again.

"Take the pain pills I gave you. Two every four to six hours." He was using his "doctor to difficult patient" tone. I rolled my eyes thinking the glasses weren't so bad after all.

"Okay… if I need them," It seemed like a good time to pull out my excellent compromising skills.

"Take them because they'll also reduce the inflammation." Before I could protest, he covered my mouth with his fingertips. I resisted a sudden and surprising urge to kiss them. Instead, I nodded.

When we reached my room, I thanked him. There was so much more I wanted to say, like how gentle he was, how wonderful it was to see him again and how beautiful the stitches were. My only regret was that he would not be the one to remove them. I would have that done after I returned home, and I was seriously thinking of having them bronzed. I unlocked the door and turned towards him.

"Will..."

Before I could say more he put his warm hands on the sides of my face and tilted my head down to kiss me on the forehead. It was a longer than usual forehead kiss. His lips were soft and tender, and his moist breath stirred my hair, tickling me. He tilted my head back up then and kissed my nose. I stared up at him, unable for once to think of anything to say. He gave me a tired smile and then winked and walked off down the hall. I watched until he turned the corner, remembering the old wife's tale that warned against watching someone until he was out of sight. It was bad luck and meant you would never see that person again. I watched Will leave seven years before, his red taillights disappearing around a curve in the road. I hadn't believed the superstitious story then, and anyway I did see him again. But now, I was afraid that twice would prove the tale.

I opened the door, turned on the light and pushed my aching body slowly into the room. Horrified, I gasped at my reflection in the full length hall mirror. My hair looked like I'd been riding a motorcycle through a hurricane, there were blood stains down the front of my blouse and the trauma induced paleness of my skin against the dark, plastic goggles made me look like a raccoon after an eating frenzy. This was the image that would be burned into Will's memory.

Chapter 16

The Last Night

My blouse stiff with blood and the stitches in my shoulder screaming, I collapsed on the bed. Memories of the night he left me seven years before rushed into my mind.

We spent that night alone, speaking words that no longer mattered. The silence in between was loaded with the ticking of the clock. Our hands touched, but our fingers were already strangers, and the sticky hours melted into an unbearable thickness. At ten o'clock, we could no longer stand the waiting abyss. There was no turning back from his leaving, and I think we both wanted it over.

I will not cry, I thought. *I cannot stand this if I cry.*

But I did cry – the loss so intense and emptying that my sobs caught inside me and made no sound, not until the unwanted tears washed over my face. Will drew me tightly against him, pulling me into him and crushing me painfully until I could not breathe. His face was invisible through my tears, and I was never sure if I heard him tell me goodbye.

And then he was gone. His warmth drained from my body, and a cold eeriness crept in. I stood singly. I was one. My heart would not beat – until I remembered the winding road that would lead him away from me. I ran to the window and watched his lights disappear in the valley below, and with them the light he shed on my life. I remained there long after he vanished, listening to the weeping of my heart.

Chapter 17

The Big Empty

I woke early on the final day of the conference. My first thought, before I even opened my eyes, was that I would be on the evening flight heading back to *my* world. For once, I wasn't looking forward to going home. I felt empty and wished my time with Will could have allowed us to connect at that special level again, to recapture how exclusive and remarkable those first few months were. Everyone always says you can't go back, and I didn't want to. I'd seen enough of him though to know how much we had both changed, and that seemed so worth exploring. It was just that some finality, some closing, would make it more bearable. I knew Will's schedule was impossibly busy. And he had, after all, tried to see me again the evening before. Still, Will had told me before he left for the hospital when Sophie cut her leg that seeing me was "difficult." So maybe I was an intrusion he would rather not have to deal with. How could feelings survive what we had put them through? His proposal months after he returned home was more than likely a result of loneliness. His friends had probably gravitated to different lives and different cities. His feelings had been recollections glazed with the sugar coating that seeps into memories.

I dressed, opened my half-filled suitcase and listlessly continued packing. Before I left the room, I checked my phone's message light one more time, but it just stared at me like an unblinking salamander eye. There would be no more opportunities to see Will. I had to admit that the little time we'd had together had only created a desire for more. And, I was relieved when Will told me he wasn't married. Still, I had no more intention of involving myself in a relationship now than I did seven years ago. So what was the problem? I enjoyed my carefree and uncomplicated life. I didn't know why I wasn't like most of the girls I knew who wanted marriage and a home and a family. Was something wrong with me? I enjoyed dating and having someone around to go places with, to laugh with, to talk to, but I was a social misfit – a person who didn't fall in love. I wasn't actually sure I was capable of loving someone, at least not a serious, forever kind of love. It sounded painful, and I was an expert at avoiding relationships that might cause me pain. And so, whenever dating turned into something that began to look serious, I ran the other way.

Downstairs, the technical assistance desk I was scheduled to man had only been visited by two customers, and one just needed directions to a meeting. I never liked the last day of a conference. The approaching echo of emptiness engulfed me. Sometimes, when I arrived early for a company seminar, before the scraping set-up racket of chairs and tables and the chatter of coordinators barking orders, I would stand in one of the wide, silent hallways and listen. I could almost feel the rumble of coming voices and the thrumming of approaching feet beating a pulse on the floor. The silence was welcome then because it was a peopled future about to unfold, but afterwards, when the throngs disappeared, the silence was an echoing death rattle. It was like a petite mal. I felt deserted and empty like the hallways. But for the moment, I sat content enough in the imminent quiet, while the sun streamed in from a side window and wrapped my feet in warmth.

"Hi Jackie." The voice caught me off guard, and I jumped, knocking a pile of pamphlets off the table. I forgot my arm was in a sling and threw myself off balance reaching for them.

"Whoa," Jay said grabbing my chair before it toppled over. He scooped up the pamphlets, threw them into a haphazard stack, and then perched on the end of the table. "I tried to call you this morning, but I missed you. I heard about last night. You alright?"

"Sure," I said. I wasn't looking forward to answering questions all day about my being a glass magnet. I gave Jay the truncated version and tried to downplay the hospital part, telling him no permanent damage was done.

"Why the sling?" he asked.

"Oh, that... well, I managed to stop one particularly sharp piece of glass with my shoulder."

"Geesh," he grimaced. "So then... how's business? Customers not keeping you awake?" he asked, always one to get on with the work at hand.

"Things are really hopping here," I said.

"Actually, I'm glad I caught you alone."

I was fortunate to have a boss who did not micro-manage. Either you did your job and did it well, or you weren't on the team. He appreciated his staff, understood technology and kept his door open. Jay was easy going. I liked that about him. He had an even temperament, and I had learned a lot about systems and customer support from him. He pulled up a chair, leaned back and put his hands behind his head.

"How would you like to take some vacation time?" he asked.

"As long as it's not permanent," I said.

"You're not going anywhere. I need your help with the Cooper contract for starters. You haven't taken any time off for over a year. I think a break would do you good." He glanced at my sling and nodded. “I heard you talking to someone about the beauties of South Africa. Why don’t you take a week or two and see it while you’re here? The Chevron account is under control. We don’t need to move on Laser Tech until they resolve their software issues.” When I paused, he added, “Besides, I seem to have interrupted your breakfast with your doctor friend. Maybe this would give you two a little more time together.” Jay did a sort of Groucho Marx thing with his eyebrows. He probably thought I was love-challenged and emotionally incompetent. After all, he’d watched me make myself available for every late-night, out-of-town job he threw my way. My mind started darting about in different directions. Did I want to take a vacation virtually alone? It was pretty clear Will wasn’t interested in spending time with me. Where would I stay? This hotel was too pricey unless I could negotiate a weekly rate, which probably wouldn’t be too hard considering all the offers they’d made since last night’s accident. I had always wanted to see the pyramids, but unfortunately they were at the other end of this sprawling continent. “Where’d you go?” Jay asked, frowning.

“This is a big decision,” I insisted. “It’s not like you asked me if I’d run upstairs and check out the banquet room before dinner.”

“Well, you’ve got, umm, let’s see” he said checking his watch, “about eight hours before you need to leave to catch this evening’s flight. Think about it.”

“I’ll definitely give it some thought,” I promised.

The conference room doors opened just then and the crowd poured into the hallway. I welcomed the interruption to my somewhat depressed confusion.

Chapter 18

No He Isn't

I spent the afternoon avoiding the now empty rooms. I said goodbye to the few customers who were still milling around collecting brochures and asking last minute questions. The conference ended and only the ghostly whirring of a vacuum could be heard winding its way into a distant hallway. I headed for my room knowing the quiet would help me think, but that the silence would drive me crazy. I unlocked the door to find a beautiful bouquet of roses sitting on the coffee table. There were eleven red and one yellow rose buds. Red for passion and yellow for fidelity, or so Will had told me a long time ago.

A small card was leaning against the vase with the single word 'Jacqueline' written on it. I opened it with shaking hands.

Enjoy your life, Jackie
Love, Will

The tear startled me as it splashed onto the card. I tried to wipe it off and smeared the word 'life.' This was the final goodbye. It was over. If I stayed, I wouldn't see him again. I was the past, not the present, and certainly not the future. I took a deep breath, waiting for my usual defenses to take over and remind me that I didn't want anyone interfering with my life. I waited. The silence started sounding like noise. The emptiness of my life sped towards me like a camera zooming in on its subject. I looked around at the bed with only one side slept in, the half-filled suitcase, and the empty hangers in the closet. You can't want him because you're lonely, I thought.

"I'm not lonely!" my inner champion yelled. That's right, I thought. There aren't any holes in my life. And if there were, I certainly didn't think they needed filling by someone else. And what difference did it make anyway? Will wouldn't be seeing me again. The card made it clear – "*Enjoy your life*" How depressing. It's what you say to someone you never expect to see again. I sat on the edge of the bed wondering what it was I wanted from Will. I had turned down his proposal, and I couldn't remember feeling this need for him back then. I was numb for a few days after he left, and then I just turned off – my gift, shutting down. I would do that again.

Packing finally finished, I walked over to the window to enjoy the view one last time. The noon sun was turning the city into yellow metal, as if the gold in the ground had crept into the skyscrapers. Listless and edgy, I moved through the room straightening the bedspread, picking up a business card that had fallen on the floor, and throwing away the morning newspaper. I kept looking at Will's flowers. I could smell the delicate sweetness of the roses, and pulled the yellow one out to rub its silky petals against my cheek, so cool against the heat of my skin. I would not read the card again. I tucked it into the side of my suitcase and headed downstairs to take care of my bill. There was time for a walk before meeting a few of my co-workers and heading for the airport.

"Ms. Sinclair?" the short, dark-haired clerk at the front desk called me back as I headed out of the lobby. "I'm sorry. I didn't notice there was a message for you." A small flame of hope lit somewhere deep in my chest. I glanced at the nameless envelope. Inside was a single piece of paper.

Jackie –

Sorry I had to leave you last night, but it looked like you were in capable hands. I checked after my meeting and found out you made it back to your room. I didn't want to call and disturb you last night, and I'm back in meetings today and tomorrow. If you're around, give me a call (room 1101), or please leave a message and let me know how you're doing.

Roy

I left a message for Roy at the front desk that I was fine, packed to go, and wished I would have as good a seat mate on the way back as I did on the way to South Africa. I also thanked him for persevering through some of the more disastrous moments of my life.

"Ms. Sinclair?" The desk clerk signaled me again.

"Call for you. Just hit "1," she said, nodding towards a wall phone.

"Hello?"

"Jackie – It's Will. Just checking on my most difficult patient. How are you feeling?"

"Oh ... " I said, my heart plummeting. This was painful. Our last conversation was going to be a medical check-up. I wanted to talk to him about anything but my injuries; instead, I was having a long distance office visit. "Hi," I said lamely, trying to keep the depression out of my voice.

"Are you okay?" Will asked, diving immediately into suspicious doctor mode.

"I'm fine. You'd hardly recognize me. I combed my hair and put on a clean blouse."

"Are you having any pain?"

My attempt to hide my feelings hadn't slipped by him, only he thought I wasn't feeling well physically. Now he wouldn't let me slide by without trying to dissect every one of my vital signs. It was clear that acting was another vocation I could throw out of the possible future jobs lineup.

"I'm great," I said with as much gusto as I could muster, "Never better. I had a terrific doctor after all. And, thank you for the beautiful roses. I wish I could take them all home, but I tucked one in my suitcase to fly back with me. Actually," I added, wanting to change the subject, "you just caught me. I'm heading out for a walk to see your beautiful city one more time."

"When are you leaving?" Will asked.

"Tonight." My throat tightened. There was a long silence.

"It might be better to take it easy. Have you got someone to walk with you?"

"No, but it's a beautiful sunny day, and if I see any flying glass, I'll duck."

"Jackie, I'm serious. Is Roy going with you?"

"Roy? No, why?"

"Does he have another meeting?" The words were an accusation.

"I…have I missed something?" I asked.

"Well, don't you think he should be a little more concerned about how you're doing?" Will insisted.

"He left me a note," I said. What in the world was the matter with Will? He was acting like Roy was here as my personal assistant.

"A note." Will sounded less than impressed.

"Yes, a note, and I thanked him."

"You thanked him because he wrote you a note?"

"What are you so angry about? He went to the hospital with me, and he checked on me as soon as his meeting was over. He's been incredibly helpful. Besides, except for your excellent services, I've been able to take care of myself just fine." Why would Will think Roy should have any reason to ... ? No, I thought. Surely Will doesn't think Roy and I are ... what – a couple, dating? The rings. We had similar rings. And we both wore them on our left hands. And now that I thought about it, Roy had been around both times I'd seen Will.

"Will?"

"What?" he said, clearly annoyed.

"Are you angry with Roy?"

"Well, I think you deserve a little more consideration."

"And why should I expect more consideration from Roy?" I couldn't resist. There was silence at the other end of the line, and I began to think the boy was beginning to see the light.

"Well, Roy is your ... husband?" Will asked tentatively.

"No," I laughed.

"Then, your husband is back in the states?"

"Afraid there isn't one. Roy is a customer I met on the plane on the way here. He's done nothing but go out of his way to be helpful." This was my 'let *me* throw the drink in the sink' moment.

"Could you use some company on your walk?" Will asked.

Chapter 19

I said I was Not Going to Stay

Will met me in the lobby 20 minutes later.

"Here," he said, handing me another pair of froggy glasses.

I grimaced and shook my head. "I don't think so."

"Then you'd better have a pair of your own you can wear. Let's give your eyes another day or two of rest." I dug in my purse for a pair of sunglasses and put them on. "How's the shoulder?" he went on in doctor mode.

"Couldn't be better." A wave of dizziness hit me, and I put my hand to my head.

"What's the matter?"

"Oh, I guess... I'm just a little tired."

"Maybe a walk isn't such a good idea." He rubbed his chin, watching me.

"The fresh air will do me good. Besides, rumor has it there'll be a doctor along." I suddenly remembered when Will had written me about showing his mother my picture after he returned to Africa. She'd said I had a "cheeky" smile. I gave him one.

These last few moments with Will felt bittersweet as we walked past the towering buildings. Towards the outskirts of town, the shops were older and more run down. Glittering windows, fresh paint and pristine streets were replaced by dirt-smudged buildings covered with dozens of hand written signs and advertisements. Spray-painted screams of graffiti stained walls and windows in garish colors, and wind-blown food wrappers, cigarette butts and empty coke cans were scattered on the streets and in the gutters. A crumpled newspaper ad for vegetables and fruit rolled to a stop near our feet, then suddenly blew away in a gust of wind, scraping and scratching in a lopsided cadence against the pavement. Now, there were fewer business suits and more flashy shirts and long-chain jewelry. The looks some of the people gave us as they passed began to make me uncomfortable.

"I didn't realize how far we'd come," Will said eyeing two men in baggy pants, one covertly handing a small package to the other. He guided me across the street and headed us back towards the Carlton. The sun's heat soaked into me and made me drowsy. Will was watching me closely and had tucked my hand into his arm as we walked and talked about the city. After a few blocks, he led me into a small, cool café and ordered iced tea. I held the frosted glass to my cheek and moaned with pleasure.

"This wasn't the best idea, was it? Didn't mean to chat you up so much," Will said. We'll take a cab back."

"Okay," I said listlessly.

"No argument? Your shoulder must hurt. Did you take the pain pills?

"Yes, mmm, no ... I forgot." I took a sip of the tea. Will was staring absently at my shoulder.

"Okay, my turn. What?" I asked. Will didn't respond. I waited.

"I was thinking about you leaving. You've come all this way and haven't even seen how beautiful my country is." I was caught off guard by the unexpected tears that welled in my eyes. I dropped my head, but it was too late, Will had seen. "How much time do we have before you catch your plane?" At least he had said "we," not "you."

"I have to leave the hotel in a couple of hours. If you have to get back to the hospital, I understand." But the truth was, I didn't understand. I'd rather go home hearing he felt nothing for me than wondering for the rest of my life if I'd given up on finding out that I wanted him in my life, and that there was a chance that he might want to be in it. At least I could attempt to put an end to this now. I took a deep breath and looked directly at him, teary eyes and all.

"Scratch that. I'd actually rather spend the next hundred and twenty minutes with you." He nodded absently, but said nothing, just stared off into the distance. I had a little pride left, so I shrugged, wincing at the pain in my shoulder and stood. "I'd better start back if I'm going to make it." He reached for my hand and pulled me gently back down, but remained silent. "Help me a little here," I said, perplexed. "You're going to have to say something because I have no idea what's going through your mind."

"I met someone." Will looked me in the eye.

My heart felt like a lopsided ball. It had run the gamut - happy, sad, elated, hurt and right now, Will's words were pummeling it. Of course he had met someone. It was a miracle he wasn't married. He was intelligent, fun to be with, handsome, a doctor. I gently pulled my hand back and tried smiling.

"That's ... " I couldn't finish.

'Jackie, the timing of your trip couldn't be worse." Well, that certainly made me feel better.

"Sorry, but I don't schedule system rollouts," I said in a quick flash of temper.

"I only meant worse in the sense that your arrival coincided with Cali coming back." I'm sure I looked confused. "Cali is a girl I met last year. I'd been alone for a while. She was fun. The relationship got serious, and we ended up engaged." He looked down for a moment, "Until she got cold feet and left. She returned a week ago and wanted to pick up where we left off." Will was watching my reaction. I'd unconsciously covered my mouth with my fingers. It didn't help that my hand carried the faint scent of his aftershave.

'So ... you're engaged again?" I tried to keep the disappointment out of my voice.

"When Cali returned, my first reaction was to stay away from her. I was hurt, but she eventually convinced me that we should at least talk. We did, and the relationship looked like it was back on track. And then you showed up." Will rubbed his hand down his face.

I'd heard enough. "You don't owe me anything, Will. We were a long time ago."

He looked as if he were the one in pain. "When I got your letter, I wasn't sure seeing you was such a good idea. It wasn't only that I didn't want to open up to all those old feelings, but I was afraid to lose the memories."

"I know. Believe me, I understand. I do, but I'll be gone in a few hours."

"Jackie, I have to ask - have you moved past what we were to each other?"

I knew in that moment that I hadn't, probably knew the minute I thought about writing to let Will know I was coming. I still felt something. But now that someone else was in the picture, did I want to put myself through discovering what it was? I was hardly the type to fight for love. I was more likely to run.

"What are you asking?"

"Stay – give us a chance to find out what's between us." Will put his hand on the table and leaned forward slightly, "I'm going to be blunt." *When wasn't he?* "If you still feel anything for me, don't go. Stay, and let's spend some time together."

"And you'll be fitting me in between your time with Cali?" Will had it all his way – home court advantage, two women. All the choices lay on his side. I winced. My head felt like it was between a slowly tightening vise.

"I told Cali about you last night. She was upset. She thought we'd picked up where we left off."

"Last night? Last night you were sewing up my shoulder. Are you… living with her?" The headache was pounding.

"No, she works at hospital."

"And why would you tell her about me if you thought I was married?"

Will shook his head, "Telling her had nothing to do with you being married. I told her because having you here changed things." I drew in a deep breath. "What I mean is that after Cali left me I was lonely, not devastated." I knew my eyes were radiating wariness. Will watched me for a moment. "I think you can understand that kind of feeling, Jackie. It's about filling up loss."

"You're forgetting that you eventually wrote and told me it wasn't going to happen for us," I said, barely hiding the hurt. I had never actually said, "No," to Will's proposal. I just kept getting on with my life – college, work. When his letter came, I'd known the truth too, that too much time had passed and that our lives had spiraled in different directions. The real problem had been that we couldn't seem to find a way to fit our two worlds together. "Now you want me to stay and see if you want to walk out of my life again? What if we're just repeating the past?" The heat was suffocating, and I put the glass of tea against my cheek again. It felt like ten pounds, and my hand shook.

"I wrote that letter because you weren't ready or willing to get married then, and you weren't sure I was the right guy. That didn't give me a lot to hold onto." He frowned at my trembling hand and took the glass from me. The ice had melted. Will signaled the waiter and asked him to call a taxi. Intending to go wait outside in the fresh air, I stood and reached for my purse. A sharp pain shot though my shoulder, and I swayed toward the table. Will put out a hand to catch me, but I grasped the back of my chair and took a deep breath. I shook my head to stop the dizziness, but couldn't, so I sat back down and dropped my head into my hands. Will was at my side in a second. He pulled my chair out and leaned my upper body over my knees.

"Jackie honey... I'm making a mess of this, and I want you to understand what's happened. But first, I need to get you back to the hotel." Will turned at a call from the waiter. "Jacks, the cab is here. We'll finish this later." It was the first time Will had used the old nickname, but I didn't want to hear anymore. He helped me into the cab, and it was all I could do to sit upright. I must have dozed because it seemed we were back in no time. The ache in my head had dulled, but my legs were wobbly. What was I going to do? I'd checked out of my room, and sitting in the lobby until it was time to get myself to the airport seemed monumental.

"Jackie. Are you alright?" The voice was Jay's. This was getting worse by the minute.

"She needs to lie down," Will told him.

The two men commandeered me towards a lobby couch, lowering me as carefully as mummified Egyptian remains. Jay actually reached over and felt my forehead. That was... motherly, but weird. Will tried to convince me that I should lie down, but that wasn't going to happen. All this molly coddling was irritating. People were beginning to stare, and the headache was pounding again with the sharpness of a two bladed sword.

"I'll be okay in a few minutes. I've got to catch my plane," I told no one in particular. Jay looked at Will, and I sensed something pass between the two men.

"Jackie, you're in no condition to fly," Jay said, back in manager mode. That shot a dram of adrenaline through my system. I was not going to stay here with Will and Cali.

"Overactive doctor's imagination," I croaked through my dry throat. It was not the sort of thing I meant to say. I was hurt by Will's words, but I didn't mean to be insulting. "Sorry," I backtracked, holding up a hand. "It's just that I'm fine, and I don't need anyone to take care of me."

"She's fine," Will mumbled, shaking his head. I slumped sideways against the couch pillow and closed my eyes. "I'm not a daft soutpeel," he grumbled. "I'd have to be putsy not to see how sick you are." I opened one eye and squinted up at him.

"Never mind," he said. "But, you don't make it easy."

Within minutes, Jay had reserved a room and returned with the key. Will stuffed more pillows around me and then walked off to talk to Jay. I couldn't hear the conversation, but Will was doing most of it. Jay nodded and the two shook hands and returned to the couch where I lie swaddled.

"Jackie, let me have your airline ticket," Jay insisted, his tone making it clear he wanted no opposition from me. "I'm going to cancel your flight. You can reschedule when you're feeling better. I told the doctor that I suggested you take a week or two off. You deserve it, and it looks to me like you need it."

So… what, like these two men were making decisions for

me? I pushed myself to an upright position, hiding my shaking hands beneath me. And then, wobbling a bit to and fro, stuck my chin in the air and scowled through the spots that were swirling in my eyes.

"I can make it to the plane, and then all I have to do is sleep." There was no response from either of them. "You're just leaving me here with strangers?" I scowled at Jay in a last ditch effort. I needed more air.

"Jackie, you're not well. I can see that, and the doctor doesn't think you should be flying. Besides, you're not alone. The admin staff will be staying through the end of the week to wind things up. I'll make sure they keep an eye on you. And, it seems to me, you have a very competent doctor. Besides," he added with a little wink, "I'll expect you to have this hotel running our software by the end of the week." The traitor. He put out his hand for my ticket. Knowing I was licked for the moment, I handed it over. In return, I got a smile and my new room key.

"Try to relax and have a good time," Jay said and headed for the reception desk.

Chapter 20

Out of My World and Abandoned

I felt disgruntled and deserted, stared at by strangers and packed between couch pillows like a thick wool sweater on a summer blouse sale rack. Well, I would just rest until I felt stronger, and then I would reschedule my flight for the next day. Will reached to help me off the couch.

"You," I said pointing a finger at him, "are responsible for the dilemma I'm in. I don't know what you said to Jay, but you've clearly bamboozled him into believing I'm not well enough to catch a plane. Flying is part of my job. It's second nature to me. I could do it with my eyes closed." A searing pain shot through my shoulder, and the room slowly spun. I really wanted to lie down. Will looked at the number on the room key and guided me toward the elevators.

"I've got this," I insisted, putting up a hand. "I'm going to get my luggage and then take myself to my room for a short rest after which I intend to reschedule my flight." The speech took every ounce of strength I had.

"Mmm hmm," Will hummed, continuing on towards the elevators.

"You don't get to ignore me just because you think I might be the tiniest bit sick." The truth was, the supporting arm he had around me was the only thing keeping me upright.

"Well, first of all, Jay had your luggage sent to your room already, and second, I'm going to make sure you do rest. You can reschedule your ticket later." I drew in a breath to say something, but

Will held up a finger. "Jackie, you're exhausted, you're in pain and you've been putting up with me for the last couple of hours. You need to rest."

He was right. I just didn't want to admit feeling helpless. In my room, Will insisted on removing my shoes and covering me with the bedspread. He asked me where the pills he had given me were and watched me take them. My head was fuzzy, and my body felt on fire. I remembered this kind of fever aching from childhood. The surface of my skin felt irritated and raw, and I wanted to move and stretch it. Will sat on the edge of the bed and brushed the hair from my eyes. He frowned, put his hand back on my forehead, and then pulled the cover back and unbuttoned the top two buttons of my blouse. My ears were buzzing, and he seemed to be a long way off. He pushed the blouse off my shoulder and gently removed the bandage. I flinched. The wound was red and swollen. The next thing I knew, Will was talking to someone on the phone. It sounded like he was ordering medicine, but I couldn't keep my eyes open, and my mind drifted in and out of focus.

"Hot," I mumbled and pushed off the cover.

"I know, Jackie honey."

"Honey," I repeated and dropped off to sleep. I woke to an arm sliding behind my back and pulling me up.

"Take these," Will dropped two small pills in my mouth and tipped a glass of water against my lips. "They're just aspirin. Your wound is infected. I'm going to give you an antibiotic." He rolled up the sleeve of my blouse, and I turned my head drowsily to watch.

"Why?" I asked.

"Because the antibiotic will clear up the infection."

"No," I smiled, "Why is it infected? Didn't you give me an

antibiotic already?"

"Yes, but it didn't work. I'm going to give you something stronger." He pushed the needle into my arm, but my eyes were closed before he removed it. *All alone,* I thought, and pushed up my heavy lids.

"Will you leave me a number to call – just in case - *I hated admitting it* - I feel worse?"

"Better than that," Will smiled. "I'll be right here."

I looked up at him skeptically. "What about Cali?"

"Sshhh." He pulled a chair up to the side of the bed.

When I opened my eyes again, Will was asleep in the chair, and the sky had slipped into an overcast grey. I stretched and gasped at the stab of pain in my shoulder. Will woke instantly.

"Hi, how're you feeling?"

"Maybe better, I think." He felt my forehead.

"You still have a fever."

The phone rang shrilly. Will reached over and picked it up, started to answer it then handed it to me.

"Jackie here," I said, sleepily.

"Jackie? – It's Roy. You're still here. I got your message and thought you were heading home. I asked at the desk if you'd checked out, and they told me you'd checked back in. What's going on? Are you alright?"

"I'm okay."

"Why don't I believe you? How's the shoulder?"

"I know it's there."

"Can I help?"

"You've already thrown yourself in the path of flying cocktail glasses." My tongue didn't seem to be moving fast enough, and my words felt slurred and mumbly.

"What are your plans for heading back to the states?"

"Oh ... a little unclear just now." I glanced at Will and decided to reschedule my flight as soon as he left. I wanted to get out of the hotel and safely onto a plane before Cali showed up as my nurse.

"I'll be out of meetings about four this afternoon. Are you up to dinner?" Roy asked.

"Dinner? Oh ... have a fever – turned out to be an infection in my shoulder. Don't think I feel up to going out." Will was standing at the window with his back to me. He straightened his shoulders.

"Shouldn't you see a doctor? What about your friend?"

"I have enough antibiotics and pain killers in me to be stopped at customs for dealing drugs." I sensed Roy's smile.

"I've got a meeting in a few minutes."

"More espionage?" I asked.

"You'd be surprised. I'll check with you later," he said and hung up.

Will returned to the bed and looked down at me, his eyebrows knit together. "I've got to get back to hospital."

"All the men I know in this big country are always leaving me for work," I said, smiling smugly.

"I'll send someone from hospital to check on you."

"I don't think I'm up to meeting Cali just now."

Will shook his head. "I mean Rachel."

I suddenly felt a little perkier. "I'll be just fine, thank you."

"She's a terrific nurse. She's just protective of people she loves." When I looked questioningly at Will, he added, "Cali isn't a nurse. She works in the administration office."

"Oh . . ." I said, the connection between Rachel and Cali sinking in. "So, Rachel thought I was trying to move in on Cali?"

"More like I was moving in on you. Cali is Rachel's niece. She helped Cali get the job at hospital." Will glanced at his watch.

"Well, you have things to do," I said, "and I'm going to get out of this bed and take a shower."

"You stay right where you are, unless you want me to send for Rachel now," Will warned me. He put his hand on my forehead and nodded, and then headed for the door. "I'll knock you up later," he said glancing back at me. Okay, now I was awake. "Call you," Will said looking over the top of his glasses at my startled expression. "I'll call you later," he added, shaking his head and smiling. This British jargon was going to take some getting used to.

After he left, I sat up and waited for the spinning to slow down, wondering if Tilly had left any shampoo. When I thought I could navigate without bumping into walls, I stood up. The room was kaleidoscoping wildly and my legs were wobbling like two cooked noodles. I was too weak to do anything but slide back between the cool sheets. I closed my eyes and was instantly asleep.

Chapter 21

The Revolving Door / Fevers and Friends

A couple of hours later, I was awakened by a quick tap on the door. Before I could call out to ask who it was, a key was inserted in the lock, and the door opened slowly. A brown curly head wearing dark framed glasses peered into the room. Tilly eyed me curiously, and then bustled in carrying fresh towels.

"I heard you was sick," she said. "So I come to check for myself." She walked right up to the bed and felt my head. I figured I had the most popular forehead in Johannesburg.

"How did you know I was sick?"

"Your doctor left orders at the front desk that you wasn't feelin' so good, an' that we should bring you whatever you need. The message also got sent to housekeepin', and I come right away." She whisked around the room, straightening my covers, fluffing my pillows, and swabbing through the bathroom. When she finished, she handed me a small card on which she'd written "Tilly" and a housekeeping number.

"You jes call me anytime, and if I'm not there, summun else'll come lickety split. When you git hungry, call room service. Now you jes rest."

I had a momentary twinge of guilt for thinking she might have come to retrieve any extra conditioner. I'd clearly misread the woman. Her brusqueness was more of a bossy mother thing. She laid two mints on the bedside table and gave the covers another smoothing swipe, then bustled out turning once before closing the door to give me and the room a once-over. I waved and smiled. She "harrumphed" and closed the door. I managed a quick shower, but had just dozed off again when someone else knocked. I needed a revolving door.

"Jackie? It's Roy. Can I come in?"

"Sure. Just give me a minute to get there," I called out, running my hand through my still damp hair.

"Stay where you are. I talked to the desk, and they sent a hotel employee with me. He has a key."

I sat up as the lock flipped and a room service employee entered pushing a table with covered dishes, a bottle of wine, a bottle of Perrier and two glasses. Roy followed him in and came over to the bed. For once, he wasn't dressed in a suit. Instead, he wore a checked cotton shirt, polished cotton pants and loafers. But, as usual, the blond hair looked casual and perfect.

"Mohammad to the mountain," he smiled, tilting his head to get a better look at me. "Since you weren't up to going out, I thought you might like to eat in."

"Another rescue," I said. "Aren't you tired of always being around me when I'm at my worst?"

"You look great."

"Lying, that's a spy thing, right?"

Roy picked up the terrycloth hotel robe on the end of the bed and put it over my shoulders, and with an arm around my waist, helped me to the couch. I wasn't very hungry, but sitting up talking to Roy about the conference took my mind off Will and my missed flight.

"So, now that I've plied *you* with wine,' I said, 'how did your meetings go?"

"Very good." He was suddenly serious. "We'll have to talk about them sometime."

"So they're still off limits?"

"For now. To future ventures," he said, tapping his glass to mine. And then changing the subject abruptly, asked me how I'd ended up in technology.

I smirked. "Actually, I didn't. It was more of a 'we stumbled into each other.' After I graduated, a friend suggested I interview with his company. He knew I wanted to write, but it was a good opportunity to join a technology company with great prospects that hadn't gone public yet. He said it would be a good chance to practice my interviewing skills. The candidates were reduced to nine and neither of us thought I'd have a chance of being selected. I was lucky, and maybe it helped to know someone in the company. So here I am."

"What kind of a writer?" Roy never lost the thread of the conversation he was after.

"I majored in journalism. I wanted to write for a newspaper." I shrugged. "Well, the two aren't so far off, I guess. I just write contracts instead of news stories."

"Do you still want to write?" As usual, Roy was firing questions like a machine gun.

"I'll always want to write."

"Why don't you?"

It was one too many questions. I reached up to support my head, which fell into my hand with the weight of a cannon ball. "Sorry, I'm really out of it tonight."

"Let's get you back to bed." Roy put his glass down and stood to help me up.

A knock at the door startled us both. Roy opened it to a

familiar looking woman who first glanced with accusing eyes at him, then at the table with its clutter of dishes and glasses and finally came to rest on me, draped limply over the end of the couch. Will had made good on his promise to send someone to check on me. Rachel brushed by Roy, her street clothes swishing crisply. She deposited a small bag on the bedside table and then straightened the bed sheets, folding them back in true hospital fashion. When I introduced the two, Rachel nodded briefly at Roy but said nothing.

"I'm afraid I might have tired your patient a bit."

"Following doctor's orders isn't one of her strong points." Roy's good looks and boyish charm were lost on Rachel.

Eyeing me with disapproval, Rachel whisked me off the couch and into the freshly straightened bed, then whipped a thermometer out of thin air and popped it into my mouth. My worst fears were confirmed when she removed a needle from her bag. I felt like a shish kabob about to be skewered. Roy glanced at the needle Rachel was filling and gave me a sympathetic look.

"Well, I'll leave you to expert hands," he said. "I have a couple more days of meetings. I'll check in to see how you're doing." He glanced at the needle once more, then shot me an impish grin.

"You're burning up," Rachel scolded. "You shouldn't be entertaining guests."

"Aw diun no he ws cmig," I said around the thermometer.

"You're going to have an injection now and then start these pills in the morning." She set two white bottles on the bedside table. I closed my eyes and braced myself for the shot, but her touch was light and calming. "There, all done." She removed the thermometer from my mouth.

"Rachel – you're magic. That's the most painless shot I've ever had."

"Hmmph, 101.5. No more visitors." She carefully lifted a corner of my bandage, glanced beneath it and then pulled a package of tape from her bag to reseal it. She brushed the hair off my forehead. For the first time, I felt the gentleness of her efficiency. I smiled and snuggled into the cool bed, cooing a little to myself.

"Thank you for coming all the way over here. I feel better already," I said.

She wrapped the used needle and bandages in a plastic bag marked, "Warning," and dropped it into a side pocket of her purse before straightening her shoulders and looking uncomfortably at me for a moment.

"He's worried about you." The words did not come easy to her. "You just need a good night's sleep," she tutted and gave my hand a squeeze.

Chapter 22

We Need to Talk

I woke to light streaming in my window. Sometime during the night my fever had broken. My legs still didn't feel too solid beneath me, but I managed to get up and shower. There were four bottles of hotel shampoo waiting for me on the bathroom sink.

Later in the morning I curled up in my bathrobe on the couch and called work. Jay was in a meeting, so I left a message that I was feeling much better and would be rescheduling my flight in the next day or two. Tilly bustled in barely knocking before entering. She peered at me with a mother's discerning eye before tucking a blanket around me while she changed the sheets and cleaned the room.

"Back inta bed," she snapped.

The town was full of people ordering me around. But I had to admit, I'd never felt so taken care of. After Tilly left, I dressed and thought a short walk down to the lobby and civilization might do me good. It was a great idea until I got to the reception area and the dizziness returned. Wobbling through the lobby on trembling legs, I found two chairs in a corner and collapsed into one of them just in time to see Will come through the front doors. He spotted me on his way to the elevators and squinted at me as though he'd seen a specter.

"What are you doing down here?" Even angry, he was gorgeous.

"Getting a little exercise?" I hoped I didn't look as bad as I felt.

"You're white as a ghost. You're going back to bed."

"You Johannesburgians are very bossy," I said.

He scooped me up, but I swayed a little, and he clucked like an old hen. After a few feet, Will looked at me with raised eyebrows. "I understand you were entertaining last night." A self-satisfied smile curled around the corners of my mouth.

"What?" he growled.

"Nothing. Can't a girl spend a little time with her husband?"

My message light was blinking when we returned to my room. I hit the play button and left it on speaker.

"Jackie – it's Jay. How are you feeling? Better I hope. I just got your message about rescheduling your flight for tomorrow. Stay where you are – and that's an order. I've been trying to get you to take a little vacation time for the last year. You're in a beautiful part of the world. Enjoy it! I'll see you in a week or two." There was a short pause while I scowled and Will looked smug. "If it makes you feel any better, we all miss you. Besides, no one wants to work with Kiely. We'll put him off until you return. You seem to be the only one who can charm him into a good mood anyway. Have fun."

While I sat on the edge of the bed, Will did his doctor stuff - checking my now hopefully non-existent fever, my vital signs and shoulder, and then asking if I had taken the pills Rachel left the night before.

"By the way," I admitted, "Rachel's okay."

Will glanced at me, "We need to talk." He pulled a chair to the side of the bed and leaned forward, resting his arms on his legs. "Are you up to resuming our conversation from yesterday?" he asked.

"Alright, let's finish," I said. My word choice didn't leave much doubt about what I thought the outcome of this "talk" would be. With Cali in the picture, I felt like a rejected foreign import.

"Don't close yourself off, Jackie. Hear me out." I owed him that much and nodded. "When we left the café yesterday, you thought I'd decided to let Cali make the decision for all of us because I said I talked to her first. Am I right?"

"It seemed that way," I said.

"When your letter arrived telling me you were coming, I wasn't sure what I felt at first, except panic. I was settled in my life for once, and I didn't want the… interruption." He shook his head. "It didn't take long to realize what the real problem was. I was afraid I was still in love with you." I wanted to stop him because the way I saw it, he didn't have any decision to make as long as he was in love with Cali, but I knew he wanted to lay it all out.

"I told you I was lonely when Cali left me - lonely, Jackie, not devastated. I thought I had to open up old wounds to compare what I felt for you and what I felt for her." He ran a hand through his hair. "The feelings weren't the same, but I already knew that. Actually, I wasn't all that surprised when she left. When I met her she'd just broken off with a longtime boyfriend. I don't think she was over him. She left me to go back to him, and now she's returned to pick up where we left off. I'm not sure she knows what she wants."

Cali was a ping pong ball that just rolled to a stop on Will's side of the table. I didn't want to hear that Will would take her back. And, at this point, I didn't want to dissect exactly why I didn't want to know.

"When you showed up here in Africa, the past was right there in front of me again. The only problem was choice. I didn't have one. You'd moved on with your life, and I sure as hell didn't want to want you and lose you again. Once in a lifetime is enough. But then last night at the hospital, when I looked into your eyes," Will squinted slightly, "it was seven years ago. Nothing has changed, not for me." He reached over and tucked an errant strand of hair behind my ear. His fingertips brushed my neck and a spiraling chill snaked down my back. I shivered. Will was gauging my condition as the doctor he had become, but he was also watching my reaction as the man he was. "Every time I touched you or leaned close to you last night, your heartbeat sped up. I don't believe that was fear." I didn't trust myself to respond, and even if I had, I wasn't sure how much I wanted to admit. Will glanced at my lips and then back into my eyes. "I thought it was over between us," he said. "I was wrong."

I wanted to silence the part of me that was arguing in my head, the part that remembered our painful past, telling me to be careful, to protect myself. I wanted to break free of it and hear the voice it constantly drowned out, that difficult to hear voice that always asked the same question – "What do you want?" I looked away from his eyes to think for a moment.

"We let each other go," he said, understanding my hesitation. My head popped up, and he held up a hand. "I know, I was the one that walked out of your life, but I was here, waiting for you when you decided to live your life without me." He took a long breath and released it, and then sat back. "Did you love me?" he asked, his eyes trained on mine. It was many years later when I realized Will already knew the answer to that question. He was only asking me if I did.

And there it was - the topic I never dealt with because I'd covered up what I felt for Will knowing he was returning to Africa, permanently. When Will wrote six months after he left and proposed, I continued to deny whatever it was I felt. He was so far away, and if I accepted, it meant facing the loss of family, friends, my country and maybe even my plans for college. I convinced myself he was just lonely after returning home. The real kicker, and what I didn't know back then, was that I had a distrust of men and relationships that my mother had fed me like baby formula from the time I could first remember. I didn't know how to cut through the years of layers and filters that opinion created. I only knew that I had to protect myself by maintaining emotional distance. Funny how safety nets can become solitary dungeons.

"Did you love me?" he asked again, his gaze piercing the air between us.

"I don't know," I whispered. He reached for my hand and laced his fingers through mine.

"Why?" That was the question I didn't want to answer. This was way out of my comfort zone.

After a moment, I scooted so that my back rested on the thick pillows that lay against the headboard. I took a deep breath and looked out the window. "After you left, I used to dream about you. You were always in the distance looking at me, smiling, but never moving towards me." A chill ran up my back, and I wrapped my arms around myself. Will pulled the bedspread over me, and took my hand again. He nodded for me to go on. "You remember how strict my mother was? There was no feeling sorry for myself because you were gone. It wasn't allowed. The face I put on for her gradually took over, and I convinced myself that I was fine. I had a college degree to earn and a life separate from yours ... forever." I shrugged. Will watched me, emotionless. "I told you I didn't see your proposal coming, and that was because I had no reason to believe you felt that way or that I'd ever see you again." I smoothed the bedspread and realized my hand was shaking. "I never wanted to get married." I winced. "My parents' marriage was a sad situation. I couldn't imagine going through something like that, giving my independence to someone else, exposing myself to that kind of pain. So please," I glanced away, "what I felt for you was tied up in all of that." I needed him to understand what I could not feel.

Will suddenly blinked and started, then moved to sit on the bed, leaning forward and pulling me into his arms. I put a hand on his chest. "If you want a life with Cali, I understand." Will straightened and sat back.

"Cali was never in love with me, and I would have been settling if I'd stayed with her. I knew that the morning I met you at the hotel for breakfast. I don't want to lie to myself anymore, Jackie." Will's eyes held mine. "I never stopped loving you." He reached for me again, and this time I didn't resist. "It's alright," he murmured. We stayed that way for a long time, and then Will pulled the pillows down on the bed and lowered me onto them. He lay down beside me, and careful of my injury, fit his body against mine, and we fell asleep.

Chapter 23

The Bet

Opening my eyes in the late morning, I found myself alone. I checked the clock and saw the cancelled airline ticket lying next to it. I picked it up and stared at the destinations – Dulles… San Francisco. I was still holding it when I answered the knock at the door.

"You're leaving?" Will's face turned a dusky red. I followed his eyes to the ticket in my hand. "I thought you were going to stay and give us time."

Beyond Will telling me he still loved me, I had no set expectations of how our lives would fit together any better now than they did seven years before. Déjà vu, I thought, time running out and one of us leaving for home. I wanted so badly to hold onto him, and at the same time I wanted to find my way to the cold comfort and empty security of my kind of safety.

"You're asking me to take a leap of faith," I said.

"Yes." His eyes drilled into mine.

"We could both end up hurt again."

"Yes."

"I'm scared," I admitted.

"I know," Will said. "So am I. But the risk of that is worth a second chance." Will was betting on an outcome I couldn't predict, and I preferred better odds.

"I just want to be on the winning team," I told him.

"I'm counting on the fact that we'll both be."

Will had worked out time off, how I don't know, and we parted with plans to spend some time together, a road trip to see Will's Africa. He would pick me up the following morning at 6:00, just enough time to shower, dress and pack after his all night shift.

Planning time together was a shot in the arm, and I felt good enough for a little outing. After ordering a bouquet of roses and lavender in a hand-painted vase for Rachel from the lobby florist, I took a cab to the hospital to deliver them in person. Almost to Rachel's station, I was approached by a young, pretty blonde girl.

"Hi," she said brightly, "are you looking for someone?"

"Thanks," I said. "I'm just delivering some flowers." Rachel looked up, and I waved. The girl's lids lowered, and she followed me to where Rachel sat.

"Thank you for everything you've done, Rachel." When I handed her the arrangement she smacked her lips and brushed a hand at me.

"You didn't need to do that. I was glad to help."

"You know my Aunt Rachel?" The girl was leaning an elbow on the countertop and openly checking out the slacks and blouse I was wearing.

"This is my niece, Cali Elburt. Cali, this is ... " Rachel began.

"Aren't you the one who slipped, or got cut up by some flying glass?" Cali interrupted. She'd known who I was all along.

"That would be me," I said. I suspected not much got by Cali when it concerned Will. And, I suspected she didn't like me giving her aunt anything.

"Well isn't that just the cutest little bunch of flowers," she said.

Chapter 24

An Offer

True to his word, Roy called after his meetings ended and left a message asking me if I felt up to joining him for a short dinner. He made reservations at a small French restaurant a block from the Carlton. Our table was near a fireplace in a quiet corner. The waiter appeared, and Roy ordered a wine from the south of France. Besides software, hardware, corporate negotiations and the media world, Roy was evidently also a wine aficionado. We sipped the warm Bordeaux and spoke of everything but work.

So," Roy said in one of his abrupt changes of subject, "what are your plans?"

"I've decided to spend some time in this beautiful country," I smiled.

"Would this have anything to do with your doctor?"

"Do you ever beat around the bush?"

"Doesn't get me many answers," he said.

"Actually, I'm thinking of a safari."

"Making those choices," he nodded, raising an eyebrow.

"Maybe just setting things right."

"I thought you might." I gave him one of my profoundly skeptical looks. "I know you better than you think I do," he said and shrugged. I was chagrined at the thought that both he and Will seemed to think they knew me so well, but I couldn't help listening to a tiny voice that admitted they both might be more tuned into my feelings than I was – very unsettling.

"Do you head to the States tomorrow?" I asked.

"Yes, more meetings in New York, and then I'm off to our Chicago office to finalize an expansion." That was vague, and I wondered if it had anything to do with Ability. "No questions?" he asked.

"Yes, lots, but you don't answer them," I said.

"Well, that's about to change."

I leaned forward. "Carte blanche?"

"Well, not quite," Roy hedged, "but give it your best shot."

"Okay, is Caduceus about to absorb Ability?"

"No."

When he didn't elaborate, I dove back in. "You said expansion. So then, I assume that means Caduceus is going to add South Africa to its playing field."

"If Caduceus is going to keep pace with new technology, we need to invest in the latest developments in satellite high speed and wireless interconnectivity and beyond. We're jumping into the media business." It made a lot of sense. The Caduceus product focused on satellite communication.

"Will you be partnering with CNN?" I asked.

"A South African version of it. It's still under wraps, and I'll need you to keep it that way for now," he said.

"I will," I promised, surprised he was sharing the information with me. "So, how will this new acquisition affect your job?"

"I'll be theading up satellite news operations in Europe and Africa, with home bases in Johannesburg and New York. It's one of the reasons I wanted to speak with you tonight." Before he could say more, the waiter returned to take our orders.

"Mademoiselle?" The waiter gave a slight bow.

"I like living dangerously. The gentleman will be ordering for me." I said smiling expectantly at Roy.

"We'll begin with the escargot," Roy said, not missing a beat. My smug smile turned into a tiny frown.

"I don't think I'm hungry enough for hors d'oeuvres."

"Just as I thought." Roy nodded.

Having no intention of being beaten at this game, I asked, "Do you serve those as a main course?"

"Yes, of course," the waiter sniffed.

"Well then, perhaps the gentleman would prefer that." Roy's glance flicked my way and the hint of a smile touched his mouth.

"I think we'll both just have Caesar salads, filet mignon aux oignons et gratin dauphinois… and, umm, mousse au chocolat." He looked at me with raised eyebrows.

"Sounds wonderful." The waiter snuffed a bit more and with a slight bow, left us. "I would have loved ordering the snails," I said in a confidential tone, "but they always leave me with such a craving for ice plant."

While the waiter cleared the last of our dinner, I saw Roy glance at the ring on his left hand. A pained look briefly crossed his face. He realized I'd seen it, and turned the conversation back to work.

"I have a proposition for you, Jackie. Your background in computers and journalism is a good fit for Caduceus's new division. It would allow you to bridge the gap between technology and the media. You could use your sales and negotiating skills and fulfill your journalism goals." Roy sat back and took a sip of his wine.

I was stunned by this dinner turned into job offer, but I was also intrigued. "It sounds interesting."

"Well, the new division will include an international

investigative branch. Africa, as you know, is at the boiling point - relations with Britain, the poverty, demonstrations and underground activity, disease and the tempers beneath it all."

"It's a huge challenge for Caduceus to take on," I said. Roy tilted his head and looked at me.

"Which is why we're looking for someone in the field who can liaison with the States, someone who can clearly present and document the information. The job will entail splitting time between South Africa and New York. There may be occasional trips to our European office." Roy was still watching me closely. "I think your background in technology, your willingness to travel and your interest in journalism is a good match for the position."

I liked what I heard, but the challenge was on two fronts for me – the job and the time Will and I needed. "I'm flattered you've considered me," I said after a few moments. "I'd like to hear more."

Over dinner, Roy sketched out a clear picture of the job, the travel required and the necessity of being unencumbered by commitments. He wanted to fill the position as soon as possible. I was impressed with the scope of the expansion, the opportunity and the salary.

"I'll be back in two weeks," Roy said over dessert. "In the meantime, take your vacation. Get some rest, and call me with any questions. You've got my number."

Chapter 25

The Road Back

Good to his word, Will knocked gently on my door at six the following morning. I was up, showered, packed and ready to go. We were like two kids on the last day of school, our delicious two-week summer vacation stretching ahead of us. The excitement of escaping from the jobs and the people in our lives, and the nervousness of being together again was exhilarating. Johannesburg's golden red sky opened for us like a newly cut pomegranate, the hotel's open elevator doors awaited our arrival and the valet tipped his hat as we exited the lobby. Grinning at each other, we threw my luggage into Will's older model blue Chevy.

"Mmm, American made." I raised my eyebrows and smiled smugly. "It's the best."

"So it is true then?" Will smiled back. "I do know best."

"Obstinate man," I muttered. And with that, we sped out of Johannesburg as if the morning sun's flaming rays had set it on fire. We were barely out of town when Will reached across the seat and held out his hand for me to take. I threaded my fingers through his, the touch was tinged with memories and the promise of possibilities. I laid our entwined hands in my lap, but his unexpected warmth seeped through the thin material of my slacks and embarrassed me, so I moved our hands to the seat. He glanced at me over the top of his glasses, a considering look in his eyes.

"Hungry?" he asked after a moment.

"A little, but I'm not sure I could eat just yet." My nerves always ruled my stomach.

After about a mile, Will pulled to the side near a grove of trees. He turned off the engine. My heart started pounding, and I wondered fleetingly if this trip had been such a good idea. Suddenly shy, I didn't know where to look or what to say. Will turned slowly towards me and reached across the top of the seat putting his arm around my shoulders. I was eighteen again, unable to breathe, sitting at the side of the road near an apple orchard.

"Jackie?"

"Mmm?" I pretended to watch a small bird on one of the tree branches outside my window, but my toes were curling inside my shoes. When he said no more, I took the bait and looked at him. It was going to be one of those indelible moments - the little flicks of time that replicate themselves on brain tissue, like the picture I had of Will lying on the picnic blanket in his leather jacket. *Please, God, don't let this one create a sore spot.*

"I know we haven't been together like this in a long time," Will said, "but it's still only me." My eyes darted to the safety of the glove compartment door, which I examined as intently as if I were looking for the answer to the riddle of the Sphinx. "We have to put the past in the past, Jackie, or we won't be able to move ahead."

"I know," I grimaced, "but it's been so long."

Will suddenly removed his arm from my shoulders. It surprised me, and I wondered fleetingly if we both had cold feet. I turned to look at him. He was studying me, and there was conviction in those honey gold eyes. Will put his hand beneath my chin, drawing me towards him. He met me half way and gently touched his lips to mine, and then looking into my eyes again, pulled me full against him and kissed me as soundly as I have ever been kissed. It caught me by surprise, and I froze for the tiniest moment as the locked door at the back of my mind clicked opened. The entirety of us hit me – this exceptionally precious man, the lips that still knew mine so well, the incredible fit of our bodies, and the extraordinary ability of his arms to pull me both into him and back through time. I remembered it all, and without thinking, responded body and soul. The intervening seven years flew out the window, down the road and dissipated into thin air. When the kiss ended, we were left breathless, staring into each other's eyes. Then suddenly, we both burst out laughing.

"Better now?" Will asked.

Chapter 26

Blood Ties

After an hour of driving, exhaustion caught up with Will, and he admitted needing a short "kip." I drove for the next couple of hours while he slept. What a stolen moment in time – traveling in a foreign country, no one able to reach me, no work requests and no responsibilities other than to keep the car pointed north and enjoy the beautiful scenery. I glanced at Will, asleep and vulnerable beside me. Moaning quietly, he opened his eyes and seemed momentarily confused when he saw me, then blinked slowly and smiled before dropping back to sleep.

We arrived at Will's parents' home in mid-afternoon, a single story house situated among rows of flower-filled hothouses. A florist shop stood in the distance, close to the street. Will pulled into the side driveway and stopped near a glassed-in porch. Inside was a table covered with a blue and white floral, of course, tablecloth. Will was excited and all but pulled me into the house. No one was home, so he gave me the grand tour ending with his room. I immediately looked for the bed stand where Will had written me that he kept my letters. Will followed my gaze.

"I had your picture on top, even talked to it sometimes," he said, staring as if he still saw it there. The admission came at a cost. I turned to leave the room and its agonizing memories, but he wasn't through. I was to know it all. "I still remember the smell of the perfume you put on your letters. I kept them in that drawer." Lost in the memory, Will nodded towards it. "Whenever I missed you, I'd open the drawer, and the perfume would fill the room. I could actually picture you here with me… for a moment." He inhaled as if the scent still lingered. Caught in his memories, I sniffed and was surprised to smell only long, silent absence. "The letter you wrote to tell me you had accepted a job offer in the states after your college graduation…" he hesitated. "I don't know what I expected, but not that. It was so final. You weren't coming, ever. I took it to my room and read it over a thousand times, until it got too dark to see. I never put that letter in the drawer with the others, just crumpled it up and threw it. I found it a long time later when I pulled out an old pair of boots from the back of my closet. I stuck my foot in and felt something. It was your letter…hated those boots after that. I felt like they betrayed me, waited until some unsuspecting moment when my guard was down. I thought for a while I could hate you, too." I shuddered at the rawness in his voice. "My God, Jackie, what did we give up?"

"Not this moment," I whispered. A door somewhere in the house opened and closed.

"Hello? Will?" Footsteps came searching.

We stood staring into each other's eyes before Will called out "We're here."

The Absalom found us first and went crazy jumping and barking when she saw Will. A smaller version of the dog followed, scurrying around my feet. Behind it was Will's mother. The top of her head barely reached my nose. She looked crisp in a beige skirt and white blouse, and her hair, the exact chocolate brown of Will's, was professionally done. She gave Will a quick hug.

"You meet at last," Will said pulling me beside him and introducing me to his mother. She put out her hand, and when I reached out, she took mine in both of hers and smiled. Her friendly gaze almost hid the scrutinizing look underneath. I wondered what she knew about the relationship between Will and me. Did she know he had proposed? Had he confided in her? Why hadn't I asked Will to tell me more about her before we met?

"Will, shame on you for making Jackie come all the way to Africa to see you. I'm very happy to meet you at last, Jackie. Thank you for taking such good care of Will while he was in your country." There was the tiniest inflection in her voice when she said "your country."

"It's nice to meet you, too, Mrs. Kincaid. As for taking care of Will, I think most of the thanks goes to my mother's cooking."

"I've never been a really good cook, but after Will returned and I heard about those wonderful dinners, I knew I was in trouble." She laughed. "Let's go into the kitchen and have some tea." We sat at a small table, and Will scooted beside me, resting his arm on the back of my chair. I was struck by how comfortable Will and his mother were with each other. There didn't seem to be a parent-child feeling to their relationship, just mutual love. When the tea glasses needed refilling, Will took care of it, and when the phone rang, Will offered to get it.

"Hello?... Hey, Tom. Yes, just for the day. Yes, I brought Jackie...Sure, come on over." Then the family did know about me.

"Tom and Lynn are coming over later," Will called to his mother, then glanced at me.

"Ask them if they can stay for dinner," she called back.

Will had written me about his brother, Tom, and his wife, Lynn. I wasn't ready to explain or even talk about our relationship with anyone except Will. It still felt too early for the invasion of family, no matter how well intentioned. Well, no choice now. The troops were on their way.

"I've got to make one quick call to the hospital to check on a patient," Will apologized picking up the phone again.

"So, how do you like your visit so far?" his mother asked.

"The little I've seen of the country is beautiful – mostly the Johannesburg area and the ride here. I spent the better part of my days in meetings and lectures or answering customer questions." I took a sip of tea.

"What do you do?" She leaned back in her chair, but her upper body remained stiff. I had the feeling she was trying to look relaxed for my sake.

"I manage the western sales and support in the U.S. for a technology company. I was here to speak about the new software." I knew from my own parents' reaction to anything about technology, that I might not be making much sense to her. If I wasn't, it was hard to tell. There was an intent intelligence in her eyes, and she listened thoughtfully. She continued to watch me for a moment. I changed the subject. "Your home feels like you brought the garden inside." She smiled and glanced toward the hot houses.

"Thank you," she said, drumming her fingers on the table in a little dance, like a woman with something on her mind. "I'm happy to have you here, at last," she added.

"Is floristry a family business, Mrs. Kincaid?" I wanted to know anything that would fill in the backdrop of Will's life. This was my chance to see Will through her eyes.

"Please, call me Connie. My father started the business with a small flower stand when I was a child. It grew." She waved her hand absent-mindedly at the garden. "We hope to put in more hothouses later this year so we can grow most of our own flowers." She shifted forward, back still straight, and looked directly at me. "What are your plans while you're here? "

"We're heading to Timbavati for a quick tour," Will chimed in, returning from his hospital call. I inhaled sharply, and the two similar faces glanced at me. I could feel my heart beating in my throat, and I was sure my face was a conspicuous shade of pink. What was Will's mother thinking of me taking off with her son – just the two of us?

"And," Will went on, "as soon as Tom found out food was involved, he accepted your dinner invitation." Will grabbed a chair, but before he could sit down, the kitchen door opened and a brown-haired man, his skin darkened by the sun, came in. He took off his wide-brimmed canvas hat and hung it from a peg on the wall. His eyebrows shot up and stretched the wrinkles at the sides of his eyes. White streaks where the sun had not reached, shot out like rays.

"Hi, son," he said shaking hands and patting Will on the back.

"Jackie, I'd like you to meet my dad, Karl." A slow smile crept over the older man's face.

"Pleased to meet you at last, Jackie." Karl's hand was warm and rough as he shook mine. "You're a long way from home."

"She's going to let me show her how beautiful this country is." Will sat down beside me and rested his arm on the back of my chair again. The three sets of eyes studied me. I felt like a pot of petunias being judged at an Interflora Convention.

"Well, your mother's got the guest bedroom all made up. How long will you be staying?"

"We're heading out tomorrow," Will told him.

"Oh?" his father said, rubbing a hand across his chin. I could see the beginning of stubble and the gesture scraped like sandpaper.

"What's on the agenda?"

"Timbavati for starters, and then..." Will looked at me and smiled slyly, "And then we'll see."

"Is the 'and then we'll see' going to require mosquito netting?" I asked, leveling Will with a suspicious squint. *Was I talking about beds?*

"Anything is possible, Jackie honey," he said, smiling at my reddening cheeks. His parents glanced at each other.

"Should I be concerned?" I grimaced, looking at Karl.

"More than likely." He winked, and his face lit with humor, all the tiny sun lines turning upward like a dozen smiles. I guessed this was what Will would look like some years down the road.

"Karl, why don't you show Will the new dahlia varieties? Jackie can keep me company in the kitchen while I start dinner." So, Will's mother and I would continue the strange dance we had begun, moving cautiously toward common ground. I smiled at Will and tried to keep the nervousness out of my eyes. Of course he saw it, this man who read me so well. He leaned over and kissed me on the cheek.

"See you soon," he whispered against my ear and gave it a gentle nip. I jumped slightly, looked down and reddened again. I felt like a chameleon.

As soon as the men left, Connie handed me an apron. I was put to work peeling apples for bobotie, a lamb stew whose ingredients surprised me. I watched as Connie added raisins, curry, almonds and chutney. My culinary skills were rustic at best. Growing up, I preferred working in my father's shop cleaning carburetors or watching him rebuild an engine rather than learning to cook. It irritated my mother no end. I once told her I thought I was very good at stirring. The remark earned me an impromptu cooking lesson. Connie and I worked in silence for a short time while she mixed up a batch of cornbread, or mealy, as she called it.

Is this your first trip to Africa?" she asked suddenly.

"Yes." I could feel the next question coming.

"How long have you been planning this vacation?"

Close enough. What she wants to know, I thought, is did I intentionally plan to come over here and steal her son away. I could understand her concern, and for all she knew, I might be trying to seduce Will back to America. I preferred Roy's direct approach. It saved time and shortened the interrogation.

"I actually hadn't planned on staying after my company's conference, but there was a small accident which caused me to miss my flight."

"An accident? What happened?" she looked up with concern.

"Some flying glass, nothing too serious."

Connie frowned, "Are you alright then?"

"Almost good as new." My shoulder twitched.

"So," I continued, "missing the plane, and the fact that my boss thought he could work me harder when I got back if he talked me into taking an overdue vacation... ouch!" I nicked myself with the knife. Connie took my bleeding finger and rinsed it under the faucet. She was just putting a Band Aid on it when Will and his father returned.

"I'm not going to have to sew you up again am I?" Will asked frowning.

"Nope, doctoring seems to run in the family." I held up the bandaged finger. His parents glanced at each other again and then Connie looked at me.

"The flying glass thing," I nodded.

"Alright," she said with authority. "All of you take a seat. Just let me check on dinner, and then I have a few questions." Why not? The key witness had arrived. And so, the tale of my work related trip to Africa and the past few days was told minus a few details like the night after my fever broke when I fell asleep in Will's arms.

"So," Karl said drawing out the word, "you wrote Will that you were coming here for a computer conference?" I nodded, thinking that would clearly make me the guilty party if all did not go well. "And you had breakfast with her?" he asked Will in the same pondering cadence.

"That's right. And then later that morning, Jackie helped me take care of a woman who fell in the lobby and cut her leg." Will winked at me.

"You left that part out," Connie said. Will and I shrugged.

"Mmm," Karl exhaled slowly, still tracking his initial train of thought. "Since you've been here, Jackie, there's been a cut leg, a cut shoulder and now a cut finger." He turned to Will, "You spend much more time with Jackie, son, and you're going to need to open a blood bank."

Chapter 27

A Genre of Love

A chatter of voices drifted through the screened window followed by footsteps on the porch. Tom, Lynn and a little girl with long looping curls all seemed to enter at once. When the child saw Will, her eyes and mouth simultaneously popped open.

"Unkoo Wiyl, Unkoo Wiyl," she screamed jumping into his waiting arms. She held her little bow lips and chubby cheeks up for his kisses. He obliged her, nuzzling the little neck and tousling her hair. She squealed with delight, wriggling to get down, and then toddled over to me and pointed a finger.

"What lady?" she asked.

"My name is Jackie. What's your name?"

She eyed me curiously, then stuck a finger in her mouth and mumbled, "Thindy."

"I love your beautiful curls," I told her.

She dimpled shyly, and then stuffed the end of one lock into her mouth. Patting my knee, she wobbled off to be picked up by her grandmother.

When Tom was introduced to me, he bundled me up in a bear crunching hug. He was a bit taller and heavier than Will, with a ready smile and a round nose that his dark framed glasses kept sliding down. Chatting easily about a variety of subjects seemed to be one of his favorite pastimes. "So you're the little lady from America that thinks she can put up with my brother," he laughed.

"More like he's putting up with me," I said.

"Yeah," Will wrapped an arm around me, "you're a real thorn in my side."

"Florist talk?" I asked.

"Ah, I think you're going to have your hands full with this one," Tom grinned.

Lynn was quieter and a little shy. She wore no makeup and kept her head slightly down, even when we were introduced. Her reserved demeanor and pulled back mousy brown hair hid her prettiness. I wondered if her simple clothes and functional shoes were a way to avoid attention. She spent most of her time chasing after Cindy or picking up scattered toys.

As the day drew to its close, we remained in the kitchen, talking while Connie finished preparing dinner. We ate casually at the inside porch table where the windows afforded a view of the setting sun glinting off the hot houses. Karl said grace, and when we finished passing the dishes around, Tom's plate was piled high. Connie suddenly popped up from her chair.

"I've forgotten the mealies in the oven." She returned in a moment with the bowl of steaming cornbread and handed it to me. I took one and started to pass it to Tom, but there wasn't one square inch of space left on his plate.

"Like me to put one in your pocket?" I asked.

"Well, if you slather it with butter and keep it on your plate, you can just feed me a bite now and then," he smiled.

"I'd be happy to if I wasn't so afraid of losing part of my hand with it."

Tom eyed the mealies wistfully. "I guess I'll have to pass for now, but when you've all taken one, just set the plate right here in front of me. And, Jackie, pass me the butter," he said, popping a chunk of lamb dripping with gravy into his mouth.

Sometime during the meal, amidst the food laden table and the talking and laughing, my mind wandered to a spot outside. I imagined I was peering hungrily through the paned windows, looking in on this loving family - at the cozy glow, the sumptuous stew and the contented diners. Just for a moment, I felt like the little match girl, watching and wanting to be a part of the warmth.

I sensed Will's eyes on me and turned to smile at him. He was slow to smile back, but when he did, it held a note of melancholy that caught in my chest. I frowned, and he winked at me with a tenderness that made my heart stutter.

We all helped with the dishes, except for Will's dad and Cindy, who both fell asleep in his recliner browsing through a flower catalog. I was sorry to see Tom and his family leave. Their open-hearted acceptance of me, and Tom's contagious enthusiasm, created an almost immediate friendship. There were hugs and kisses, an incredibly wet one from Cindy, and then waves and more blown kisses from the porch before the house quieted down.

Chapter 28

Before We Begin, No Turning Back

Will carried my luggage to the guest bedroom. After all the noise and laughter of the evening, I was surprised to still see a troubled look in his eyes. A small stream of fear snaked through me. I put my hand on his arm.

"What's wrong," I asked, my stomach clenching. He walked to the window and stood looking out for a long time.

"A month ago, I knew what to expect. Now…" he turned to face me. "Things are unsure again."

"Would it have been better if I didn't let you know I was coming?"

"No. I would take this moment with you again… even if…" He shook his head.

Will was having second thoughts. Maybe he was regretting leaving Cali. I knew I was playing into all my old fears, but Will had said everything was unsure now. A sudden intense cold swept through me. I didn't want to be somewhere I wasn't wanted.

"Will," I braced myself to keep my voice from trembling, "if you're having second thoughts, it's alright. I understand. Just… do whatever you need to do. I still have my plane ticket, so I can leave anytime." I held my head up and nodded, but I couldn't meet his eyes. There was a moment of heart-stopping, for me, silence before Will's angry words.

"What do you mean 'it's alright, you can leave anytime?'" His voice raised an octave. "You're talking about walking away from each other again?" His eyebrows climbed to the top of his forehead and crashed into each other. "I don't think it's an accident that you're here. I think it's a miracle that we have a second chance. This is about fighting for what we almost lost, not hopping on a plane at the first sign of difficulty. This is about both of us ... "

Relieved, I put my hand over his mouth to stop the tumbling words. My other hand flew to my chest, and a whoosh of air escaped. A door down the hall opened and then closed after a moment.

"I ... thought you regretted ... maybe Cali," I ended lamely.

Will took hold of my shoulders. "We have to trust each other, Jackie." His voice was fiercely intense, but his words were soft and low. "If I say something that hurts you or you don't understand, ask, don't give up."

I shook my head. "So, why are you so unsure?"

"I'm not, you are. I feel like it's seven years ago all over again."

My feelings—love—being backed into a corner, not my strong points. I felt like it was seven years ago, too. Will didn't misread my momentary hesitation. He knew I needed to trust that I was safe with him. "We haven't been together like this ... " I pointed back and forth from one of us to the other, "I never knew us as..." I stopped, unable and unwilling to define our germinating relationship.

"Give yourself time to get used to me again, Jackie. If you react to every bump in the road by running away, we'll lose each other again." He put his hands on the sides of my face and kissed me softly.

"Don't lose me then," I whispered. "Don't let go."

"I tried not to the first time." His words were punishing, and they hit their mark.

"You said we wouldn't look back."

"I said we needed to let go of the past. That's different. We need to look back so we don't make the same mistakes."

I laid my forehead against the solidness of his chest and let out a long sigh. Tiny threads of doubt began to snap and break away. His desire and conviction was a magnet, weaving and strengthening the iron filaments of my own certainty. "I'm not hopping on a plane," I said and threw my arms around his neck, holding on like a drowning soul on a floating log. He kissed the side of my neck, and then careful not to touch my wound, gently laid his hand beneath my throat. I could feel my heartbeat against his palm. "It's going to be a long night," he nodded with an almost accusatory look, and leaned down to kiss me. I had no inclination to stop him despite my open bedroom door.

"Long night," I murmured. The door down the hall opened again, and Will reluctantly released me. He kissed me lingeringly once more, his lips warm against the coolness of mine, and then he closed the door behind him. A few moments later there was a gentle tap on the door.

"Jackie?" It was Connie. "May I come in?"

I opened the door, but she remained in the hallway. "Please," I said gesturing towards a chair. She walked to the window to adjust the blinds, and then turned towards me, her hands clasped. I closed the door.

"May I be frank?" So Will had inherited his straight forward approach from his mother.

"Of course," I said. She came towards me and took my hand in both of hers as she'd done when I arrived.

"You and Will, your circumstances are ... challenging." The word seemed to define most of the areas in my life at the moment. "You have serious decisions to make in a very short time. First of all, I want you to know that I can see why Will is in love with you. And, I can see that you're concerned about spending time alone together and how that might appear. Don't worry about it – we're not." Her eyes took on a faraway look for the briefest moment. "Not many people get a second chance. Take it – if you're sure it's what you want." She released my hand and squared her shoulders. "That's the part I'm concerned about – whether or not you're sure." I released the breath I'd been holding. Mother and son – both had come to cast a light on the path ahead. "Before you say anything," she added, "I want to tell you that I don't know exactly what happened between the two of you in America, and I don't know why things didn't work out afterwards for you. That's between you and Will, but whatever it was, or is – make the decision. I don't want to see either of you hurt any more than necessary."

"It's very... complicated."

"Love is," she said. "But if being together requires commitment and loss, then the reason should be love." She was fighting for her son, and she was letting me know that she was ready to play by the rules too. There was no doubt the decision would affect us all. If Will and I made the relationship work, one of us and one of our families would experience loss, and therefore we both would. If we decided to say a final goodbye, and it would need to be final, we would all suffer anyway. A decision needed to be made, and the absence of 'loss' and 'love' was no longer an option. But, Will's mother was right. Love was the redeeming goldmine. She watched me, reading I believe, the thoughts flickering through my mind.

"Will and I are up against some of the same problems we faced seven years ago." Connie frowned. "But I'm hoping we're better equipped to deal with them now. I do know that this second chance is precious." I stared into her eyes for a moment. "You're telling me love is the answer."

"I believe, for you, love is the question that determines the answer."

This understanding and courageous woman was willing to risk the happiness and peace of her own heart for Will. I hoped I had the same courage.

Chapter 29

To There and Back Again

I woke to the sun streaming in my window and the sound of a shovel methodically chopping into dirt and dumping it into a wheelbarrow. The smell of something bready drifted into my room. After peeking down the hall and seeing that all the doors were open and the rooms empty, I showered quickly and was nearly through dressing when someone knocked on my door.

"Breakfast is ready and if you don't come out, I'm coming in to get you," Will threatened.

'Last shoelace," I called back. I threw open the door and was grabbed around the middle and pulled into a hug.

"Mmm," he murmured, burrowing his lips into the crook of my neck. "I missed you last night."

"Are you two coming, or am I going to have to send Tom after you?" Connie called from the kitchen.

"Is Tom here?" I whispered.

"He said he wanted to make sure he didn't miss telling you goodbye." Will snorted. "More likely he wanted to fit two breakfasts in this morning."

"Here I come. Get decent," Tom warned us.

"Not much chance of that happening with you," I said, tickling Will so I could wriggle out of his arms. I took off toward the kitchen, almost making it through the door before his arm snaked out and pulled me back into the hall. He trapped me against the wall and resumed his noisy nuzzling.

"I think I just lost my appetite," Tom groaned from the kitchen.

"Highly unlikely," Will murmured. To my horror, my stomach growled.

"Feed that girl," Tom demanded.

We found Tom seated before yet another loaded plate, this one piled high with scrambled eggs and sausage. "Hey California girl, you ready to wrestle with the rhinos?"

"I think I just did," I said, raising an eyebrow at Will. He plopped into a chair and pulled me onto his lap. "Are you always this feisty in the morning?" I squirmed to get up, the inevitable hot blush creeping into my cheeks.

"Morning?" Tom complained. "It's practically supper." A heaping plate of crumpets suddenly appeared.

"I'm trying to get Tom fed before he takes a bite out of one of you," Connie said setting the tower in front of him. I sat down and passed him the butter.

Tom helped Connie clean up while Will showed me the nursery. In the crispness of the morning, the warm, moist air in the hot houses was a welcome cocoon of fragrance. Only the crunching of our footsteps in the gravel broke the silence. I walked down each row, sniffing the medley of reds and yellows and pinks.

"These are the new varieties of dahlias," Will explained as he leaned over a tray of seedlings that had just popped their heads above the soil. He bent closer, squinting into the individual tray cups for a moment before turning to watch me as I continued perusing the blooms. A particularly beautiful yellow dahlia tipped in bright orange caught my eye. I looked back to ask Will its name just as he decided to sit in an open spot on one of the planting tables.

"Aaargh ... what?" Will yelled, scrambling off the table and nearly upsetting the seedling trays. A small garden snake stuck its head up flicking its tongue and eyeing him indignantly. I guessed it was the poor little fellow's best attempt at giving Will the cold shoulder. It slithered off between the potted sprouts with great pomp and circumstance, stopping once and looking back disapprovingly as if to say, "Bipedal invader!"

"And I'm letting you take me into the savage bush lands of Africa?" I shook my head doubtfully. There was a gliding shuffle in the flowers on my right. "I'll be outside," I whispered to Will, the door closing behind me before my words reached him.

Will caught up to me, and we wandered through the gardens, occasionally holding hands or leaning against each other. I wanted to see every greenhouse, smell every flower, open every door that Will had opened uncountable times. I closed my eyes and inhaled the earthiness of dirt and fertilizer and the heady fragrance of the blooms. It occurred to me that I was standing where Will had stood, inhaling the precious flower scents he had smelled while we were apart. He stood here alone, while I stood alone in my world. Who had been the first to feel the hopeless despair when our fragile connection fractured and drifted into a seemingly impassable chasm?

"I always wondered what your world looked like. I should have asked you to send me a picture. Of all of it," I added wistfully. Will had lived in my world. When we were apart, he could picture me moving through it. I had only his words to bring his world to mind. Will turned me towards him and wrapped his arms around me. We stood like two garden statues cemented together, gazing into each other's eyes.

The goodbyes were heartfelt. Karl patted my shoulder and

then awkwardly put his arms around me for a moment. "You tell Will to put a needle and thread in his bag."

"A little gorillicillin wouldn't hurt either," Tom added, crushing me in a lion-sized hug.

But it was Connie who spoke silently to my heart. She hugged Will, and then murmured softly to him. Everyone was aware of the possible finality of these goodbyes. Connie put her arms around me and whispered in my ear. I looked at her and our eyes held for a long moment. When the car turned the corner, I looked back to see her standing alone, still watching. Our gazes locked, but neither of us smiled.

Chapter 30

Not Until You've Walked in Another Man's Shoes

We told each other about our jobs, laughed about Tom's appetite and followed our progress on the map Will had brought. It was as if everything between us was starting fresh, and like the car moving forward, we also began to leave the past behind.

"Tell me about this safari," I said. Will didn't answer for moment, reminiscing I guessed.

"Timbavati is a game reserve. We took a few vacations there when Tom and I were kids."

"Are we loaded on a jeep with our tourist cameras, safari hats and guides, just like in the movies?"

"Pretty much." Will chuckled and shook his head. "Tom and I had a favorite guide, a Zulu fellow named Masuwra. We were daredevils back then, and Masuwra spent half his time keeping us out of the jaws of trouble. One year, we snuck off while lunch was being prepared and found ourselves facing a couple of hyenas, which by the way, have the strongest jaws of any animal." Will took his eyes briefly from the road and laid a hand on my knee in, what I assume, was a warning.

"No plans to get friendly with them," I promised. Will gave me a wry smile and went on with his story.

"Tom and I were so scared we couldn't move. One of the hyenas looked like it was going to charge us. It was circling, getting closer and closer. The next thing I knew, Masuwra came running from behind us waving his arms and making all kinds of noise, banging a stick against his gun. The hyenas stood their ground, so he shot into the air, and that finally bloody scared them away."

"Did he kick you out of his safari?" I asked, enjoying hearing what Will had been like as a boy.

"No, but we worked in the kitchen for the next two days, and we weren't allowed out of the jeeps by ourselves when we did go out again. It wasn't so bad, though. The kitchen staff taught us some Zulu, and they had a pet monkey named Zara. So when we weren't working we had the monkey to keep us entertained."

"Mmm," I sighed, relaxing in the warmth of the sun coming through the car window. "Remind me to thank Masuwra."

"No one knows much about him," Will went on. "Word is, he was some sort of shaman way back."

"You mean like a witch doctor?"

"No – more than that, if the stories are true."

"But he's not a shaman now?"

"I've seen him do some things I can't explain." Will shook his head. "Saw him stare down a lioness once when a tourist tried to get friendly with one of her cubs."

"He just looked at her, and she left her cub unprotected?" I asked.

Will scratched the back of his head. "It sounded like he was talking to her in Zulu, and she seemed to understand. Calmed her until one of the guides got the tourist back into the jeep." Lost in that long-ago time, Will half-chuckled to himself. "I decided to sneak out one night after everyone was asleep. Guess I thought I could find some lions or wild beasts. Barmy idea. I heard some mumbling off in the distance and saw a fire with someone moving around it. The grass was tall enough to hide me, so I crept toward the fire on my belly.

Great white hunter." Will shook his head and laughed. "Yeah. Anyway, it was Masuwra dancing around. Every now and then, he'd throw something into the fire and it would flare up. He was chanting some Zulu words I couldn't quite make out, and wearing an animal skin like a cape. I must have dozed off after a bit. When I woke the fire was out and Masuwra was – well, he looked like he was talking to the sky or maybe his Gods. And then something started crawling up my leg. I was afraid to make any noise and give myself away, but the thing was on its way up my shorts. I was just about to jump up and start slapping at my knickers when Masuwra was suddenly standing over me. Scared me to death. He held up a finger and mouthed for me not to move. That was no small task. The crawly little bugger was inching its way toward parts I feel very protective about. Masuwra started singing, which made no sense to me. I pointed to my pants and made a horrible face, but he just kept singing. The sounds were strange, kind of calming. I actually started to relax a bit. After a while, I couldn't feel the creepy bugger moving anymore. I was afraid it might have set up housekeeping. And then, Masuwra reached down beside my knee. The nasty little beastie dropped out of my shorts and right into his hand. He kept singing to it and disappeared into the night."

"What was it?" I asked grimacing.

"Don't know, but I suspect it was poisonous. I just took off like a bolt of lightning. That was my last nighttime safari."

"More time peeling potatoes in the kitchen?" I smiled.

"No. Masuwra never mentioned it."

An hour later, we stopped in Lydenburg, a small town about 140 km east of Timbavati. We ate lunch at a café with a rickety porch and then headed for a sports shop.

"You're not planning on wearing those takkies are you?" Will pointed at my tennis shoes.

"Takkies?" I mumbled, shaking my head. These tennis shoes can go a million miles," I insisted indignantly. I pitty-patted around the sidewalk to demonstrate their durability.

"It's not how long they'll hold up. They won't protect your ankles and the material is penetrable."

I glanced warily at my shoes. "Are we talking about large-toothed animals with foot fetishes?"

"If you stay in the jeep the entire trip, you'll miss some of the more incredible sights." Will cast another disparaging glance at my feet and shook his head.

"Same question - are we discussing toe munching reptiles?" I examined my shoes with new eyes.

"Actually, I plan to be the only one nibbling on your toes. In any case, I want you to get a pair of boots."

"Bossy man," I mumbled, but reason and fear won out over independence. We found a shoe store where the salesman was only too happy to tote out several styles of hiking footwear. I tried on four different high top, leather boots, and was partial to a beige and brown pair.

"You can't go wrong with these," the salesman quipped. "They're thick leather with a silk lining – very comfortable, very safe."

"Yes, but will they protect me from human teeth?" I asked.

We arrived at the Timbavati base camp in late afternoon. Will had hardly turned off the motor and gotten out of the car, when a tall, well-built black man appeared out of nowhere. His grey hair, shaved close to the scalp, accentuated his high forehead and prominent brow.

"Dr. Will," the man nodded, breaking into a wide grin that pulled his cheeks into two round balls. "It is good to see you."

"Masuwra," Will clapped him on the shoulder. "I hoped you were our guide."

"I was not, but when I found out you were coming, I made new plans."

"Masuwra," Will put his arm around my waist. "This is Jackie." The guide's glance slid to me. His head did not turn, but his eyes moved slowly from my face down my body and then up again, suddenly snapping back to my tennis shoes. A pouting scowl covered his face.

"Damn," I muttered under my breath, and reaching behind me through the open car window, brought out the boots and held them up. Masuwra's face broke into a wide grin, his amazingly white teeth gleaming in the sun's slanting rays.

Chapter 31

Tall Tales

"We will leave at first light," Masuwra told us as a tall, muscular boy easily swung our travel bags out of the car's trunk. Masuwra took the boots from me and tucked them under the boy's arm.

"This is Njau. He will take care of you. He speaks some English, but mostly Zulu and a little Swahili." The boy gave us a quick nod, but kept his head and eyes down. Masuwra told him to take our bags to huts number one and three. The boy cocked his head and asked a question. Masuwra shook his head and repeated "one and three." We followed the boy down a dirt path to a group of five small mokhoros, or round huts.

"This house," he pushed open the door of the small screened structure, "is for Mrs. Dr. Will."

The bed was covered with a leaf print blanket and draped in mosquito netting. I set my purse on the small rattan chest, which folded out into a desk. Above it, an intricately carved elephant on a pull chain dangled from the overhead fan. I suddenly realized that I should tip the boy, but through the small bathroom window, I could already see Njau and Will entering the adjacent hut. Suddenly feeling slightly displaced, I sat on the end of the bed just as I had done before leaving the Carlton Hotel in Johannesburg. My thoughts then were of losing Will and returning home to the emptiness I'd convinced myself was comfortable. So much had changed in such a short time. I had to admit that the possibilities had increased in the positive, but what lie ahead still remained an unknown. The door rattled.

"Ready for dinner and then maybe a walk?" Will asked through the screen.

I could smell the cooking meat before we arrived at the small outdoor camp "kitchen." Njau and the other staff were grilling steaks on a surprisingly modern barbecue, while the other four safari guests were seated under a tree, drinks in hand, talking.

"Oh, I've shot wild boar bigger than that," a middle aged, sunburned man boasted. "Been kicked by a giraffe once, too. Broke my leg in three places. No, there's no reason to be concerned," he assured a worried-looking, white-haired woman wearing a jungle print blouse. "You just need to know your animals and," he laughed, "always be prepared to run." He punctuated the remark by downing the remaining third of his drink. "Ah, here they are," he boomed spotting Will and me, "the last of our party. Come join us for a nip." He gestured with his glass at one of the staff for a refill. Sitting beside the sunburned man was a younger version of him. The boy, who was looking at the picture of a bird in the book he was holding, was in his teens, thin and a bit gawky. From the size of his feet, I guessed it wouldn't be long before he towered over his father.

"Oh, how nice," the woman gushed. "Another female. I was feeling quite outnumbered. It's my third safari, and I always enjoy having another woman along to talk to." I smiled and squeezed Will's hand a little tighter. "I'm Martha Magisage and this," she grasped the elbow of the elderly, rather tired-looking man beside her, "is my husband, Thomas."

"Tom, just Tom will be fine," her husband corrected, reaching out to shake hands with Will.

Martha was thin and motherly with hair perched atop her head like a dollop of whipped cream. "And you are?" she went on before either of us could introduce ourselves.

"I'm Will and this is Jackie."

"Charlie, here," the sunburned man chimed in a little too loudly. He pushed himself forward and shook hands, and then tipped his head towards the boy beside him. "My son, Stanley." The teenager awkwardly shook hands with Will and then returned to his book. "So, you're the doctor," Charlie went on. "Can we get some drinks over here for the doctor and his wife? How's my refill coming?"

"Why don't you sit next to me, Jackie," Martha insisted from her lawn chair on the small patch of mowed greenish-brown grass. I glanced at Will and smiled, knowing he could read the regret in my eyes as I released his hand. The minutes were ticking in my mind just as they had the night he left. When would I be able to look at Will and not feel like the sand in the hour glass was running out?

I learned from Martha that Tom had retired two years earlier from a high-powered, well-paying job that had allowed them to meet other high-powered people in a multitude of exotic locations. There was no need for me to talk beyond professing my wonder and amazement over their myriad adventures and insatiable thirst for travel.

Will was captive to a similar travelogue from Charlie, who hardly took a breath between hunting sagas except to drink and occasionally glance at his son and say, "Isn't that so, Stanley?" or, "That stag must have weighed nearly nine hundred pounds, wouldn't you say, Stanley?" The boy sat quietly, looking uncomfortably bored. I could only guess that his father's boisterous personality and engulfing physical presence had been an overpowering influence in his life. Stanley never acknowledged his father's glances, or attempted to answer the rhetorical questions.

Dinner was delicious, huge juicy steaks, a creamy rice dish, leafy green vegetables and loaves of steaming bread. It was beyond me how Martha managed to clean her plate in record time and continue recounting her many exploits non-stop.

At last, Will glanced at me with the tiniest hint of a nod. "I think we're going to call it a night." I was thankful that he had the forethought not to let on that we intended to take a walk. I had no doubt it would have turned into a group gallop in which Will and I would once again be captive to tall tales.

"Let's just have one more drink, Doctor," Charlie brayed, slapping Will on the back and signaling to Njau.

"I'll take a rain check on that." Will stood and came around the table to fetch me. Charlie made sure he caught Will's eye and winked lewdly. Broken veins, witness to a few too many 'one more drinks,' ran across his cheeks like little red rivers.

When we said our goodnights, I leaned down next to Stanley's ear and whispered, "I'm guessing you're going to be able to teach me a lot about the animals. I'm looking forward to it." The boy looked startled and then blushed, smiling into his lap. Charlie peered at his son. Our small interchange seemed to disturb him. I suspected Charlie didn't like not being the center of attention.

Will and I wandered for a while, coming to a stop behind a large leadwood tree, before we put our arms around each other.

"I think Masuwra keeps tranquilizers for the animals," Will said raising an eyebrow.

"Doubt it will mix well with alcohol." I wrinkled my nose. Will kissed it and then pulled me against him and into a long kiss. Lost in the moment, I didn't hear the voice until Will gently pushed me away from him.

"I think they went this way," Martha chirped. "There they are." Unfortunately, Martha's two previous safaris had honed her tracking skills. "I'm glad we caught up with you before you went to bed. We," she wiggled her fingers absently in the direction where dinner had been served, "were just talking. Since the majority of us have done the usual safari things, you know, like drive down the same old trails and see all the same old animals, well, we thought it might be more interesting to take some of the back roads, see some of the sights other tourists don't get to see." She stopped and inhaled quickly. "Of course, it's only fair to ask you, Doctor, and your wife, if you agree." Finished, she shook herself like a hen with a flea.

Will glanced at me, and I smiled and nodded. "We'll look forward to it, Martha." Will put his arm around my waist and turned to leave, but Martha wasn't quite finished.

"Oh," she added in a huff of breath, "One more thing, a favor really. The porter boy... what was his name, Tom?" Tom looked as if he'd had a long day and gazed blankly at his wife. "Tsk," she waved the enameled nails dismissively at him. "Oh well, it doesn't matter anyway. Well, Tom caught a bug at our last stop and has been snoring something awful, keeps me awake all night. I haven't slept a wink in a week, and I was just wondering, if you're only using the extra cabin you have for baggage or whatever, if we might just take it. I could really use a good night's sleep. We'd pay for it of course and for any inconvenience." She smiled expectantly at Will, clearly use to using money as a means of getting her way.

"I'm so sorry to hear that," Will said. "We'd both be more than happy to accommodate you... " Martha smiled, took a breath and started to say something, but before she could, Will shook his head. "But, I'm going to have to say no." He managed to look extremely contrite.

"Well, as I said, we'd be more than happy to make it worth your while." Martha repeated as if she were speaking to someone with auditory processing issues.

"We appreciate that, but..." Will leaned forward and lowered his voice, "for medical reasons, we need separate rooms." I cleared my throat to cover a smile and looked down. Martha's shoulders jerked uncomfortably, and her eyes narrowed as she moved back slightly. She "harrumphed" and pulled her lips into a fine line, looking back and forth as if there were an answer to her dilemma somewhere on the ground.

"Well," she said looking up at last, "our cabin has two *single* beds." She squinted and nodded as if she understood the problem completely.

"I'm afraid that won't help." Will explained. "I have an advanced case of satyriasis complicated by chronic dyspnoea." I had no idea what Will was talking about, but I thought I would explode in peals of laughter if I didn't do something to distract myself. I couldn't resist, so I pulled up the sleeve of my blouse and started scratching the inside of my elbow, eyeing it suspiciously.

"Is it... contagious?" Martha wrinkled her nose and ran her tongue over her front teeth in an open-mouthed grimace.

"Not always," Will said in his best medical voice, "but it can be incredibly painful." Martha, now clearly in escape mode, glanced around like a meerkat checking the horizon. Tom's attention had finally been engaged, and from the look on his face, he was in on the fun and enjoying every minute of it.

"Well, I'll just have to put up with the snoring," Martha snitted angrily. "C'mon, Tom." She yanked his sleeve and bustled off in the direction of their cabin. I could barely hear her whisper, "Do you think we can have our linens laundered in town while we're here?"

Will grabbed my hand and quickly led me around a bend in the path and away from any other prying ears and guest huts before stopping and looking at me with smug innocence. I fell into his arms, and we laughed until the tears ran down our faces.

"Have you already infected me with this dread disease?" I asked when I could finally catch my breath.

"Not hardly."

"Why not?" I inquired reaching up to kiss him.

"Because satyriasis is a condition that affects men."

"Go on," I murmured, intent on my task.

"Satyriasis is an uncontrollable sexual desire."

"Hmm," I mused, "hopefully a chronic condition. And what was the rest of it?"

"Oh, chronic dyspnoea?"

"Yes, that."

"It means - you take my breath away."

"I see. And how long have you had this condition?"

"Close to seven years now." The humor was gone from Will's voice. I reached up to wipe the last vestige of a tear from his cheek, but he pulled my fingers against his lips and kissed them. "You're going to realize you love me," he whispered, his breath a soft caress against my palm.

The grasses swayed in the evening breeze and the sun unrolled its final light before us like a golden carpet. Wrapped in each other's arms, I could feel Will's body tense, and I knew he wanted to tell me something, but seemed to be troubling over how to say whatever was on his mind.

"Jackie honey, the separate cabins....well, I think it's best for now."

I could hear my insecure inner voice starting up – he doesn't think this is going to work; he doesn't love you. *Shut up*, I told it*, and listen for a change.*

"It's not that I don't want you. God knows I do. And don't start thinking I don't think this will work between us. It will." He gave me an I-know-what-you-were-thinking look. "It's just that I think we need to take some time to get used to each other again first." He looked at me to gauge my reaction, and then snorted softly. "I'm not telling you anything you haven't already decided, am I? I should have known. I was afraid you'd see this as me not being sure about us." He swung me gently back and forth in his arms, gazing across the plain. There was more on his mind.

"Besides," he said at last, "this isn't where I want us to be when we make love for the first time, not here. It's beautiful and very 'African safari,' but that's the problem." He looked into my eyes. "When we make love for the first time, I want it to be on common ground – not my world or your world, but our world."

"Is there such a place?" I asked.

"Our world?" He smiled and nodded, "Just around the bend."

The evening chill was a reminder that we had an early morning, and we reluctantly relinquished this stolen moment of private serenity. As we strolled back to our huts, I shook my head, thinking of Martha and Tom.

"If I ever start treating you like that, straighten me out, will you?"

"You won't. It's not in you to be like that, honey. But," he added with a less than chaste glint in his eye, "If I see the faintest hint of it, I'll just pop you into bed and make love to you until you don't have the energy."

"What makes you think you won't wear out first?" I asked smugly.

"Satyriasis," he said.

Chapter 32

Safari

I slept deeply and woke to the sound of scurrying feet and the thudding of boxes and equipment being loaded into our safari jeeps. I was stretching luxuriously when Njau tapped on my door and called out "Breakfast!" I called from my netted nest for him to come in. The doors had no locks, nor did there seem to be any need for them. Njau moved silently and gracefully, setting a tray of hot coffee and biscuits on my bedside table. The biscuits were very hard and reminded me of Italian biscotti, so I dipped them in my coffee.

"Mmmm, delicious, Njau. What are these?"

"They are called rusks. Cook makes them with anise and raisins and sunflower seeds. I am happy you like them, Kabibi."

"How much time do I have before we leave?"

"One half hour." He turned to go.

"Njau?"

"Yes, Missus?"

"I just wondered... you called me Kabibi. What does that mean?"

"It is Swahili for Little Lady." I smiled thinking it was the first time I'd been called little. I was 5 feet 6 inches and weighed 125 pounds. Compared to Njau's towering height and size though, I guess it made sense. But, word spread, and the name stuck.

Will was standing by the jeep speaking with Masuwra when I reached the little convoy. The guides were checking rifles. "Those are only for emergency," Will said, joining me. Charlie was already in big game hunter mode talking to his son.

"Now Stanley, you see that .416 Rigby the boy there's got? That gun will drop a bull elephant." Charlie walked over to the jeep and took the rifle from the guide. "Of course, I'd still put my money on a .375 H&H in a Ruger M77 safari grade." He looked through the gun's sight and aimed at something on the horizon. "It's got a manageable recoil and weight. Now you take that and back it up with a 44 mag pistol on your belt as a little reassurance, and you're ready to hunt. You can load the mag with snake shot for small critters and hard cast bullets for larger game. But if you're after Cape buffalo," he cast a piercing glance in Stanley's direction, "you're better off with a .458 Winchester. You can shoot a Cape and it'll keep running. I saw one take seven shots before dropping." I suddenly felt like I was going to lose my breakfast. Stanley looked a little pale around the gills too.

Martha appeared wearing the latest in safari couture, insisting that Tom 'hurry up.' Glancing at Will, she immediately commandeered the front three person seat, insisting Stanley ride with Tom and her. As we loaded into the jeep, Martha inadvertently brushed shoulders with Will. She sidestepped, glancing precariously at him, and then turned to me crooning primly, "I hope you're taking precautions, dear."

"Too late," I confided. At her look of horror, I added, "I gave it to him."

I offered to sit in the middle of the back seat, but Will wanted me on the outside where I could see better. That left Will next to Charlie, but he seemed to handle the incessant chatter about past hunting exploits with a calm I would have found hard to maintain. Our tracker sat on a seat attached to the front fender. The two jeeps, ours loaded with people, and the other with supplies, two guides and kitchen staff, headed off leaving swirling dust in their wake. It wasn't long before our guide was pointing out the remains of an early morning lion kill. We drove on down the bumpy road and found tracks leading to a grassy expanse. The heat was increasing, and the lions would be heading for shade. Charlie's gruesome hunting monologue kept up until the tracker pointed to a small grouping of trees and asked us to remain quiet. Lounging in the shade were three lionesses and two cubs. The jeep slowly inched ahead. It was thrilling to be so close to the magnificent creatures. One lioness was trying to sleep, but one of the cubs was insistently jumping and nipping at her ears. She patiently nudged him away with her head until, eventually growing tired of the little cub's antics, she gave him a nip. It only seemed to encourage the playful attacks, until suddenly, the lioness let out a short, sharp growl. The cub's eyes widen and it sat down on the spot putting its small head on its paws and falling asleep almost instantly. We all laughed, everyone except Charlie.

"First light, that's the time to hunt," Charlie told Stanley, slapping him on the shoulder. "It's the best time to get a shot at a lion." The boy didn't look back at his father, but I could see his Adam's apple bob as he swallowed and grimaced.

I hated leaving, but there was so much more to see, and although Will had been on other safaris, my own wonder was reflected in his eyes. I was starving after the light breakfast and happy to find that we were in for another African treat. We stopped under one of the sparse spots of shade where the guides covered the jeep's hood with a tablecloth and set out more coffee and tea, raisin and wine scones, freshly baked muffins and jam with sun warmed butter and hard boiled eggs. It was a feast.

Stanley gobbled his breakfast and was already scanning the

horizon with binoculars.

"See anything?" I asked. He jumped slightly and blushed. Still holding the glasses against his eyes, he pointed toward the grasses ahead of us.

"Just some Kori Bustards." He glanced shyly at me. "Would you like to look?"

"I'd love to," I said and took the glasses he offered me.

"They're feeding on insects now, but they're also meat eaters if they can find any carrion. They're one of the few birds that suck water instead of scooping it up." Stanley was animated for the first time.

"Are those little furry things, babies?" I asked.

"Yes. They stay with the mothers for several weeks."

"Where are the fathers?"

"They don't stick around after the courtship, but that's interesting to watch. The males puff their necks up, sometimes four times their regular size, and they bow to the females."

"Have you actually seen the courtship?"

"Oh, yeah, several times."

"How do you know all this, Stanley?"

He shrugged. "I started watching birds as a kid. I have tons of books. I joined a birding club, but..." He glanced at Charlie and didn't finish the thought. I had an inspiration.

"Stanley, would you mind sitting with me so that you could show me some of the other birds?" He looked up, surprised.

"Sure, I mean there are lots more varieties here than at most of the other reserves. I can probably show you some oxpeckers when we get to the river, if there are any rhinos or flat dogs around." Seeing my puzzled look he added, "You know, crocodiles. There might even be some Pel's Fishing Owls, too." His rush of words and beaming face made me laugh.

"Sounds perfect," I said, enjoying his sudden spurt of enthusiasm.

Before we loaded back into the jeep, I explained to the rest of the group that I had coerced Stanley into sitting next to me so he could teach me a little more about the animals. I was careful not to say birds, as I suspected Stanley's interest in them was a sore spot with Charlie. Will and I were the last to climb aboard and he mouthed, "Thank you."

"Just killing two birds with one stone," I whispered.

An hour later we stopped and got out to stretch our legs near a watering hole. Masuwra signaled for me to follow him to some high brush where he held a finger to his lips and pointed to the brush where a lioness was crouching waiting for thirsty prey. About five minutes later, several impalas entered the clearing to drink. The cat tensed, ready to spring. Her slight movement caused one impala to look up in her direction. When the impala spotted its predator, the lion simply sat up looking bored and checked out the landscape until the herd left. She then crouched back down to wait for her next mid-afternoon snack opportunity.

I looked questioningly at Masuwra. "Why didn't the lion go after the impala?"

Masuwra watched the crouching cat for a moment. "That is because the lioness may be queen in her jungle, but she is not the fastest runner." He glanced at me out of the corner of his eye. "If there is something you desire, then it is wise to understand your prey."

We continued along the dusty and sometimes sandy trails, the rhythmic bouncing of the jeep and the heat lulling me into a half sleep, when suddenly Stanley called out in excitement.

"There!" His voice cracked, ending an octave higher than it started out. "It's a Ground Hornbill." I followed his gaze and saw a bird that looked like it was wearing a hat of bright red leaves. It was pecking and darting among the grasses. The driver slowed so we could watch and Stanley could fill us in on the bird and its habits. Charlie looked the other way, preferring to scan the horizon for bigger game. About a half mile further, we stopped to watch a herd of wildebeest. When we had taken all the pictures we wanted, the driver headed down a muddy slope where we found a buffet waiting for us under the shade of a huge fig tree. It was hard to believe we were sitting in the middle of a savanna dining like kings. The food was incredible.

"Njau, what kind of steak is this? I love it."

"It is monkey gland."

I choked and coughed, trying to swallow, and then reached for my water glass and took a long drink. I looked up to see Njau walking away, but not before I saw the slight smile on his lips. I squinted suspiciously at Will, who lowered his head and looked a little too interested in what was on his plate.

"What did I just swallow?" I asked warily, noticing Will had not touched his 'steak'.

"I thought you wanted to experience Africa." He was all innocence.

Njau returned with a pitcher of water and refilled my glass. "You cannot cross a river without getting wet, Kabibi." He set the water pitcher in front of me. I eyed the mystery meat, or whatever it was, with trepidation.

"Monkey gland is steak, Jacks," Will finally admitted looking amused. "It's the marination that makes it taste so good, some kind of spicy chutney sauce."

I gave him a squinty-eyed smile. "I can't wait for you to try some of our Rocky Mountain oysters."

As the staff was breaking down the picnic gear, a foraging warthog popped its head out of the brush several yards away. I had never seen a warthog and was surprised that it actually had warts on its head. The guides grabbed sticks and guns and chased it away.

Three rhinos ponderously plodded through the bushes on the far side of the hole and splashed noisily into the water, wiggling their ears. Their wet, armor-looking skin glistened in the late day sunlight. It was heartwarming to watch Stanley's excitement as he pointed out the oxpeckers with their red bills and yellow circled eyes standing atop the rhinos' backs munching on tics.

We were dusty and tired at the end of the day, ready for a shower. Stanley joined Will and me for a short walk before dinner. I asked him why Charlie had brought him to a game reserve when it was clear his father preferred to be hunting.

"Dad thought seeing the animals hunt and kill each other would make me feel like he does about hunting. I won't – ever. Dad thinks real men hunt. I tried, but I can't do it. I don't want to kill animals." Stanley sighed, "I really disappoint him." He kicked at a pebble in his path, missed by a couple of inches and then stumbled on it. "Gee, anyway, my aim's so bad I couldn't hit an elephant with a fire hose." I wished more hunters felt the way he did.

"So, what happens next? Will you go on a hunting trip?"

"Probably, but he'll only be disappointed in me." He sighed again.

"You're wonderful just the way you are, Stanley. As a matter of fact, you're my hero," I assured him.

And with that, we followed our noses to the wonderful smelling meal awaiting us. After dinner, we turned our chairs toward the savannah and watched in awe as the infinite lights of heaven suddenly pierced the raven blanket above us like a burst of applause. The magic of the moment mesmerized even Charlie.

Chapter 33

Now or Never

The following morning we left at sunrise and within the first half hour, spotted hyenas stealing the remains of a kill from two lionesses. The hyenas tore ravenously at the bloody bones, leaving little for the scavengers, which Stanley informed us were called Lappet-faced vultures. They looked like little men dressed in white pants and fluffy neck bows as they squabbled for position over the skeleton. That afternoon, our tracker pointed out a herd of zebra, and farther on several elephants that were curious enough to come within yards of us. I was overwhelmed by the beauty and grace of the animals, and surprised how nonchalant and often disinterested they seemed with our presence. More than once, I found Will watching me instead of the animals.

Shortly before dusk, when the air began to cool, we stopped near a watering hole. Will and I, accompanied by Masuwra, wandered a short distance. Suddenly, Masuwra signaled us to stop. In the foliage on the other side of a large grassy expanse, a mother giraffe and her child were munching on leaves. The mother turned her head slowly and regally, staring at us through large, liquid black eyes. The young giraffe kicked up its back feet and frolicked beside her. She gracefully leaned her long neck forward and licked the side of its tiny, wide-eyed face.

Masuwra nodded to the left, and we followed his gaze to two cheetahs crouched in the grass. My stomach clenched, and I grasped Will's hand. Without warning, one cheetah sprang toward the baby giraffe. The mother ran forward and shot out a hoof sending the cat flying. It landed on its feet and crouched, ready to attack again. A momentary splash of color moved in the grass as the second cheetah crept soundlessly toward the giraffes, but it darted away when the mother kicked at it with both back hooves. She stood then, chest heaving, preparing for another assault. My own chest tightened in response. The first cheetah inched forward, its eyes fixed on the baby, now scurrying frantically back and forth through its mother's legs. Its enormous black eyes were wild with fright. The second cheetah moved quickly to the side. The mother turned, smacking it hard in the chest. It let out a high pitched scream as it flipped through the air, landing a few feet away. But the moment of distraction was just enough to leave the baby unprotected. The first cheetah sprang forward and clamped its steely jaw around the toddler's upper leg, dragging it a few feet before the mother could intervene and chase away her child's attacker. The baby was on its back in the tall grasses, a single small leg shuddering in the air.

Unable to stand anymore I cried out, and then clasped my hand over my mouth as one of the cats glanced in our direction, the look of the hunt still in its eyes. We froze, no one breathing during the endless gaze, until at last, the deadly stare left us. I inched backwards intending to return to the jeep, but Will grasped my shoulders and pulled me against him to face the grisly scene. I struggled to release myself from his grip, but he wouldn't let me go.

"I don't want to watch this," I gasped, outraged. How could Will do this to me? The mother giraffe's fight to save her baby was heart wrenching.

"This is life," he whispered, his grasp on my arms making it impossible for me to turn away from the deadly scene. I was furious with him, but I raised my head and watched, if for no other reason than, ironically, to defy him. Masuwra stood beside us, neither condoning nor condemning Will's or the cheetahs' actions.

Spellbound by the majestic life and death struggle, a lone zebra watched from a few yards away as the mother giraffe moved in an awkward circle. But it was impossible to keep both cats back as they stalked her child from opposite sides. The cheetah behind her rushed back in and dragged her baby into the brush where it strangled and killed it. From our vantage point, we could see the cats standing over the lifeless body, scanning the nearby area for other predators. Convinced there was no imminent danger, they lay down and greedily consumed their kill.

I was both horrified and mesmerized by the sight of the cheetahs buried muzzle deep in the open belly of the baby giraffe. Drawn by her grief, the mother stood a few yards away, proud neck bowed in hopeless despair as she watched the powerful predators devour her child. One cheetah raised its head at her nearness and clawed the air, hissing. The moment's rawness, so apparent in the palpable torment of the mother giraffe's anguish, was sharpened by the cheetahs' grimaces and the shiny newborn blood that coated their teeth and gums.

At last, Will's grip loosened. I flung myself from him and stumbled back to the jeep. I stood shaking, lost in the gruesome images when a large, brown hand with flat oval nails came to rest on my arm. But instead of startling me, it stunned with its warmth and gentleness. I looked up, already knowing its owner. What was it about Masuwra that seemed to soften the breeze and make the trees sigh? He smiled at the disgruntled look on my face.

"The good lesson is the hardest," he said. While in principle I agreed, I wasn't ready for anyone to convince me that there was anything good about what I'd seen.

"I understand that my world is different, kinder in some ways. And I also understand that there's no supermarket in the savannah. What I can't digest is the savagery," I shuddered.

"We arrive," Masuwra said, gesturing for me to sit beside him on the sunny grass, "with one gift. You are wearing it. When we leave, only our soul returns. It is our job to honor the body, but also to honor the earth mother." He shrugged and tilted his head. "Sometimes, we must honor one with the other."

"But why is it so difficult, Masuwra?"

His arms were resting on his raised knees, and he brought his fingertips to his lips for a moment as if in prayer, then made a small clicking noise before answering. "If an animal kills another and eats it, it is nourishment and continuation. If an animal kills another and eats it, and all you see is pain and death, then all you know is suffering."

"But there's always a winner," I said. "Why is that fair?"

"We are never owners, Kabibi. That which comes to us, must always be returned." He squinted into the distance, and then rose to his feet and moved quietly away.

I sat rigidly apart from Will on the way back, shaking, barely able to keep my fury under control. When we reached the camp, I worked off my anger by helping prepare dinner. It was only when I realized the irony of the situation that the betrayal I felt eased. I looked at the impala carcass rolling lazily around on the spit above the open air barbecue. Wasn't I also eating off the land? My inner voice rose in bitter resentment. *Yes,* it answered. *But our prey was purchased from outside the reserve. Its life was taken without pain or even unnecessary fear, and we did not take a child from its mother.*

I had no appetite for the meal, and instead walked to the nearby stream, watching its softly flowing current. An unsuspecting leaf had snagged on a small log jammed against the bank. How long could it hold on against the flow? And why, in our own struggle to move forward, did Will and I keep encountering obstacles. Would there always be so many barriers for two people from different worlds? I heard Will's footsteps in the dry grass. He came to stand beside me, his gaze following mine to the deterred little leaf.

"You had no right to do that to me." My words were knife sharp.

"Survival isn't always pretty," he said after a moment.

"You think watching the wretchedness of a mother lose her child is necessary for me to understand that life can be cruel? I know loss." My eyes held seven years of it. Will flinched.

"I suppose I deserve that." After a moment, he reached to take hold of my shoulders, but the memory of that gesture was too fresh, and I pulled away. Will turned to face the water again and rubbed his forehead like he'd lived a thousand years. "Trust me, Jackie honey, loss is a cruel teacher. You and I have very little time, and we've wasted so much already."

"You want me to trust you? Well, you just proved that I can't." The anger had made me speak more loudly than I meant. I glanced back toward the camp, but it was deserted except for Njau, who was cleaning up after dinner with his back to us. I picked up a rock and threw it into the water.

"Jackie, nature is a balancing act, and I won't sugar coat it for you – eat or be eaten. I guess that sounds cynical, but life will always renew itself. Know that, and you'll find your own strength. You told me you want to feel safe. Well, that won't happen unless you're willing to risk everything you have for what you want. Until you can do that, you won't trust yourself, and that's a world more important than trusting me. Our own way is going to be tough and rocky too. I need you to survive it, love."

"Our way... or your way?" I asked, suddenly feeling a chill.

"I'm a doctor. This is Africa. It's not the world you're used to." A stab of panic shot through me.

"Then it is your world we're supposed to survive in. Haven't we been down this road before?"

Will watched me for a long moment. "I'd hoped today... what happened... might help you understand. Every day is a tragic life and death struggle for these people. I can help." I started to turn away, but Will put his hands on either side of my face and pulled me back to look at him. "I don't want to do that without you." All I could think of was what a fool I'd been to get myself into the same spot I'd been in seven years before.

"You knew," I said, pulling away from him. "You intended all along for us to stay in Africa, in your world. I was never part of the equation." I swallowed to drown the furious tears that filled my eyes.

"The problem isn't where we are together, Jackie. The problem is you don't know if you want to take the risk."

"And what are you risking, Will?" My voice trembled with hurt betrayal.

"Ah," he sighed. "That's just it. I'm risking it all. I'm asking you to do what I can't - to give up what you love." The naked truth and yearning in his eyes stopped my breath. I shook my head to clear my thoughts, and then turned back to the river where his words mingled with the murmur of the water. "Make no mistake, Jackie," he said moving to my side, "if you choose to leave, I'll follow you to the ends of the earth, but it will always be to bring you back to our world."

Will meant for me to be accountable, just as he held himself accountable, for the fact that time was running out. We had only these few days together to resolve the obstacles before us – the still irresolute history of our past, the work we both loved, the job offer he didn't yet know about, and now, the letting go of my world. Will had made me watch the gruesome scene so that I might face my own demons, make my own choices, but most of all, know my own heart. Our relationship was a dike with more holes than we had fingers. We both feared separation and time, but the leaks must be plugged, the choice made. And once made, there was no letting go. It was now or never. The flowing water tossed and burbled, disappearing around the bend. I turned to face Will, my voice low and threatening.

"Don't you ever treat me like that again," I said, knowing he saw the storm in my eyes.

Will laid a hand on my cheek. It was cool against the throbbing heat of my skin. "I'm sorry, love. I won't - but never doubt that you are safe with me." I pressed my lips together in the last vestiges of anger. Will gently drew my still rigid body into his arms, and I felt myself relax against his warmth. In the moonlight, I watched a second leaf float towards us and catch behind the first.

"It would be awful to be thrown alone into the current."

"Not with me behind you," he said.

Chapter 34

Snug as a Bug in a Rug/ Behaglich

I woke up to the howling wind and a tap at the door.

"Come in Njau," I called, expecting to see him carrying the usual tray of hot coffee and biscuits. I was surprised instead to find raincoats in his hands.

"A storm is coming, Kabibi, but it should pass quickly," he told me, bowing his head slightly and laying one of the coats over a chair. "Please come to the dining room. You will eat there this morning." He disappeared before I could answer him.

The wind whipped my clothes against my body on the short walk to breakfast. I stepped into the warmth of the dining room to find Charlie and Stanley on the opposite side. Stanley stood with sloped shoulders, head down. His cheeks were crimson. It was clear by Charlie's blotchy red complexion that Stanley had somehow angered him. The harshly whispered words were easy to pick up as the acoustics in the round building magnified sounds. I took a magazine from one of the tables and walked to a window where I could at least appear unaware of their conversation.

"I've already made the reservations, and I'll expect you to start using those binoculars to hunt game, not look at a bunch of ridiculous birds."

The door opened and a muggy gust of wind all but blew Martha, Tom and Will into the room. I glanced at Stanley and saw his father give him one last threatening look before turning towards the new arrivals. Like a mime running his hand in front of his face,

Charlie's angry countenance turned into a jovial smile.

"Looks like we've got a bit of weather ahead of us today," he boomed, slapping Will on the shoulder and reaching out to shake Tom's hand. He glanced at me and smiled uneasily.

"The poor kid," Will whispered planting a quick kiss just below my ear. A line of goose bumps popped up and ran down beneath my collar, causing me to shiver. "Cold?" Will teased, tracing the line of bumps lightly with his finger. I squinted menacingly at him.

I made it a point to sit next to Stanley at breakfast. He hardly touched his food and answered my questions with nods. I gave up and dropped into a companionable silence, listening with a half ear to the breakfast chatter. Apparently rain was approaching, but it was not expected to reach us. The raincoats were only a precaution.

In late morning, we were lucky to spot a small herd of elephants near a watering hole. One of the smaller females danced friskily down to the muddy pond, trunk swinging, ears flapping and hips wiggling in time to her cocky gait. Her jaunty mood and trunk dipping maneuvers were a comical sight, until our driver started the engine in order to move to a spot with a better view. The dancing elephant spun nimbly and bellowed, running toward our jeep. The driver immediately turned off the motor, and Masuwra told us to "Hush." My heart pounded as the musical mammoth rushed within a few feet of me, stopping suddenly to glare like a performer whose audience was putting on coats to leave mid-scene. Our driver tried moving the jeep about ten minutes later only to have the toe-tapping behemoth charge us again. Clearly insulted, she scowled indignantly, then threw her head back and trumpeted before turning her back on us and disappearing into the brush.

Lunch was served under the shade of an enormous fig tree.

Will and I sat with Stanley, who was making up for the breakfast he didn't have. A movement in the sky caught his eye. The boy glanced at his father and then defiantly took out his binoculars to follow the flight of a large eagle as it circled high above us. A moment later, Stanley handed the glasses to me, nodding at the ground several yards away.

"It's after that guinea fowl - there" he whispered excitedly, pointing to a bush. I stood and moved slowly forward, training the binoculars in the direction he was indicating. The incredibly large eagle dove sharply, easily grabbing the running bird with its talons before soaring away. "The martial eagles can carry off antelope, he trilled in admiration, his voice cracking as he completely ignored his father's angry and belligerent stare. Stanley retrieved his glasses from me and headed a short distance away to inspect the rustling of a red headed bird in the branches of a nearby tree. I watched him, knowing that despite his trepidation during Charlie's morning tirade, Stanley's fascination and knowledge of birds would not easily be crushed or denied.

"Good," I muttered to myself. "You hang in there, Stanley." I felt rather than heard the sudden presence to my right.

"When you live with a lion, you must wear the skin of a crocodile." It was Masuwra's voice, as quiet as my own. Moments later, the urgent chatter of our guides caught my attention. They were pointing to the northwest where dark, angry-looking rain clouds appeared to be heading in our direction.

"Is this the storm that wasn't supposed to hit us?" I asked Will, raising my voice against the whine of the wind. The sooty murkiness rolled towards us. Will grasped my hand and pulled me to the jeep.

"Here, put this on," he insisted, all but stuffing my arms into the sleeves of the green raincoat. As he put on his own, the drenching downpour overtook us. The jeep's worn and faded canvas shade was little protection against the onslaught, making it necessary for the group to take cover against the man-sized fingers of root at the base of the huge fig tree. Will backed me into a hollow and shielded me with his body. He wrapped me in his arms and pulled my head against his chest. The deluge was so profound that were it not for the raincoats we would have been soaked to the skin in a minute. Sheltered against him, harbored in our tree niche with my cheek against the slick wetness of his jacket and his solid warmth protecting me, I could feel the pelting rain pummeling his back. Even the wail of the wind and the thrumming of the downpour did not drown the sound of his heartbeat, so snuggled against him as I was. The sanctuary and seclusion within his arms was incredibly sensual, and I would never again hear the drum of rain without remembering the feel of his body against mine. I had no desire to leave my cozy cocoon, and I didn't realize until Will chuckled, that the drenching rain had passed as quickly as it had arrived, and that I was still clinging to him like hope to a golden moment.

"Scared or comfortable?" he asked softly.

"Oh," I said feeling a little embarrassed. I released him and retreated mentally to my safety zone, intending to joke about how brave I was. Nothing came to mind, and the silence of my normally battling inner voice surprised me. But it remained mute, and I realized I liked the feeling of being together, of being part of something outside myself, part of something that did not wholly and only include me, not out of selfishness, but surprisingly because I liked having someone else make me feel safe, someone with whom I could give and take without fear.

Tom had not fared as well. When he realized Martha had left her raincoat behind, perhaps in deference to her safari attire, he staunchly insisted she wear his rain jacket. He was drenched, the water from his clinging safari shorts running down his spindly legs.

"Tom, you're soaking wet," Martha scolded, as if he were unaware of his sodden state, or that she was the cause of it.

"It would appear so," he mumbled, frowning at the muddy pondlet he was inhabiting.

"You poor thing," Martha crooned, suddenly sympathetic. She pointed at Njau and insisted he "get something for Mr. Magisage." Tenderly tucking her already sniffling husband into the jeep, Martha swaddled him in two tablecloths from lunch. By dinner time, Tom was in the throes of a nasty, nose-dripping, glassy-eyed fever. Martha turned into Florence Nightingale, coddling and fussing over her husband and conferring with Will over every cough and sniffle. Even Rachel would have admired her zealous and meticulous ministrations.

Charlie retired early to his hut, probably the result of three double martinis and his disconsolate brooding over his son's inability to appreciate the joy of the kill. Stanley followed shortly afterward.

With the camp to ourselves, Will and I stood near the open fire pit watching the flickering flames.

"Alone at last," I sighed.

"No," Will murmured, "together at last."

Chapter 35

A Far Off Cry

Masuwra was suddenly standing beside us. "I am sorry to interrupt, but I must speak to you," he said looking directly at Will. Masuwra glanced at me through half lowered lids before dropping his eyes to our entwined hands. "I have come to ask for your help." Will's hand tighten around mine. "There is great sickness in the homes of my people. Many have died, and many more will die. I am asking you, Dr. Will, to come with me and use your medicines." A muscle pulsed in the bronze cheek.

"What sickness is it?" Will asked.

"It is the umiyane."

Will frowned. "Where is your village, Masuwra?"

"Not so far, less than a day's journey from here. It is called iNgwavuma."

Will ran his hand through his hair. "Are there any doctors there now?"

"Only sometimes from the hospital in Manguzi. It is almost two hours to drive there for treatment, but no one owns a vehicle. It is a two day walk for those who are strong enough."

Will drew a deep breath and shook his head, "Masuwra ..."

"My people are dying."

Will looked at me.

"Can you help?" I asked. He nodded.

"I'll be right back," he said, and left with Masuwra.

Wrapping my arms around myself to ward off the coolness of the night air, I moved nearer the fire. As I stared into the glowing embers, I couldn't deny the feeling of disappointment and the creeping fear of separation. I berated myself for the self-indulgent thoughts. People were suffering and dying. That was all that was important. If Will could help, then I would do everything I could to support and encourage him. But to have our time cut short, to risk losing each other again – it was frightening. Stop it, I thought. If we're going to make this work, then I need to become a part of Will's life. But, what about him, I wondered? How will his life become a part of mine? I held my hands out to catch the last vestiges of warmth. Suddenly, Will's arms were around me, and I leaned back against his solidness.

"I just spoke to one of the doctors at Manguzi Hospital. The staff is stretched to the limits. They're going to order more quinine drugs and try to send someone out to iNgwavuma in a couple of days." He pulled me closer.

"Why are they sick," I asked, turning in his arms to face him.

"Umiyane – mosquitoes. Malaria is epidemic in the rural areas. The mosquitoes get into the water and the sewage – they kill thousands of Africans every year. iNgwavuma is a poor village. The blacks there still live like they did fifty years ago – huts, no plumbing." I could see the desire to stay with me and the depth of his commitment to his countrymen battling in his eyes.

"What do you need to do?" I asked. Will blinked slowly.

"I called a colleague in Johannesburg. He's going to overnight some drugs and medical supplies to Manguzi Hospital. If I pick them up in the morning, I can drive them out to iNgwavuma. I'll stay just until a backup doctor arrives." His voice was apologetic.

"I'm coming with you." He released me abruptly and stepped back.

"Absolutely not." This was the voice of uncompromising authority. The words rankled a bit.

"If we're going to be together in this, then let's be in it together. I can help, and don't tell me you don't need two more hands," I insisted.

"Jackie, there's no running water, let alone clean water. There's no electricity. There's probably one loo for every twenty people, and it's only a long drop hole in the ground. Besides, you're just as susceptible to the mosquitoes as the natives."

"And you're not?" I shot back. "If you can stand it, so can I. Show me how to be safe and what to do. I can handle it."

"Safe," he muttered. "Malaria is deadly. I won't expose you to it."

"Will, it's all right. My doctor gave me chloroquine, that and every other vaccine he had access to before I came here." I frowned. "What about you?"

"Some of our training for tropical medicine is in outlying areas. We're vaccinated, but even that's not foolproof. Besides, I don't want you seeing that kind of poverty and death." The remark brought a surge of anger.

"What a hypocrite you are, Will Kincaid. You wanted me to see life and death on the safari, but you're afraid to show me the poverty and death your own people face."

"I'm not trying to hide anything from you, Jackie. I love my country, but these deaths are unnecessary. There's not enough money for vaccine, and not enough doctors to give the vaccine that's available." He shook his head. "It's different for you. In America you learn about the horrors of African slavery. Well, in Africa, poverty is slavery. No one should have to experience either. I chose to deal with the sickness and pain. I don't expect you to deal with it too. I'm not going to put you in harm's way, and Bob's your uncle."

"Harm!" I said, squinting at the British expression. "The cheetahs could have turned on us at any moment."

"No. Masuwra and the guides had guns," he muttered absently, his mind already on the hours ahead.

"Well, there you go. We don't need guns now." Will's eyes snapped back into focus, and he grabbed my arm and shook it.

"Disease is deadlier than the cats, Jackie. They can both sneak up on you, but disease – it's inside your body before you know it, before you have time to defend yourself." I was ready with a million reasons why I could help and be safe, but before I could say another word his face softened and he groaned in a rough whisper, "I couldn't stand it if anything happened to you." I looked into his eyes and saw his fear for me.

"So keep me with you, and I'll be safe." I pulled his lips to mine and kissed him. He didn't respond at first, and then suddenly slid his fingers into the hair at the back of my neck, pulled me hard against him and kissed me. I tasted the fear and the love, but there was also sadness and need. I wrapped my arms around him and lost myself in that kiss. I knew in that moment I would have gone anywhere with him, risked anything for him.

"All right," he said, pointing his finger at me, "I'll take you to Manguzi Hospital. You can stay at one of the doctor's homes until a replacement relieves me." The thought of imposing on some unsuspecting family for the next couple of days didn't much improve my state of mind.

"And if another doctor doesn't show up? Then shall I just go home?" I crossed my arms and raised an eyebrow.

"Someone will come," he insisted. I waited. "You'll be a distraction."

"Quite possibly," I said, "but I'll be the most helpful distraction you've ever had." Assuming I had found a crack in his defense, I jumped back in. "I'm here because I choose to be. Don't protect me from who you are." He crossed his arms and then squinted menacingly at me, making me expect more justifications in his growing list of reasons why I should be confined to the doctor's barracks. I meant to win this argument, but his ultimatum startled me.

"If you don't do exactly as I tell you . . . . ." His voice had a seriously sinister ring to it. I took his earlobes between fingers and thumbs and pulled his lips down to mine.

"I will be the best student you're ever likely to train."

"I don't know how you've gotten around me," he grumbled.

"Maybe you've met your match, Kincaid," I said. "Now let's get this show on the road."

Chapter 36

A Distant Sacrifice

While Will made arrangements for the trip, I returned to my hut and began packing. I didn't hear Masuwra until he tapped on the door frame.

"You will accompany the doctor?" His voice coming through the screen was quiet and intimate in the padded softness of the night. I nodded and walked towards him, surprised that while he'd known Will as a child, had even reprimanded him on safari, that he now referred to him as "doctor." But then, I had no doubt Masuwra held a deep respect for all the creatures of the earth. He pushed the screen open and gestured for me to come out. We sat on the steps in stillness for a time, Masuwra's watchful eyes searing through the darkness - *"Tyger! Tyger! Burning bright/ in the forest of the night..."*

"This will be difficult for you," he said, breaking the silence.

"Probably," I agreed, "but I want to go."

"Why?" he asked

"Because... I want to learn more about his world, about his need to help the people." Masuwra looked at me, and it felt as if he had climbed into my thoughts.

"A hunger can get inside you," he said, "and consume you." A tiny shiver ran up my back. He stared into the distance as if he were listening to a voice I could not hear. I wasn't aware of when he started speaking again; I only know that the timbre of his voice and the cadence of his words had lulled me into his story.

"... the Namagua shepherd boy lived on a mountain in

KwaZulu Natal where he tended a herd of very unusual goats. Most goats can survive almost anywhere, but the shepherd's goats could only survive in the very thin air of the mountain top. In the valley below lived a shepherd girl who also tended a herd of very particular goats who could only eat the richest, greenest low grasses. One day, one of the boy's goats lost its footing and fell off a cliff. It landed on a small patch of grass halfway down the mountain. On this very same day, one of the girl's goats wandered up the mountain and was standing in the patch of grass where the boy's goat landed. The boy ran down the mountain to rescue his lost ram and met the girl who had climbed the mountain to find her lost nanny. The boy and girl fell in love, but did not know what to do about it because they lived in different worlds. Five months later, the nanny gave birth to a very unusual goat. It could not breathe the thin air at the top of the mountain or the rich air at the bottom of the valley. The low green grasses were too rich for it and the brown grasses at the top too dry. The shepherds could not understand a way to mix their herds and be together, so they each spent part of their day in the middle of the mountain with the goat-from-two-worlds.

Many years passed, and the boy grew bent and grey, and the girl grew old and fragile. One day, she could no longer climb the mountain. The old man waited for her until the sun set and the night grew dark and cold, but the old woman never came. When the sky filled with stars, the man took the now ancient half-way goat with him to the top of the mountain and slept next to it to keep himself company. Unable to breathe the oxygen-thin air, or tolerate the tough, brown grass, it was not long before the much loved goat died. No one ever saw the old man again. But for many years afterwards, in the sigh of the wind that blew down from the mountain top, people claimed they could hear the young shepherd calling to the girl in the valley below."

When the story ended, I sat for a time with my eyes closed. A sudden gust of wind blew through the camp, and I caught myself listening for the shepherd's call.

"Is half a world ever enough?" I asked. But, like the wind, Masuwra was gone, and the only sound was the night cry of a creature and the distant answer of its mate.

Chapter 37

Innocuous Inoculations

Before dawn the following morning, Will tapped lightly on my door. Barely awake, I stretched into a lion-sized yawn and then got out of bed and padded across the room barefoot to let him in. He raised his eyebrows and smiled as his eyes traveled down my thin nightgown.

"I thought we'd get an early start," he said. I tried to straighten my hair and rub the sleep out of my eyes. "Don't bother," he smiled when I'd done the best I could. "I intend to keep you in a disheveled state permanently."

There was another light tap on the door. I looked down at my nightgown and shrugged. Njau entered carrying a tray of steaming coffee, venison sausages, honey bread and melon. There were two plates, two sets of silverware and two mugs. Clever man.

"What a feast, Njau," I said, eyeing the sumptuous meal.

"You will need much strength today, Kabibi honey." At the name, both Will and I glanced up, startling Njau.

"Is this not correct?" he asked looking from Will to me with distress. "It is the name I hear Dr. Will use for moments of importance, like at the river. Today is also important. You will help our people." I put my hands together as if in prayer and held them against my lips, biting the insides of my cheeks to keep from smiling at the touchingly sweet remark.

"Thank you for honoring my woman, Njau," Will said with sincerity. This seemed to please the young man, and he smiled proudly before leaving the hut.

"Your woman," I groused in mock anger.

"Yes, my woman," Will said, raising an eyebrow. "Do you have a problem with that?"

I wrinkled my nose. "Sounds a little proprietary, don't you think?"

"Absolutely," Will said carrying the tray of food to the bed. He put a sausage on a plate and set it before me, and then took a knife and fork and cut the sausage into bite-sized pieces. I watched as he stabbed a chunk and then held it to my mouth.

"Why is this reminiscent of you force feeding me pain pills?" I asked, suspicious of so much solicitation.

"I'm demonstrating the perks of being 'my woman'." He shrugged. "Imagine it – a lifetime of having every desire and whim fulfilled." He took the piece of sausage off the fork with his teeth and offered it to me.

"Forget the whims," I said, putting the sausage back on the plate. I threw my arms around his neck and gave him a good morning kiss to remember. Moments later, tangled in the sheets, we both jumped as the screen door knocked against its frame several times.

"The jeep is loaded and ready to leave." We could see Njau's wide smile as he peered through the screen.

Forty-five minutes later we were on our way to Manguzi with Masuwra following in an older model jeep. The trip took four and a half hours. As we neared the small town, the paved roads turned into dirt, and small groupings of huts began to appear. The Manguzi Hospital was pitifully small compared to the city hospitals. The supplies had not arrived, but were expected "soon." Masuwra guided us through the 107 bed facility where patients were recuperating side by side in large rooms. There were no curtains or sense of privacy, but none of the patients seemed to mind. Nearly everyone had a smile for us. The maternity ward held only eight beds, all of them full. Each doctor cared for approximately 40 patients. None of the physicians seemed to be specialists as they each took on whatever emergency or illness presented itself.

I moved among the patients with Will as he gave shots, treated sores and sutured wounds. We wore masks and gloves, but I was able to do little more than hold their hands and assist with bandaging. I was touched and thrilled to help these beautiful people whose smiling faces held a poignant mix of hope and strength. When the medical supplies arrived shortly after noon, I was watching Will deliver a baby. When he held up the tiny infant for the mother to see, he glanced at me with a tenderness I had only guessed at. The look captivated me with its sweet promise and nearly brought me to tears.

The next hour flew by as Masuwra, Will and I loaded the vehicles with the supplies sent from Johannesburg. There was some negotiating for certain medicines, but Will still managed to leave with a full load. It took another two hours to reach iNgwavuma.

As soon as we arrived, three men from the village, two of them thin and sickly looking, helped set up a temporary clinic that consisted of nine poles stuck in the ground to support canvas walls and a shaded roof. Masuwra had brought the tent materials in his jeep, along with two chairs, two fold-up tables and four cots. While the supplies were unloaded, Will visited several of the single room dwellings to determine the most urgent cases and do what he could to treat the sickest among them. Many of the sick lay on the dirt floors of the crowded shacks, their shaking, dehydrated bodies burning with the deadly malaria fever. My stomach churned at the stench that permeated even the outside air. The lack of food and water were appalling. The mud-filled, stick walls supported roofs of thatch and corrugated metal that looked as if they had already spent the better part of their life somewhere else. Most huts housed up to ten people and had only one or two small openings in the walls.

"No, you mustn't drink this water. It's bad," Will insisted, picking up a small boy who was scooping brown liquid into his mouth from a slimy looking mud puddle. He set the boy down a few feet away and squatted before him, "Amanzi kubi," *bad water*. The boy looked at Will and shrugged, then scurried back to the slimy wetness, cupped his hands and continued to drink. Will retrieved the boy again and handed him to a woman standing nearby. "Masuwra, please explain to these people that drinking dirty water will make them sick."

"There is only a small stream about one kilometer from here. Many are too sick to make the walk." I could hear the anger and frustration for his people in the words.

"Then tell them they must boil the water before they drink it." Will grabbed a dented pot hanging on a nearby hut and poured water into it. He took it to a fire pit and mimed building a fire and putting the pot over it. The people watched, expressionless. Frustrated, Will headed for an old rusty, metal barrel full of water near the back of one of the buildings. He peered inside and then pointed to the top of the water, "Nunus," *insects,* he told them. A frazzle-haired older woman near him shrugged and walked away. Several others turned to leave just as Will put his hands against the rim and started to push it over. Two of the men rushed back and shoved Will away from the barrel. Masuwra's voice suddenly boomed through the small village.

"Ukuvala!" *Stop*.

He strode toward the two men, pushed them to the side and

emptied the barrel with one shove. The brackish water slapped against the side of the hut. In the same fluid movement, Masuwra leaned and picked up a large, pottery jug, swung it onto his shoulder, and walked out of the village down the long dusty road. In a few moments, several villagers tiredly picked up water vessels and followed.

Will spent the next few hours treating fevers, holding the heads of those who vomited, giving intravenous fluids to others with diarrhea and dehydration and inoculating the people who waited in line for his white man's medicine. More than once my stomach rolled, and I thought I might be sick, but I steadied myself, determined to help. Will was tireless, but by late afternoon, there was still no end to the long line of patients outside the little canvas clinic. Following Will's instructions, I organized the supplies, sterilized instruments and learned the names and uses for the vaccines. Will also taught me to fill the syringes and set up the intravenous tubing.

Suddenly, two men pushed through the doorway. They were carrying a blue-lipped woman who was gasping for breath. I watched Will as he quickly examined her, and then told the men that he would have to cut an opening in her throat and insert a tube to let air into her lungs. He called over his shoulder for me to continue with the inoculations.

I froze, and then glanced at the syringe I'd just filled as if it were about to jump off the table and bite me. I turned to Will, intending to point out that a course in giving shots was not a general education requirement for a Journalism major, but he was already looking at me with raised eyebrows.

"I've got to do this tracheotomy quickly, Jackie. You said you wanted to help. Here's your chance." Just the slightest smile danced across his mouth as he returned to prepping the woman for the procedure. At my silence, he glanced up and saw the confused terror on my face. "Picture the deltoid muscle" he said, as if he were simply suggesting I count available cotton balls. There it was again - that hint of a smile. I suspected Will was enjoying himself. I would deal with that later. Right now, I needed a little more instruction.

"My memory could use a little refreshing," I called back, smiling sweetly. His look of innocence wouldn't have fooled a gnat with a lobotomy.

"That's the muscle that covers the shoulder and just below. Picture an upside down triangle at the top of the arm and give the shot near the middle of the top. Keep the needle at a 90 degree angle with the arm, and plunge it in a little less than a half inch."

Plunge. Did Will say *plunge*? I wasn't an Olympic diving champion for heaven's sake. The top of my arm cringed. But the calm voice went on.

"Make sure you empty the syringe before you remove the needle."

Several of the villagers, who for once I hoped spoke no English, were now watching me. I smiled and nodded to them as if I'd just received a black belt in giving shots.

"How will I know if the needle is in the right place?" I squinted menacingly at Will.

"Once the needle is in, pull back slightly. If there's blood, start over with a new needle and serum. If there's no blood, you're good." Will winked at me and went back to his work. Infuriating man. He was in serious trouble.

Taking a deep breath and squaring my shoulders, I smiled at the young woman standing before me who, I assumed, thought I knew what I was doing. I picked up the loaded needle with trembling hands, and swabbed her arm with alcohol. I could feel a ring of perspiration across my forehead. Masuwra, who had been standing just outside the door, entered and took hold of the woman's hand, smiling into her eyes and speaking to her in a gentling voice. He glanced at me, his gaze holding mine, until I gave him four little nervous nods. It's now or never, I thought. I held the needle up as I had seen Will do, and then tapped it and extruded a small stream of serum to check for air bubbles. Taking hold of the girl's upper arm, I gently pinched, hoping that might dull any pain I was about to inflict. I swallowed, and then slid my left hand to the underside of her arm and used my right to gently *plunge* in the needle. The girl jerked, causing the arm muscle to tighten, and I'm sure, increasing the pain. Masuwra, bless his heart, kept at his distracting ministrations. I pulled back slightly on the needle, praying there would be no blood. The African Gods answered my plea, and with one last, deep breath, I pushed down on the plunger, injecting the serum.

"Mmm, there," I said more to myself than to the girl, and quickly removed the needle. I stood staring at the arm, holding the syringe like a 1950's movie star with a cigarette.

"Breathe," Will smiled, not even looking up from his corner of "our" medical center.

Chapter 38

Night Crawlers

The day released itself into a red-orange sunset that silhouetted the umbrella-hatted trees, and the sweating earth gave up its fragrance of dry, baked grass. Someone produced a kerosene lantern, probably one of the more modern pieces of equipment the village had. Will worked relentlessly, holding his hand against fevered foreheads, peering into infected mouths and ears and laying his stethoscope against chests that wheezed and struggled for air. I managed to get him to eat some dinner Masuwra brought us, but I had to half feed it to him while he continued to diagnose and treat the ghostly thin inhabitants of iNgwavuma.

"This is the last patient, then you must rest," Masuwra told Will a short time later. He helped the elderly man onto one of the cots. "I have told the others to return in the morning." The sick man wore an old army jacket that hung on his frame like a storm-weathered sail. Behind him was a grey-haired woman. Will finished bandaging an open sore on the arm of a young boy. "Uyaphila," *You will be fine,* he told him. Will turned and crouched beside the elderly man. The man coughed. It was a hacking, raspy sound.

"His name is Tafari," Masuwra told Will.

"Unjani, Tafari?" Will asked, encouraging the man with a gesture towards Masuwra, to explain what was wrong with him.

The frail old man spoke between labored breaths, while the grey-haired woman smiled sadly and rubbed a loving hand across his forehead. When Tafari finished, she leaned over and whispered, "Mudiwa."

"Beloved," Will translated, looking up at me with a tired smile.

Tafari was suffering from an advanced case of tuberculosis. There wasn't much that could be done with the medicines at hand. Will smiled at Tafari, patting his arm, then stood and turned toward Masuwra. "This man needs to go to Manguzi for treatment."

"I will see to it," Masuwra said.

Bone weary, we cleaned and sterilized the little infirmary as best we could, and used the water we brought with us to wash up and brush our teeth. I wasn't too thrilled about using the long drop toilet, and even less thrilled to know that Will intended to stand nearby while I did. Despite having to hold my breath, I was pleasantly surprised to find that long drop toilets are pretty much effective at muffling sounds.

Masuwra had set up a small tent for us and the unused supplies. He moved the two cots from the infirmary into it for the night. The tent was barely tall enough for Will to stand up, but it was cozy and private and kept the mosquitoes out. Will gave me a moment to change into night clothes before returning and pushing the two cots together. He slipped out of his outer clothes and amid the conversations and occasional infants' cries that floated to us on the air, we lay on our sides nose to nose, our fingers entwined, talking softly about the day. Although he could barely keep his eyes open, Will's mind was still running at breakneck speed.

"We've got to get more medicine. I'll make some more calls tomorrow. There's a store with a phone a few miles down the road." His words began to slur a bit, and his voice was a whisper. "These people need clean water, and some sort of sewage system... but the government doesn't have the money..." His eyes closed. The thick lashes rested above the bruised-looking skin beneath them. Even in the darkness, I could see the heavy stubble that left a dark smudge on the lower half of his face. Will's fingers slowly relaxed in mine, and I thought he was asleep until a few moments later when his eyes slowly opened.

"I'm sorry you're in the middle of all this," he whispered.

"And if I want to be?" I said, pulling a portion of my blanket over the cot ridges separating us so that I could scoot closer and lay my head on his shoulder.

"You were wonderful today. It's made a difference, you know." He kissed the top of my head then reached to pull me closer. He slowly unbuttoned my nightshirt and pulled me against him. The silky, cool feel of our skin touching was magnetic. I barely noticed the slightly salty taste of his lips as his hand glided gently down my side. Will rose on one elbow and put his other arm behind my waist to pull me onto his cot. His elbow was near the edge between our cots, and with our added weight behind it, the narrow lounge tipped precariously and then shot up and sideways, dumping us in a mound of twisted blankets on the floor. Will landed on top, knocking the wind out of me. We were twisted in the covers and around each other like a trail of ants circling a cookie jar. Before we could disentangle ourselves, a loud engine and a painfully bright pair of headlights moved from one side of the tent to the other, coming to rest on the front flap. The tent, with its multitude of medicine bottles, lit up like a many faceted diamond in a glass case. The engine stopped. Two doors opened and then slammed shut as Will tried, without much luck, to unravel us, all the while muttering something incoherent that sounded suspiciously like Zulu.

"Hullo?" a man's voice called. The tent flap suddenly opened, and we looked up into two impishly grinning faces.

"Sorry it took so long to get here, but looks like you've got things . . . all wrapped up," the thin, red-headed, young man said, his mouth twisting into a lopsided smile. His faded green t-shirt hung loosely underneath an equally worn and faded sort of lab coat. A drooping name tag hung from an ink-stained pocket.

"Just grab the end of this blanket," Will growled, shoving a lose corner at him.

"Oh. Here, let me help." It was the short, older woman, peering from behind the man. She was clearly having trouble keeping a straight face. She grabbed the other loose end of the blanket, and with one yank, the two wrenched off our cover and sent me rolling against a stack of boxes where I came to an abrupt stop when my head banged against the corner of one of them. The tug had the opposite effect for Will who, still tangled in the woolen folds, whirlpooled away from me. He was now hopelessly wound in the blanket as tightly as a tourniquet. I sat up, clutching my pajama top and rubbing an already swelling bump just above my ear. The young man chuckled, and leaned over to help, but Will shook his head, giving him a no-thank-you wave with the tips of his fingers, the only parts of him, besides his head, that were showing.

"Well then, we'll meet you two outside after you've straightened things out." Will's face was the shade of my mother's Thanksgiving cranberry sauce, and I bit my lip to keep from smiling.

"Bloody blooming blanket," Will groused, thrashing about like a well-developed pupa trying to emerge from its cocoon. Frustrated, he snorted and lay back, then rolled himself free. He tossed the blanket, muttering more Zulu.

"Let me see that." He reached to explore the bump on my head.

"Ow!" I yelped.

"Sorry." He poked a bit more gently. "I need to do a better job of keeping you away from pointed objects."

"It's alright, Will - just a little tumble. My world has bumps and warts, too."

"A few too many when I'm around," he muttered, still upset.

"You okay?" I asked.

"Yes, fine" he said, rubbing a hip.

"I thought so," I sighed, giving him a half-lidded smile, "seeing as I cushioned your fall." I couldn't resist. One of Will's eyebrows shot up, and the threat of a smile touched his lips before he threw his head back and roared with laughter. He sat back then and wiped an errant tear before laying his hand gently on the side of my face and whispering, "I love you, lass." He slid his hands up my sides under my night shirt, his thumbs tucked under my breasts, and pulled me into a kiss that made me completely forget our newly arrived guests, where I was, or anything else for that matter. A throat cleared outside the tent, which started us laughing. We tried to stop, but ended up snorting and snickering. Eventually, we put our clothes and tent in order, dusted ourselves and our egos off, and headed out to meet our visitors.

"Sorry for the interruption," the man said reaching out to shake Will's hand. "I'm Mark Catterling, one of the Manguzi intern volunteers, and this is the area nurse, Joyce Severs."

"Will Kincaid, I'm a resident at Johannesburg Hospital. This is Jackie Sinclair." Despite the casual greeting, Will's rosy flush gave away his mild embarrassment.

"Understand you two are on vacation. Nice of you to jump in and handle this," Mark said.

"We didn't expect you until tomorrow, but we're glad to see you anytime -- well, almost anytime," Will added wryly. The two men discussed medicines and procedures while Joyce and I poured four cups of lukewarm coffee from a thermos in their truck.

"You brought a lot of supplies," I said glancing at the boxes piled behind the front seats.

"We weren't sure what was needed, but this should see us through the next couple of days." She straightened a leaning bottle inside one of the open boxes. Her weathered hands were freckled, the knuckles slightly knobby with arthritis.

Masuwra had been busy re-stoking the fire so that we might talk for a bit by its warmth and light. Mark was from Cape Town, and planned to specialize in subtropical diseases. His work at Manguzi hospital provided a veritable smorgasbord of maladies from which he could glean expertise. Joyce had been working with the urban poor since her twenties. I guessed her to be in her late forties. Neither Will nor I explained our relationship, and both Mark and Joyce, despite their earlier amusement over the situation in which they found us, seemed to sense our need for privacy and did not ask. We talked until we were all yawning and the challenging day ahead beckoned. It was decided that Will and I would help with the patients until mid-afternoon the following day and then head on our way, stopping at a nearby town where there was a phone to call for any needed supplies. Masuwra would stay to assist at the clinic and translate. We helped Mark and Joyce set up their tent and then banked the fire before heading to bed.

"I'll be on call if you get... tied-up." Mark smiled impishly.

"Devil of a chap," Will mumbled, holding open our tent flap for me. Just as I was about to step in, he grabbed my arm so tightly I could feel a bruise forming.

"Stop," he whispered. I froze and then heard a sliding scuffle off my right. "Don't move."

I caught the shine of slithering in my peripheral vision. I've always been deathly afraid of snakes, and Will's extreme reaction led me to believe this was no pet hot house serpent stargazing in the moonlight beside my foot. I was afraid to breathe for fear the slight movement of my chest might incite it to strike. I slowly glanced sideways at Will, hoping he knew how we were going to move out of the serpent's strike zone. He was watching the snake. Actually, he looked fascinated, as if it were some laboratory test that was about to produce an epiphany for him.

Behind us, Mark popped his head out of his tent and started to say something, then spotted the snake and swallowed his words except for one barely audible, "Bollocks."

A bead of sweat slithered down the side of my neck and ran along a back muscle that was threatening to cramp. I heard Mark move slowly out of his tent. The snake turned slightly, bringing its sleek little head upright into strike position. It was when it opened its black mouth that I remembered reading about African black mambo snakes in one of my tour books. Black mambos were deadly poisonous, and they could strike repeatedly. My spinal cord was rattling inside me, and my mouth went dry. I felt myself sway. Will tightened his grasp on my arm, causing me to wince involuntarily just as an errant spark from the fire exploded in a shower of color.

The last thing I remember was the snake lunging towards me. And then, I was on the ground with Will and Mark leaning over my leg. My ears were ringing, and I couldn't seem to breathe. Will was talking to Mark about something that sounded like "antivenom." His left hand was on my head brushing the hair off my face while he moved back and forth first peering into my eyes and then staring at my leg with Mark.

"It's all right, Jackie honey. It's all right. You're going to be just fine." Despite his in-charge and somewhat calm demeanor, his voice was terse and anxious. He grabbed a blanket from the tent and put it beneath my head, all the while firing questions at me. "How are you feeling? Are you nauseated? Can you feel this?" he asked pinching my leg a few inches below the knee. He looked into my nose, startling me and making me sneeze. He prodded my stomach.

"Ouch."

"Does that hurt?" Will asked, his eyes boring into mine.

"It should," I said in a shaky voice. "I think you cracked a rib when you fell on me." There was a lot of tugging going on by my foot. Will and Mark scoured my skin for any break, finding only a small reddened area but no open wound.

"Well, that takes the biscuit," Mark said sounding surprised. "Look at that." He held up the boot he had removed from my right foot – the foot the black mambo had struck.

Joyce was scanning the surrounding area with a flashlight. At Mark's words, she turned the light on the boot he was holding, focusing it on two small holes, one on either side of an eyelet. Will snatched the boot and flipped the top back to show the inside. Neither fang hole had made it through the thick leather.

"Careful," Joyce warned, "There's venom on that boot." Will dropped it, and we all stared at it, this hero boot lying on its side in the dust. "An eighth of an inch either way," she said in disbelief, "and one of the fangs would have pierced her ankle through that eyelet." Suddenly, Will sat back hitting the ground hard. He dropped his head between his knees.

"Thank God," he nearly sobbed. And then in one continuous movement, he rolled to his knees and pulled me, like a rag doll, into his arms. We were both shaking, our teeth clattering like lids on boiling pots.

"Wh...Why are my ears ringing?" The trembling words were rough against the dryness of my throat.

"Masuwra shot the mambo," Mark said pointing at the limp, headless coil a few feet away.

"This snake does not like people," Masuwra said from the shadows where he was scanning the surrounding area, "but the village was built where it breeds. The sparks from the fire scared it." Before I could thank him, he scooped up the snake remains and disappeared. I couldn't tell if I was shaking my head in disbelief or if it was only my heartbeat pounding against the walls of my body.

"Water," I croaked. Joyce left and returned in a moment with water and two pills.

"Something to relax you," she said. "It's just a couple of my valium." I could imagine the need for the tranquilizers in the world she faced each day. Eyeing the ground cautiously, Joyce and Mark headed to their tent. "It's a damn miracle," I heard her whisper into the blackness of the night. There was something about the way she said it or the look in her eyes, but this woman had seen the dregs of life, and her words coated my skin with goose bumps.

As exhausted as he was, Will woke me every hour or so as a precaution, checking me over as gently as a mother with a newborn. Shortly before dawn, I looked up into his peering eyes and scooted onto my side to make room for him on my cot. I drew his head onto my shoulder.

"Sleep now, Mudiwa," I whispered. "I'm fine."

Chapter 39

The Life in my Arms

I woke alone in the morning, the heat of Will's body gone. The cot he'd slept on was also gone, leaving a gaping hole in our little house. I snuggled deeper into my cocoon of blankets and listened to the chatter of undecipherable sounds. I could hold these peoples' hands, give them medicine, sleep in their village, even empathize with them, but I could not understand their words, not yet. The laughter of a child, universal in its song, pierced the cool morning air, and I smiled. When I finally sat up, a wave of dizziness hit me. I hung my head and shook it trying to dispel the sensation and clear my mind. The tent flap opened and a hand of warm sunlight reached me. Will came in and sat beside me.

"How are you feeling?" he asked.

"You left me," I pouted. He winced and pulled me against him. "I'm all right, Will."

"I want you to take it easy today." It was his doctor's voice.

"So, you don't need me to perform some intricate surgery or find the cure to a disease?" Will's face reddened.

"Ah, the shots." He smiled sheepishly.

"I was mortified – sticking needles into people. You're in bad trouble, Will Kincaid."

"How's that?" he asked, smiling.

"Ha! Like I'm going to let you know exactly when I'll extract my revenge. Just be on guard, doctor."

"Torture me with kisses," he said and pulled my lips to his. The kiss was gentle but passionate, and the moments passed before he pulled back sighing reluctantly. He stood and reached for my hand to pull me up. "We'll need the cot, so let's get you set for the day."

"Uh, if that involves you standing guard again..." I waved a finger in the direction of the long drop, "think I've got it figured out, and I've no intention of falling in."

Fifteen minutes later, I was headed to the clinic when a tall, painfully thin woman clutching a small bundle came running towards me through the field outside the village. Her words, forced out between panting breaths, were frantic, and her eyes radiated such panicked fear that tears filled my eyes. I shook my head in frustration, unable to understand her, but the message was clear when she thrust her bundle towards me. I peered into the slit at the top and then carefully pulled back the tattered blanket. Two enormously huge eyes stared with glazed innocence. The cracked and swollen lips of the tiny, open mouth were like dried rose petals above the sunken cheeks. One hand lay against the side of the emaciated head, the wrist so delicate that I thought it would break if I touched it. The child, whose age I could not guess, was so thin and dehydrated that the blanket pulled its skin into multiple folds like the bellows of an accordion. I nodded to the mother to follow me and walked quickly to the clinic. So many patients were in line, that I had to scoot sideways through the door, the mother moving silently behind me, holding onto the back of my blouse.

When Will saw me enter, he handed something to Joyce and came over to me. Glancing quickly into the blanket, he gestured to the medicine table, the only spot left to lay the child, but my arms wouldn't release the tiny life that struggled within them. I willed myself to send strength into the fragile body, whose every breath seemed like its last. I cooed incoherent sounds and moved my head trying to get the baby to focus on me, wanting desperately to find some sign of fight in the dull and hopeless eyes. A tear slid down my cheek and dropped onto the baby's shoulder, startling me. I was sure the thirst-racked skin would immediately soak it up, but the tear just sat, waiting like me for some response. It finally rolled off and disappeared into the blanket. I looked up at Will as he gently held his stethoscope to the rib-lined chest. He straightened up, nodded at Joyce, and then slowly looked at me. His eyes told me everything I didn't want to hear.

"Nothing?" I whispered, sucking in a shaky breath. The mother's eyes were darting back and forth between the two of us.

"Maybe if I'd seen him sooner." Will picked up the tiny hand, and the delicate fingers tightened slightly around his. I looked up with hope, but Will closed his eyes and shook his head. He took off his glasses and rubbed the spot on his nose where they sat.

Joyce, her wiry grey hair flying wildly around her ears, brought a metal stand with a bag of clear liquid swinging from it. She carefully and gently fed a tiny needle into the elfin arm. I watched as the liquid slid down the tube and disappeared into the child. The large eyes moved listlessly toward me and stared.

Will was holding the mother's hands, his eyes filled with frustrated tenderness. "Phephisa," *sorry*, he told her shaking his head. She started to sink to the floor, but Will caught her, picking up the nearly weightless woman and carefully laying her on a now vacated cot. "Ngathanda ukukupopola," *I would like to examine you*. His smile was tired as he smoothed back the hair that escaped from her head scarf.

Still holding the child, I backed into a corner where the mother could see us. I wasn't aware of the time that passed as I rocked and crooned to the fragile life in my arms. I could neither stand to see the ravaged body, nor look away from it for fear that if no one was watching it would give up what little fight it was still able to wage. When Will finished examining the mother, he gave her some medicines and, with the help of Masuwra, instructions for herself and her son. Masuwra carried the woman to his relative's hut. I followed with my precious bundle, holding up the attached bag that offered what little hope still remained.

Several people lived in the 10 by 15 foot room. A small window and the open door did little to dispel the nauseating smell of sickness. Will had given the mother a sedative, and while the exhausted woman slept on a bed of worn blankets at the back of the room, I sat against the outside of the hut, harboring her child in my arms as it struggled to draw each breath. I hung the bag on a jutting piece of stone above our heads, then reached into my back pocket and pulled out the lip balm I kept there. Putting a small amount on my finger, I gently dabbed it on the tiny cracked lips. Every few minutes, I dipped the tail of my blouse into the bottle of water Will had tucked under my arm and touched it to the swollen tongue. I knew it wasn't enough, but I begged and pleaded with the child to swallow a little.

"C'mon baby, please baby, just a little… just a sip. Please, oh please, precious little person." Shaking, I wiped my eyes on the shoulder of my blouse and tasted the salt of my tears. The afternoon wore on as I rocked back and forth against the bumpy stone wall humming some long forgotten nursery song.

I woke to the touch of a hand on my arm and looked up to see Will kneeling on the ground before me, his eyes searching my face.

After several seconds, he slowly reached towards me and gently took the dead child from my arms. I did not try to stop him, nor did I cry. I simply dropped my empty hands into my lap. When he returned, I was still sitting against the wall watching the warm breeze blow through the grasses beyond the village.

Chapter 40

Continuous Journey

I put my suitcase in the trunk of the car. Will and Mark were going over the lists of needed supplies. Joyce stuck her head out of the clinic and seeing we were ready to leave, headed towards me. She hugged me for a long moment, and then, embarrassed, stuck her hands in her pockets.

"Never believed in coincidences or luck. I think things happen for a reason," she said, squinting at the sun's rays glinting off Masuwra's jeep. "You really shouldn't be here, you know. It's not your world... and last night..." Joyce shook her head. "I don't know what's in store for you, kiddo, but it must be on the 'need to do' list." She shrugged then and gave me one of Mark's lopsided smiles. "Take care of yourself," she called over her shoulder as she headed back to the clinic.

I saw Masuwra returning from the river with two large buckets of water. He took them to a fire where a pot of water was already boiling. Two women were also returning from the stream. They took their water directly into their huts.

"Masuwra?" He straightened and turned to me. "Thank you. There is no way for me to tell you . . . " I stopped, no words adequate enough, and put my hand on my heart.

"Why do you thank me for not allowing a bad thing to happen?" he asked.

"But, you saved my life. I need to thank you." I held out my hand to shake his. I didn't suppose it was the way of things here, but it was my way, and I wanted to let him know how much I appreciated what he'd done for me. He looked at my hand, but made no effort to take it.

"You do not yet understand, Kabibi," he said and smiled gently. Confused, I shook my head. His eyes searched mine for a long moment, and then he laid his fingers on my forehead. The touch was only a whisper and yet electric. As the seconds passed, I had the strangest sensation of being drawn by him, pulled outside of myself somehow, as if the two of us were caught in a vortex, swirling downward. Just before disappearing into the blackness of its depth, I sensed my connection to him. It was as thin as tissue and as thick as ligament. It spanned time and space. We were one and the same in our different worlds and bodies, and I trembled at the immenseness of us. We were not so alone in this vast universe as I had imagined, not sole, but souls entwined like reeds in a flowing river. And then suddenly, I felt myself rushing upward towards the light, which now seemed different, as if each person, each blade of swaying grass, moved to the same synchronistic flow, a communal undulation in which I no longer sensed my own separateness. My words had, after all, been unnecessary.

I was startled back to the present when I felt Masuwra grasp my hand. I looked up to see him smiling at me. Will stood waiting, watching the two of us from a few yards away. He nodded once to Masuwra, and then we left.

Chapter 41

A Mouthful of Misunderstanding

Will and I drove south to Lavumisa, a small border town between Swaziland and KwaZulu Natal, where he would call for more medical supplies. I sat near my window, staring mutely at the passing fields, hands listless in my lap. My exhaustion was filled with numbness, and my thoughts drifted in memory from hopeless faces and vacant eyes to thankful smiles and defiant spirits.

"Come here, Jackie honey," Will said softly, holding out his arm to me. He seemed so far away as I slid across the seat. When I laid my head at last against his shoulder, it was as if he drew all the tension in my body into himself. The release drained me, and I felt the sadness and fatigue slowly melt like dripping wax.

We spoke no more as the rolling thrum of the tires on the road lulled me into a troubled half sleep in which I wondered if Will regretted having to leave iNgwavuma because of me. I would have stayed, and told him so, but he had insisted this was "our time." I think we both felt a little guilty about leaving. Perhaps I was holding him back from the work he loved and the people that needed him. The car came to a stop, and I sat up and smiled sleepily at Will. He reached into the back seat for his medical supply list, then kissed me before getting out of the car. He made his calls from a small store with a rickety looking porch whose squeaky door announced patrons. It was nearly a half hour later when the door opened again.

"Done," he called, returning to where I stood leaning against the side of the car. I couldn't help my heart-pounding response to the look of him: the rhythmic sway of his hips as he walked, the intenseness of his gaze and the confidence that seemed to stream through him. He watched me watching him and smiled slowly.

"Hungry?" he asked.

"Only a little."

"Well, love, I'm going to feed you, doctor's orders."

We returned to the small store. Will bought groceries, and then asked the tall, thin, grey-haired man behind the counter, who spoke with a thick accent, for a padkos, or lunch of sandwiches and drinks. A few minutes later, the man smiled, baring a mouthful of missing teeth.

"Here is padkos." He handed me the sack and smiled saying, "sanibonani."

Since the drive ahead would take two hours, Will thought we should eat on the way. While we drove, I unwrapped our picnic and handed him a sandwich. I pulled the edge of my bread up and peered inside.

"These aren't banana sandwiches," I said surprised.

"Banana?" He glanced at me over the top of his glasses.

"Well, isn't that what the owner of the store told us?" Will looked puzzled for a moment and then burst out laughing.

"*Sanibonani* means 'good day'."

Chapter 42

Phoenix

Will drove us to a town perched on the edge of the ocean where he had rented a small cabin. It sat, buffeted by wind, on a cliff. We carried our bags into the tiny living room and then collapsed on the couch near the window. I must have fallen asleep to the soothing slap of the waves below. When I awoke at twilight, my head was on a pillow in Will's lap. He was staring out to sea.

"What happened after I left?" he asked quietly.

"What do you mean?"

"After I left the States, did you meet someone else right away?"

I had, or more exactly, someone had met me. I hesitated, not wanting to talk about dating so soon after he left, but then we both thought we would never see each other again.

"I want to know," he gently prompted me, brushing a finger along my cheek.

I sat up, apart from him. "A couple of months after you left, I met Kurt." Kurt had just shown up in my life one afternoon as I was leaving class. He'd insisted on carrying my books, taken them from me despite my own insistence that I could carry them myself. Kurt walked me all the way across campus to my car. Before I drove off, he leaned over and kissed me on the cheek. And he'd been in my life, one way or the other, ever since.

"Was it serious?" Will's voice brought me out of my reverie.

"Kurt was always there for me."

"And I wasn't."

"No," I whispered.

Will took off his glasses and set them on the table. "Is he still part of your life?" I nodded. "Well, I can't say that I like the chap, but I'm grateful he's been there for you. And were there others?" His voice was barely audible.

"Some," I said, "but I always ended the relationship whenever it got serious. I'm not proud of that, but the closeness was… too confining. I didn't want to deal with it." I held my hands up against an invisible force.

"You didn't end our relationship."

"I didn't need to. You were leaving." I looked away. "I didn't want to." Part of me felt as if Will and I had been together a lifetime, but another part was still hesitantly putting the letter in the mailbox.

"What do you want from your life, Jackie?" I wasn't expecting the question, and it took me a moment to answer.

"I want to be able to take care of myself, to be good at doing what means the most to me. I'd like to look back on my life and know that I've helped others." I gazed out to the darkening ocean. Will waited. "And to be loved, always. That most of all." My words surprised me.

"Are we going to be able to get beyond my leaving, because I think your 'for always' comes from that?" He touched my arm with the tips of his fingers. "Before you answer, Jackie, I want you to remember that I hadn't told you that I loved you before I left. We'd made no promises to each other."

"No, we hadn't."

"I did love you," he said. Will waited for me to look at him, but I couldn't. Not knowing if he loved me had been the life preserver that kept me afloat on my sea of self-deception. "Jackie, look at me." I bit my lip and looked askance at him. "No, Jackie." He turned me to face him and lifted my chin until I looked him in the eye. "I may have been gone when I told you I loved you, but that doesn't mean my love is any less enduring than it would have been if I'd told you while I was still with you. I loved you then; I love you now, and I'll love you always, even if you get on the next plane and fly out of my life forever." He thought for a moment and then ran his fingers through his hair. "You don't have much trust for most things, and maybe I'm a part of that, but you're going to have to take a leap of faith and believe that what I'm telling you is the truth." The air was heavy, and in the back of my mind, I could hear the ticking of a clock. "Because," he continued, "if you do fly out of here, I won't have the time you need for me to prove it, and we'll have lost before we started." His eyes bored into mine.

"How do you know you'll love me tomorrow?" I asked.

"That's the leap of faith for you, not me, Jackie. I'm not questioning it. You are."

"Why don't you have to make a leap of faith? Why?"

"Jackie honey, you don't either. Whatever is in your heart is already there. Accept it, and good news or bad, I'm still going to love you because that's what's in my heart."

The sky was dark now. I stood and walked to the window to clear my thoughts. I heard Will click on the light. In its glow, the glass reflected my unexpected tears like spun silk threads.

"I adore you," I said in a half whisper. But it wasn't enough. Will came to me and turned me to face him.

"Don't give me part of you. We're worth more than that, and

we need a far sight more because we're going to have to make the world our home."

I opened my mouth to speak, but my thoughts were jumbled and incoherent. I looked into Will's eyes thinking I could read our future there, but I couldn't. He could no more promise me what was in store for us than I could tell him how to save a patient with an incurable disease. I shook my head in confusion. Will dropped his hands from my shoulders and a veiled look passed over his face. The simplicity of the movement and the sudden absence of his touch threw me back in time to the night he left. The connection I had to him then came rushing back. It was not the collective oneness Masuwra had shown me. It went beyond a universal bond. It was the knowledge of the single framework within which Will and I existed, had always existed, and the graft that had been made long before this lifetime. When Will left, I thought the connection had been severed. Now, his words had opened the long hidden wound, freezing me in separate moments. My mind locked onto both the memory of him leaving and to this moment rife with possibilities. The two points in time drew closer and closer in my mind, but for a moment, I couldn't navigate the sense of them. And then, every bit of me smashed forward, every raw nerve, every broken fragment, every crumbled longing tore through me, bursting with the force of an explosion. The gossamer curtain that had whitened and dulled the outline of my world ripped wide open. I loved Will. I knew it the night he left, but my mind had snapped shut against it. I gasped as the sudden, crushing pain of that denied love thudded into my heart. But, as hearts do, mine was already struggling to heal itself. How could it not? I was standing before the man it hungered for, the man whose heartbeat complemented its own. There was no better medicine.

Will remained perfectly still, except for the slight movement of his hand towards me when I gasped. I glanced up, tears sliding down my cheeks. Will looked into my eyes and knew, and I saw the tears that filled his own. Still trembling, and in a voice raw with that long hidden truth, I told him at last what he had waited so long to hear.

"I love you. I always have."

Will blinked twice and then grabbed me, burying his lips in my neck. His breath caught, and the sound echoed through me. He pulled me into himself and kissed me almost brutally, and the fierce words he spoke afterwards were feverish. I only caught bits," love you ... mine ... let ... go." We were both shaking when Will took my head between his hands and looked intently into my eyes. There was no mistaking the question.

The sudden insistent ring from the kitchen startled us both.

Chapter 43

The News

"It's for you," Will said, handing me the receiver. At my confused look he added, "I left the number with my answering service."

"Jackie!" The woman on the other end of the line sounded a little panicked. "It's Jackie," I heard her tell someone. "We've been trying to reach you."

"Sherry? Is everything all right?" It was the receptionist from the Ability office in California.

"Jay wants to talk to you. He's heading to his office now. I'll connect you." There was a momentary pause, and then Sherry added, "Take care." The phone clicked twice.

"Jackie, sorry to break into your vacation. Where are you?"

"In a little town called Lavumisa. What's going on?" I asked, my heart beginning to race.

"Your father called. It's your mother. She's not well. You need to get in touch with your family right away."

"Is it serious?"

"I think you're going to need to head home right away. Let me know whatever I can do to help."

"Thanks, Jay," I said and hung up to redial.

"Mmm, hello," my father said, answering as he always did by prefacing the greeting with a soft murmur.

"Dad? It's Jackie. How's Mom?"

"I've been trying to reach you," he said.

"I know. I just got a call from work. How's Mom?"

There was a short silence, and then his voice crumbled, "The doctor's given her three days."

I swallowed, striving for some semblance of composure, afraid to speak for fear my voice would make this harder on my father. I willed the trembling away and asked as calmly as I could, "Is she at the hospital now?"

"Yes," he said, his voice watery. "I'm heading back there now."

"I'll need to grab my things and book a flight. It's probably going to take me at least twenty four hours to get there. I'll be there as soon as I can," I promised.

"That's good," was all he said.

"How are you doing, Dad?" There was no answer. "I'll be there soon. Just take care of yourself. I'll call you when I land."

"What's the matter, Jackie?" I must have looked pale because Will put his arm around my waist just as my knees buckled. "Tell me." I raised a hand, but no words came. "Take a deep breath, sweetie," he said. I did, and then turned away from him and walked a few feet off trying to calm the shaking that was coming out of some cold place inside.

"Don't do that," Will said.

"Don't do what?" I asked, my mind a jumble of thoughts – plane tickets, hours . . . my mother...

"Don't turn away from me when you're hurt." The words didn't compute in my world. I never relied on anyone but myself.

"What are you saying?"

"I'm reminding you that there's the two of us now." He took

a step closer, holding his hands out, gauging my reaction to him.

"I know that, but..."

"No...you don't," he said.

"What do you want me to do?" I drew back slightly.

"I want you to know I'm here for you." I stood perfectly still, my muscles frozen and tight. "Tell me," he said again, gently wrapping his hands around my arms.

"My mother is dying." The words were eerily calm. Will's body jerked. I don't remember the words he murmured to me before he wrapped his arms around me.

All the flights for the rest of the day were booked, but I was given an emergency bereavement seat later that night. I packed my suitcase in silence. I couldn't have talked if I'd wanted to because my teeth were clamped together to keep them from rattling. After the car was loaded, I returned to stand in the comforting embrace of the cottage, this somewhere place where I had found my own truth. I wanted to remember its beauty, but more importantly, I wanted to memorize the feel and smell of it. As I closed the door, I thought I heard my mother's voice speaking to me from far away, urging me to hurry.

We spoke little on the trip to Johannesburg. Will encouraged me to sleep or at least rest, but I couldn't. I couldn't quell the tremors running through me, and I didn't want to lose the time with him. He held my hand, and whenever I caught his glance, I would nod and smile to let him know I was all right. We arrived shortly before the flight and found seats near the departure gate.

"I'm sorry I'm not going with you," he said. We both knew that last minute tickets half way around the world were too expensive for Will's salary as a resident. "But I'll be with you every moment, standing by you, holding you." After a moment he added, "When... everything is worked out, you'll come back to Africa." It was a hopeful statement, not a question. The remark surprised me, first because I thought he shouldn't doubt that, one way or the other, I would find my way back to him, and second, because I hadn't thought that far ahead. I opened my mouth to answer, but a loud voice announced that Flight 6822 to San Francisco was ready for boarding. I looked at Will, my mind racing. "I don't... I'll need to check in at work. Oh...and I've got to call Roy about the job," I added thinking out loud. Will's head snapped up. The loud voice was calling row numbers for boarding.

"Roy? What job?" Will asked sharply.

"I can't find my ticket," I huffed in exasperation. I started emptying my purse, knocking out a candy bar and a tube of Chap Stick, handing things to Will.

"Jackie," the insistence in Will's voice stopped me. "What job?"

"Roy offered me a job the last night I was in Johannesburg. I'd intended to tell you at the cottage, but there wasn't any time. He offered me a job as liaison for his company and the new division they're forming. There it is!" I let out a huge sigh of relief and pulled the ticket out of the side pocket of my purse. The picture I'd brought of Will at the beach fell to the floor.Will picked it up and stared at it for a brief moment, and then shook his head in exasperation. I started toward the gate, trying to quickly explain about Caduceus's interest in satellite technology and plans for an office in South Africa, but the news of my mother, and the despair I felt leaving Will was muddling my brain. The blaring voice was making it difficult for Will to hear me. I lined up behind the last few stragglers.

Will's voice was calm, but there was anger in it. "Did you accept? Where will you live?"

"I haven't accepted. I only promised to think about it." There were two passengers ahead of me now. Will pulled me against him and kissed me.

There was only time for him to say, "Call me when you land."

"I will," I promised." When he released me, the cool breeze in the causeway pulled me into its beckoning grasp.

Chapter 44

Home Again

California

The flight was endless and my thoughts relentless - *She can't die. Will she still be alive when I get there? How much time...* The ear-numbing drone of the plane engines would not cease their sluggish roar, would not stop vibrating against my own internal clamor. The sky lightened, darkened and then lightened again. I shook my head when the flight attendant offered me a meal. I only vaguely remembered landing once in some country my mind did not acknowledge. Later, when exhaustion consumed me, and I slept fitfully, my dreams filled with dark swirling pools and white mists. I woke to find a cup of tea some kind soul had left on my tray table. I took a sip of the lukewarm liquid, but it tasted bitter, and I left it. I hadn't realized how tensely I had been holding onto myself until the pilot announced that we were entering the United States. The torment of the previous hours was nothing compared to the last five which were nearly unbearable knowing how close I was to home and to reaching my mother.

The custom lines were as endless as the flight, and it wasn't until after I picked up my rental car that I realized I hadn't called Will or my father. I didn't stop to find a phone. I just drove the two hours to the hospital, arriving shortly after dark.

I freshened up so my mother would not see my exhaustion and fear, then asked for directions and headed to the third floor. The subdued murmur of a television, a hacking cough, the smell of overcooked mashed potatoes and the slide of a body adjusting itself in a bed, clicked through my brain like the sound of cards in a bicycle wheel. I grimaced at the stale, flat air, and entered my mother's hospital room.

Chapter 45

Heartbeat

My brother's profile was back lighted by the far window where he stood gazing into the distance. His intense discomfort of hospitals, coupled with the imminent loss of the woman who had loved him so dearly, was evident in the hunched stiffness of his shoulders and the fierce distress in his eyes. He didn't hear me enter and remained lost in thought.

Except for her labored breathing, my mother slept serenely, a small mound in the big, white hospital bed. My father sat beside her, pale and drawn. We held each other for a long moment and then took up watch on opposite sides of her bed. My mother had a long history of heart problems: tachycardia, fibrillation and then a massive heart attack which she suffered alone for nine hours, calling no one for help. It was an attack that left the bottom third of her heart lifeless. Her doctor's prognosis was severe physical impairment and imminent death. But, so like my mother who fought everything and everyone who threatened her need for control, she fought the diagnosis and then lived ten more years in a typical act of total defiance. She found no comfort in relationships because the insecure nature instilled in her by a depression era childhood and the death of her mother when she was only 12, caused her to replace love with suspicion, and warmth with anger. Her life had been, in many ways, a battlefield where the only acceptable victory was power and control. They were the only antidotes to the safety and need for respect she craved. She lived her life wrapped in a cocoon of mistrust and self-doubt. Our relationship existed on rules and complaisance. She ruled, and I had learned as a small child not to defy her or cross the boundary uninvited that held love and acceptance on the other side. Punishment was physically harsh, but the withheld love was far more painful. I clung to each word spoken from the lips that had often been larger than life - the coral colored lips that yelled and accused and despised.

We were lost to each other, and I could not find a way to reach through her hurt and anger. She wanted a family and a home of her own to rule, but she saw the people who came with them as flawed and unworthy. I strived to be all that she wanted me to be, but her expectations were an unfillable abyss. I spent my youth trying to replenish that bottomless gorge with, what must have been to her, a teaspoon. I came now, not out of duty, but because it was one last hope, one last chance to see if the love was there. And I came because she was my mother, and I was a dutiful and loving daughter.

I was still standing partially blocked from view by the curtain that surrounded her bed when I realized she had woken. Her gentle words were for my brother who she had always called "The King." Seeing his distress, she comforted him, telling him that she would always be with him, and that he would know it because he would be able to feel her hand on his cheek whenever he missed her.

She saw me then, and I went to her, kissing her and smoothing back her beautiful thick, blonde hair. I took her hand, and she looked into my eyes. It was one of the rare moments in my life when she looked to me for the strength she knew I had. Her face held no glimmer of weakness, yet I knew that she was calling me to her side, to walk unfalteringly through these last hours with her. It was my gift and my curse to have taken the harshness between us and made myself nearly unbreakable. I sat at the side of her hospital bed, waiting through the frequent naps for the short periods of wakefulness. After one particularly long sleep, she awoke to find me crying, my cheek pressed against the limp hand I held.

"What is it?" she asked.

"I'm going to miss you so much," I choked, hating the moment of weakness, but needing her to allow it. My mother stared at our clasped hands for several seconds, and then holding them together in the air, pointed to the strikingly similar little fingers.

"When you miss me, look at this." After that, and always afterwards, I could never look at that finger and not see my mother's hand.

Chapter 46

The Message

Slipping out after she fell asleep, I found a phone and called work for messages. There were over thirty. Will had called twice, and the last message was from Roy.

"Hi, Jackie. It's Roy. I called Ability this morning to see if they had a number where I could reach you and heard the news about your mother. I'm sorry. I guess this means you've cut your vacation short and headed back to California." There was a slight pause. "I'll be in California week after next, and at the risk of incredibly bad timing, wonder if we might meet then. Of course, I understand that will depend on your situation. You've got my number. Let me know what your schedule is, and let's see if we can get together and continue our discussion. Again, I'm very sorry about your mother. If there's anything I can do, please let me know. Talk to you soon."

Why was everything happening at once? I put through a long distance call to Johannesburg Hospital. The line crackled and clicked before the operator picked up. Will didn't answer his page, and so I asked for Rachel.

"Third floor nurse's station."

"Rachel, it's Jackie. How are you?"

"Jackie, I'm so sorry. Will told me about your mother. How are you holding up?"

"All right… tired, sad, but okay. I'm trying to reach Will. Is he available?"

"Oh, sorry. He's in surgery. I can take a message for you." I bit my lip, disappointed. I wanted so badly to hear his voice.

"Yes, please tell him I'm home. I'll try to reach him later." I paused, hesitating to say more, after all she was Cali's aunt.

"Anything else?" Rachel asked. The sound of her voice made me feel she had become my confidant, and that she suspected I had something more personal to say to Will.

"Mmm, yes. Please tell Will that Roy will be here in California, and that I'll talk to him about the job offer then." Better to keep Will posted, besides what difference would it make if Cali knew I might be changing jobs? Five minutes after Rachel hung up, Cali turned the corner.

"What's this?" she asked her aunt, noticing Will's message.

"Nothing to concern you," Rachel said, unsuccessfully stopping her niece from grabbing it.

"So, Jackie went home. I knew she would. She doesn't belong here." Cali grinned triumphantly.

"Stop acting like that message is a proposal from Will." Rachel took the paper from Cali and put it back on the spiked peg marked 'Dr. Kincaid.' "You're family, and I love you, Cali, but I swear there are times you act like you're six-years-old." Rachel might as well have been scolding a patient on a salt free diet who'd already eaten a jar of pickles.

"Don't worry, Aunt Rachel. I'll make sure Will gets the message." Cali leaned over the counter and deftly slid the message off the spike.

"You keep out of this, Cali. I mean it," Rachel called after her niece's retreating figure. With no children of her own, Rachel had lavished more than a mother's amount of affection on the girl.

I suppose this is partly my fault. I've spoiled that girl rotten. Rachel shook her head as Cali disappeared down the hall.

Chapter 47

Always There

Perched on the end of my mother's bed, I watched her drift back to sleep. At the sound of a quiet knock, I turned to see Kurt heading toward me, his straight, dark brown hair falling over one eye and the familiar half smile on his face. I reached out to take his hand, but he stepped against me and took me into his arms. I hadn't expected him to come, and the embrace caught me off guard. I froze for a moment and then sank against him with a sigh. His feel was familiar, his arms a circle of safety and comfort. I laid my head against his chest knowing he would not release me until I moved away.

"How did you know I was here?" I asked.

"I always know where you are," he answered, echoing our long ago past. "How's your mother?" I could feel the rumble of words through his sweater and stepped back to look up at him.

"Sleeping again," I whispered, unconsciously rubbing my little finger with my thumb.

"I'm so sorry, sweetheart." Even though we hadn't dated since college, Kurt had never stopped the endearments, nor had I wanted him to, but now it felt wrong.

"Thank you for coming."

"So, did you see him?" Kurt asked. I furrowed my brows in question. "The fellow from Africa, the one you dated before me." How like Kurt to figure out what was going on in my life and then grill me for details.

"Yes." It wasn't the time to talk about Will, besides so much had happened in the last two weeks. Holding the memories inside felt like the only warmth I had.

My mother's breathing was suddenly louder and more difficult. I sat down again, gesturing to the only other chair. Kurt glanced at it and then sat on the arm of my chair, his hip leaning against my side, his hand clasping the back of the chair. I straightened and slowly inched forward hoping he wouldn't notice.

"Are you going to stay tonight?" he asked.

"Yes. They're bringing in a guest bed. I don't want to leave her." I knew he would make some sort of offer to stay with me, but I wanted this time alone with my mother and family.

"I'll stay with you," he said. It wasn't an offer. It was a decision.

"Oh … no, I can't let you do that." I knew my father would also stay and the thought of the three of us crowded around her bed for the entire night was claustrophobic. Before he could say more, I touched his arm and shook my head with a '*please understand*' smile. I hated that the closeness he so desired made my chest tight.

"I just want to make sure you're okay," he said.

"I know. I'll be fine."

Kurt stood reluctantly, slowly running his hand across the top of my shoulders, leaning over to kiss the top of my head. I stood up, but far enough away not to encourage another embrace.

"Thank you for stopping by. You're such a special friend." He flinched at the word 'friend'.

"I'll be back tomorrow," he said, ignoring what he did not want to hear.

Chapter 48

A Gaggle of Geese

Early the next morning, the hospital interns were completing rounds with one of the doctors. They flocked into my mother's room like a gaggle of geese, little white coattails flapping, heads bobbing up and down, right and left, as they jostled for position. Clustered, with altos to the right and sopranos up front, and with my mother as their audience, they consulted their metal sheet music. Each offered a melodious opinion at the direction of the lead doctor who waved his yellow pencil and scratched marks on his own score chart. The orchestration ended in two minutes, and then they flew out to serenade elsewhere.

Book Two

Chapter 1

The Message – Johannesburg

Will

Felt good to remove my surgical mask and stretch after the appendectomy on the 17-year-old boy. It'd been tough concentrating. Jackie kept popping into my mind. I could understand her not calling with all she's dealing with, but she never answered my question about returning to Africa. And then she dropped that bombshell about a new job with Roy. He seems like a nice enough guy, but I don't like the way he looks at her. Don't know that I much like the idea of Jackie working for him. I'll try reaching her again. It's driving me crazy waiting to hear from her.

I headed back to my apartment, grabbed something to eat and was cleaning up from dinner when the doorbell rang. I opened the door and found Cali smiling in a personal way that made me uncomfortable.

"Hi Will. I heard you were back, and I thought you might have missed this message." She held a pink piece of paper against her chest in a way that made it impossible to see who it was from. I wanted to lunge for it in case it was Jackie, but it looked like that was exactly what Cali wanted. The pose was obvious, and I wasn't in the mood for whatever she was selling. Besides, she knew how I felt about Jackie, and the talk we'd had about ending our relationship didn't leave any room for misunderstanding. I held out my hand for the message, but she dropped it to her side.

"May I come in?"

"Is it from Jackie?"

"Well, if you let me in, I'll tell you." On the chance that it was, I stepped back and gestured for her to come in. She glided in looking around the room like she was expecting Jackie to pop out of the floor like a rabbit out of a magician's hat. Cali took her time taking off her sweater and setting her purse down on the coffee table, but the purse tipped sideways and hit the floor landing upside down. She muttered something and bent to pick up all the stuff that'd fallen out. When she dropped the message, I grabbed it and read it. It didn't make sense to me – the job, Roy, California... Now I really wanted to talk to Jackie.

"Look, Cali, I'm pretty beat. I was about to take a shower. Maybe we can catch up at the hospital tomorrow. Thanks for bringing the message over." The innocent look rolled right into sympathetic.

"I'm really sorry she went back home." I brushed at the air dismissively, but I know I looked upset because Cali slid a hand behind my neck and starting massaging it. "It's too bad things didn't work, but she's where she belongs." I pulled away and walked to the window to try and sort things out. There was a young couple arguing on the sidewalk below. The girl pushed the boy away and stalked off. My mind was racing. *What was Roy doing in California? Had Jackie already accepted his job offer? If she had, where was she going to live?* My thoughts were interrupted by a drawer opening in the kitchen. I looked over to see Cali with a wine opener.

"Cali, this isn't a good time." She looked at me in a calculating way.

"Of course, I understand. Maybe we can have a drink after work tomorrow. You go ahead and take that shower. I'll let myself out."

I wasn't much listening, more like grinding my teeth. After

Cali left, I headed for the shower, turned the water on hot and let it pound against the back of my neck. I'd known Roy was going to complicate things from the start. I figured it must be around noon in California. Jackie would be at hospital with her mother. I'd give it an hour and then try to catch Jackie after lunch.

Chapter 2

The Go-Between

Cali rang the doorbell. She couldn't find her car keys and assumed they had probably slid out of her purse when it fell on the floor. She rang the bell again, and then reached into the small zippered pocket on the inside of her purse for the key Will had given her to his apartment several months before, when it had been good between them. Cali had purposely kept the key, hoping things would eventually work out with Will, hoping Jackie would do just what she had done – go home. She heard the shower when she opened the door. The keys were behind the leg of the coffee table. Cali retrieved them and was about to leave when the phone rang. She glanced towards the bathroom, then shrugged and picked up the receiver.

"Hello."

"Oh… hello." The voice sounded surprised. "I'm calling for Will Kincaid. Do I have the right number?"

"Jackie, how nice to hear from you," Cali purred. At the pause, she added, "It's Cali." A slow smirk pulled her lips sideways.

"Hi, Cali. Is Will available?" The voice was tight, and the words were hesitant.

The smirk was still on her lips, but not in the innocent voice Cali used to answer. "He's in the shower right now. Do you want me to get him for you?" The pause was longer this time.

"No, don't bother. I'll take care of it."

"Are you sure?" Cali asked, but the line had gone dead.

Cali started toward the shower, then paused biting her lip. After a moment, she smiled, then turned and quietly let herself out, locking the door behind her.

Chapter 3

The Loud Whisper - California

Jackie

I was still seething after my conversation with Cali, when the phone in my mother's hospital room rang.

"Mmm hello?" my father spoke softly into the receiver, but the noise had awakened my mother, and she pointed to her water glass.

"Let me get you a fresh glass of water with some ice," I offered. "How are you feeling?"

My father waved his hand in the air. He raised his eyebrows and mouthed the words, "It's Will." I froze, and watched as he held his finger to his lips for me to be quiet so he could hear.

"She's doing as well as can be expected," he said looking down.

I started shaking my head frantically. "No," I mouthed and waved my hands back and forth. "No!" I'd called my parents from Africa after the convention and told them Will and I would be spending some time together, but that was all. My father's eyes were watching me.

"Thank you, Will. Well, it's hard on all of us.... .uh, Jackie's not here right now," my father told him hesitantly. He listened a moment, then, "I... don't know exactly when she'll be back. Yes, I'll tell her you called... Yes... goodbye."

"Sorry, Dad. I just don't feel like talking to anyone right

now." He looked at me thoughtfully, but said nothing. Will called twice the next day, and every day for the next week. I stopped answering the phone. Then the calls stopped.

Chapter 4

You're on Your Own

The crisp sheet of the hospital bed felt cool as I sat resting my head on my arms, watching my mother sleep, watching her leave. And Will – I'd let down my defenses, loved him, and then to have him take back up with Cali the minute I was gone. Every drop of emotion was wrung out of me. I was like an empty and colorless vase whose painted scene had long ago worn away. As sad as it seemed, I was relieved to concentrate on my mother. A finger of sunlight moved slowly across the floor. When the beam reached my mother's pillow, I got up and adjusted the blinds. She moaned gently and opened her eyes.

"Hi. Sorry. I didn't mean to wake you."

She didn't answer at first, and I thought she had fallen back to sleep, but she asked from behind closed lids, "What time is it?"

"About two o'clock. It's a beautiful day," I told her, then wondered if talking about beautiful days would remind her that there wouldn't be many more of those for her. "Are you thirsty?" My mother's lips pressed together in a way that reminded me of the tight lipped looks that often covered her face whenever she was disappointed or angry with me.

"No." She frowned. "Well, maybe I'll have a little sip." While I was helping her grasp the straw with her weak, shaking hands, the doctor knocked and came in.

"Having a little drink?" he asked, looking at his chart. "Any discomfort? Any pain?" Not responding to my mother's lack of response, he moved to the bed and slid an arm behind her and pulled her forward, putting his stethoscope against her back. "Uhhmm, hmm." He laid her back against the pillows. My mother's sunken blue eyes reached out to him, but as always, when she wanted to present a strong front, she remained outwardly calm. But now, there was a searching, pleading look in her eyes. The doctor patted her arm and smiled down at her, "I think we can let you go home." A spark of hope passed through her eyes, but no encouraging words came from the doctor. Her lids lowered, and she picked at the blanket.

"Will I see you again?" she asked.

The doctor looked at me, "I'd like to speak to your mother alone."

"Of course, I'll just be outside," I told her.

I waited in the overly hot corridor, hating the medicine smell and all the equipment sprouting tubes and nozzles like potatoes left too long in the vegetable bin. Walking to release my pent up feelings, I tried to keep from looking into the other open doors, but my eyes were drawn to the dramatic scenes playing out in the rooms. The sight of the patients, some sleeping open-mouthed on their sides, others trying to eat from mostly prone positions, and the strained look on the visitors' faces depressed me. I turned around and headed back just in time to see the doctor leave my mother's room. He glanced my way and came towards me.

"We're going to send her home this afternoon. We went over home care. Hospice will take over from here." He smiled and put out his hand.

"Thank you... for everything, Doctor." I shook the hand that seemed like my mother's only life line. He started to walk away.

"Uhm, excuse me, Doctor. Will you be prescribing medicine for her? Do we call you when things get worse?" I hated how alone I felt for her.

"No," he said. "Hospice will meet with her sometime in the next hour or so." And with that and another cursory smile, he melted into the white hallway, his doctor's perfectly pressed coat snapping to the disappearing cadence of his footsteps.

Chapter 5

The Final Journey

I stood stuck to the speckled linoleum, staring after the disappearing figure, then squared my shoulders, put a smile on my unwilling face and entered the room. My mother's gaze was fixed on an otherworldly realm that I could not see.

"So, we're going to get you home. It'll be nice to climb into your own bed again." It felt like I was pushing each word out of my chest. "We'll open the windows and let in some of this healing sunshine." Why did I say healing? My mother's vacant stare moved to my face. She blinked and shook herself back to the present.

"Dr. Savage wanted to tell me goodbye. He said he won't be my doctor after this." I saw the betrayal in her eyes. The thoughtlessness and lack of compassion stunned me. Why didn't he tell her she could call him if she wanted to? He'd walked out on her at the worst moment of her illness. "He said I won't call him anymore." Her trance-like voice interrupted my angry reverie. She picked some more at the blanket. "If I need anything, Hospice will take care of me." For a moment, she was involved in an internal conversation. "I asked him a long time ago, that when it was time, to promise to keep me comfortable. Do you think I can call him if I have a question?"

"Of course," I lied.

The next two hours were filled with Hospice representatives and hospital administrators, nurses unhooking intravenous tubes and my mother's staring eyes. We listened, or at least I did, as each administrator talked kindly about equipment for the home, medicine deliveries, nursing care, always carefully avoiding the only topic that mattered – the end of my mother's life. While the nurse finished preparing my mother for the final trip home, I ran out to my car and dug through my suitcase for the warm up suit, a gift I'd bought for her in Johannesburg. In her room, I unwrapped it to show her the aqua-blue outfit that matched her eyes.

"I brought this back for you," I said. "It's soft and comfy. It'll be easy and quick to get into for your ride home." She looked at it and nodded. I helped her put on the jacket, zipping it all the way up for warmth. She moved to the side of the bed and pushed her legs over. The pants and sleeves were too long. I was surprised because I was always careful to buy petite clothes for her. "I'm sorry it's so big." She looked down at the suit, but said nothing. I don't think she even saw it.

Chapter 6

Five More Days

When we returned to my parents' home, I tucked my mother into one of the oversized chairs she loved in a sunny corner of the family room. I covered her with one of the many afghans she'd crocheted, and she looked small atop the huge cushion, like a tiny doll with big, wide eyes and fluffy blonde hair. I cannot imagine the shock and fear she was experiencing facing the last hours of her life. She never cried, or broke down or mentioned the time she had left. Later that night, not knowing how to comfort her, I moved her to a chair in front of the television to watch, with my father and me, a favorite show. It was some relief to lose myself, even momentarily, in the sitcom, but at one particularly funny part, I glanced over to see if she was enjoying the show. She wasn't even looking at the screen. I felt so helpless and foolish to think that I could somehow provide relief for her in those last hours of her life.

The following day she stayed in her bed, sitting up to meet the Hospice nurses and visitors, to be part of the various sick bed deliveries and to chat with friends who dropped by. As we talked and reminisced, I brought in a small bowl of peaches, hoping she would feel like eating something. I don't know why, but instead of handing her the bowl and spoon, I started to feed her, startled that she allowed it. She just went on talking while I spooned the fruit into her mouth.

My mother lived five more days, sleeping most of the time. The nurses had ordered morphine and encouraged me to give her regular shots. Her breathing became more labored, and whenever the nurses stopped by, or I called them with a question, they continued to encourage me to increase the morphine to keep her comfortable.

On the third day, my mother stopped waking and could no longer talk to us. I will always remember the heart-breaking look on my father's face when he realized he would never speak to her again. That night, I told my father that he needed a good night's rest and that I would switch beds with him and sleep with my mother. I privately called the Hospice nurse and told her I was afraid of my mother dying during the night while I was with her. She told me not to worry – that if it happened, it wouldn't be the frightening event I thought it would. Sometime during the night, despite the morphine and the wandering review of life her mind had taken, my mother wanted to sit up. I balanced her on the edge of the bed. She looked so peaceful and gentle with her eyes closed. I had never seen her like that. Standing in front of her, I pulled her head against my chest, and rocking softly, sang a lullaby to her. The sliding silkiness of our nightgowns pressed together while her head lay quietly against my heart, was a closeness so unknown to me. When her body relaxed into a slump, I carefully laid her back on the bed.

"I love you," I said.

"I love you, too," she answered from the bridge of our two worlds.

Chapter 7

A Last Breath

On the morning my mother died, I was sitting with her when my father came in to relieve me. I had been running back and forth to the kitchen, preparing sandwiches and baking cookies for the guests who, like a low tide, continued to gently come and go. When my father settled himself in a chair alongside her bed, I went back to the kitchen and put another batch of cookies in the oven. Busy with other food, I nearly forgot them. I grabbed the potholders and started toward the oven. In that moment, I felt the most insistent urge to return to my mother's room. Knowing the cookies would burn if I left them any longer, I opened the oven door and quickly reached in to remove them.

I heard a very loud and demanding voice say, "Now." I slammed the oven door shut, leaving the cookies to burn and hurried into my mother's room. My father was leaning forward over my mother listening to her labored breathing. I climbed up on the bed and put my arm over her legs, pulling them against me. She took three more loud, racking breaths, and then the room filled with the most deafening silence I have ever heard. I glanced at my father. His stricken face will always be with me. I buried my head in the bed blanket then and cried into the eerie silence.

It made no difference how estranged our relationship had been, or how many years it had remained so. One simply cries for one's mother.

Before they took her body away, I fixed her hair and straightened her nightgown. I folded the sheets back smoothly, knelt on the floor beside her and held her hand until its increasing coldness broke into my thoughts. I cried then, harder than I have ever cried before or since, sobbing in loud incoherent gulps. I vaguely remember my brother and father entering the room at different times, but I couldn't stop the tears that came from the sorrow of losing what I had never had. I don't know how long I had been kneeling there when a hand was firmly, but gently placed on my right shoulder. It pushed my collar down and startled me. I reached up to lay my hand over it, but no one was in the room with me.

Death is a strange acquaintance. He comes in his own time and on his own terms to help us remember that we must let go of this life, but he rarely stays long enough to become recognizable or familiar to those of us still here. And so, we are left wondering who the visitor was, and when he will come again.

Chapter 8

An Ocean of Showers

The next three days were filled with visitors and calls, funeral arrangements and bouts of grief that rose to the surface at odd moments suddenly and unexpectedly. I sat on the front porch making a last minute change to the eulogy I would give the following day. Kurt had stopped by and was sitting beside me, ready to help if I needed anything.

"Why is it," I asked him, "that you always seem to be here for the crises in my life? I'm your worst nightmare."

"You're my best dream," he answered, and scooted his chair closer to help me edit my words.

I barely heard the crunch of tires on the driveway. When the front gate opened, I looked up slowly, still lost in thought over the wording. Silhouetted against the setting sun, I didn't recognize the man at first. My exhausted brain sensed the familiarness, but the form didn't register because he didn't belong here, not anymore. And then a ray of sun slipped through the arbor leaves and lit the face I had thought I knew so well. It was Will, looking tired and wrinkled. He was supposed to be an ocean away. As he walked slowly towards me, I could see the circles beneath his eyes. What was he doing here, eleven thousand miles from his home?

"Hi," he said when he reached the bottom step of the porch, his eyes flicking quickly to Kurt. I saw by the way Will was watching me that my stillness confused him. I suddenly couldn't look at him, and I felt the heat of a flush on my face. Will came up the steps and stood looking at me. When I didn't respond, Kurt glanced at me, and then stood up putting out his hand.

"Hi. I'm Kurt." The sudden realization of these two men together brought me to my feet.

"And Kurt, this is Will," I said tight-lipped. My nerves were jangling, and I held my breath as the two men stared at each other. After a moment, Will reached an arm out, and they shook hands giving each other a short, smileless nod. I was suddenly furious. The anger I had pushed aside these last days now surfaced. "I'm sorry, Kurt, but could you … ?" I gestured toward the house. I didn't have much to say to Will, but say it I would.

"Call me if you need anything," Kurt said turning toward the door. Will reached for me, but stopped when I pulled the notebook to my chest and looked down.

"What's wrong, Jackie?"

"Maybe you should tell me,"

"Why don't we sit down," he said almost politely. It wasn't a question.

"I'd rather stand."

"Your mother … " he said then, again reaching for me. I shook my head. He watched me, expressionless, for a moment, then looked stricken. "I'm so sorry, honey." I kept my death grip on the notebook and looked away.

"I may be a little jet-lagged, but this isn't exactly the reception I expected. Why didn't you call, Jackie?"

"Oh, but I did." The words were righteous.

"I expected your silence to have something to do with Roy, but maybe I should have been more concerned about Kurt."

"Really? Well, I'm surprised you could tear yourself away from … " I wasn't going to say her name.

"From what?" Will asked, frowning.

Kurt came to the door. "Jackie?"

"It's alright Kurt. Could you give us a minute?" He paused a few seconds and then retreated into the house. I stared at the door.

"A minute." Will gave me a gauging look. "I just flew half way around the world and you're going to give me a minute. Jackie, are you going to look at me?" I took a jagged breath, bit my lip and then looked up defiantly. Will looked hurt. I checked an impulse to reach out, reminding myself what he had done to me, and the fury returned. He moved nearer.

"Don't," I choked out.

"What's going on?"

Well, nothing is going on here, that's for sure. What's going on, is going on in Johannesburg." I shook my head angrily. "How could you? I believed everything you told me. What you've done, hurt, and I had all this to go through." I flung an arm in the direction of the house.

"Jackie, I would never hurt you." The words were almost angry.

"I wasn't gone what, half a day, before you ran back to Cali? Did you really think I wouldn't find out?" Will's eyebrows shot up and his mouth opened slightly.

"Is that why you wouldn't take my calls?"

"Absolutely," I said with a calm I didn't feel.

"After you left, I stopped off at my parents and told them you'd flown home to be with your mother. There was no point in being off work, so I headed back to hospital. I was worried about you, and I thought being busy would help pass the time. That's it. So how does Cali fit in?"

"Well, showers for one thing," I said.

"Showers?" he looked bewildered. *Great act.* "Jackie, I have no idea what you're talking about."

"Fine. You want me to say it, to prove to you that I know you went right back to Cali?"

"Yeah, I'd really like to hear this," he said with a wry smile.

"Don't you patronize me, Will Kincaid. I called you at the hospital and left a message with Rachel."

"With Rachel?" The bewildered look returned, but only for a moment. I watched his eyes search back and forth before he slowly folded his arms across his chest.

"I called again at your apartment, but evidently I interrupted you and Cali." Will started nodding slowly, the momentary faraway look turning into disgust.

"Uh huh," I said, seeing the nod and feeling vindicated.

"I'm surprised," he shot back, "that you cared enough to call, considering you'd already made up your mind to work with Roy."

"Oh, no, we're not changing the subject…What do you mean work with Roy? And even if I was, *that's* no longer any concern of yours."

"Well, I think it is." His take-no-prisoners look infuriated me.

"How egotistical! You can dilly dally with Cali," *I hated that the words rhymed,* "while I'm supposed to be missing you. You told me it was over between the two of you."

"Well," he glanced pointedly toward the screen door.

"I haven't done anything but let you back into my life. And that was a huge mistake." I turned away from him. "One I'll regret for the rest of my life."

"Sit down, Jackie." The command, though quietly spoken, was definitely not the right tone to use with me in my present frame of mind.

"What do you think you're doing?" I demanded.

"Straightening this whole thing out."

"I don't think so," I said.

"Jackie, please, just sit down and listen." I slapped my notes neatly on the chair seat and perched on the arm, staring at him with enough anger to melt a lesser man. Will ignored it. He pulled the other chair to face me and sat. "I got your message telling me you were working with Roy."

"I never..."

"Just listen." Will held up a hand. "You'd promised to make that decision with me." My mouth opened and Will raised his eyebrows. I huffed and folded my arms, trying to look bored with the entire conversation. "When I called you back to find out what was going on, your father answered and told me you were out. But I could hear you talking in the background, so I knew something was wrong. And since you wouldn't answer any of my calls... well, here I am."

"I'll bet that didn't tickle Cali. Does she even know you're here?"

"I'm getting to that part."

"I don't need any details, thanks," I said, but Will forged ahead.

"Cali showed up at my apartment one night with a message you'd left at the hospital. She told me you'd also said you were working with Roy in California."

"That's not true."

"I know that now," Will said.

"So, you didn't have to make the trip. I could have told you that over the phone."

"You could have, if you would have taken any of my calls." He tilted his head and half-smiled.

"Why should I? You had your pernicious girlfriend to keep you company."

"Jackie," Will said, exasperated at last, "Cali has nothing to do with us."

"Right, because there's only the two of you now."

"Why did you bring up the 'shower'?" Will asked, ignoring my remark.

"Well, that would be because Cali offered to get you out of it to take my call."

Will's face turned purple, and he mumbled a string of angry words that included "conniving" and "key," something in Zulu and several renditions of "bloody." He snorted. "I thought she left, but she must have come back in after I got in the shower. I didn't know you called or that she talked to you." I stared at Will trying to compute this very different story. "Jackie, I can understand your reaction to Cali, but what about to me? Do you think so little of me, or what's between us, that you believed her?" He stood and looked out from the porch, his hands on the railing. After several moments, while I tried to grasp the twist of events, he ran his hand through his hair and turned, his eyes boring into mine.

"So, you ... never ... ?"

"No, Jackie, and you were wrong to think it of me." The disappointment in his eyes hit my stomach like a block of ice. "You didn't trust me with Cali, and you've made it difficult for me to trust your feelings."

"My feelings," I said in a choked whisper, "wouldn't have been crushed if I didn't care." It was a lame argument, but a true one. He had come after me, followed me to the childhood home where we had first known each other. And there was the cost of the tickets he could not afford and the time off work. I could only imagine the grueling schedule that would make up the hours of his life when he returned home. Will was watching me with wary eyes. I winced. "I was wrong, completely and totally wrong - blind. I trust you. I trust us," I said. His eyelids lowered, and I grimaced with hard-earned understanding and a lot of guilt. "And you're here," I added in a voice full of contrition. He shook his head and let out a long breath.

"When you left Johannesburg, Jackie, I wasn't sure you were coming back. And then when you wouldn't answer my calls ... Of course I'm here." He looked at me for a long moment. "I've come to take you home." Before he could reach for me, I threw myself into his arms. "To the ends of the earth," he murmured. In that moment, our world righted itself. His kiss drained me of the anguish of the past days, and left me feeling raw and vulnerable. As the last cool rays of sun washed off the porch, Will tipped up my chin and looked me in the eye, "Now, about Roy and Kurt," he said.

Chapter 9

Decisions, All at Once

It was an incredible relief to have Will with me for the funeral and the reception. Two days later, I suited up and met Roy at one of Sandstorm's satellite offices.

"You've lost weight," he said, eyeing me with concern.

"Only a little."

We talked for two hours. Roy had several questions about my time in Africa. As for the job, as I had hoped, it would entail interviews, investigation and writing. There would also be travel, but to what extent, Roy was not yet sure. The salary, benefits and stock options were wonderful. And then came the question I knew he would ask.

"How's your doctor?"

I nodded and shrugged, "Good."

Roy looked at me from beneath lowered brows. "Good – it's going to be a problem traveling good?"

"I guess that depends on where the traveling takes place," I answered.

Roy leaned forward, resting his elbows on his desk. "Jackie, I need to know you'll be available whenever and wherever news occurs."

"I understand," I said, trying to find a balance in my mind for these two incredible opportunities in my life.

"Do you?" Roy probed. "There can't be encumbrances on your time. When I give you an assignment, you need to start packing.

The position is all the things you told me you want. But, you have to commit one hundred percent." He stood and came around to sit on the front of his desk before me, arms folded. "So, what's it going to be, a relationship or a job that can make your career?" He stared into my eyes.

I held up my chin and straightened my back. "It is everything I want." *Everything except Will,* I thought. "It's an incredible opportunity." I paused. "I'd like to have a couple of days to think it through."

"I'd hoped you'd have an answer for me today. I'm flying back this evening, and I wanted to let Charles know the position is filled." Charles Stannish was president of Caduceus. I was concerned that my hesitance might seem a lack of enthusiasm.

"This is not just an incredible opportunity, it's a commitment," I countered. "My answer will also be a commitment."

Roy rubbed his chin for a moment, never taking his eyes from mine, then nodded, "Fair enough."

Chapter 10

The Pier

Will was waiting for me outside the Caduceus building. We had dinner in the garden patio of a small restaurant near the beach. During dinner, I told Will I had promised to give Roy an answer in a couple of days. It would mean being based in New York, but that the majority of my time would be spent in South Africa, particularly the first six months while I got up to speed. Will listened, but made few comments.

After dinner, we walked along the shore. A group of teenagers sat around a blazing fire on the upper beach drinking beer and roasting hot dogs. Their laughter drifted out to us and was soaked up and carried away by the small waves that slapped against the sand at our feet. Will took my hand and kissed it and headed for the deserted pier where we had walked so long ago. The weathered wharf rocked against the lapping water, its small boat children tied to it like nursing pups, rubbing and bumping each other to jostle for position. At its length, a single light cast a misty glow over the water. Will had been noticeably quiet throughout the evening, and when we reached the end of the pier, he stood silently looking up at the stars. Lulled by the rhythmic swaying, I was surprised when he suddenly turned me to face him. With the light behind him, his eyes were endless pools of black. I started to smile, but stopped when I saw the slight furrow between his brows. He touched a finger to my cheek, and then traced the line of my jaw.

The frown deepened. "Jackie, I still believe Africa is where I can do the most good."

Half worlds, I thought.

"I know you're the one giving up so much, but if you accept Roy's offer, we'll both have the careers we want. I don't have to wait any longer for you to finish college, and you don't have to wait to see the world. We can do that together. More importantly, we have the love now that I thought we had then. What I'm trying to say is, I don't want to lose you again, and I don't want a future without you. Share it with me. I love you so much, Jackie. Marry me, once and for always. Marry me."

The starlight caught in the tears that filled my eyes and momentarily blinded me. I loved Will, and I wanted to be with him, but I had to think this through - this collision course of personalities and professions, of different worlds and distant separations.

"We'd be living on different continents, at least for a while," I said.

"Yes."

I stared at the ocean with its tiny, uncountable drops of water all moving together in one beautifully fluid dance and waited until my thoughts rested against its quiet and ancient rhythm.

"Such an unpredictable road ahead," I whispered. Will's eyes never left my face. I looked at the stream of light from the single bulb above us to the illuminated water below. I could see a short distance into its depth, and while I might not be able to see what lay ahead in my own future, I knew if Will was there, I was willing to take the risk that what was beyond would hold the love and dreams that I wanted. I was startled from my thoughts by the sudden slap of a wave against the pier. I looked back into the eyes that were asking me to share a future. "I can't imagine this life without you. I love you. Yes."

Will released the breath I hadn't realized he'd been holding, and took my face in his hands, "Then promise me you'll marry me as soon as you return to Africa."

"As soon..." I said. And then, standing on our rocky island beneath the heavens that encompassed both our worlds, I made one more promise. "One regret I refuse to have Will Kincaid, is that I never kissed you enough."

Chapter 11

New York

The next two weeks were hectic. I gave Jay notice. He was less than pleased and asked what it would take to convince me to stay, but he knew that Ability couldn't offer me the opportunity Caduceus was. I spent the days making sure my accounts were transferred and saying goodbye. The following week, Roy returned to California and met me at the Caduceus office. He enthusiastically welcomed me aboard, but admitted he would have preferred that my doctor and I remain friends. Twice while we were talking, Roy touched his third finger, absently spinning the ring which was no longer there. He caught me watching and shrugged, looking uncharacteristically uncomfortable.

"My wife and I have separated. It doesn't look like things are going to work out." No wonder his reaction to my news about Will and me.

Roy sent me reams of documentation to read and study. The situation in Africa was intense. Its long history of conflict and encroachment by the French, British, Indians and Dutch in the 1600's had eventually resulted in the British annexation of most of the lands of South Africa. And with the annexation had come a virulent apartheid that stripped the black Africans of basic rights and often buried their cultural traditions. Even the now widely spoken Afrikaans language was a mix of that used originally by the San and Khoikhoi tribes and the mother tongues of Dutch, Europe and South Asia. Many African tribesmen who once lived off the land had become cattle and sheep herders known as trekboers, others were drawn to the cities as laborers in the diamond and gold mining revolution of the late 1860's. The Zulu nation was the last to fall to the ever creeping hand of the United Kingdom. In the early 1900's, the struggle for equal rights and the formation of the African National Congress (ANC) were followed with unspeakable violence as the nation fought its way to a balance of power between those who could claim ancestry far into the African past and those who would claim imperialistic salvation. The letters Will had written me after he left were filled with political frustration, particularly as his state of Rhodesia fought for its independence from British rule. I immersed myself in the history and current politics between packing boxes and preparing to move.

Will and I talked every day. He was eager for my return, and understandably more than a little anxious about it, especially when I told him I was giving two weeks' notice at Ability, but also taking two more weeks off to relocate and find an apartment in New York near the Caduceus headquarters.

"I don't see the sense of keeping an apartment in New York. You won't be there much, and it would be easier to rent a hotel room," Will argued.

"The only home we'll be keeping is ours," I assured him, "and besides, the apartment is more of a company rental for convenience. I'll be there before you know it," I promised.

The days flew by for me as I said my goodbyes and closed up my California apartment. Two weeks later, I arrived in New York, and two days after that, dressed in a dark blue suit, I wound my way through unopened moving boxes in my new apartment and hailed the cab that took me to my first day of work. I waited for Roy in his office where a floor to ceiling window overlooked Central Park. I peered at the minutia on the street far below. Yellow cabs were everywhere, like bees in a hive pushing against and around each other to deposit their loads of honey.

"You made it," Roy nearly bellowed as he strode into his office. He reached out and took my hand in both of his.

"Your view is a little like the African bush," I said glancing back out the window.

"Well, Central Park can be a little wild."

"No, I mean the streets, the way the people move through the city like beautiful beasts intent on the hunt." Roy followed my gaze to the streets below, and then looked back at me as though he were seeing something in me for the first time.

"Are you moved into your apartment?" he asked.

"There're still a few boxes to unpack, but the phone's hooked up, the lights are on and the heater works. Snug as a bug," I said.

"I want you to be settled, Jackie." Roy frowned. You need a home base, somewhere to come back to after you've been out there chasing stories."

"I am, or at least I will be soon, but then I'll have a home on each side of the Atlantic." The small indentation between Roy's eyes deepened slightly.

"Let's get you introduced to your new colleagues."

In the next hour, it felt like I met more people than I had at the Johannesburg conference. Roy offered to take me out to lunch, but the visiting South African office manager, Todd Overbeek, insisted that we had many things to discuss, and took me out instead. The afternoon filled itself with conference calls and getting up to speed on upcoming assignments. Before I knew it, I was hailing a cab home.

I plopped my briefcase and purse on the hall table and kicked my shoes off into the dark and lifeless apartment. Trying to find the light switch, I forgot about the boxes and painfully stubbed my toe just as the phone rang. I limped back to the hall table and felt my way to the receiver, suddenly wanting desperately to connect with another human being.

"When are you going to get here, darling girl?" Will's voice was as welcomingly warm as the apartment was cold.

"Oh, thank God," I said, running my hand over the wall and finally finding the light switch. "Can you hang on for a second?" I headed for the heater control.

"Are you alright?" Will asked.

"Yes, just really glad to hear your voice."

"Tough day?"

"Not so bad." I sighed inwardly. "Just… no, everything's fine."

"When are you coming?" Will asked again.

"Roy wants me here through the end of the month, but that's only another week and a half." I grimaced.

"You need to be *here* in my arms."

"I need to be there in your arms." The emptiness of the apartment crept inside me.

"What can I do?" Will asked softly. I couldn't decide if his voice was comforting me or making the loneliness worse.

"Just be there when I finally make it across that big salty pond between us. And tell me about you; tell me everything." When I hung up, I was feeling better, but before I could head for the kitchen, the phone rang again.

"Did you make it home through the jungle okay?"

"Hi, Roy. Yes I did, but it's colder than the arctic, and I just stubbed my toe on a box."

"Still accident prone?" Roy laughed.

"Didn't have you to throw yourself in front of it and save me."

"No broken bones, then?"

"Nope, I was just about to limp my way to the kitchen."

"First week in the big city, dangerous obstacles - if you're not too done in, why don't you let me at least save you from hunger?" he offered.

Exhausted, I ran my hand over my hair. "It's a great offer, but I'm going to have to learn to keep myself out of trouble. I think I'll just curl up with a hot cup of tea and read through some more of the small library you sent over. But, thanks anyway."

"I understand." His voice seemed a little flat. I suppose he had his own lonely night to face. "See you tomorrow."

"I'll be the one on crutches wearing four sweaters."

Chapter 12

What Have I Done?

Two nights before I left for Johannesburg, I was curled up on the couch reading when the thought of leaving my country, my family and my friends hit me with the force of a tidal wave. I suddenly wanted to hear my father's voice. I reached for the phone and called him.

"Hi, Dad."

"Jackie, well, isn't this a nice surprise. How's life out there in New York?"

"Oh, great," I answered, swallowing a lump in my throat.

"Everything okay?" We were too much alike for him not to innately understand that something was amiss.

"I just wanted to hear your voice, make sure everything's okay with you." I could hear my father thinking.

"Having second thoughts?"

"No, not really. I guess I'm just a little tired. It's a lot to get used to. You know, new job, new city."

"New life," he added.

"Pretty much, but I'm hanging in there. And you know I'll be back to see you soon."

"Good. I'll look forward to that. And I'm doing fine, Jackie. Don't worry."

"Thanks, Dad… I miss you."

"Miss you, too. You take care of yourself."

"I will. Love you." And then he said goodbye as he always did.

"Love you more."

I hung up, wrapped my arms around my legs and laid my forehead on my knees. An hour later, snuggled into a pillow on the couch, a persistent ringing entered my dreams. By the time I realized it was the phone, it was too late. I got up and went to bed.

Chapter 13

Across the Salty Pond

It had been the same dilemma. I couldn't decide whether or not to pack the inevitable pair of red shoes I always seemed to have, but now I could see the outline of one heel pushing against the side of my suitcase as I hurried toward my gate at New York's JFK airport. I could hardly wait to see Will. The flight was only about three-fourths full, so I had two seats to myself by the window. The excitement stayed with me until we landed. And then, as we taxied toward our gate in Johannesburg, disquiet curled around the edges of my consciousness. The lost, slightly panicked feeling I had on the couch two nights earlier returned. Here I was in Africa. Nothing felt familiar. I couldn't remember Will's face for a brief second, and that scared me. I shook my head and swallowed. *Get a hold of yourself, kiddo."* My hands were shaking. I *can always change everything back to the way it was if I need to,* I reasoned. An invisible vise wrapped around my chest. The man across the aisle stood to remove his bag from the overhead bin. My own movements to rise seemed jerky and awkward.

I focused on my feet as they carried me out the exit ramp, my mind chanting in time to each footstep, *I'm fine. I'm fine.* When I reached the end of the ramp, the thought "home" flashed fleetingly through my mind, which home I have no idea.

I saw Will standing near a pillar, his eyes searching for me. My earlier intent to rush to him was gone, instead I felt rooted to the spot just outside the end of the ramp. And then he saw me. He smiled, his eyes squinting slightly as he walked towards me. He simply gathered me in his arms and pulled my head against his chest. "It's alright, Jackie honey. I'm here. It's alright now."

Chapter 14

Finding the Way Home

Will talked as we drove. I knew he was giving me time to acclimate, and I was relieved that there were no questions about my quiet arrival.

"I was thinking you could stay at my apartment since I'm at hospital so much," he said.

"The, um, secretary at work made a reservation for me at the Carlton," I blurted out. I felt Will turn and look at my slightly shaky smile and averted eyes. When we reached the Carlton, he helped me check in and carried my bags to my room. He stopped in the hallway, handed me my luggage, took my key and opened the door.

"Goodnight, Jackie," he said, and kissed me on the forehead. As I watched him walk silently down the long, carpeted hall, something loosened inside me. I took a deep breath and let it swoosh out. Will was walking away – my mind kicked into the present and out of the safety net it had been lying in. I dropped the bags where I stood.

"Is that the best you can do?" I called after him, trying to sound indignant. He took a few more steps, and then turned those honey gold eyes in my direction.

"You know better than that," he said, with a look more pillaging than a Saxon army.

"It's all a little vague, actually," I protested. "You wouldn't want to ... remind me would you?" Will pursed his lips and stood there looking like he was trying to decide if surgery was possible with a cheese spreader and a rubber band.

"Fine," I said as nonchalantly as possible. "I guess I'll just turn in then."

"You planning on doing that alone?" he asked.

I shrugged. "There was a pretty cute bellboy down by the reservation desk." Will walked slowly back to my door and, crossing his arms, leaned one shoulder against the frame.

"Not an option."

"You're the one walking away."

"I was going to give you until I reached the end of the hall."

Arrogant man. "You don't always know best." Will put his hand behind my neck and pulled me into a kiss that was knee buckling.

"Definitely not compatible," I sighed.

Will nudged both suitcases into the room with his foot and backed me in along with them. He turned, closed the door and pushed me against it, trapping me with his body. Just as he leaned in to kiss me again, an irritating buzz sounded.

"Bloody hell," Will groaned and reached for his pager. He read the number. "I've got to go, Jackie. I'm sorry. It's one of my patients." He slowly tucked my hair behind my ear, kissing the spot just below it, the one that always sent chills down my back. Smiling proprietarily, he headed back down the hall.

"If you see the bell boy..." I called after him.

I heard him mumble something that sounded like "I'll shoot him."

A half hour later, Will was reading a patient's chart one last time before surgery.

"I thought you had the night off," Cali said, appearing from around a corner.

"No I was just dropping off Jackie."

"So you didn't stay home to help her unpack?"

"She's at the Carlton." Will handed the chart over the counter. "Rachel, would you make sure that Mr. Williams receives these medication changes after surgery?"

"Yes, I'll take care of it myself," Rachel told him, shooting Cali a warning look.

Will took Cali's arm and moved her down the hall where they couldn't be heard, then released his grip. Rachel couldn't make out what Will was saying, but from the look on Cali's face, it wasn't a declaration of love. She did, however, catch his last words.

"Don't interfere again," he said before heading to the doctor's lounge to suit for surgery.

Chapter 15

My Girl

A knock on my door woke me the next morning. Before I could answer, a key jiggled in the lock and in walked Tilly.

"Tilly! It's me, Jackie."

"You still sick?" she demanded, acting like we'd seen each other the day before.

"N…no."

"Then why you still in bed?" Same old wonderful Tilly, but I was up for the banter.

"Any chance you remembered to leave some shampoo in the bathroom?"

"Well, you won't know that les' you git up and git ta goin." Her lips twitched.

"Yes, ma'am," I said, hopping out of bed.

"I'll be back in half-n-hour." She shook her finger at me.

Will showed up tired and exhausted just as I finished dressing. Without a word, he gathered me into his arms and kissed me. A moment later Tilly walked in, vacuum in hand.

"Tssuh! Body can't hardly clean a room without people all over the place."

"Tilly, this is my doctor."

She looked Will up and down. "You jus' lucky you fixed up my girl here," she fussed, referring to my infected shoulder. "Otherwise, I'd a had to git Miz Molly to come over."

"Who's Miss Molly?" I asked.

"She our doctor. Fix anyone, anytime, an' a lot quicker than some others. She don't need all them needles and pills." Tilly sniffed at Will, who was staring wide-eyed at her, before she went back into the hall for more supplies from her cart. He winked at me, and I gently touched one of the dark circles beneath his eyes.

"Looks like you'd better get some rest."

"I'm knackered - six-hours in surgery."

"I understand," I said and then grimaced. "Am I going to be saying that a lot?"

"I'm great at making up for lost time. I'll be back before you know it." He smiled and leaned backwards to stretch.

"Yep, I've heard that before. Now, go. Get some rest." I turned him toward the door. "We have a life to start living together."

Will turned and looked at me with such longing that had I not gestured toward Tilly standing in the doorway tapping her foot, he might have given her the shock of her life.

Chapter 16

A Scuffle or Two

The next morning I headed downtown to cover a protest rally I suspected was backed by the ANC. Throngs of black Africans and coloreds, those who were a mixed race, many of them European and Khoikhoi or Bantu, were listening to a man standing on top of an old dented car. Arms flailing and no microphone, he was yelling to the crowd. The mass of bodies before me was swaying. Some of the protestors had their arms around each other's shoulders, others were jumping or jabbing the air with pointing fists. There were crudely made cardboard signs from the hopeful, "Be reasonable Our Requests are Reasonable," to the confrontational, "The Call Has Gone Out," and "People Unite and Fight." I moved closer to the group to make out the speaker's words above the protesting voices. Someone to my right yelled "Stop the genocide in the jails."

Knowing I was covering the rally, I'd forgone my usual work suit for slacks and a blouse, but still everything about me stuck out in the crowd, my straight brown hair, the color of my skin, even the cut of my clothes. I skirted around the edge, staying several feet away from the protestors, and moved closer to the front. Several policemen with batons and guns were moving toward the throng. I'd brought a camera and had just started snapping pictures, when a small group of teenage boys suddenly pushed through yelling "Fight, fight for equal rights." Within seconds, the crowd picked up the chant. Bodies danced and jumped to the rhythm, and the shouted words intensified to the edge of hysteria. The protestors were now a pulsing current of pushing and shoving. The speaker scuttled off the car roof and hot-footed it to a nearby building. I snapped several more photos and turned to move back, but something struck me from the side and knocked me off balance, slamming me elbow-first into the concrete. I tried to get up but the crowd surged toward me, and someone grabbed my camera. I shot my fist out into a chest and grabbed the camera strap, yanking it back. Before I could rise, I was surrounded by the crush of pressing bodies, legs painfully banging into me. A foot crunched down on the fingers of my left hand. I quickly pulled my elbows against my sides, but before I could cover my head, something hard slapped against my cheek shoving me sideways. I rolled into as small a ball as possible. Moments later, I sensed a break in the swarm of bodies and tried scrambling to my feet, at first half crawling, scraping my knees, then half rising, running like a hunched over Neanderthal, but finally shoving my way through the bodies to the far side of a tree a few feet away. Glancing back, I saw the rowdy throng swirl toward me again. I took my next breath running like I'd never run before. I didn't stop until the searing pain in my lungs nearly doubled me over. I knew people were staring, but all I could think of was to get back to the office, to safety and people I knew. I hailed a cab and frowned in confusion at the driver's open-mouthed stare.

"What happened to you?" he asked.

I guessed I looked a little disheveled.

"I ran into a few protestors," I told him and, sighing with relief, laid my head against the back of the seat. When I arrived at the office, I was met with more odd stares and a gasp from Rita, the receptionist.

"What's wrong with everyone?" I insisted.

"You're kidding, right?" she said peering at my cheek.

I put a hand to my face. The movement sent a shot of pain into my elbow, and I looked down to see the back of my sleeve torn and covered in blood. That was when my legs buckled. Someone grabbed me from behind, and the next thing I knew, I was sitting in a chair with six sets of eyes staring into mine.

"Pictures," I said, holding up my camera. "I have pictures."

Todd took me to the Johannesburg Hospital where my elbow was stitched back together while I held an ice pack on the cheek I now realized was swollen and turning an ever deeper shade of purple. There were no broken bones in the hand that had been stepped on. Rachel, who knew everything that went on in the hospital, showed up and insisted on fussing over me and threatening the doctors in case they didn't admit me for the night to be monitored for a possible concussion. I begged to go home, but no one listened. Rachel went off to try and reach Will out in the field. I slept most of the afternoon, until my phone woke me.

"Hello." The dryness of my throat made it sound like a hiccup.

"Jackie?"

"Yes."

"My God, are you all right?" It was Roy.

"Mmm hmm," I said, pushing my stiff body into a sitting position.

"Todd called and said you were caught up in some kind of protest, and you're in the hospital. I've been trying to reach you. What happened?" he demanded.

"What time is it in New York?" I asked.

"What happened?"

And so, with as little detail as possible, I related the morning's events. "I gave the story to Todd," I ended. There was a long pause. "Still there?"

"I didn't send you to Africa to join the ANC." Roy sounded angry. "You could have gotten yourself killed."

"I got a little close to the action today, but I'm fine. I'm taking care of myself."

"Like you did today?" I didn't have much of an answer for that. "When you feel up to it, I want a complete run down. You scared me to death, Jackie."

"I'm sorry, Roy, but I'm fine—really."

"The good news, I guess, is that you have your own doctor to take care of you."

"He doesn't know I'm here. Rachel tried to call him out in the field, but they haven't been able to locate him yet."

"That's unfortunate." The words held no surprise. "I hope you don't have to get used to that. I want you to take whatever time you need." At least I wasn't fired.

Shortly after dinner there were two knocks on my door. Cali's blonde head poked its way into view. She grimaced.

"Wow, you look awful. I heard you tried to outsmart a group of upset protestors. Looks like they won." She managed another pained expression. I had a sudden urge to throw a bedpan at her.

"I'd say I held my own."

"Wait 'til Will sees what a mess you are."

"Is there something you wanted, Cali?"

She pulled her shoulders back and crossed her arms, while her mouth made little sideways trips back and forth, and one foot beat out a nervous tap on the floor. "Well, I just thought I should apologize for…" She shook her head as if she already regretted what she was going to say, and her eyes flicked to the door like a kid in the principal's office. She inhaled long enough to fill the lungs of an adult rhinoceros, and then launched into a full-blown apology.

"I guess I made things pretty tough for you and Will. And, well, I'm sorry." I waited while she exhaled all that air she'd sucked out of the room. "I guess I could blame you for stealing Will away from me, but it wasn't like that. I'd had my chance." She half smiled. "Well, I guess that was only because you'd walked out of his life. Truth is," and the air left the room again, "I would have never been what you are to him." She shrugged. "I'm really sorry."

I didn't doubt her sincerity, and I appreciated the courage and honesty it took for her to apologize, but we were both pretty uncomfortable. And it wasn't like I could make a quick exit, stage left. So there I sat, knowing I was at the podium next. It was easy enough to accept the apology, but I didn't exactly feel like offering her a year's supply of hair bleach to prove it.

I simply nodded and said, "Thank you, Cali."

She reached over and straightened the blanket on the end of my bed, while I brushed off an invisible ball of lint from my faded blue hospital gown. We looked up at the same time, our gazes locking in a shared moment of cease fire, until Cali gave a little start and nodded toward the door.

"Well, I'll catch Will when he returns and bring him up to date on your little skirmish."

"Thanks, I can handle that myself."

"Sure," she shrugged walking towards the door. "Let me know if you need anything."

I was still shaking my head when a nurse walked in with some pink pills.

Chapter 17

Taking Wing

The night seemed endless. I was too hot, and the constant thrum of rubber-soled footsteps, distant coughing and the changing gears of trucks in the street below, drifted into my troubled dreams of flailing arms and legs. I was relieved to see the sky begin to lighten. And as I had so often done, I lay awake in the waning moment of darkness, that juncture when night surrenders to day and time balances in still expectation. With the pendulous past and present held at bay, muted mind gives voice to the heart. In that instant, desires are liberated, and the soul is free to soar. No matter how fleeting, I am always captured by the exhilarating boundlessness, as if in that moment, creation can be touched.

Chapter 18

Powder Kegs

Rachel offered to take me back to the hotel on her lunch break, but this time I won the cab debate. The phone was ringing when I entered my hotel room. I picked it up holding onto my sore ribs.

"Jackie? You made it back to the hotel. Are you up to a visit? I just got in." It was unlike Roy to sound so anxious.

"Yes, of course, but I thought you weren't due in Johannesburg until next week."

"I wasn't. Fifteen minutes okay?"

I flipped back the long arm lock on the door so that it was slightly ajar and headed gently towards the couch. It was then I noticed the large floral arrangement on the side table. It actually hurt to pull the card from the imbedded clip.

Jackie – Looking forward to having you back soon,

Roy

Gingerly settling myself on the couch, I dozed off just as footsteps came down the hall. Roy knocked and then slowly pushed the door open. Looking uncharacteristically crumpled, he crossed the room open-mouthed and sat down beside me.

"Good God, Jackie," he said, his eyes lingering on every bruise and scrape.

"Yeah, you didn't mention this in the job description." I

smiled and winced again. He looked at me, reprimand and relief in his eyes. "I'm alright," I nodded. He started to say something, but changed his mind and sat back. After a moment, he shook his head and then filled me in on the outcome of the protest. Several people had been arrested, and three badly injured. One of my pictures had actually caught a policeman hitting one of the protestors, and the story I'd given Todd made the local paper with my name in the byline. Roy looked at my left hand and grimaced, then reached over and gently picked it up. He ran his thumb over the bare third finger.

"No ring?" he asked.

"The doctor was concerned about swelling. I put it on this chain." I pulled out my grandmother's ring from beneath my blouse.

"No engagement ring?" A movement near the door caught my attention, and I looked up to see Will watching us.

"Jackie . . . they told me at hospital, but I wasn't expecting . . ." He was across the room and kneeling before me in a blink.

"Roy," he said and nodded before taking my hand from his. He checked my hand front and back. "Let me look at you." He put his fingers beneath my chin and turned my head to the side, then gently probed the swollen cheek.

"Ouch."

Roy stood to leave. "Well, I'll check with you later. Make sure she takes care of herself." Will nodded again. I thanked Roy for the flowers. He looked at me for a moment, and then closed the door behind him.

Will examined every finger, every rib and even peeked under my elbow bandage. "What were you thinking, Jackie, getting in the middle of a protest? Tutu's right, this city is sitting on a powder keg of emotions waiting to blow up." The remark reminded me that'd I intended to set up an interview with the man who made that statement, Desmond Tutu, the gentle speaking black bishop, unquestionably one of the greatest and most controversial anti-apartheid proponents. "Jackie – are you listening to me?" Will was still scolding, "You can't just go running around poking your nose into hostile situations and getting coshed."

"Well, evidently my nose is the only thing you haven't checked, because it's just fine," I shot back feeling a bit indignant at his reprimand.

"Jackie," his voice was calmer, "you could have..."

"I know, gotten myself hurt."

"You are hurt. You could have gotten yourself killed." Will stood up, glancing at the flowers. "You haven't even been here a week and look at you. I leave town for a couple of days and come back to find you bruised from head to foot."

"I didn't get these bruises because you left town. I have a job to do, and I ran into a small bump in the road."

"I treated a motorcyclist who ran into a truck. He was in better shape than you are."

I groaned my way to my feet. "What else is wrong?"

Will shook his head and grimaced "I propose to you and as soon as you arrive in my country, I leave you alone. I wasn't here to take care of you when you were hurt, and ... Roy's right, you don't even have an engagement ring."

"Oh, that," I said, looking at my bare finger.

"I haven't forgotten," Will said, smiling sheepishly. "I had my grandmother's ring reset for you. I'm supposed to pick it up today."

"Oh!" And now my eyes filled with tears.

"What can I hug?" Will asked.

"Pretty much everything." He gently wrapped me in his arms, and the warmth of him was a welcome balm to my bone-deep soreness.

There were two quick knocks at the door before Tilly backed in pulling her cart behind her. She turned, took one look at my face, and zeroed in on Will.

"What you done to my girl now? Look at that face. What kinda doctor you anyways?" She bustled over and raised her nose in the air to peer at me through the bottom half of her glasses. "What happened, darlin'?" she crooned.

"Just got myself caught in a crowd." I put a hand to my swollen cheek so I could smile. She poked Will in the chest.

"And just where was you when all this was hapnin'?"

"Not where I should have been," he said, looking like a puppy near a puddle.

"Well, ya got that right," she huffed, turning back to me. "Just le' me git ya all comfy." When Tilly had me tucked back on the couch, she leveled a caustic eye at Will. "This girl needs a lotta watchin', and yer not doin' much of a job of that. I don' wanna see nothin' else hapnin' to her."

Tilly headed for the bathroom mumbling about the "good use" of men. From the sounds of clanking glasses and slapping cleaning cloths, I'd say the bathroom took quite a licking. Will was sitting beside me when she returned to bang her vacuum against every table and chair leg in the room, ordering Will to lift his feet.

"I'm watchin' you boy," she said.

Chapter 19

Coming to Terms

Will returned the next morning to take me to his apartment for the day. He said it would give me a "change of scenery" while he was at the hospital. He insisted I bring along something to wear for dinner out.

We ate at a nearby Italian restaurant, ordering heaping plates of spaghetti and meatballs and a bottle of wine. We talked about the rotating doctors' program Will was a part of, and the travel my job would require, all the while holding hands and leaning across the table for an occasional kiss. With an apologetic tilt of his head, our waiter appeared, informing us the restaurant was closing. We hadn't noticed the empty tables or the time.

Bundled in coats, Will led me out through the restaurant's back door where a tiny path meandered through a garden of young cypress and trimmed rose trees. There, alone beneath a beautiful moon, Will handed me a small velvet box. Inside was his grandmother's engagement ring, a stunning sapphire set between two diamonds.

"It's beautiful," I said, tipping it back and forth to catch the light.

Will took it from the box and slid it on my finger. "It's only a symbol, Jackie. The promise is in my heart."

"And in mine," I said reaching up to his waiting kiss.

Arms linked, we headed back to Will's car so he could drop me off at my hotel. Halfway there, I stopped to look at a protest poster attached to a street sign, "Black is Beautiful," it read in big, bold letters. Underneath was information on a rally the following week. Will steered me away from the sign.

"Don't even think about it," he said. I didn't respond. "You're not seriously considering going to that rally?"

"I have no intention of getting myself in the middle of another stampeding crowd," I told him.

"Meaning?"

"Meaning I have a job to do, and I've learned my lesson about protests."

"You're not listening to me. I don't want you near any more rallies," he insisted.

"I appreciate your concern," I told him, "but I intend to do the job I've been hired to do."

"I'm not going to have my wife in the middle of an out-of-control crowd. You were lucky this time. You're not going to any more."

"What I'm not yet is your wife, and when I am, I still won't let you order me around." Bossy, frustrating man. Will kept walking, and despite the heated topic, he appeared completely calm, which was more infuriating than his presumption that he could set the curfews of my life. "When you're through doing that 'father-look' thing, Kincaid," I wiggled my finger in front of his perfectly straight and slightly upturned nose, "I'll be happy to accept your gracious acquiescence that you know how capable I am of handling my job."

"Which is, to be at my side," he said.

"At your . . ." I spluttered. "I'm not a side car on the bicycle you're riding through life."

"What about a family?" he asked, a smile playing around the edge of his mouth.

"I'm not exactly planning on being Betty Crocker right away either. So what's this all about?"

"Just planning our future."

"Feel free to include me on that," I said.

"Only trying to make sure the mother of my children won't be running off to rallies every time she sees a poster tacked to a pole."

"Mother of your children . . . ."

"I'm pretty clear, based on my medical studies, that certain activities we'll be engaging in soon have been linked to procreation." He smiled and made a little humming noise. I gingerly pulled my bruised body away from him and came to a dead stop

"Ah, another medical epiphany." It was time to get the conversation back on track. "So, no more talk about rallies."

"Not as long as you let me know about them ahead of time – every time."

"All right, whenever I know ahead of time . . . "

"No, Jackie, the deal is, you call before you go."

"So, you're giving me an ultimatum, Kincaid?"

"Just including you in the planning," he countered, knowing he had pushed all of my buttons he was going to for the night.

Chapter 20

The Last Doubt

And then the day of the wedding arrived, bright and sunny and promising. It wasn't a large group, close friends and family, some of the interns and doctors Will worked with, a few colleagues from Caduceus, two close friends from California and Rachel and Cali, who showed up with her former boyfriend. Best of all, were my brother and father, whose trips were Roy's wedding gift. Roy called the day before to tell me he was stuck in Zurich and couldn't make it.

Will and I were married in a small chapel outside of Johannesburg. I took hold of the arm my father held out for me, but the aisle ahead looked endless. I took the first few steps watching the toes of my shoes push the front of my satin, floor length gown forward. I looked up, surprised to see Tilly, sitting in the back, smiling at me through teary eyes. She nodded at Will, but there was something of the evil eye in it. Someone murmured, and I glanced ahead to see a woman I did not recognize mouthing the word, "Beautiful." It was what everyone said when they saw a bride. Beaming faces, all smiling except for an elderly man with thinning hair and stooped shoulders, who was frowning. A flash went off and left little floating white spots in my eyes. How many more feet to the altar where Will stood waiting? A wave of panic slapped into me. This moment I had fought against for so long, the moment I had always believed meant giving myself away, had arrived. The final surrender. My hands were ice cold, my knees wobbling in their sockets.

And then I saw him. He was standing in front of the bottom step, smiling at me - the dark hair, the honey gold eyes, the cummerbund of his tuxedo flat against his trimness, the beauty of him. My heart stammered once, and then resumed a reassuring loud and steady drumming. My father gave my hand a last squeeze and kissed me before releasing me to Will who tucked my arm through his. The heat of him startled me. As Will moved toward the altar, my hand betrayed me and pulled him back. He turned, a question in his eyes. I leaned forward wanting to say something to him, but I didn't know what it was until I whispered, "For always ..." The words were hesitant, almost a question.

Will had moved his head down and forward to hear, but now he pulled back to look at me. The tiniest hint of concern passed through his eyes. Did he think I didn't want to go through with the marriage? Did I not want to? My face flushed and the heat of it made me feel faint. I swayed towards him. Will gently grasped my elbow, steadying me. But my eyes must have had another message, because Will slowly smiled and whispered so only I could hear, "Always and once, love." He waited until I returned his smile. And then, amidst the music and the whispers our conversation had induced, we turned together toward the altar.

Chapter 21

Getting it Right

Will wouldn't say where we were headed except east, but he promised me a nice hot bath. For the last few miles, the road wound through a valley and then climbed a modest mountain range where a thatched roof cottage sat on stilts at the edge of a quiet, little pond. A small bridge crossed the stream that fed the pond and led to a path that wound back down into the valley. Centuries of rain had settled the hills into their bottoms like a child's cheeks full of milk. Blue and white wildflowers popped through the grasses and disappeared on the other side of the bridge.

"The cottage belongs to the parents of one of my fellow interns," Will told me. I unwrapped myself from his side and stepped out of the car into the cool evening air.

"It's wonderful, Will." I whispered, afraid to disturb the silence.

An ancient looking tree grew on one side of the cottage. Two of its three trunks shot up and over the little house like fingers about to pick it up and cart it off. Once inside, we found ourselves standing before a large window overlooking the valley below where two small hills nestled side by side. The green valley floor swept up and over them like a blanket covering two reclining lovers.

"You must be exhausted. I've dragged you through wild jungles, makeshift medicine tents and a wedding ceremony." He commandeered me toward the couch, slipped off my shoes and tucked my feet up beside me. After bringing in the rest of our things, he rummaged around in the kitchen and brought out two glasses of wine, and then settled himself behind me so that we faced the view. We sighed in tandem like an old married couple at the end of a long day. Will held up his glass for a toast, but the seconds passed as he stared gravely at the spot where the two rims touched.

"What…?" I asked.

When he spoke at last, the words were a whisper, "I'm so sorry."

"Why?"

"I told you how selfish I'd been the first time I proposed, expecting you to give up everything. I said this time was different, that we'd bring our worlds together. Well, that hasn't happened, at least not yet. You left your family, your friends, your country; you changed jobs. I didn't want it to be that way, love. All I can offer you right now is to be your home." Will took my glass and set it with his on the table, then turned me to face him. "I regret that I've taken you away from the life you know. I only want you to be happy."

I brushed a lock of fallen hair off his forehead. "Will, regret is a reminder that we went after something our heart desired, and it didn't turn out the way we thought it would. It's a tap on the shoulder, a voice in the mind that says 'keep trying.' But you already know that. You made this second chance happen. I would have regretted it if you didn't." I ran my fingertips across his lips. "*Not* going after our dreams is the real disappointment. Besides, how could we ever regret what comes from the heart?"

Will let out a long breath and then wrapped his arms around me. Lost in our own thoughts, we watched the last round of sun dissolve into the horizon. I handed Will his glass, and tapped mine against it.

"To the beauty of regret."

Chapter 22

A Shade of Moonlight

Down the hall, a large bed sat beneath draped white netting. In each corner of its solid wood headboard was a hand carved lion head. But the piece de resistance was the bedroom wall that slid completely open to reveal the lush horizon. An enormous, four-legged tub sat dead center in front of the open wall, allowing bathers to gaze across the ten-foot deck and out to the valley beyond. Will reached into the closet and brought out two oversized, white terry cloth robes. “This is all you’ll need,” he said, handing one to me. I changed in the bathroom, and padded out barefoot a few minutes later.

“You’d better put your shoes back on,” he said.

I blanched, remembering the snake. Will was at my side in a moment. “No, no. Nothing like that,” he insisted, kneeling to slip my shoes on my feet. He picked up a small bag and then flipped a switch on the wall, and small, hidden lights lit the path leading to the pond. We followed the lights over the bridge and down the gently sloping mountain. We’d been walking for less than a minute when a flowing movement caught my eye. A specter-like figure, dressed in a long skirt, was floating down the path ahead of us. Her white skin glowed in the moonlight. She turned and looked at me for the briefest moment before disappearing around a small bend, but it was long enough for me to see the despair in her colorless eyes. I let out a small shriek and pointed ahead. Thinking I had just spotted our destination, Will smiled and kept walking. I grabbed his arm and pulled back.

“Did you see that...that… woman?” Will’s body tensed, and I

watched as his eyes scanned the area ahead.

"Nothing here but us," he said after a moment, sounding relieved. I looked again, but saw no one. Whatever it was had disappeared near a small grotto in the side of the hill. Will led me off the path and through a low gate that guarded the small cave. We entered the circular room and were immediately enveloped in a moist warmness that radiated from a pool of water. The low ceiling enhanced the cocoon like atmosphere, and the steam rose in swirls up our bodies like the hands of a masseuse.

"It's a mineral spring," Will explained. "The water from the pond filters down until the underground heat forces it back up here inside the cave. This bath was carved out of the mountain around the turn of the century by some of the Trekkers who originally settled here." The hush of his voice bouncing against the circle of stones gave the hillside niche the feel of a small cathedral. I watched as Will took matches out of his pocket and lit several candles set along the edge of the pool. He turned and kissed me gently before stepping back and dropping his robe to the floor. The slant of the moonlight through the grotto entrance turned his skin into creamy marble, and I watched as the flickering candlelight danced across his chest.

He reached for the belt of my robe, but I moved back slightly, surprising both of us. Will glanced at my face and then gently tightened the belt. Taking my hand, he led me to the stone steps. I watched as the muscles in his legs flexed beneath the slimness of his hips. When he was waist deep in the water, he turned and motioned for me to sit on the edge. He pulled up the back hem of my robe and folded it beneath me as I settled myself on the rocks at the edge of the pool. Toes first, I dipped into the warm water. It rolled up my legs like honey, helping to calm the anxiety that had seeped inside me. I leaned my head back and sighed with content. Will's fingers touched my neck where my robe had fallen open, and I looked down when I felt his chest against my knees. He slowly ran his fingers along my sides to my waist and loosened the belt, then reached up and pulled my head down for a kiss. When I put my hands on his shoulders, he released my head and slipped his hands into my robe and around my back, gently sliding his hips between my knees. The steam spiraled around us as his hands traced the contours of my body, sliding into my waist, drifting up my back and down again, gliding along my now bare thighs. The pace of our breathing increased until it filled the small room like the rhythmic sound of waves scraping against sand. Through half closed eyes, I traced the constellations of tiny water droplets that coated his hair. Will's hands circled my breasts, coming to rest open-palmed beneath them. He leaned over to kiss each, drawing his tongue in lazy circles around the nipples. I leaned into him, arching my back. I moaned, and it echoed against the walls and came back to us as a sigh. And then, looking into my eyes, Will slipped the robe off my shoulders and slid his hands beneath me, pulling me forward against his stomach. He wrapped my legs around his waist. Then, taking my mouth into his, he slowly lowered me down his body into the warm water and gently onto him. I gasped at the sudden sharp pain, and Will froze, startled.

"You … never?" A minute wave washed against us and scattered the candlelight.

I shook my head trembling, whether out of fear or passion or both, I had no idea. He did not separate us, but instead moved slowly forward, careful not to move our positions, until my back was against the smooth stones. He began to kiss me, softly at first, drawing me deeper and deeper into his own passion. When the hunger of our mouths was no longer satisfying, he began a slow, rhythmic movement with his hips. The pain was only a fleeting soreness now, and my hips began their own ancient dance against him. He lowered me gently at first, sliding deeper and deeper into me, until I lost the sense of my own separateness.

"Open your eyes, Jackie." It was a long moment before his voice reached me through the vaporous gauze, as thick as the steam our pool exhaled, that had enveloped my senses. But the command brought me back from my otherworldly realm of pure physical sensation, and I forced the thick, moist air into my lungs to help find my way to his words. I knew the look I returned was sleepy-eyed and faraway. Will ran his thumb across my lips, and I could taste the bitterness of the mineral water on the tip of my tongue. It stung me and woke me to the intensity of him. He continued to move inside me, faster and harder, our skins slippery in the silken mist, until at last, he touched some long slumbering flame within me that responded to his own demand. And when that moment came, I saw myself in his eyes. I felt consumed and depleted, and yet, sated and restored.

I came back to my senses later as Will carefully withdrew from me and carried me through the thick warmness of the bath to an underwater bench where he settled me on his lap. He pushed my dripping hair back and looked at me.

"Are you all right, love?"

I nodded, watching the play of candlelight on the pool's surface. *All right, but different now.*

"I didn't know," he said softly. I pulled my fingers through the water, watching the small ripples float off like echoes. "I thought…"

I glanced at him. "I know, the other men I dated. I told you, when it got serious I ended it."

He brushed back a tendril of hair that had fallen over my eyes, and asked, "Do you remember the day I told you that I wished I could be the first?"

"Mmm hmm," I blinked and felt tears at the back of my eyes.

"Do you know why I wanted to be the first?" I looked skeptically at him, and he raised a questioning eyebrow.

"Well, maybe you thought it was something you were good at. But," I shook my head, "it seemed to me you were saying once was enough."

A half-painful expression crossed his face. "Well, you're completely wrong, love. I wanted the first time to be something sweet and special for you." The skeptical look was still in my eyes. "No, not because I was trying to tell you I was good at it." He cocked an eyebrow. "But now that you mention it…" I tweaked him in the ribs. He laughed, and the warmth of it shot out to the walls around us, reaching back to wrap us in its embrace. "It was because," he said, serious again, "making love is beautiful, and I wanted you to experience that, to have that for a lifetime." His hand slid up my thigh, brushing across me and gliding up my stomach. He lifted me just far enough out of the water to kiss the small hollow between my breasts, and then stood me in front of him.

"It was more than that," he said, coloring slightly. "It was selfish of me, but I thought if I was the first, you would be mine no matter who came later." His eyes half closed, he nodded to himself, the words barely a whisper, "Mine forever."

I shrugged. "I would have been anyway." The remark surprised him, and I smiled. He laid his hand over my heart.

"Well, love, we belong to each other now." And then he said what he knew I most wanted to hear, "I'm not going to wake up some morning and stop loving you." He gazed into my eyes with that truth, and it released the fear I had carried for so long. I put my arms around his neck, and as we both leaned into the kiss, he took hold of my legs and pulled me back astride him. Whatever our future held, it was going to be a wild ride.

Chapter 23

Shades of Tomorrow

The moon moved above the little cave, leaving only the candles to illuminate our bath.

"I'm starving," I said just as my stomach growled. Will's chuckle rumbled against my back.

"Me too."

I hated leaving our warm, watery nest because I knew there would never be another night exactly like this. I closed my eyes and relegated every moment to memory. Will got out first, shivering in the cold night air, and held my robe for me to rush into. I was tightening the belt while Will put out the candles when a cold misty breeze and a swishing movement caught my eye. It was the sad lady in the long skirt again. She looked right at me and then turned and glided down the path into the valley. I drew in a sharp breath.

"What's the matter?" Will asked putting out the last candle.

"It was her again, the woman I saw when we got here." Will's right eyebrow twitched as he walked warily towards the cave entrance. I followed him, but when I looked again, there was no one on the path.

"Are you sure you saw someone? The steam from the bath can look like all sorts of things," he said.

"It was the woman. She was wrapped in a shawl, and she was as white as milk, but I could see every feature on her face, even her eyes. They were cloudy, like she was blind. She seemed so sad." Will shuddered, staring at me with a half-puzzled, half-disturbed look. "You don't suppose we had an audience, do you?" I grimaced.

"No." He took my hand, "Let's go have some dinner."

The kitchen was small and old-fashioned with a butcher block built into the counter. Double doors led outside to a wood slat patio where two chairs with canvas seats and backs sat near a small round table under the thatched roof.

Will insisted on making his "reasonably good" spaghetti. I made a salad, and we ate in our robes in front of the fire, alternately laughing and gazing into each other's eyes between sips of champagne. A wisp of smoke wafted up the chimney, and I remembered the woman. I looked speculatively at Will.

"You wouldn't be afraid of ghosts, would you?" He glanced at me, and put his head down. I smiled, "You *are.*"

"It's not so much that I'm afraid of ghosts, as that I have a healthy respect for upsetting them."

"I think you know more about this specter than you're letting on." He waved dismissively. "C'mon, Will, tell me. I love ghost stories."

He blew out a long breath. "White lady sightings are not that uncommon here."

"Like the one I saw?" I asked, a shiver running through me.

"So I'm told."

"Have you ever talked to anyone who's seen one?"

"No. Enough ghost talk." He poured more champagne into my glass.

"You'd better tell me the rest so I'll know what to protect you from," I teased. "Besides, it sounds like a great bedtime story."

"Just what I had in mind," Will said gathering the front of my robe in his hands and pulling me towards him.

"Not going to bed until I hear it."

Will glared at me and then settled my body against his, "Just remember, it's only a story." I snuggled in. "When the Voortrekkers came through here in wagons, there was a young couple that was married just before joining the train. A few days into the trip, the trekkers were attacked by Zulus when they drove their covered wagons across the tribe's land. The newlyweds survived, but the young woman was blonde with blue eyes, and the natives thought that meant she had special powers, so they took her prisoner. Her husband went after her and was captured by the tribe. They were going to kill him, but to save his life, the woman told the Zulus his death would bring them bad luck. They feared her enough to believe her. The Zulus took him way up into the mountains and left him. A year or so later, more trekkers came through, and there were massacres on both sides. The tribe the woman lived with was wiped out, but according to legend, she survived. One of the trekkers claimed he saw her afterwards holding her dying husband, who'd found his way back to her. He'd been shot by an arrow and was bleeding to death. After he died, she washed off his blood in a nearby river. In the trekker's account, it looked as if her own blood washed into the river along with her husband's because she turned white. She disappeared shortly after and was never seen again. Some people believe she's the white lady, still searching for her husband.

I shivered. "And she's cursed with wandering forever, never finding him?"

"Don't know. Others who've seen her say her eyes are clouded because she sees into the future and foretells omens."

"Like?" I prompted him, owl-eyed.

"Like loss, change, death."

I froze. She had looked right at me.

"Now you see, I've scared you, and that's exactly what I didn't want to do. Forget it, love. It's just an old wives' tale. Besides, you've already had a lot of change in your life."

"So, let's change the subject," I said, wrapping my arms around myself against the finger of ice creeping up my back. "A toast," I picked up my glass, "May the only spirits in our life be truth, passion and love."

"And may you always haunt my dreams," Will said kissing my neck.

I sat up and turned to face him. "Since we're drinking to good causes, here's to Stanley, may he be named Time Magazine's Ornithologist of the Year. And," I added with a cheeky smile, "to cots, may they all have training wheels." Will snorted and then turned to stare into the fire before offering his own toast.

"To those who endure and never give up." His voice was soft and heavy now.

"To second chances," I whispered.

"And first loves," Will said pulling me into his arms once more.

Chapter 24

An Unorthodox Education

I half-woke in the morning with my cheek against the furry softness of Will's chest. Something was tickling my nose, and I sleepily batted at the annoying tormentor, but the tickling persisted. Eyes closed, I reached up to grab whatever it was.

"Ouch!" a deep voice yelped.

Male voice, unfamiliar mattress, strangely soft and prickly pillow - a mental alarm sounded, and I came up and off the bed like a stone out of a slingshot, landing elbow first in the middle of Will's chest.

"Ooomph!" Will's breath exploded as he also shot upright knocking his head against one of the protruding carved lions in the headboard. Rubbing both the top of his head and his chest, he opened one eye and glared at me questioningly. My hand flew to my mouth. "I'm hoping you have some alternative techniques for waking me up," he said.

"I'll work on it," I smiled.

"Get over here," Will held up an admonishing finger, "carefully."

I did my best to look contrite, but failed miserably. "Poor thing. I suppose you'll expect breakfast in bed now," I said gently kissing the red spot on his chest.

"Well, I am feeling mighty hungry, but it's not food that's on my mind." That said, I was pulled beneath him before I could blink and lost in a tangle of legs and kisses. I remember the call of a bird, the scratch of Will's beard and the feel of him inside me. Beyond that, I had no sense of time passing.

The sun was just beginning to peek over the skylight above us as I awoke for the second time. I was lying on my stomach beside Will, the blanket at my waist. Will was asleep on his back, one arm flung across his eyes and one hand on my thigh. Slowly and gently I rose on one arm, and pulling my hair to the side, placed tiny kisses from his shoulder down to his stomach. I was about to retrace the path and head for his mouth when a sleepy voice interrupted my journey.

"You're a quick study."

Chapter 25

Silent World

We ravenously devoured a noon breakfast under the thatched roof of the porch while a sudden rain storm drenched the valley below. A rainbow drew itself across the sky casting pink hues where it touched the sides of the valley. The clouds cleared as quickly as they had appeared, and we raced down the small trail joking about finding the pot of gold at the rainbow's end. The hued arch stayed ahead of us, enticing us closer and closer to the valley floor through the freshly washed plants and rain studded diamond spider webs.

Our laughter and words came to an abrupt stop as we negotiated a sharp jog in the trail and found ourselves standing on a small precipice where the hills released themselves into the valley. It was as if the carpet of green grass below us had been pulled up and laid at our feet. The verdant lushness poured across the open field and laid itself against the blue of the horizon. To our left, a small, smooth cliff jutted out like an ancient guardian gazing over the valley. We climbed up to perch on it like two stone sentinels waiting for time to reshape the hills. It was after the sunlight had moved against the rock wall beside us, that we were both startled by a small "clink." A chunk of rock had fallen leaving a small cache in the cliff face. Something glinted from inside. Will scooted over and peered cautiously into the dark hole before reaching inside and pulling out a small stone.

"Whoo," he breathed, bouncing the object in his open palm, and then dropping it. Curious, I moved over and gave the stone a quick poke.

"Wow, that's cold," I said, still feeling the iciness in my fingertip. Will looked at me and frowned, then tentatively touched the stone again.

"Barmy. Thought it was too hot to handle." He picked it up and held it out to me like an offering in his open palm. The oblong stone, wider at one end, was about two inches long. When Will brushed it off, we could see that someone had carved what looked like the letter "L" with rounded ends into one side of the stone. The other side was carved with a dark circle in a diamond and what looked like butterfly wings on each side. I could imagine ancient hands polishing the smooth pale surface. Will put it in my pocket, and I forgot about it until much later. When the sun began to cook our skin, Will reached for my hand and led me back to the coolness of our cottage.

What was left of the afternoon, we spent in a small swing on the kitchen porch, my head on Will's shoulder. I ran my hand across his chest.

"Hmmm," I sighed lethargically.

"What?" the breath of his question was soft against my hair.

"It's strange," I whispered, "this being able to touch someone whenever you want." Even after all that had happened between us, some vestige of my safety net threw itself out, and I sat up and frowned. Will gently pulled my head back onto his chest.

"Whenever you want," he said.

When the sun sank toward the end of the valley, and the cooling plants released their heady scents, we built another fire and roasted chunks of cheese over it, feeding them to each other on crusty pieces of French bread. We were silent then, both drawn into our own thoughts as we watched the fire's flames lower themselves into the burning embers. We had taken the leap, given in to the pull of the current and gone around the bend. Will suddenly shook himself and stretched, then stood reaching for my hand. He led me to the bedroom where he turned on the water in the large tub and opened the sliding wall to the moon and the purple twilight of the valley. I disappeared into the kitchen and returned with candles and matches. With the light off, the tiny flickering flames turned the room into our own diamond-studded, spider web. Will took hold of my blouse and pulled me within inches of him, then slowly slid each button free, all the while looking into my eyes. Free of our clothes, we sank into the exhaustion sapping warmth of the water, and nestled into each other like threads in a strand of yarn.

Years later, whenever I looked back on the times Will and I spent together, this single day would remain foremost in my mind. But it wasn't the making love and sleeping until noon, the small lush valley that took our breath away or the cozy little cottage. What locked it into my memory were the quiet intimacy of the hours, the need to do nothing but be together and the satiating completeness of being with him. Will had said we would find "our world." I knew now that it was not a place, but instead a fusion of souls and a passion of minds.

Chapter 26

I Thought I Could See Forever

The phone message light was blinking when we arrived back at our apartment the following Sunday night. Besides a few calls from well-wishing friends, there was a message from Todd letting me know about a department head meeting at 8:00 the next morning and a call from the hospital. An amputation was scheduled for the following day, and the physician slated to do the surgery was down with the flu; could Will fill in? The recorder clicked off, and we both stood, staring at the machine.

Will leaned toward the couch, gathered up the afghan, and held out his hand. Lacing his fingers through mine and putting our hands against his chest, he led me out the door and up the stairs to the rooftop. The air was crisp, and the deep purple outline of the distant mountains against the midnight blue of the star-studded sky above, were mirrored by the lights of Johannesburg spread below us like a celestial carpet. We curled up in the blanket against a warm vent.

"How did you know about the rooftop?" I asked.

"I wanted my wife to have a home with a view."

I nestled into him. "Promise me we can live right here, just like this, forever."

"If I thought it would keep you away from any more rallies, I might consider it," he said, kissing the top of my head.

"Only to keep me away from rallies?"

"You'd have to stay right here, sort of like a side car," he warned.

It wasn't until the following week that I realized I'd misplaced my favorite jacket and assumed I'd left it at the little thatched cottage. I never thought to check the roof.

Chapter 27

Come Home to Me

The relentlessness of Will's hospital schedule meant he often returned home shortly before dawn, gently sliding into bed beside me and pulling me against him before falling instantly into a deep sleep. The comfort of Will's arms and the warmth of his body always called me from my dreams, but I didn't mind waking. I loved the sleep that came back to me in the early morning hours. It felt stolen, as if I had challenged the night with my vigilance and won back a hidden pocket of time from its folds of darkness.

As a medical student, Will was often scheduled for surgical rounds in the outlying hospitals. But as the months passed, he sometimes visited the sick in the ghettos and outer villages on his time off. In the beginning it was only for a day or two every month or so. He was drawn to the people who had such need for the doctors they rarely saw. The trips increased until he was gone at least once a month and then twice a month for several days. Except for leaving me, he looked forward to working in the outer clinics. He returned home exhausted and, as the weeks passed, troubled more and more over the villagers' struggles. There was never enough time, enough medicine or enough money.

Knowing Will was returning, I hurried home one evening after a late meeting to find the lights on and the apartment empty. On a hunch, I climbed the stairs to the roof. Will stood against the far wall lost in thought. I hesitated, puzzled by his faraway look.

"It was lonely – coming home to the empty apartment," he said without turning.

"I had the same feeling when I walked in and didn't find you." He smiled and reached into his jacket pocket, "For you." He handed me a small box. Resting on white satin, and encased in silver, was the strangely marked stone Will had found in the cliff near the cottage.

"Where did you find this?" I asked, delighted to see the stone again. "My pocket had a hole in it, and I thought I'd lost it. I looked all over the cottage before we left."

"Well, it must have wanted to come home with you. I found it in the car."

"That's strange. I wasn't in the car until after I noticed it missing."

"Turn around, love, and I'll latch it for you." The stone was warm against my skin, and beneath it I could feel the beat of my heart.

"Thank you. It's beautiful." I put my hand over the stone and frowned.

"What?" Will asked.

"I don't know," I laughed. "It just feels vaguely familiar, like I've worn it before." I shook my head and smiled. "Silly." I rarely took the necklace off after that.

A sudden gust of wind whipped across the roof top and Will pulled me into his arms, resting his cheek against my forehead.

"Want to talk about it?" I asked.

After a long moment, Will drew in a deep breath, "A man lost his wife and son from fever at hospital today. I was too late to do anything."

"I'm so sorry, Will." I pulled him more tightly against me.

"They were dehydrated. The boy was skin and bones, and his

mother was…I could have helped, Jackie, if I'd only known – at least I could have made them more comfortable."

"And no one sent for a doctor?"

"Maybe, but they rarely show up, and the people have no way to get to a clinic or hospital other than on foot. Which is why," Will grimaced, "they usually trust their own sangomas." At my confused look he added, "Some call them witch doctors. The natives trust them more than the hospital doctors. It's only when their money runs out, that they come to us. By then, it's almost always too late."

"Can't some doctors go to the villages?"

"They've got more patients than they can handle at the clinics. Hundreds, sometimes thousands, come every day. And, we need to see them where we're set up for testing and surgery."

"But you go."

"I can at least treat some of the infections before they become life threatening - immunize them, teach them prevention." Will huffed. "They rarely listen. Even when they do, the water's filthy, infested with mosquitoes, and they live in such cramped quarters that disease spreads like fire."

"You have taught them, Will. You've saved lives."

"And I'm glad for it, but it's not bloody enough by a far shot. Most of their time is spent figuring out how to feed themselves. Building a fire and boiling water is just one more thing to do." Will closed his eyes and rested his cheek against my hair. "If I didn't have you to come back to… " The remark startled me and raised goose bumps on the back of my neck.

"Then what? You wouldn't come back? You'd stay in the field?"

Will tipped my chin up. "Jackie love, you're what draws me

back. I find myself again with you."

"Come with me then," I said, and led him across the roof, down the stairs and to our bed.

Chapter 28

Without You Days

Will finished his residency and accepted a position at the Johannesburg hospital as a surgeon, specializing in tropical diseases and medicine. At first, the new job kept him home, but his desire to work in the ghettos and bush villages, became more and more important to him. Now that he was free to arrange his schedule, he was often gone one week a month, and within six months, he was spending closer to two weeks a month traveling to the poorer rural areas, often sending, or bringing back the sickest to the clinics and hospitals.

My own travels increased, too. At first, I flew to New York every two months, but my forays into the political and cultural struggles of South Africa meant my input was often needed at strategy meetings at headquarters. In Johannesburg, the city tensed like a panther waiting to strike. Street cars were filled on payday with Black gang members called tsotsis, who threatened the workers returning home, demanding their paychecks. I wrote about Black activists like Stephen Biko, who rallied his countrymen by inspiring their pride. I interviewed ANC leaders as their movement lost and gained power. I turned in uncountable human interest pieces on families ravaged by hunger and kept in the ghettos by apartheid laws. Whenever they would talk to me, I interviewed angry protestors and injured marchers. I had never worked as hard or cared so much about other people's suffering. And through it all, I watched the creeping flow of the ghetto into the city.

My stateside apartment became my home away from home. I missed Will terribly, and my New York shelves filled with African books, carved giraffes and cheetahs, stunning handmade gifts Will brought back from the natives and dozens of photos of Will and the country I now also loved. At first, whenever we were apart, Will and I called each other every night when it was possible, but more and more often, Will was not near a phone or his schedule and the time difference kept us from staying in touch. The lonely chill of the apartment seeped into my bones and my mind, and I often stayed late at the office writing and researching anything and everything about Africa as it thrust itself through the apartheid turmoil. The truth was, it made me feel closer to Will.

Perhaps to fill the void in his own life, Roy often work into the evenings. He would sometimes wander into my office to talk or to ask me to join him for dinner. We were a sad pair, both trying to keep the conversation light and on a topic other than the loneliness we both felt. One night, walking back from a late dinner, Roy tucked my arm through his.

"This is a fine mess we've gotten ourselves into," he said.

"My mother used to say 'This, too, shall pass'. It always does, you know." His eyes rested on me for a moment.

"How's Will handling the time apart?"

"Pining away for me, no doubt." The remark was meant lightly, but it sounded wistful, and I quickly added, "His work is making a difference for a lot of people."

"And how are you doing?"

"I'm doing just… peachy keen." Roy arched the eyebrow he saved for when he was making a point. "I am. I may be a little lonesome at times, but I'll be in Johannesb… home and see Will in a couple of days. Oh shoot," I grumbled, remembering that Will had called that morning to let me know he would be spending the rest of the week in the field. "No, I guess I won't. There's an outbreak of malaria, and Will and his team are setting up another immunization in the north." I shrugged, trying to hide my disappointment.

"Why don't you spend the extra time here? No point in going back to another empty apartment. Besides, I could use your help on a half hour segment we're doing on Biko. His Black is Beautiful campaign is gaining momentum."

"Yeah," I laughed. "Thanks for the offer of extra work, but I have a couple of interviews set up that I'm not going to miss. And besides, you know as well as I do that there's a league meeting with Biko at the end of the week. They're threatening to arrest him. I want to be there. They just won't let up on him." Roy rubbed the back of his neck and squinted at me. "I'll be fine," I said with some exasperation. "Anyway, you know me, the epitome of shrewd caution." Before he could say anything else, I pointed to the doorway ahead. "Home sweet home. Thanks for an enjoyable evening."

"Jackie," Roy was determined to have the last word, "Cover the protests; don't join them. If you have an interview with anyone you consider... no make that anyone I'd consider, dangerous, take someone with you. And spend as much time as you can with Biko, preferably not in a jail cell, then get your trouble-magnet, shrewd self safely back here."

Chapter 29

The Other Side of the Dark Continent

The hollowness of the Johannesburg apartment intensified my jet-lag. I couldn't sleep more than a couple of hours at a time. I tried cleaning, reading and watching television, but nothing filled the void Will's absence left. Finally, around noon on Sunday, I headed to the office. The building was deserted except for a janitor who left shortly after I arrived. The air conditioning was off, and the stale air and silence pressed into me. I turned on the secretary's radio to some soft background music and sat down listlessly at my desk. Might as well do some checking on my sources. I made a couple of calls before reaching someone whose cousin knew someone who might help. It was always the same – everyone guarded, everyone suspicious.

I didn't realize how much time had passed until my stomach growled, and I looked up at the darkened windows. The loneliness I had been fighting since I'd arrived hit me like the humid weight of a New York summer. Eager to hear voices and see people, I saved my files and quickly packed my briefcase. Just as I reached to turn off the office light, the phone rang. I all but ran back to my desk to pick it up, hoping it was Will and that he would not hang up before I could answer.

"Jackie? What are doing at the office at this hour?" It was Roy.

My throat closed, and I could feel a wallop of self-pity rising. I had to swallow twice before I could answer.

"Just catching up on a few things." I hoped my voice didn't give away the crushing disappointment I felt.

"You all right?" Roy could tune into my feelings like a fan to a favorite radio station.

"Sure... great." *Change the subject.* "I could ask you the same question. It must be what," I said glancing at my watch, "six in the morning in New York?"

"I'm here in Johannesburg. The quarterly reports are due out this week. I was just going to leave you a message to let you know we're doing a reorg. I wanted you to know about it before the inevitable rumors start."

"Problems?" I asked.

"Not for you. Will you be in the office much longer?"

"I was just leaving."

"Why don't I head down and meet you. Fifteen minutes okay?"

I sighed inwardly not wanting to stay in the emptiness any longer. But then a little company might be good. Fifteen minutes later I heard a key turn in the door down the hall, and then Roy was leaning against my office door with a sweet boyish smile he rarely used during business hours. He didn't say a word, just walked over to me and took my jacket off the back of my chair.

"It's Sunday, Jackie. We're getting out of here." Right on cue, my stomach growled again. I grinned and shook my head, embarrassed. Roy raised an eyebrow. "So you can still smile."

"Oh... I used to smile all the time, but then they cut back on paper clips."

"Maybe you're trying too hard to hold things together." I rolled my eyes, but let the remark go. He put a hand lightly at my waist as we headed toward the door.

"Thin," he grumbled. "Why do I get the feeling that the only time you eat is when I feed you?"

"This must be about the reorg. You're just fattening me up for the kill."

"No work talk," he insisted. "Besides, I'm not letting anything happen to you." He flipped off the light and closed the door behind us.

And there wasn't a mention of work almost all the way through dinner. While we ate, Roy told me about a weekend trip water skiing with friends, an opera that had nearly moved him to tears and a neighbor's son, a "cute kid named Harry," who'd kicked a ball through his front door window. Harry's mother watched from across the street as the boy mumbled a tearful apology on Roy's porch. Roy assured Harry that he had already planned to replace the window because it had a crack in it. Afterwards, they sat on the front porch eating vanilla ice cream and discussing the New York Jets.

I told Roy about my afternoon giving shots, about Masuwra, and finally, the evening I still remembered with dread, when the black mambo struck. Roy listened, smiling occasionally and shuddering once or twice. Half way through the snake escapade, I sensed his mood change. I tried making light of it, but it was too late.

"And that's what your life is like when you're with him?"

"Sometimes, life just happens. I can't control everything. I wouldn't want to." Was I defending myself or Will?

"So when he's not exposing you to something life threatening, he's just not there."

"That's not fair," I shot back in Will's defense. And I was irritated that Roy kept referring to Will as "he."

"When are you going to see him again?"

"Soon… next week...He's saving lives," I added, resenting that I sounded like I was making excuses for him. What had been a relaxing, fun evening, had just turned sour. "I think I'd better get home now." Roy put his napkin on the table and signaled the waiter.

Outside, the night air was cold. We walked in silence for a block before Roy pulled my hand around his arm. He looked at me without apology, and then huffed with exasperation.

"Late nights at the office, empty apartments. Not good, Jackie"

"I have a job that fascinates me, a husband I love who loves me, and apartments on two different continents. Who could ask for more?" Why did the question feel hollow?

"Admit it, Jackie, you're married to a husband who's usually missing in action."

"Roy," I stopped and held up a warning hand meaning to lay it against his chest to end his words, but I stopped before touching him. "Don't push it."

Roy looked up at the stars and shook his head. "No." The word was only a breath. "You're not being honest with yourself."

I turned and started walking. "You're getting personal. This is personal."

"I mean to be," he said catching up to me. "You're hopping from one country to another hoping that in between jobs you'll actually get to spend time with the man you're married to."

"You gave me this 'hopping from one country to another' job," I accused him.

"All right then, let's take a different tact. Why haven't I seen you relax and laugh like you did tonight since… " he pulled his shoulders up around his ears, "I don't know when? Why are there dark circles under your eyes? Why have you lost so much weight?" He stopped me with a hand on my arm. "Why haven't you asked yourself these questions, Jackie?"

"Is my work not up to speed? Are my assignments late? Am I not always where the news is happening?" I made quotation marks in the air. "Those are the questions I ask myself."

"Wrong questions."

"You're my boss. I don't need to be psychoanalyzed." I wanted him to stop.

"Don't you ever think about going after what you want?" He stuck his hands in his pockets and looked at me.

"What are you talking about? I have gone after what I want." I scowled.

"Have you?"

"Of course, I just told you."

"You told me what you have." His words infuriated me.

"Dog with a bone," I mumbled to myself.

"We're a special kind of people, Jackie."

"Really?" I said, exasperated. "And what kind of people is that?"

"We're people who dream big – people who know what they want. We find it and grab it, no matter how tough. We're Americans, Jackie." His steely gaze held mine. "I won't say anything else now, but don't expect me to keep silent forever."

"I can walk myself home," I said heading toward my apartment, and I didn't look back.

Chapter 30

The Bubble Bursts

Will called me the next morning at work.

"Jackie. You're there. I didn't think I'd catch you – only have a minute.

"Where are you?"

"I'm still at hospital. The black students marched – kids, Jackie!" he said, his voice heavy with frustration. "Their bodies are lined up on the morgue floor… most killed by bullets… some shot in the back. It's bloody awful." His voice was like crystal at the cracking point, ready to explode, and I knew he was running his hand through his hair. "Nothing's left of the Diepkloof clinic but a shell, and one of the hospital buses from Orlando was burned out. The overflow of injured are coming here. I only left the operating theatre to call you." There was a moment of silence and then Will's voice, away from the phone - "No, get her ready for surgery, and get a tourniquet on that boy's arm. I'll be right there." There was scuffling and the sound of wheels rolling quickly into the distance. "I've got to go, honey. I'll call you as soon as I can."

"You won't have to," I said, my words tumbling over each other. "I'm just leaving…." but the line was dead.

I'd known that I'd be heading to Soweto. It was all over the news. The new education law to teach in Afrikaans had ignited a long smoldering and near explosive fire of resistance. The resentment of using a believed oppressor's language for learning was outrageous to the Blacks. What had started that morning as a peaceful student protest march had turned violent. I was gathering what I needed when Roy walked into my office, hands in his pockets, and confirmed that I was covering the story.

"Already getting a few things together," I said, scanning my desk to make sure I wasn't forgetting anything. I stuffed camera, recorder, papers and pencils in the traveling bag I kept at the office for last minute assignments. I glanced up after a minute, realizing Roy hadn't moved, had just been standing there watching me gather my things.

Problem?" I asked.

He looked like he was, about to say something, then changed his mind. "No." He turned to leave, but stopped at the door. "Keep the cameramen in sight." He nodded two or three times and walked out, hands still in his pockets.

We arrived in Soweto within the hour. John and Sam, the camera crew, set up and began filming and snapping pictures. The streets were littered with bloodied bodies. Parents were searching frantically, screaming the names of their children. Those that could, walked or dragged themselves to shelter. There was gunshot and screaming in the distance. The dirt streets, where the protestors had marched, were littered with charred wood and broken glass. I watched a group of small children, their laughter and screams as hypnotic as the cadence of a catchy tune, rock the scorched remains of a car. Too young to understand the depth of the devastation, they played with the burnt remnants of their world like toys. Sam panned to the prone body of a man whose back was a bloody mess of seeping whip marks. The man curled into himself and rolled towards the camera, moaning. His cheek looked crushed and, stripped from the waist down, I could see burns on his genitals. Sam stopped filming. There'd been no mercy from the apartheid regime police despite the protestors' lack of weapons. Further down the street by an empty field of weeds, a young boy was sitting in the dirt. Sprawled next to him was the dead body of a girl. He turned slowly when I approached him, and then jerked slightly at the sight of me – a white woman holding a recorder, followed by two white men with television cameras.

"They shot my sister. We din' have no warnin'. They jes' swat us down like flies," he said and started to sob.

The stories were the same everywhere. It was only when the police started firing randomly at the protestors that the students picked up rocks and pieces of wood and threw them at the police. Tear gas was released, and the protestors ran. I remembered Will's words that some of the children had gunshot wounds in their backs. We couldn't get near one area where the furious students outnumbered the police. They barricaded their hard won plot of ground and were destroying anything and everything, especially if it looked like government property.

The students' intent to march peacefully had not stopped the police from violence. But when I spoke to the victims, I could see they were beaten, but not broken. There was defiance and hope in the angry faces. Now it begins, I thought. The Blacks have reached their limit. They'll fight violence with violence, and it will be a long, vicious battle.

I signaled John and Sam to follow me through a small alley to shortcut our way towards the gunshots and took off first. Crouching behind the corner of a building, we watched a car driven by two young Blacks try to run down police. Shots rang out and the car swerved and crashed into a building. The bloodied head of the driver slid down his window. I was suddenly knocked backwards when two older, colored boys ducked into the alley. They spun around and saw us. The one in front lunged at me, but John threw his shoulder into the boy's stomach, throwing the youth sideways, and throwing himself, head first, into the wall. The other boy grabbed at Sam's camera. We fought them off as best we could, while John and Sam tried to cover me. I heard the smack of a fist against flesh and saw John's head whip sideways.

"We're news people," I yelled. "We know what happened to you. We don't like it. We'll report the truth."

I must have yelled it a half dozen ways while they continued to shove and taunt us before the boy in front threw up a hand and told his friend to stop. They eventually listened and then told us their stories, but wouldn't give us their names. It was just as well because their stories belonged to the colored community. That morning, the boys left school and joined in the peaceful march, but when the bullets tore through the bodies of their classmates, an incredulous anger had driven them to retaliate. Helpless against the gunshot, they grabbed whatever they could and fought back. I noticed then that blood was oozing from a small puncture wound in the smaller boy's arm. There were more gunshots on the street. The larger youth grabbed John's camera, and the two boys disappeared down a turn in the alley.

The side of John's face was swelling into a purplish mound, and he had to keep pressure on a cut near his ear to stop the bleeding. Sam had escaped with a few scrapes, and somehow I'd managed to sprain an ankle and had to use Sam as a crutch on the way back to our news van. Just as we caught sight of it, a rowdy group of young Blacks came down the road from our left. We ducked behind a building, but one of them saw us and yelled to the others to follow him. They had bats and were clearly riled, strutting and boasting about their conquests. I was scared, and I could tell Sam and John were, too. The boys stopped in front of us and stared for a moment before the one in front sneered.

"Look at these white cowards. They crouchin' like scared kittens." The other boys laughed. "Maybe we should teach 'em a lesson 'bout who's in charge heah."

"Wait!" It was John's voice. He stood, still holding his bleeding wound. "Don't do this."

"You scared?" the boy taunted, slapping John on the arm with his club.

"We came to help."

"Yeah, right. No white man gonna help no niggah." The boy pushed John, and he hit the side of the building. The impact stunned him, but he shook his head and turned back to face the angry boys.

"We came here willingly from the television news – put ourselves at risk. We're not armed." John moved his hand slowly toward me gesturing at my recorder, "You can tell your story." The boy paused and frowned. "It's true," John told him. "Why else would we come here where you control the streets?" Sam and I slowly stood up, watching the boy as he checked out our equipment. My knees were shaking and my mouth went dry. Sam grasped my arm and held onto me. I could feel the tremor in his sweaty hand.

"Why you lisnin' to them?" a heavy set boy behind the first asked. He pushed through and smiled at me in a way that made my stomach churn. His hand was in the collar of my blouse before I knew it. He pulled, and the top button flew off pinging in the dirt. His eyes narrowed as he caught sight of the necklace Will had given me. We both reached for it at the same time, and his meaty hand wrapped around mine. He squeezed, sneering at me. The pressure increased until I thought my bones would crack. Sam shouted at the boy to stop, but one of the others shoved him away. The crushing pain was so intense I could feel sweat forming on my forehead. Then suddenly, the pain subsided. I thought the boy had let go, but when I tried to release the necklace, I realized his hand was still wrapped around mine, and that he was staring at our clasped fists with a stunned look. It was then I felt the stone vibrate and begin to heat just before the boy screamed and snatched his hand back. He stood there, open-mouthed, gaping at the series of raised welts on his palm. I had felt the searing heat, but the stone had burned him.

"You some crazy bitch," he spat, eyeing me with anger and fear. He reached back with his other hand meaning to slap my face.

"That's not the message you want to send," a voice yelled from across the road. "Whatever you do next is what will be on the news tonight. Your actions will be watched by the whites and the Blacks."

"Who you?" the first boy yelled, squinting into the sun to where Roy stood, camera in hand, across the road.

"I run the television station and decide what news airs," Roy told him, sounding more at ease than I thought he felt. His usual coat and tie were gone, and his shirt was open at the neck. "This is an opportunity to say what you want and have thousands of people hear it."

"How we know he not lyin'? The heavy set boy sneered.

Roy pointed to the news van a few yards away. The station's logo was in large blue letters on the side. The boys stared at it and hesitated.

"Now say what you have to say, and we'll report it."

"Is some kinda trick," the heavy boy said.

The first boy shoved him away, "I got something to say." I turned on the recorder, my shaking finger slipping twice, and handed him the microphone. He took it and then turned to face the camera Roy was pointing at him. "This is James Wakeman, and I got somethin to say. Aint nobody gonna keep us down. Nobody…"

While the boy spoke, Roy came slowly across the road, continuing to film. When he reached us, he took the recorder from me and gave it to Sam, then nodded for John to get me to his car. When the filming was finished, I heard Roy tell James he could call the station and ask for him if he had anything else to say. Roy handed him a business card, while Sam reattached the microphone to the small recorder.

"You jes make sure that all gets on the televishun," James called after Roy and Sam as they headed towards the van.

Sam took John to Baragwanath Hospital, while Roy and I followed in his car. We drove in silence for what seemed like an hour before he stopped and pulled over beside the road. Roy sat with his hands on the wheel, the engine's idling the only sound between us. He turned slowly and looked at me. For a second, I thought he was angry, and that made me angry. I was just doing my job. Well, maybe a little more than my job. Okay, that maybe wasn't the smartest thing I'd ever done. But before I decided to worry if I had a job, Roy shook his head and let out a whoosh of air filled with exasperation and relief. I started to shake deep inside, and the percussion of it passed through me and out like airwaves from a sonic boom. I tried to think of something to say that would be remotely appropriate, but I couldn't think of a thing. I just sat there, my entire body trembling. Roy reached into the back seat for his jacket and put it around my shoulders and then pulled back onto the road.

The hospital was jammed with people, half of them injured, and the other half wandering around, their stunned, horrified expressions reflecting the violence they'd been through that day. And while Baragwanath might be a hospital where much needed medical help was available, we were still white people in a city full of colonial hatred, so I told Roy we should probably drive around to the back entrance. We parked in the safest place we could find and took what equipment we had with us. We headed to the doctors' lounge. I stopped a passing nurse and told her I was Dr. Kincaid's wife. She told me Will was in surgery, and not expected out soon. The nurse gave John a quick once over and promised to return. An hour later she showed up with a harried looking doctor and a tray of medical equipment. Roy left to call the office while John had his face stitched and the nurse packed ice and put a brace on my ankle until I could have it looked at properly. The doctor and nurse left immediately for what was going to be one long shift. There was no telling when Will would be free, so we decided to find Roy and head back. We grabbed our equipment and headed, in my case hobbled, to the door just as it swung open. It was Roy. He told Sam and John that he would see to it that I got back. Roy decided I should have a wheelchair and was about to go looking for one when the door opened again and an exhausted looking Will pushed through. He was about to pull off his green operating cap when he spotted me and started.

"Jackie ... ?"

"Your wife needs some attention." Roy spoke softly. The statement wasn't lost on Will. I shook a hand in the air and explained it was only a sprain. I was going to add that our cameraman had by far gotten the worst of the situation, and then thought better of it. All I needed was another lecture on getting myself into precarious situations.

Will was kneeling in front of me in an instant, staring into my eyes with a "not again" sort of concern. While he examined my ankle, I watched the concern turn into anger. "Well, it's not broken, but you've likely some damage to the ligament." I had the feeling the last words were more for Roy's benefit than for mine. Will stood and faced Roy, "I'm surprised to see you out in the field. Don't you usually manage these things from your office?" The words were clipped, and Roy straightened slightly.

"When I'm needed, I show up." It wasn't so much a statement of fact as an accusation.

"I'm not the one putting her in harm's way." Will's voice was as cold as steel on ice.

"I'm right here in first person," I broke in, miffed with the two of them. "And I've heard all I'm going to. It's bad enough that I put myself in harm's way, but having you two try to blame each other really takes the cake." They turned at my words and scowled at me. The twin looks made me feel like I'd volunteered to perform Swan Lake in the middle of a mine field. I shook my head, agitated, "In case either of you haven't noticed, I'm fine."

A nurse stuck her head and shoulders through the door, spotted Will, and told him his patient had been prepped. Will nodded, and then knelt again in front of me. He took my face in his hands. "You go home, put your foot up and stay put. I'll be there as soon as I can." And then, looking into my eyes, he gently kissed me and tucked a strand of hair behind my ear. As he left for his operating theatre, he glanced pointedly at Roy. "Jackie won't be at work tomorrow."

Roy rubbed a hand across the back of his neck and sat down beside me, resting his elbows on his knees.

"Why *are* you here?" I asked.

"We got more reports on the violence, and I was concerned about you – about the team," he finished.

I looked at him and shivered. "Thank God you showed up. Thank you, Roy." After a moment, I laid a hand on his arm. "It's maybe not a good policy to hire people you worry about."

"It's a full time job with you." He looked at my ankle and huffed.

"Well, I could research African eating habits – have my own cooking show."

"Exploding soufflés and flaming dish towels… No, I don't think so." Roy grimaced. "C'mon, let's get you home." He reached an arm around my waist and pulled me up. "You can't get into too much trouble there," he mumbled.

"I heard that," I said.

Over 360 Blacks were killed in the Soweto protests that day. Nearly 20,000 students had marched and set into motion a surging rage - a storm of such frenzied fury - that it would eventually blast apart the chains of bondage and leave a stain of blood across the nation. In the days following the Soweto uprising, the protests spread to the cities. Prime Minister Vorster's intention was clear. The government would not be intimidated – stop the protests and violence or law and order would be restored at any cost. Although the government sent in armed vehicles, it was still several days before the standoff in Soweto ended. The protests and speeches were banned, but Biko ignored the edict. Eventually, he was arrested and brutally beaten to death by the police. But instead of a warning to the Blacks, it only served to increase the building tension and growing unrest. The black schools were closed, giving a quarter of a million students plenty of time to continue the uprising they'd started. The relentless marches and riots became an everyday occurrence. It was a long, bloody time until the South African apartheid regime finally collapsed, and when it did, so did its racist colonial state.

Chapter 31

Miss You Nights

I fell into a restless sleep and woke in the late dusk of evening. Wrapped in an afghan, I limped up the stairs to the roof where the stars umbrellaed above me and pirouetted westward to slip behind the mountains. For a moment, it seemed as though the night sky parted, and I could see into the operating theater where Will was bent over a patient. I felt the intenseness of his eyes peering through his dark-framed glasses, and tasted the acrid smell of the blood that stained his surgery smock. A sudden surge of warm air gently pushed my mind back to the empty rooftop. Had this breeze also blown through the windows and long hallways of Baragwanath Hospital and now come to haunt me? It blew like fingertips through my hair, leaving goose bumps on the back of my neck.

Two nights later, the door opened, and I looked up to see Will. His face was etched with exhaustion, and his clothes were as crumpled and tired looking as he was. I opened my arms and reached for him. Dropping his bag, he took three giant steps and knelt beside the couch, pulling me against him. His kiss was hard and salty.

"Missed you," he said pushing my hair back to look into my eyes. He kissed me again, more gently this time, but with the same intenseness. As tired as he was, he ran a hand down my leg and removed my shoe to check my sprained ankle.

"It'll do," I said taking his face in my hands. I smoothed back the hair from his forehead and felt him sway a bit.

"I'm a sweaty mess, love. Come scrub my back while I take a bath?" A few minutes later, I was balancing on the rim of the tub rubbing shampoo into a creamy lather on Will's draped head. I let my hand fall to the hair on his chest, and swirled the suds in lazy circles.

"Not enough of you in my life," he mumbled from behind closed lids.

"No." I whispered.

He raised his head for a kiss and pulled me towards him. The next thing I knew, I was sitting on Will's lap, my slacks soaking wet and my sweater thirstily drinking the soapy water.

"Wha...?" I cupped a handful of water and sent it flying towards him.

"Seems to me, you're in no position to push your luck," he said, wiping some errant drips from his chin.

"Well, seeing as you're on the bottom this time, consider yourself at great disadvantage," I warned.

"How's that?" He smiled like a cat with a bowl of cream.

"I could keep you here for days, and you wouldn't be able to take off and leave me behind." The words were out of my mouth before I could stop them.

"Is that what you think – that I leave you behind when I'm at the clinics?" I grabbed the sides of the tub and tried to pull myself out, but Will threw out an arm and blocked my effort. "Is that what you think?" he repeated.

"You disappear more than you reappear these days."

"I want to be with you every moment I can."

"I guess it's a matter of priorities," I said testily. His eyes narrowed and then he pulled himself upright causing me to slide sideways and water to slosh out of the tub.

"That's not true, Jackie. I would rather be right here with you than… " At the pause, I raised my eyebrows.

"Maybe you'd rather be out there than with me, Will."

He grabbed my arms so tightly that I winced. Will ignored it and gave me a single shake. "No… no, Jackie. I was just thinking, sometimes I come home and you're gone too. We knew this would be a problem. We have to ride it out."

"Until when… forever?" I pulled away from him, hating this conversation that never seemed to have an answer.

"Most of the people I see would have no medical help if I wasn't there." He took my face in his hands and made me look at him. "And I need you to be here when I come home."

"What about when I need you? There are other doctors who could help."

"You have me."

"No, I have a job and two empty apartments. No home, except when you're here."

"And wherever you are is home for me, too," he answered.

"Don't do that. Don't use words to make up for your absences." I pushed against his arms and grabbed the sides of the tub. "Please! Let me up."

"No. Stay and fight for once," Will said, keeping me pinned against him.

"Fight?"

"Yes. Don't run." I pulled away, but Will would have none of it. "What do you want, Jackie?"

"Fine then. I want you to be here – with me." The silence hung as damp as the air.

"I can't do that right now, Jackie."

"You mean you won't," I said.

Will let out an exasperated breath. "How willing are you to stop traveling? We've got compromises to make, love."

"Yours or mine again," I said angrily.

Will dropped his hands into the water. "You're right. We'll work on our schedules. We'll figure out more time together." The idea was great in theory, but I didn't believe for a moment that two people with jobs as time-greedy and unpredictable as ours could promise anything.

Will pulled my lips close to his and looked me in the eye. "We're not letting go of each other, Jackie. This is for always." He kissed me then, slowly caressing my mouth with his. Somewhere in the middle of the kiss I heard him mumble, "Seeing as I haven't got a calendar on me, I say we don't waste a golden opportunity," and for the moment, all was forgotten.

Removing clothing quickly in the heat of passion is hard enough, but trying to remove wet clothing while sitting in a tub on someone's lap, is like unwinding yourself from a tangled leash while your dog is in attack mode. Mini tsunamis slapped the tub, and dollops of water hit the floor. The soap made our skins slippery, but Will managed to hold me against him, and whenever the tidal waves of water moved us, we floated with them like twisted tree limbs riding through a sweeping flood. Later, with my head on Will's shoulder, and one leg draped over his in the now tepid pool, I shivered. Will leaned forward and turned on the hot water. The heat crawled luxuriously up our bodies, and moments later Will was asleep.

The long absences in our marriage were taking a toll, and I resented the amount of time we were away from each other. I could handle the hours and even the unexpected absences as long as I knew that within a short period of time we would be together again. It was the days and weeks we spent apart that frightened me. Half the time we couldn't even reach each other by phone. I shivered again, but this time the water was still hot.

Chapter 32

When and Where

The heat of the coffee mug warmed my cold hands as I sat at the kitchen table lost in thought the next morning.

"Penny for your thoughts?" Will said, leaning against the kitchen door where he had been watching me. When I didn't answer, he poured himself a cup of coffee and sat across from me, a small grin playing at his lips. "I'm racking my brain trying to think if I did something last night that upset you, but I thought everything went swimmingly." When I didn't smile, he waited.

"I've been sitting here thinking about how much time we're apart," I said. "It's more every month."

"The time we do have together is better than what most couples have." Will brushed a crumb from the table. "It won't always be this way."

"You can't promise that. Your job means too much to you."

"Not as much as we do," he said.

"I know we planned to make it through this – but it's harder than I imagined, and . . . " Will frowned. "And I'm not sure you won't - just not come back someday." The silence was filled with the fear we both felt.

"Are you asking me to give up working in the clinic?"

"No. You'd only be unhappy, and I couldn't stand that." I got up and dumped the rest of my coffee in the sink. "I'm going with you."

"Where?" he asked, startled.

"To the villages and the clinics. I'll talk to Roy. The network needs a story on what apartheid is doing to the people who don't know where their next meal is coming from. Maybe I can help your work and at the same time be with you – at least for a while."

"You mean you intend to interview the ghetto people? No. Most of them don't speak English well enough to answer your questions, and those that do will be suspicious of your motives. It's...no ... it's too dangerous, and I don't have time to keep an eye on you."

"You don't have time to keep an eye on me? Well, what do you think I'm doing while you're in some, God knows where, village or clinic? Who do you think watches over me then?"

Will stood and put his coffee mug on the counter. "You don't understand the danger. You think they're going to talk to you, tell you their problems?" His voice rose an impressive octave. "Bloody hell, Jackie. They don't even trust you. You're white. You're the enemy. And one thing's for sure, they don't want the enemy in their neighborhoods, and I don't want my wife in danger."

"Fine, then you do whatever you need to, and I'll take care of myself." If Will could help the people, so could I, and I'd do it alone if necessary. "At least I'm willing to rearrange my life in order to spend more time with you, which you by the way, don't seem to care about."

Will pressed his lips together looking like he was about to explode. "You know as well as I do that I'd spend half my time worrying about you and the other half patching you up." After a moment, he took a softer tone. "Jackie, I'd take you with me in a minute, want you with me. I wish I could, but you ... " he tapped my nose with his finger, "won't do what you're told."

"What I'm told," I grumbled. My mind flashed to my sixth grade classroom when the teacher had slapped the back of my hand with his ruler for passing a note between two friends. "Starting a family, giving up my job and staying home waiting for you to show up whenever the whim hits you, are not going to fix this problem." Will pulled me into his arms, and I could feel the fast beat of his heart, strong and unyielding. "I'm going to get that story, and I don't need a babysitter," I mumbled into his chest. As I spoke the words, I knew there was another reason the story was important to me. The racial discrimination that separated the African peoples was also separating Will and me.

Book Three

Chapter 1

Back Then – Baragwanath Hospital

Will

I watched the mirage-like heat waves snake up from the highway ahead, and figured I could sterilize my surgical instruments on the metal roof of the truck. My shirt was plastered to the seat, so I leaned forward and let the breeze from the open window cool my back, and then rolled my head to release the ache in my neck. It wasn't much help. My schedule had been grueling, and the brain-numbing bounce from the ruts in the road was making me drowsy – that and the engine's drone. Reminded me of a Bantu woman I'd heard humming to the child on her hip while she queued at the clinic.

Jackie was asleep with her cheek against the back of the seat. I took my eyes off the road just long enough to watch a piece of her hair slip out of a kirby grip. The strand swung back and forth to the sway of the truck. I shook my head at the bruised circles beneath her eyes. She was trying to handle it all, and as much as I hated to admit it, her unhappiness over the time I'd been away from home was wearing on her. She acted tough most of the time, but every now and then she'd let down with me, like the night I fell asleep in the tub. Not much of a homecoming for her. I've done a bang up job of throwing her life into a tailspin. Bloody hell of a situation for her. She's handled most of the changes pretty well, but not the loneliness. It's eating away at her, and it's why she throws herself into work like she does. I just hope it's enough for now, at least until I can figure things out. It has to be.

"Where are we?" Jackie opened one eye and squinted.

Her hair was flattened against the side of her head where she'd laid against the seat. The darkness beneath her eyes made her look like that painted Geisha doll I bought her in Chinatown before I left the States. I told her we still had a half hour or so of driving before we got to Baragwanath Hospital. She scooted across the seat, settled herself against me and fell back to sleep. The thought of taking Jackie anywhere near the slum areas and having her deal with people who weren't going to like her because her skin was the wrong color made my skin crawl. I might be tempting the Gods, but I'm selfish enough to want her with me.

I drove around the dozens of people unloading at the bus station across the street from the hospital. The area was a mecca for booth vendors hawking everything from cigarettes, soda and fried bread to herbal cures and voodoo trinkets. There's so much superstition. I couldn't begin to count how many patients had come in after some witchdoctor had filled their tuberculosis ridden lungs with his magic medicine smoke. I know there are cures that defy the odds, but I'd take my medicine over theirs any day. Jackie was awake, scowling out the window at a bucket of intestines one of the vendors was selling.

"Chitlins," I said. Her look turned suspicious. "Chitterlings actually. Hog intestines." Jackie's nose wrinkled. "It puts a real funk in the air when they're cooking. They're also the reason some of these people are here. They don't properly clean them before they eat them, causes a yersinia bacteria infection that acts like an appendicitis attack. Wanna try some?" I grinned like the Cheshire cat.

"Keep driving, Kincaid, and remind me to pack a lunch next time," she said.

Jackie grabbed her notes and camera and followed me into the hospital. In admissions, there were the usual lines of sick people, and as always, the gunshot and stab wound victims, and worst of all, the ones who waited too long for us to help them. The orderlies put red stickers marked "Urgent" on their foreheads and pushed them in wheelchairs or raced them down the hallways on gurneys. I always hated the sound of the orderlies yelling to clear the way. Jackie was snapping a picture of the footprints and colored lines painted on the floors to direct people. It's practically always a mad house.

"Dr. Will, can you take a look at this?" one of the nurses asked. "His name is Kwekwe." I glanced at Jackie, but she was already busy taking notes. A man on a stretcher was moaning something about being bewitched. I'd bet this fellow had already been worked over by his local witch doctor. When the sangomas' cures didn't work, the disease was blamed on a curse or a spell. That was my department – curing curses and spells. A bloody froth was bubbling from the man's mouth, and he was shaking with fever and chills. He rolled to his side and vomited on the floor. I couldn't understand what he was saying. His bruised-looking skin was a classic symptom of meningitis, but I needed to be sure. I told the nurse to move him into triage and get me an LP tray so that I could tap him. I caught Jackie's eye and pointed to the patient. She gave me a go-ahead nod.

The man continued to thrash, so I signaled two passing orderlies to help hold him still. When we sterilized his back with saline, I saw the marks, straight lines radiating out from the spine. It was a witchdoctor's work. He was marking the site of the sickness. I had seen the scratches more than once. In fairness, I had to admit, more often than not, the spot the lines radiated from was the site of the problem. There was also a slash across the spine – probably to let out the "bad spirit." I looked closer. The draining cut had barely missed slicing through the vertebrae. The man started screaming and lashing out at us. His writhing was making it too dangerous for me to insert a needle, especially near his spine. I'd have to sedate him, maybe inject some pain killer, too. I asked one of the orderlies to translate for me.

"I'm Doctor Kincaid. I'm going to remove some fluid from your back to find out why you're sick. I'll give you medicine to relax you and keep you from feeling pain." The man's eyes were dazed, but some quirk of his mouth made me think he understood. When he was sedated, I inserted the needle, gently moving around the spinal bones until I felt the telltale pop of the epidural layer. The spinal fluid was cloudy, a pretty clear indication of bacterial meningitis. And that wasn't good news. I bottled the fluid and sent it to the lab for analysis. Kwekwe was going to be with us for a while.

I looked for Jackie after the procedure, but she was nowhere in sight. I put in an order for the medical supplies I needed for our trip and went looking for her. A couple of corridors away, I saw a camera flash and found her, pen and paper in hand, questioning Stan Wickerling, an intern on rotation. Stan was monitoring about a dozen men who were lined up in chairs, intravenous chest and abdominal tubes draining fluids into bottles at their feet. Most of them were in a dozed slump. Jackie was frowning at Stan.

"You mean all these wounds are from fighting each other, and you see this many new victims every day?"

"Well, not every day, but sometimes more than this show up." Stan shrugged.

Neither Stan nor I could count how many fight wounds we'd

treated. Friday nights were the worst. For most working people, a weekend was a welcome relief, but in the ghetto, it was a reminder that there is no relief. When Jackie saw me, she shook her head and gave me the same incredulous stare she'd been giving Stan.

"I know," I admitted. "It's difficult to understand, but crime's the brother of poverty. More often than not, it's why there's a Joe Bloggs in the morgue." Jackie frowned.

"Oh, you mean John Doe," she murmured after a moment.

Maybe this trip was a good idea after all. Maybe Jackie would understand the hopelessness that fed these people, and how nearly insurmountable helping them was going to be. "I think we'd better get going, lass," I said, taking her hand. Her fingers were icy. Before she could answer, one of the wounded men started yelling, clutching his chest and waving his fist at her.

"He is saying she cannot put his name on her paper," the black orderly translated. "He is worried the police will take him to jail, and he will never see his family again."

Jackie shook her head, "Tell them I won't use their names. Tell them I'm trying to help them, to let people know how difficult their lives are."

While the orderly translated, I tried to explain to Jackie that the men didn't fight each other to prove who was toughest. They fought because they were angry and frustrated. They were beaten down by the white man, and so they beat on each other to fight the injustice.

Another man starting yelling. He jumped up from his chair, one hand over the draining tube in his chest. He started toward Jackie, dragging the bottle his lungs were filling behind him. I took the writing pad from her and ripped out the sheet of paper, tearing it in several pieces. I handed the pieces to Stan while the orderly wrestled the man back into his chair. I put an arm around Jackie and headed for the door. When we were half way down the hall, she stopped and glanced up at me with frustration. I took off my glasses and looked at her. After a moment, her shoulders slumped.

"Well, at least you didn't throw me on a gurney and roll me out. I'm sorry, Will. I didn't mean to upset the men, but did you have to tear up my notes?"

"This is exactly why I was concerned about bringing you," I told her. "You don't understand these people, Jackie. Wounded or not, they're dangerous. Poor or not, they have pride. They'll fight anyone who threatens that. Writing about their gang wars and drunken brawls is only going to make it worse for them."

"I understand that, but I can't help unless I know what they want – what they need."

She was right. The blacks' struggle for independence was complex at every level, from the ghetto to parliament, and no one really understood the misery except the Blacks. I saw it every day - the pain that was acted out in violence. And that pain was the key to understanding why they landed in emergency rooms, and why some of them, more each day, risked protests that ended with their bodies beaten into bloody messes on some dusty road. But, while Jackie was figuring it out, and whether or not I had the time or energy, I needed to keep an eye on her. She had a way of getting into the middle of things and sometimes finding herself dangerously caught up in them. I'd be glad when this trip was over, and I could only hope she'd write her story and move on to something else. I handed her writing pad to her with the page of notes she'd taken still attached. She saw it and squinted at me.

"I'm on your side, love," I reminded her.

We decided to stay the night, and spent it in a small stucco building adjoining the hospital. It was the housing for the doctors who were on circuit to the clinics. The walls were paper-thin, but we were too exhausted to care about the lack of privacy. Shortly after midnight, Jackie started talking in her sleep, mumbling something that sounded like "empty rooms." I pulled her against me, and it was then I noticed how thin she'd become. All I wanted to do was protect her, but I was afraid I wasn't going to be there when she needed me most.

Chapter 2

Soweto -- Jackie's Notes

The notes were on the bed by the clothes she'd laid out to wear before she got in the shower. I took them to the window where the light was better.

Across the road from the hospital is Soweto's ghetto of multicolored wood and cardboard houses. They dapple the land like a patterned quilt of flotsam and jetsam, floating over and around the hills. The oddly shaped pieces of corrugated iron that act as roofs are held down with rocks, weathered crates, broken televisions and even rags. Some of the shacks are little more than lean-tos, the open side held up by a single board. With little to no electricity, the insides of most homes disappear into darkness. Battered grey latrines stand like weary Civil War soldiers at the outer corners of the sagging neighborhood.

What differentiates each house, are the aromas. Wafting against the buttery corn smell of mealie bread is the damp stank of human sweat. Two doors down, I have to swallow to stop the nauseous feeling brought on by rancid frying meat. Strangely, the sharp and acrid odor of wet dirt, where someone has dumped water, quiets the queasiness.

A large, rusty truck has found its final resting place between two leaning houses, which look as if they would collapse without it. There are curtains of a sort draped at each side window of the truck, and from its slightly rocking motion, I assume the owners are home. Down the dirt road, worn and just-washed clothes hang on a line strung between two roofs. The slight breeze that blows through them brings the smell of dirty water. A heavy set black woman in a white dress squints into the sun and glares suspiciously at me, her slightly open mouth exposing pink gums. (I am suddenly aware of my brace-straightened teeth.) A sickly-looking tree ekes out an existence among the shanties. It casts scant shade against the hot sun.

I feel like I'm spying on Jackie, but I figure the more I understand what she's after, the better I'll be able to protect her.

Chapter 3

A Mark Twain Lesson

After breakfast, I packed what was needed to set up a medical station in the Soweto neighborhood. Even though the hospital was so close, most of the residents didn't come for immunization or medical help. Once a month, the hospital reached out and set up a day clinic. Jackie, Stan and I wound our way along the outskirts to a small, deserted lean to that was left empty, or at least deserted for the day whenever we came. We kept our hospital bags visible while we moved through the dusty alleys so the coloreds would know who we were. I knew from past experience that word would spread within minutes, and most likely there'd be a long line before we arrived to set up.

Jackie was good with the people. She smiled a lot and tried to pick up some of the language. The people found her efforts funny, but she was a good sport. She seems to have an innate sense of their sicknesses and hurts. She'd make a good nurse or even a doctor. That'd make things easier for us, but she's a journalist born and bred.

At the end of the day, it was hard to tell the people still waiting that we were out of medicine, but the fading light made it impossible to keep working anyway. A man I'd treated earlier returned just as we finished packing the few odd supplies left over. I remembered him because he'd carried his four children, a pigeon pair on his back and a cute poppet in his arms. The littlest, clinging to his leg, rode on his foot. The kids all had colds and runny noses, and they all looked scared to death. When the man got to the head of the line, he carefully unwound each child from his body and lined them up.

Not one made a peep while I vaccinated them. And now here he was again standing in the doorway looking nervous. I started to tell him we were out of medicine, but he shook his head.

"Ah'm Amzie. You giv' medicine to my chilen." He shifted his weight. "I come tuh invite you to mah home fo' dinnah," he said as formally as if he were issuing an invitation to a state function.

I wasn't too keen on being in the ghetto at night, but the people, for the most part, knew me, and the hospital was just across the road. Besides, it was unusual for these people to allow whites into their homes, and Jackie was eager to learn more about them, so I accepted. We returned our medical equipment and then went back to our room. After a quick shower and change of clothes, I found Jackie ready to go, still wearing the pants and blouse she'd worn that day.

The man's house sat near the fringe of the neighborhood. Its wooden walls were covered with faded, flaking blue paint, and the corrugated metal roof was tied down with rope wound around stakes pounded into the ground. Inside, the tiny house was worn and sad looking, but looked clean enough for me to operate. The pigeon pair sat against the wall playing a board game on the frayed carpet. A handmade blanket covered the worn couch, and a baby was asleep in a small crib. Several pictures, including the wedding picture of the man and his wife, hung on the walls. Dinner was served on a rickety-legged table covered by a bright red and yellow oil cloth. I could see Jackie mentally cataloging it all as she greeted Pearl, Amzie's wife. She offered to help with dinner, but the woman wouldn't let her, so she headed to the corner where the children were playing. She sat on the floor beside them trying to figure out the rules to their game. When the meal was ready, the children rushed to the table, but were told to wait until the guests had been seated. The meal was simple to us, but I knew the family would have less the following week.

Pearl set a bowl of chitlins on the table, a special treat meant to show their appreciation. I smiled at Pearl and passed the bowl to Jackie. She paled and looked away for a moment. I touched her foot with mine.

"Looks wonderful," she said. "I'm just so tired from the long day, that I'm not really very hungry."

"Then a little good food is exactly what you need," I told her, tapping her foot again. She stiffened and smiled, then took a small chitlin and put it on her plate. She kept the smile on her face while she chewed. She swallowed and took a deep breath. When there was only one chitlin left, two of the children reached for it. Pearl slapped their hands away and offered it to Jackie. The gesture wasn't lost on her. She colored, but she took the chitlin and ate it while the two children watched.

We didn't speak on the way back to the hospital housing. I thought at first she was angry, but the drooping set of her shoulders told me something else was brewing. She made it as far as the door to our room, then stopped and turned to me. I opened the door and pushed on the small of her back. It wasn't until that moment that I realized how angry I was, which was probably why I didn't see that Jackie already knew it. Spending countless hours with these people, healing them, trying to give them hope, whatever gap I'd bridged, she done a good job of destroying. I closed the door, and then the dam burst.

"You couldn't have made Pearl feel any smaller. She was putting food in front of you that meant her children would have less to eat next week. You still don't get it, Jackie. Amzie and Pearl welcomed *white* people into their home. They had to face their neighbors' wrath to do that. Do you know how many white people are invited into the ghetto? Practically none, but you managed to fix that tonight. I'd say the average now is a resounding zed. You insulted a good woman and embarrassed me." Jackie's face collapsed, and the look will haunt me until the day I die. But I went right on with my tirade. "You say you want to help these people, to show the world how beautiful and strong they are. Tonight you proved you're as prejudiced as the next guy. How can you fight the fight against imperialism and be an imperialist? You think I don't know why you didn't change into clean clothes tonight? You didn't want to get their dirt on you."

Jackie didn't wipe off the tear that rolled down her cheek. She just picked up her jacket and left, closing the door quietly behind her. I sat for a moment fuming, but I didn't want her out there where it wasn't safe. I headed outside, but she'd already disappeared. I checked the truck and the area around the clinic and finally found her inside the hospital sitting near a coffee machine. I sat down beside her. It was a while before she said anything, and when she did, it wasn't much more than a whisper.

"I've been trying to convince myself that what I did was justified – that it even made any sense. I tried thinking bacon, bacon, bacon what's the difference anyway – oh yeah, life threatening bacteria. A little medical knowledge is a very dangerous thing, you know." She gave me a self-deprecating smile and hugged the jacket in her arms. "You're right, Will, I am a phony. I thought I could understand these people, write about them, make other people understand." Jackie sighed and shook her head. "Huck Finn," she hiccupped and blew her nose on a wad of tissue in her hand. "He ..."

"I know who he is, Jackie honey," I said.

"I'll never really understand, will I?"

I put my arm around her. "Neither will I."

"I'm sorry, Will. Maybe I should take what I have and write this story from home."

Home - we looked at each other. I'm not sure either one of us knew where that was anymore.

Chapter 4

Panic

Jackie was still asleep when I headed to hospital the following morning. I wanted to wake her and find out what her plans for the day were. After last night, I was pretty sure she wouldn't be organizing any peaceful protests, so I left a note asking her to come to hospital as soon as she got up. I could only hope, for once, she'd do as I asked.

There were more patients than usual. The line wrapped through the corridors and overflowed into the front of the hospital. When I finally glanced at my watch, I was surprised to see it was early afternoon. I managed a break about a half hour later and headed back to our room. The bed was made, and our clothes hung on the door hook, even the stack of medical journals I'd brought were stacked neatly on the bedside table, but I wasn't surprised that Jackie was gone and so was her notepad and camera. I picked up a medical article I'd brought with me to read, and then slammed it back on the table. It was nerve-racking not knowing where she was. I should never have agreed to bring her along. I didn't have time to go searching for her and was about to return to hospital when the door flew open and Jackie came in, arms loaded with flowers and packages. She saw me and started.

"I thought I'd take these ..." she glanced at the gifts and shrugged. "Will you come?" she asked with half painful eagerness.

"Not this time." I'd fought for her twice, and I'd fight for her again. But I wouldn't spare her this. "As soon as I can take a break, I'll walk you over and wait for you."

The afternoon was filled with emergency cases – a serious head wound, a small boy unconscious from malarial dehydration and two burn victims. My time was spent moving between operating theaters, and when I looked outside again, it was dark. I checked with the nurses, but Jackie had not stopped by or left a message. Worried, I left in my operating clothes.

Our room was empty except for Jackie's blouse, pants and knickers that lay crumpled on the floor at the bottom of the bed. There was blood on them. Grabbing my coat, I headed out to look for her. I asked everyone I passed if they had seen a young white woman fitting Jackie's description. No one had. I began to worry that I might be sending out a signal that a young white female was alone somewhere in the area. I kept pushing at the fear – the thought that was nagging at the back of my brain. Jackie had taken the flowers and packages to Amzie's house. I had no choice but to search the ghetto. The sweat ran down my face, soaking the neck of my scrubs. I skirted the neighborhood, glancing down the alleys and then headed toward Amzie's house hoping he would help me search. I was furious with Jackie and swore when I found her there'd be some serious changes, starting with a discussion in which I would be the only one talking, and then she was heading back to Johannesburg. If something had happened to her… but I didn't want to think about that.

I found Amzie's house and knocked on the door. He answered, but wasn't surprised to see me. The right side of his face was cut and his eye swollen.

"You get the message I lef' for you at hospital?" he asked.

"What message?" Before he could answer, I blurted out, "I can't find Jackie."

"She was heah," Pearl said coming to the door.

"When?" I asked.

"Sometime afer lunch," she said pointing to several items of food and a bouquet of flowers. I should have known Jackie wouldn't wait for me.

"Did she say where she was going when she left?"

"Tuh see you at hospital."

"She never showed up. I found clothes with blood on them in our room. Was she hurt?" They stared at each other for a long moment.

"Ah think you better come in," Amzie said, and stepped aside for me to enter.

He told me that Jackie had come to his house with gifts. She stayed to visit. Shortly after she left, they heard several loud voices arguing – men calling out to each other to fight. They heard a woman scream, but weren't sure it was Jackie. Amzie said he would stay indoors and close the windows when these types of fights began, but because he feared for Jackie, he called to a neighbor and the two men rushed down the street to see what was happening. When they were near the loud voices, Amzie and his neighbor could see Jackie crouched behind a pile of empty crates. Three big men from outside with clubs and guns were about thirty feet ahead of her, headed straight for where she was hiding.

My mouth went dry, and I could feel the sweat under my arms drenching my scrubs. "Did you see if she got away from them?"

Amzie continued, determined to tell the story as it happened. Jackie, he said, was looking around for a way to escape. When the men spotted Jackie and started to get rough with her, Amzie and his friend tried to stop them.

"Then what?" I demanded. If something bad had happened to Jackie, I wanted him to just say it and get it over with so I could get to her.

Amzie frowned. "Da men, dey beat us bad. Dey lef' us in da street. I didn' see Jackie afer dat."

"Amzie will help ya fine yer wife," Pearl said placing a hand on her husband's shoulder.

We took off running. I wanted to check our room again. Jackie hadn't returned. I headed to hospital hoping she was there waiting for me. She wasn't, and there were no messages, except the one I hadn't received from Amzie.

"Ah go ast mah friends ta hep search," Amzie said.

"I'm coming with you."

"No!" It was emphatic. "Today, you a doctuh from hospital, but tonight you a white man in a black ghetto."

Since he couldn't change my mind, he insisted that I wait at his house. On the way there, we stopped at the homes of four of his friends who agreed to help us search. I insisted again on going with them, but they wouldn't allow it. They said it would make trouble for them, and I would be in danger. I waited at Amzie's house crazy with worry. An hour later they returned but hadn't found any sign of Jackie. I was nearly sick thinking what might be happening to her while I was sitting there doing nothing. I had to find her. I headed back to check the room once more, and then call the police.

Chapter 5

The Mind's Labyrinth

I saw the light from under the door the minute I entered the hallway. Half mad with worry and half scared out of my wits that she wouldn't be there, I yanked the door open. Jackie was sitting on the bed hugging her knees and staring at the curtains that covered the window. Her lack of acknowledgement to my noisy entrance sent a chill through me. Still breathing heavily, I walked slowly toward her and sat down. I could feel her shaking through the mattress.

"Jackie?"

Her head turned slowly and she looked at me with a vacant stare. I shook her gently, and she seemed to come back to herself. "Will." It was barely a whisper.

"What happened? Where have you been?"

"I thought…" she started, then turned to stare at the curtained window again, like she was watching for someone or something. Her elbows were both scraped raw, and bruises like fingerprints were on her arms and her neck, a smear of blood on her cheek.

I tried to take hold of Jackie's hands, but she only tightened the grip she had around her knees. When I brushed the hair off her forehead, she jerked away from me. I started talking quietly, slowly repeating the words, "You're safe here, Jackie. It's all right." She cringed whenever I made the slightest move towards her. I kept thinking about what I'd put her through these last months. The shaking increased until her knees knocked and her skin was covered in goose flesh. I wanted to get her to hospital where I could at least give her something to calm her, but I didn't want to try to move her just yet, and there was no way I was going to leave her to get the medicine. We sat like that, with me trying to calm her, for several minutes while Jackie shook.

I was a surgeon. I had reached inside my patients to remove what should never have been there, but this torment inside Jackie was a phantom agony I didn't know how to grab hold of. I thought it might help if I could put my arms around her, but when I moved to sit behind her and pull her against me, she froze. When her shaking started again, it was stronger. That was when I locked my arms around her and pulled her back against me. She fought me, twisting and turning, gasping to catch her breath. She tried to pry my hands apart, and in her panic, it was all I could do to hold on. I kept my voice low and told her over and over that she was safe, that I wouldn't let anyone hurt her. Then suddenly, her frantic struggling stopped. We were both panting from the exertion, and the sound filled the room. I waited several seconds before relaxing my hold. Jackie remained motionless for a moment longer, and then without warning, she rocked forward pushing her feet into the mattress and throwing herself backward against me. The unexpected force caught me off guard, and we catapulted off the bed. We hit the floor hard, knocking us both breathless, but it gave me just enough time to flip Jackie on her side so that we were facing each other. I threw one leg over her and grabbed her hands pulling them together between us.

"I won't let you go until you calm down," I said, hoping I wouldn't panic her any more than she already was.

"No. Let… me… go. Let me go," she hissed clenching her fists. Her twisting struggle was wearing red burns on her wrists, and she cried out in pain. I loosened my grip, but Jackie continued to fight me, stopping every few seconds to catch her breath, until at last, worn out, I felt the tension leave her muscles, and she collapsed against me. We stayed like that, her head drooping against my chest, her hands limp, until I was reasonably sure she would let me lift her to the bed. I lay down beside her and pulled the edge of the blanket over us. It was a long time before she fell asleep. When she did, she kept mumbling, but I couldn't understand what she was saying. She cried out, "No," once, and then started trembling again. I held her against me so tightly I was afraid she couldn't breathe, but it seemed to soothe her.

The early morning light was coming through the curtains when I woke with Jackie still asleep in my arms. My shoulders were stiff from staying in the same position most of the night to keep from waking her. When the sun lit the room, Jackie moaned and opened her eyes. Heavy-lidded, she looked at her surroundings as if she were checking for something. She started to move and then winced. I didn't know what to expect. Bloody hell, I didn't even know what had happened. I moved slowly and kissed the top of her head. She didn't respond. I was suddenly furious with myself for letting her come, and I was scared – scared that she might not come back to me. I didn't know what to do, so I just held her.

One of her hands lay open against my chest, and when she patted me, I nearly cried with relief. She pulled out of my arms moving hesitantly as if testing her body. I removed her clothes and put her in the shower. She just stood beneath the steamy water hugging herself. Whatever had happened still had hold of her. I got in the shower with her and started soaping her back. She didn't pull away from me, but I sensed that she was walking a razor sharp edge. On the one side was whatever had happened last night, and I hoped to God that I was what was standing on the other side. I smoothed the warm soap suds up and down her arms until she let them fall to her sides. I moved closer, not touching her, but close enough for her to sense the heat between our bodies. My eyes were burning from the soapy water that bounced off her shoulders. After a while, she leaned back against me, but when our bodies touched, she jerked, goose flesh rising on her arms. I gently turned her to face me. It was then I realized she'd been crying. There was no sound to her grief, but it tore at me like a scream. I kissed her face and her shoulders until she responded. Her kisses were urgent, and I could feel the knuckles of her clenched fists on my back. I picked her up and backed her against the shower wall and made love to her. She made no sound, only kept her arms and legs wrapped tightly around me and her head buried in my neck. When the water turned cold, I shut it off and wrapped her in a towel. We dressed in silence.

"We're going for a ride," I told her.

We drove for an hour, and during that time Jackie said nothing. I turned onto a dirt road that led to a park of sorts, an open area surrounded by brush and trees that was occasionally used for staff outings. I led her to a knoll of dry grass by a small pond where we sat with the cool morning sun on our backs.

"Tell me," I said, not sure at all I wanted to hear what she had to say.

She swallowed, and then in a halting voice like wind in dry grass, related the events of the previous night.

Chapter 6

A Two Way Street

"I wanted to apologize for being rude to Pearl and Amzie, so I took them flowers and some food from the market. I didn't have any trouble finding their house, but it was farther from the road than I remembered. When I left them, I must have taken a wrong turn and headed into the neighborhood. By the time I realized I was lost, it was getting dark. I asked two boys, who were playing kick ball between the houses, how to get to the hospital. They laughed at me. One of them called me a stupid white woman. I saw him wink at his friend before pointing to a small alleyway. I thought they were sending me the wrong way, so I turned to go back the way I'd come. They followed, running around me, kicking the ball and blocking my way. I tried not to let them see they were frightening me. And then I heard the cars and knew I had to be close to a road, so I headed in that direction."

There was a splash in the pond startling us both. I realized I'd been holding my breath, and my fists were clenched on the ground.

"I was so close to the road. I could see them crossing through the traffic. Three men. They were carrying clubs and guns, cussing and boasting about how they were going to hurt 'them.' I hid behind some old boxes, but they found me, and then Amzie and another man showed up. The three men… beat Amzie and his friend. I tried to run, but one of the men grabbed me from behind and shoved me against the wall of a house. They started… they were yelling, pulling at my clothes. And then, the door of the house opened and two big black men holding pipes came out. They told the three men to leave and a fight started. I thought I could run, but the light was gone, and I hesitated. It was so dark. I couldn't see my way. A woman stuck her head out the door of the house and signaled for me to come inside. I slid against the wall and ducked into the house. There was a young girl inside. The woman shut the door behind me and started rummaging around in an old chest. She pulled out a gun. I guess the girl turned out the lights then because it went dark except for the light of the fire in the stove. The woman pushed me and the girl into a bedroom at the back of the house and shoved a bed against the door. We could hear the grunts of the men outside and the thumps of their clubs. And then everything was silent. We hardly breathed, just waited in the darkness. After a while, after the men that lived in the house didn't come back, we knew, and we waited for the others to come after us. We heard footsteps, and then someone started banging on the bedroom door. I looked at the woman and knew from the look on her face that it wasn't her man, and that he and his friend must be lying outside hurt or maybe even dead. The three of us put our weight against the bed, but the men used their clubs to break the latch. They pushed the door open, shoving at it until we slid backwards. I felt the floor shudder when they came in – two of them."

Jackie swallowed and grimaced like her throat was sore. I wanted to touch her, but I was afraid it would distract her, and she wouldn't release the events from her mind. She wasn't crying exactly, but I could tell from the small gasps she made and from the look in her eyes that she was reliving the whole thing.

"I heard the girl scream and saw the smaller man throw her to the floor. He was moving on top of her. He was… The woman begged him to leave her alone, but one of the other men shoved her into me, and we landed on the floor. I could hear the girl… oh God, I could hear the girl begging the man to stop, and then she started to scream. I was so scared for her. And then someone was in the doorway again. It was one of the men from the house. His face was bloody, and he was covered with dirt. He jumped on the other man, and they hit the floor hard. There was just enough light from the doorway so that I could see a lamp with no shade lying on the floor near me. I grabbed it and backed up to the wall. The small man had... finished with the girl and came towards me. I knew what he was going to do, so when he got close enough, I jabbed the end of the lamp into his stomach as hard as I could. He doubled over, and when he did, the woman slammed him on the head with the gun. I don't know why she didn't use it, maybe there were no bullets, maybe she couldn't do it. The man fell to the floor and didn't move. The girl was whimpering by then, and all I could think of was to make sure the man didn't get up again. I swung the lamp as hard as I could on the side of his face. It cut him, and blood gushed out all over. He put his hand to his head and then looked at the blood on it. He grabbed my leg and pulled me to the floor. He was still bleeding, but he just looked at me and laughed. And then he started to... I was confused and it was dark. At first I thought he was trying to choke me, but it was the necklace."

Jackie reached up and took hold of the stone, rubbing her thumb over the carved symbols. Caught in the events of the night before, she took several short, erratic gulps of air before going on.

"I reached up to pull his hands away, but it was the cord that was choking me. The stone was caught on something. The man saw it and grabbed it. I could see its reflection in his eyes. I remember thinking how strange that was because it was so dark, and because he just sat there staring at it. I thought... "she paused and frowned, "I thought I heard people chanting. I think he heard it too because he looked around the room. The woman saw he was distracted and ran into the living room and picked up a piece of burning wood from the stove with her bare hands. She brought it back and held it against the man's back until his shirt caught fire. I could smell the burnt flesh. I didn't know whose it was. And then, thank God, some men from the neighborhood came. The woman told one of them to get me out of there. The man was angry. I'd caused so much trouble for them." Jackie made a little laughing sound that was no more than a huff. She shook her head. "He practically dragged me to the road. When he saw I was safe, he left. I went to our room, but you weren't there. I changed my clothes..."

Jackie stopped and looked up at me, apology written all over her face. My accusation after the dinner at Amzie's about her not wanting to get their dirt on her, hung in the air between us.

"It's not the same," I said. She looked down and pressed her lips together, and then went on.

I went looking for you, but ended up sitting in a corner somewhere in the hospital. I finally went back to the room. That's the last I remember until this morning." Jackie covered her mouth, and the hand trembled, bouncing against her lips. "It was because of me – what happened to that girl – to that family."

I gently pulled her into my arms, and wished I could absorb the memory of it because I knew it would live inside her forever. After a while, I realized I was the one that was shaking. I thought at first it was only because I was scared of what else might have happened to her, but it wasn't just that. I was angry – boiling with Jackie for putting herself in danger, but even more, I was furious with the bloody fucking men. Jackie could have been killed, and now she was blaming herself for what they did. I wanted to rip those filthy pigs apart with my bare hands. What was I doing helping these people? I thought of the black men who came by the dozens to hospital expecting me to sew them back together, their hearts and lungs slashed open by their own people. How many had I saved? All I wanted to do was take Jackie as far away from here as possible, away from the people she wanted so badly to help. But what she whispered next chilled me to the bone.

"I can still hear the three white men with the guns yelling at me over and over, "nigger lover, nigger lover..."

Chapter 7

Taking On

I returned to rounds the following morning leaving Jackie in an office on the second floor of the hospital. She said she needed to write it all down. It was as good a form of medication as any I could give her. For once, I wasn't worried that she'd take off, but that didn't stop me from telling the receptionist to call me immediately if she did.

The patient load was crazy. I managed to break free around noon and called Jackie to meet me in the doctor's cafeteria for lunch. She only picked at her food. When we finished, I told her the girl who'd been raped was here at hospital. Jackie paled.

"Is she . . . ?"

"She's shaken, but her physical wounds will heal. The doctors and her family will help with the emotional trauma." I covered Jackie's hand with mine. "I told her I'm your husband." Her hand slid out from beneath mine, and she crossed her arms and gazed out the window. "She doesn't blame you, love." Jackie slowly turned and looked at me with eerie calm.

"I blame me," she said.

Jackie spent the afternoon with the girl in her hospital room. She never told me what they talked about, or if they talked at all. I hope they healed each other's wounds a bit – the bruises that would never fade and the cuts that would never mend - the ones I couldn't see.

The emergency room was a mad house for the rest of the day. A bus had lost its brakes and hit several pedestrians. One of the injured was a young black woman who'd been crossing the street with her baby straddled on her back. The woman tried to shield the infant boy, but she was thrown several feet and brought to hospital with broken bones and internal bleeding. The child had a concussion and would have to be watched throughout the night. The bus driver, a big, heavy fellow, was close to hysteria when they brought him in. As I was giving him a sedative, the emergency room doors suddenly flew open and the injured woman's husband, a tall, thin black man, rushed in screaming her name. When he saw her lying on the gurney hooked to an intravenous drip and oxygen, he spun around and grabbed me by the shirt, demanding to know where the driver was. There was no calming him down, but it wasn't hard for the husband to figure out who he was looking for because the driver started crying and apologizing. The woman's husband lunged at him and started pummeling him with his fists. One of the orderlies grabbed the husband's arms, and I put myself between him and the driver. The rest happened so quickly I hardly had time to move. The husband yanked his arms free and reached over to a setup tray, grabbing a bloodied scalpel. Too late, I reached for his arm, but he shoved me, throwing me backwards. The orderly and another doctor wrestled the man to the ground. I scrambled to my knees and saw blood on the floor near his arm.

"Someone get me a tourniquet," I yelled.

Blood was spurting onto the floor, and from the corner of my eye I watched a nurse grab the man's arm and inject it with what I assumed was a sedative. I pushed up his sleeve to check the severity of the wound, but couldn't find one. Slightly dizzy, I sat back, hypnotized by the rhythmic gush and spreading pool of red. The last thing I remember thinking was that the blood was mine.

Book Four

Chapter 1

A Distant Drumbeat

Jackie

A nurse told me the husband lost his footing when he wrenched himself out of the orderly's grip. The knife he was holding flew out of his hand and caught Will across the neck, nicking his carotid artery. One of the nurses had clamped her hand over the torn vessel until Will could be rushed to surgery. I waited outside the operating theater barely able to breathe until word was sent that the tiny rip in the artery had been repaired, but Will was in critical condition.

Will was barely breathing, and only the darkness of his hair kept his pallid face from disappearing into the crumpled whiteness of his pillow. The ashen skin of his hand was cold and hard, and I meant to warm it, but my own hands were like ice. I clamped them around his anyway, mooring him to my own resolve. Will suddenly wrenched his hand from mine, and I looked up in hope only to see that his entire body was twitching. He was staring at the ceiling as if in a trance, and then his eyes rolled up. His body stiffened and the hand I'd been holding flew sideways, the knuckles painfully pounding into my cheekbone and nearly knocking me off my chair. I threw myself over Will, pinning his arms between us, but I couldn't control his wild flailing and yelled for the nurse. Two arrived, and shortly afterward, the doctor on duty.

"We need you to leave now, Mrs. Kincaid," the doctor said, glancing at the heart monitor with its erratically jumping line and frantic beeping.

"Is he . . . what's wrong with him?" I gulped as the off-white curtain slid around Will, shrouding him from my sight. Another nurse carrying a tray disappeared behind the curtain. There were shuffling noises, paper ripping, the bed's wheels jerking against the floor.

" . . . outside . . . more comfortable," someone said, placing an arm around my waist and moving me toward the exit. Suddenly, I was alone in the waiting room. The sides of the chair I was sitting in felt miles away, and the cold of the empty waiting room made me feel small and helpless. My eyes were riveted on the emergency room doors that separated me from Will. Was it hours that passed? Someone offered me coffee. I don't remember who or when, it was just a memory of warmth in my hands. The doors opened at last and a tall, thin man in a pocketed white coat, a stethoscope around his neck, came towards me. I rose stiffly, and the now cold coffee I'd forgotten, spilled into a brown puddle at my feet. The man and I watched a moment as it spread under the toe of my shoe.

"Mrs. Kincaid?" I nodded.

"I'm Dr. Cranford. Your husband is sleeping. He's had a seizure, probably a reaction to the loss of blood and the length of time his heart stopped."

"His heart stopped?" The words came out, but my lips barely moved.

"I'm sorry. I thought you knew. His heart stopped from the blood loss before we got him to surgery. We don't know exactly how long his brain was without oxygen. It may have been three or four minutes. We won't know if there's any permanent damage until he wakes."

"When will that be?" I asked.

"He should come out of the anesthesia in the next 24 hours.

For now, we're watching him. He's comfortable. Why don't you go home, get some rest. Leave your number. We'll call you." It was what doctors always said in the movies.

"You said, 'should come out of the anesthesia.' What does that mean?" I wanted the doctor to say the right words – the words that would tell me that Will would be all right. But he was noncommittal. They would watch and "hopefully" Will would wake up.

Twenty-four hours. There were no windows to show me the day's progression, and the only clock was at the far end of the hall. I had to lean out from the little cubicle, release Will's hand, to see it. I wasn't willing to do that, so I sat beside Will's bed watching him breathe, watching the monitors and tubes that might as well have been attached to my own body. I had to go to the bathroom and was sure when I left that some unknown cold would seep into him and take him away from me. I nodded off once, my head resting on Will's side, and woke when a new nurse came to check the dripping tubes. I counted the hours and moments by the monotonous beeping of the heart monitor. And then, without warning, an eerie silence struck. My eyes flew to the monitor's lifeless line.

"No. No! Will, breathe! Breathe damn it! Breathe! Nurse!" Footsteps came running. I was pushed out of the way, and a machine with two large paddles rolled into our tiny world.

"Stand back!" someone shouted.

The curtain was open now, and I watched as Will's hospital gown was yanked from him. A clear gel was squirted on the paddles before they were placed on each side of his chest.

"Clear!"

And then the machine clicked, and Will's body stiffened and

arched, suspended somehow above his bed, dropping suddenly and heavily against the thin mattress. The doctor and two nurses waited, their eyes on the monitor. It refused to begin beeping, and within the breathless silence I could hear the scratch of the doctor's beard against his collar. The white line continued its careless glide across the screen, while a burning white furor built inside me. *Beep*! I screamed inwardly, *Beep*! But the unperturbed line remained lifeless.

"Clear!"

This time, I felt the stiffening of the electrical shock in my own body and the slap of the mattress against my own back. And still, the monitor made no sound, the lifeless line no jump. Unable to see Will's face from where I stood, I closed my eyes instead and saw his heart lying silently inside him. And then, like a whisper, my own heart reached out to his as quietly as a morning ray of sunlight. But its call to Will was as loud and jarring as a freight train pounding through a sleeping city. *Beat,* my heart commanded. *Beat with me… Beat…* The seconds passed as my heart called out its relentless cadence. One of the nurses glanced at me, and then looked away.

The sudden burst of the white line buckling and bulging upward startled everyone but me. Instead, I felt a jolt deep within, as if my own life's blood had broken through the banks of a blocked river and poured its warmth like spring through my soul.

Chapter 2

Between Two Worlds

Will's wound developed a yellow crust and remained red and swollen as a result of the infection he contracted from the dirty scalpel. The bacteria streamed through his system like a forest fire, and when the fever spiked, he would shake uncontrollably with chills, his blood pressure dropping dangerously low. He was sent to the tropical disease unit at Johannesburg Hospital where the type of infection could be confirmed and treated. The first few days were filled with tests, x-rays and antibiotics. The bloodied scalpel had given him a nasty staph infection. Fortunately there was treatment, but it was two weeks before Will was discharged and another three before he was up and around. I took as much time off work as I could, often escaping the office in the afternoons to be with him. We spent those quiet times strolling through town or the nearby park. I was sitting on one of the benches, Will's head in my lap one warm afternoon.

"When I was unconscious," Will said, his voice shallow and distant, "it was dark, and I was floating, drifting away from you towards… I don't know, something – a long room or a hallway. I tried holding onto you." He reached up absently and ran his fingers over my cheek. "But the hallway kept pulling me closer, and I got lost in the blackness."

"Did you want to go?" My words floated off.

He nodded. "It was fascinating."

"But you came back."

"Half way down, I thought I heard a drumbeat from a distant village, and it brought me back to you."

On the walk home, Will told me he was going back to work the following week. I knew it was coming, but it didn't make it any easier to hear.

"I'll work part-time for a while," he said.

"How long?" I asked.

"I guess I'll know that when I can stay on my feet after eight hours of surgery." When I said nothing, Will put his arm around me. "It's time we got back to our lives, lass."

"I was hoping this was our life," I said.

"We'll work now and save up for our old age, and then we'll sit in our rocking chairs with our lap blankets and talk about all the places I made mad passionate love to you." He smiled and kissed my lips. A sudden cool gust of wind blew against us, causing the fallen leaves to dance and scamper away.

Chapter 3

Last Night

Will had been back to work for a month when he told me he would be leaving in two days for Baragwanath. The dreaded day of departure arrived. Will made sure that his shift at the hospital was covered and made dinner reservations at the little Italian restaurant where he'd given me his grandmother's ring. At three o'clock that afternoon, I looked up to see Roy standing at my office door, his mouth screwed to the side. He shook his head and came in.

"I hate doing this, Jackie. It's Will's last night here."

"Then don't," I said.

"I need you in Cape Town tonight to cover the Langa and Guguletu killings. The ANC is recruiting. Looks like some of the students are exchanging their books for AK-47's."

"I can leave tomorrow," I said.

"It's news now. You have time to pack a few things. You're booked on a 6:10 flight." Roy kept his eyes on mine, "Sorry. I know this was a special night for you."

I called Will, and he met me at the apartment.

"Take a later flight, Jackie," he said.

I shook my head and kept packing. "There isn't one. I checked, but I'll be back day after tomorrow."

Will ran his hand through his hair and let out a long breath. "I need to tell you that I've agreed to set up a new vaccination program."

"Now? I thought you were on surgery rounds at Baragwanath."

"I am... first."

"When were you going to tell me, at dinner tonight - at this 'I'm going to miss you, can't wait to get back to you,' romantic dinner you set up? I think I'm the only one being set up here." I threw a blouse into my suitcase.

"No one's being set up. There's no one to cover rounds. People are dying, Jackie. I can't sit by and watch."

"And you're the only available doctor – is that it?" Will reached for me, but I backed away from him. In a single swipe of his hand, he shoved my suitcase off the bed. It hit the floor on its corner and the contents spilled. A single shoe rolled off. Grabbing me around the waist, Will pulled me onto the bed. Hurt by his willingness to leave again, I shoved at his shoulders, but he only brushed my hair back, searching my face as though he were trying to find the way to my understanding. After a moment, he lowered his head to mine and kissed me.

"You can make love to me, but it doesn't change the fact that you're leaving again," I said. A tear rolled down my cheek and caught in my ear. A tiny, salty sea.

"Making love will remind you who and what we are to each other. Nothing will ever change that." He took me then, and he meant to, but there was a giving and an accepting in it, a purging sadness. It was an act of abandonment for us both, and we lost ourselves in each other.

Afterwards, with nothing settled, he walked me down to the waiting taxi. When Will closed the door, he touched the window with his fingertips, leaving small imprints in the patina of dust. I watched the play of car lights against them all the way to the airport.

The following day, I was summoned to New York. I called Will. He was between emergencies and broke free long enough for me to tell him that there was an air controller strike, and I was going to be in New York through the end of the week. I knew he was disappointed, but I could also hear his mind spinning new plans. Before the call ended, Will decided to finish his round at Baragwanath and then go straight to the vaccination setup site.

"After all," he said, "I'd just be alone in Johannesburg."

Me too, I thought - alone somewhere between two worlds. After we hung up, I wished I could slide to him through the endless wire that no longer connected us. As I turned back to my desk, the arm of my chair caught a stack of papers and sent them flying. I leaned over to pick them up and bumped my head.

"Damn," I muttered rubbing the sore spot.

I heard a shuffle and looked up. Roy was standing in the doorway, his hands in his pockets. I felt tears threatening, and the thought mortified me. I looked down to get hold of myself.

"Let me," he said, walking into my office. He grabbed the papers in one sliding movement and laid them on my desk. When I looked up, Roy was watching me, his head tipped to the side.

"Anything I can do to help?" The remark was too close to home, and I wanted space.

"Sure, double my salary and send me to a tropical island for a couple of months." But, nothing felt funny anymore.

"How does a great Hawaiian restaurant with no air conditioning sound? We can sit near the kitchen while they steam the rice." He smiled, but I didn't expect the sadness I saw reflected in his eyes.

"I'll take that as a New York 'no' on the salary, but then one out of two isn't bad. Humid weather it is."

Chapter 4

Souls' Apartheid

I flew back to Johannesburg to find that there had been three break-ins in our apartment building. The downtown crime rate was on the rise, and murders in the outlying areas were commonplace now. Prostitutes were setting up office on the street corners, and muggings occurred regularly, even to businessmen at all hours of the day. I added a second chain lock to the door and took taxis to and from work. But there was no denying that the slums were advancing towards Johannesburg like vines of ivy winding through the slats of a fence. Crime crept into the city like a pool of infected blood.

Will returned directly to the Johannesburg Hospital the following week bringing with him a young white boy who had contracted a parasitic infection. He asked me to meet him at noon in the doctor's lounge. At 12:15, he hurried into the room, kissing me briefly. He only had a few minutes before surgery. The boy's condition had worsened. His spleen was dangerously enlarged and needed to be removed. We spoke quickly, trying to fill each other in on all that had happened in the last week. Hardly ten minutes had passed when Will stood.

"Jackie, I'm sorry." He took hold of my shoulders and pulled me tight against him, his lips brushing against my ear. "I got a call from Baragwanath. They've had two dozen new cases of the infection the boy has. I need to go back and help deal with the outbreak."

"When are you leaving?" I asked, inhaling the smell of him. It might as well have been the sting of 90 proof alcohol the way it burned and bit me.

"This afternoon," he said.

"For how long?"

A nurse stuck her head in the doorway, "We're ready for you, Doctor."

That was the last time I saw Will in Johannesburg.

Chapter 5

Windswept

Over the next month, we were only able to reach each other by phone a half dozen times. I left messages, but was never sure if Will received them, although he called me twice from outlying towns. Our words walked around the important things, and our conversations were cut short by his demanding schedule. My own schedule rarely allowed the opportunity to travel to Baragwanath. It wouldn't have made much difference though, since Will was usually working with one of the preventive teams that moved from district to district.

It was no longer safe in our neighborhood, and a month later, I sent a letter to Baragwanath for Will, explaining that I'd let the Johannesburg apartment go, and that I'd moved some things into storage. I still had the New York apartment. After that, while I was in Africa, I stayed in temporary corporate housing. It was awful, and the only thing that kept the loneliness without him at bay, was work.

The weather was bleak the day the movers came. As each piece of furniture was removed, so were pieces of the life Will and I had put in place. As evening approached, I laid my key on the empty kitchen counter and closed the door behind me. While I waited for my taxi, I climbed to the roof one last time, hoping to feel what the vacant apartment no longer held. I peered at the pinprick rips of starlight spread across the sky and felt as though I were trying to peek through the curtain that separated our lives. The dry, cold wind whipped its iciness into my coat and scraped my bones clean.

I flew back to New York and put in sixteen hour days. I smiled and laughed, forcing it all, wishing I could stop feeling anything, wishing I could block the memories. I fell asleep each night on the couch reading and writing news stories, the television on low in the background for company. I often slept with the light on in case I woke in the darkness. I knew Roy was worried about me, but I sidestepped any conversation that sounded like it was heading towards how I was "handling things." There were days I could barely keep my head up. The charade of acting as though I were fine wore on me, and I would secretly count the minutes until I could retreat to my apartment and stop the pretending. But the people I worked with knew. They tried cheering me up at first, but eventually gave up and left me alone. The only time I came to life was during an interview or when I was on camera. Roy suggested I take some time off. I panicked, knowing without the distraction of work, the memories would wash over me like thick tree sap, petrifying me in a solitary world. Roy was relentless, but I stopped accepting his offers "to feed me" or "get me out for a show or a concert." Work got me up every morning, and enough work helped me fall into an exhausted sleep at night. Roy finally insisted I take time off. I called the airport and bought a ticket to California, the one place I hoped would still feel like home.

My father was happy to have me back, but I saw the startled look in his eyes when he picked me up at the airport. I knew I looked drawn and pale. It was evening when we arrived at his house, and I was glad for the darkness and late hour. I crawled into bed and slept until nearly noon the next day. My father didn't ask any questions, just allowed me as much quiet time as I wanted. I spent it walking and writing, and sent a few articles to work. Roy called and told me that he had sent me off to rest and didn't want to see any more stories from me until I returned. I called a friend, but couldn't summon the desire to go out. A week later, the phone rang. My father was in his workshop, so I answered it.

"Hello?"

"Jackie?" Will's voice, so unexpected, caught me off guard, and an ache more ancient than Africa passed through my body. "Are you there?"

"Yes." The breath of the word swept my lungs like hot desert sand.

"I got your letter about letting the apartment go. I tried reaching you in New York, but they told me you were in California. How are you?" He spoke slowly, something more than exhaustion coating his words.

"Trying to keep busy – long days."

"It doesn't help," he said, echoing my thoughts.

"How's the medical program?"

"Sometimes I think we're making headway, and then I find out the things we teach are ignored." There was a long pause. "I don't sleep nights thinking about you." And like so many things we said to each other – it wasn't the spoken words; it was the silences in between.

I knew if I admitted my own feelings, I might begin a chain reaction between us. Our relationship was like a little red ball whose rubber cord kept pulling it back, only to crash against the wooden paddle it was attached to before bouncing away again.

Instead, "Where are you?"

"At hospital in Johannesburg. Just for the day," he added a little too quickly. I could hear the apology in his voice and fleetingly thought of trying to get to him.

"When will you return?" I asked. But the question was never answered.

"Jackie?"

"Mmm?"

"Come with me." And the ball crashed into the paddle again.

"There's no room for me in your world." My own words tore at me, and I squeezed my eyes shut to hold back a racking sob. It occurred to me then that Will rarely asked, not when he proposed, not when he wanted something from me. It was always a command. But now, there was no choice.

"I'd ask you to wait," he said slowly, "but I don't see the end in this." The finality of his words sliced me open, and what little hope I had left drained out into a pool of pain. This wasn't a battle cry for more time; it was an execution. There was a long silence before either one of us could speak.

"Be safe, Will," and then the line clicked and static filled the space between us. I almost didn't hear his last words.

"I'm not going to wake up some morning and not love you."

I knew what I was agreeing to give up when I accepted Will's second proposal. I went into the marriage with my eyes wide open. I bet on the dream. Maybe it was because there was more time to consider and less time to decide. Or maybe it's like my father once told me, you can't help who you fall in love with.

Our mistake was that we had only looked to each other when we should have looked ahead to a shared future. What broke my heart, and what was so hard to accept, was how we had found our place, and then lost our way. I only know that I do not regret one moment with Will.

Chapter 6

Return to Africa

I stayed two more days, and then called work and told Roy I was going to Africa, was going to take some time. He wanted dates, places, contact numbers, none of which I could give him. I hardly knew myself where I was headed. But I didn't need to explain things to my father. He understood, and drove me to the airport.

I don't remember the drive to Timbavati, only the last curve of the road as it came into view, and with it, the memories of our safari. They ripped through me, and I nearly stopped the car and turned around. But the past, with its beckoning fingers, drew me on. I didn't think I could stand the snapshot moments that flooded my mind – Will sitting next to me in the car, the sun-streaked twilight skies, and the protection of his body as we huddled together against the pelting rain. But stand them I must.

I pulled under a yellowwood tree and got out to watch the summoning wave of the wind-tossed grass. The gentle fingers of breeze played over my skin and wrapped around me like a lost caress. Even the heat prompted the past. I reached to wipe a tear, but the old scar in my shoulder cried out, and the tear fell to the ground, planting itself in the sucking earth. Another part of me would leave itself in this land.

In the distance beside a small house, a tall, Black man stood watching me. Except for a slow, single nod in my direction, he remained motionless, a dark statue against the vast, stabbing brightness. Drawn by a sense of familiarity, I went to him.

"Masuwra."

He said nothing, but turned, and I followed him to the house's green veranda. He gestured toward an ancient looking rattan chair whose faded cushion was threadbare. We sat in silence listening to the timeless tune of small insects buzzing around us. At twilight, Masuwra stood and headed towards the plains. Again I followed, body stiff and mind numb. We reached the edge of our savannah and stood side by side, looking into the endless vista.

"He is here," Masuwra said, his spread fingers moving in a wide, slow arc, "with the others who are called to sacrifice. It is how the land survives." His calm acceptance angered me.

"It had no right to take him," I said.

"There is no fault in the giving and taking of life." The wind swept through the grasses in assent.

"Yesssssss."

"And is my heartbreak a sacrifice too?" I asked bitterly. "If it is, I take it back. I don't give it." Masuwra's eyes slid toward me.

"Survival and death are inevitable. It does not matter if you are willing, Kabibi."

"I want to see him once more." Masuwra moved almost imperceptively, his eyes focused on what I could not see. "Take me to him," I pleaded, but he said nothing. "I only want to say goodbye." It was as close to the truth as I could manage.

"That is the way of your world."

And only then could I admit why I had come. "Please, Masuwra. Help me. Help me let him go." Masuwra continued to stare at the greedy land. I waited, wanting him to know I was strong enough to follow him on this final journey. At last he turned to face me, and his eyes looked into mine for a long moment.

"Sleep now. We will leave in the morning."

The animal calls only increased my restlessness through the long night. I slept in spurts, dreaming I could not find my way through the endless legs of the mother giraffe. I woke with purplish circles beneath my eyes, and my skin had taken on the pallor of a sun bleached sky. I took my small knapsack and was waiting before sunrise on the porch when Masuwra drove up in his battered jeep. His eyes held a trace of concern as he handed me a large brimmed hat, put the jeep in gear and headed northwest.

I don't remember when we left the main road, or when we entered the plains, but I do remember the cooling heat and the night calls of the animals that first evening. We traveled deep into the darkness among the peering eyes of unknown inhabitants. We slept beneath a lean to under the shelter of trees. Masuwra killed a small guinea fowl and roasted it over the fire. I wasn't much help, and I chided myself to shake off my melancholy. I wondered later why we had not brought food. I think Masuwra wanted me to understand the give and take of the land.

We found Will in a small village where scores of natives lined up each day to wait in the relentless heat for his white man's medicine. He was thin and bent over slightly from the long hours of work. His skin was darkened by the sun. A single, black nurse worked with him, preparing the medicines and caring for the doctor who was the only hope for her people.

Masuwra and I sat under a small grove of trees several yards from Will's medical tent, and watched for hours as he treated the endless line of sick who filed through. They stood quietly, leaning on each other, holding listless, fly-covered children. Their sunken eyes stared ahead to the small tent hospital. Will did not rush them when their turn came, but listened with compassion to their complaints and sorrows. He touched them, healed them, and when nothing else could be done, held them. He did not stop to eat or drink except for a few bites or a sip of water whenever the nurse insisted. She would occasionally mop his brow with a gauze bandage or bring a chair when he could sit for a moment.

Africa had selfishly lured him with the endless needs of her people. She shamelessly seduced him with her suffering, knowing his compassion for the maligned and his passion for healing. In return, she suckled him on the milk of empathy and endurance, strengthening him with them in order to devour his skill in her predatory quest for survival. Will had found the purpose for which he was born, and it consumed him just as the people consumed his short supplies of medicine. He would eventually be used up by this endlessly ravenous land. And just as her sun sucked the rivers dry, Mama Africa, in order to nourish and heal her children, would drink until the life force of Will's existence was depleted.

The African skies darkened, and the people still waiting were told to return in the morning. I watched as Will wearily handed a painfully thin, swollen-bellied child to its mother. He hesitated a moment and then turned and looked directly at me. He appeared to lean forward, opening his mouth slightly as if to speak. But in a parody of slow motion, his shoulders lowered and his head dropped. I knew that this was all the goodbye I was to be allowed. I don't know how long I continued to sit, stunned and shaking, before Masuwra stood and reached for my hand. He looked into my eyes for a long moment, and then we left the small plot of ground to which I had been as rooted as the tree that shaded it. And finally, like Will's gaze, which had so painfully pulled away from me, I released him from my life.

Chapter 7

Healing

I don't remember how many days or weeks I stayed with Masuwra. He taught me to be patient and still so that I might hear the song of the land and understand both its harsh brutality and constant sacrifice. I worked alongside him, no longer fearing the relentless heat, coaxing the soil to nourish the life we planted in it. Occasionally, a hurt or lame animal would come of its own accord, somehow knowing it was safe, and Masuwra would do what he could to heal it. Afterwards, it would simply disappear back into its savage and beautiful world.

We spent the evenings on the veranda, breathing in the heady plant essences that only release after the heat has cooled, and listening to the land and its creatures settling into their night time hunting and foraging. I would often sit long into the night, watching the stars as they traveled across the sky. One morning, I awoke with my cheek still pressed against the rattan of the chair to find Masuwra staring into the branches of a nearby tree. He spoke without turning.

"The nests are empty. The young have gone to find their own way."

Masuwra was right. I had said my goodbyes, and I needed to move back into my own world. Mine was not so different from Will's after all. Both were infused with torment and bliss, and each breath we took filled with the pain and ecstasy of who we are. When I returned to my room to gather my few belongings, I found a gift on my pillow – an intricately carved head of an African man. Masuwra had placed two honey gold gemstones in the eye sockets.

Before leaving, I lifted my face and accepted a last blessing from the African sun. As I turned away, I saw Masuwra in the distance, spear in hand, clothed in his native dress. He was honoring the crossing of our journeys. I nodded to him, and then touched my hand to my heart twice. The honor had been mine. Masuwra had not only shared the soul of his Africa with me, but he had also brought me back from the edge of my abyss.

Chapter 8

Flooding the River

Let your love be like the misty rain, coming softly, but flooding the river… Liberian & Madagascan Proverb

I spoke to no one on the plane ride home to New York, except briefly to the kindly older woman who sat beside me.

"Are you alright, dear?" she'd asked when the final vestige of the African continent disappeared from my window and my eyes filled with tears.

"I will be." I closed my eyes and gave in to exhaustion and a dreamless sleep.

With no baggage beyond what I had carried, I was cleared quickly through customs, suddenly finding myself in the crisp and familiar coolness of New York in spring. The realization that I'd made no preparations for my arrival startled me. What had happened to the girl who couldn't leave the house without makeup and business cards? She was standing here now, having traveled half way around the world with nothing but a change of clothes and a carved African head. I shook myself, trying to push back the heavy dullness.

I took a cab to my apartment. Roy had kept his promise to have everything taken care of while I was gone. The quiet emptiness was almost unbearable. How many months since the night Will had last held me in his arms – five, six? An eternity. I gently set the African head on my bookshelf, and ran my fingertips over the face. It was then I remembered the words Will's mother whispered to me the day we left for Timbavati.

"Some have dreams," she'd said, looking into my eyes, "but Will was born to his calling."

It felt good to take off my crumpled clothes. I put them with the ones I'd brought back in my flight bag. They were a small bundle. It was how my life felt – sadly small, a little heap of rags. I wanted to return to work as soon as possible – if I still had a job. I was suddenly frightened that, without it, I might break into tiny pieces of myself, little weightless shards that would drift off. How would I put myself back together?

First thing the next morning I called Roy. He asked how my time off had been, and how I was, and I think I told him I was fine. After that, he just said he thought we should talk. He had dinner plans that night and asked me to meet him in his office the next morning.

I was anxious, assuming from Roy's tone that the company no longer wanted me. But they did, and I was relieved. I spent as much time on assignment and at work as possible. I rarely spent time with Roy anymore, except for staff meetings and planning sessions, and assumed it was because of the young, pretty blonde I occasionally saw with him. And despite my desire to be alone in my grief, I was surprised how much I missed our talks and dinners.

And then one hazy and warm afternoon about a month later, the telegram arrived from Baragwanath. Will had contracted a virulent form of malaria – would I come quickly. I remembered how tired and worn he'd looked when Masuwra and I found him. Africa gave no preferential treatment, not even to those who served her well. When I found Roy in his office and told him I was leaving that afternoon, he stared at me and then stood and walked to his window. He gazed blindly, lost in thought. When he turned back to me, his eyes were stormy blue against the paleness of his face

"You shouldn't travel alone now. Let me go with you." The remark surprised me. We had seen so little of each other since my return.

"No. Thank you, but no. I'll be fine," I said, falling back into the old pattern even though I felt frightened and alone. Roy looked like he was going to argue with me, so I shook my head, afraid to speak because I knew he would hear the threat of tears in my voice.

"I want you to call me when you arrive." The words would have been an order except for the concern in his voice.

The last thing I needed was sympathy or someone to lean on. That was all it would take for me to fall apart. I bit the inside of my cheek so I could concentrate on the pain and forget the tears. But when my eyes betrayed me and filled, I looked away. Roy saw and came around his desk towards me. He walked past me and quietly closed his office door. Then he came back and pulled me into his arms, resting his lips against my hair.

"Go ahead – cry. No one will see you here." But I couldn't let go. I needed to be strong. I looked up, smiling with tight lips. Roy winced. "Don't be stubborn. Let me help you."

"I have to do this by myself." The words were an apology. Roy slowly released me and started to say something, then thought better of it and returned to his desk. He picked up his pen and turned his attention to the document he'd been working on when I arrived. I stood awkwardly for a moment, and then turned to go.

"Leave your itinerary with Rita," he said. I nodded and looked back at him, but he was staring at the paper on his desk.

Chapter 9

Ngikukhumbulile kangaka – *I missed you so much*

I found Will in the sterile hospital room, lying on sheets crumpled by the tossing of his fevered and frail body. The doctors and nurses smiled kindly at me, and then disappeared into the whiteness of the hospital. My heart could not reach Will this time. He had gone beyond, perhaps down the hall that had once beckoned and fascinated him. I stayed through the long hours, unaware of light or dark. Occasionally, the sharp sound of a machine's squeaky wheels, a sympathetic voice or a comforting hand on my shoulder would drift into my consciousness. But I easily slipped back into my world where Will's labored breathing, bouts of chilled shaking, and the weak grasp of his hand in mine, were all I cared about.

I was standing to ease the ache in my body when Will awakened. He saw me and smiled sweetly, and he was twenty-four again. With effort, his shaking hand reached out and rested against me as gently as the flutter of butterfly wings. I laid my hand over his, and knowing he did not have enough breath to speak, leaned over and gently kissed his lips. When I looked into his eyes again, I heard the final release of breath, like a well-loved burden set down, and saw the sparkle of a tear in his eye.

Will was buried in the vast openness of Africa on a rise overlooking a sloping valley. On that day, family, friends and colleagues stood on the windy hillside, but nothing touched me more than the countless Blacks, most walking miles carrying children, who came to honor the man who had been healer and hope to them. I was still standing by the newly turned earth when the sky began to color itself with night. It was then the feral growl echoed through the cooling air. I felt no fear, not even when I heard the footsteps and saw the green florescence of her eyes. The lioness was only a few yards from me when I started and my breath caught. She leaped in a glorious arch, and her massively clawed paw ripped through the air. She landed with the regal grandeur of a queen, her trim body silhouetted against the final warmth of the African sun. The savage eyes rested for a moment on the grave, and then she slowly turned and disappeared into the hungry land.

Chapter 10

End of Season

Roy was at the Johannesburg Airport when I arrived for my return flight. There was an anguished look in his eyes, and I didn't know if the wound was his or mine. I reached out a hand to him, and he grabbed me just before I collapsed. The feel of him, his warmth, his solidness and his presence, are all I remember of the return flight.

The time in Africa had pulled and pushed at me like a wind tunnel, ruthlessly buffeting me from one memory to another. I returned to New York exhausted. And although Roy insisted I keep the company apartment as long as I wanted, I moved to one of my own – a two bedroom place not far from the office. I opted for local assignments after that. It wasn't hard to manage since discrimination was hardly confined to Africa, and it was easy enough to continue the battle from New York. As the weeks passed, I knew I was spending too much time alone. It only fed the emptiness. I pushed myself to accept dinner and party invitations from friends and colleagues. But the nights out tired me and made me feel even lonelier. I had nothing to give. I called home on the holidays and made my excuses – I was busy at work, or an assignment had just come up. And like the blanketing of the winter snows, I buried my discontent, burrowing ever deeper.

On Christmas Eve, I was peering into the front bedroom on my way to the linen closet with an armload of towels and blankets, when there was an unexpected knock at the door. I left the linens on a hall table and found Roy on my doorstep, looking like a model out of some men's magazine, a cranberry scarf tucked into a long, tan wool coat. Above the slight smile were the familiar blue eyes. I inhaled sharply, staring at him until he finally asked if he could come in.

"Yes ... of course. Come in." I felt myself blush.

He looked at my glass of wine on the coffee table and the notes I had been taking for an upcoming newscast.

"Join me?" I asked.

By the time I handed Roy his glass, he had removed his coat and scarf and a package he had under his arm, and settled himself on the couch. He swirled and sniffed the wine, then took a sip and drew in a bit of air. "Mmm ... good," he said, nodding at me as if I'd finally managed to purchase a decent wine. Setting his glass down, Roy did a double take at my coffee table. He rubbed a finger over the finish and then glanced around the room, his eyes stopping at the little Christmas tree I'd placed near the window. He shook his head and grimaced. "You could use some furniture."

I frowned and ran a quick visual check on the room. The Christmas tree was a little on the small side, and the furniture was a little sparse, but it suited me just fine. And anyway, it wasn't like Roy had a degree in interior design. I shrugged off the remark and sat across from him. We chatted for a few minutes about work, the weather and the threatened doormen strike. There was a pause in the conversation, and Roy reached over to his coat and brushed something off the lapel.

"You ought to get yourself a new coat. Something nice like this," he said, running a thumb over the collar.

A fist of indignation grabbed me. I always made sure my work clothes were appropriate. No one ever complained about the way I dressed. Roy stood and wrapped his scarf around his neck.

"You're leaving?" I asked, surprised at the short visit.

"No. It's just cold in here. You having trouble with your heater?" Before I could answer, he slid the package he'd brought onto the coffee table. "Why don't you open this? There's a nice, warm scarf inside." When I didn't move, he squinted and asked, "Don't you have anything more exciting than this planned for tonight, Jackie? It's Christmas Eve." Out of the pathetic apathy I'd been wallowing in, came an unexpected surge of white hot anger.

"You just show up in *my* apartment and complain because you think I should be doing..." I shook my head and waved a hand in the air, "whatever it is you think I should be doing." I glanced at his bare ring finger. "And just exactly why don't you have something spectacular planned for Christmas Eve?" I hadn't felt this angry in a long time. Actually, it felt good to feel something. I stood, ready to continue my tirade, my cheeks no doubt a flaming red, but there was a smugly apologetic smile on Roy's face.

"I was pretty sure you were in there," he said.

"In here," I spluttered. "Where else would I be?"

"It doesn't matter, Jackie, just as long as you're back." He watched me, like a man not too sure the coffee pot isn't going to boil over. But I guess I looked like I was only on simmer, because he went right on. "Waiting for you to show up wasn't working, so I thought I'd get personal." I remembered the night I'd accused him of being too personal. Truth be known, I didn't so much mind it now. Roy was watching me, and the look in his eyes brought to mind his words on that long ago New York night. He had said he wouldn't stay silent forever.

"Well, there isn't much to be personal about anymore," I admitted.

"Don't kid yourself, Jackie. It was personal the day we met." He waited a moment, gauging the impact of his words. "But I was in an unfortunate marriage, and I owed giving it everything I had. And you – you'd been headed somewhere else for a long time. So I watched... and waited."

"Watched?"

"Watched you fill up your life with work. You've made yourself into a quite a journalist, Jackie. You're two thirds fearless determination." He crossed his arms and gave me a wry smile. I crossed my arms right back.

"Why do I not want to hear what the other third is?"

"Because it has to do with your take no prisoners method of getting the news."

"Well, like you said – I bring in the news – in my own way."

"Exactly." Roy raised one incriminating eyebrow, "Which brings me to the waiting."

"Well, if you're waiting for me to change – you know, 'old dog, no new tricks'."

"I've been waiting for you, Jackie." Static silence filled the air between us. Our eyes, his piercing and mine cautious, sparred in a language all their own, while the sand slid out from beneath my feet. I shook my head.

"You couldn't have known how things would turn out."

Roy started to say something, but changed his mind. Instead, he closed the distance between us in two steps. Stopping a breath away, he put his hands on the sides of my face and buried his fingers in my hair. "I won't tell you I understand the pain you've been through. But seeing you go through it was my own hell." He stared into my eyes, "I'm not asking you again to let me help you, Jackie. I'm telling you I'm here."

Getting through each day on my own was the only goal I'd had in a long time. And the days were jungles full of twisting trunks and branches, the light rarely making it through the canopy above. I looked away, and a little bedraggled laugh emptied out of me.

"I'm afraid I've lost myself."

"If you're lost," he said, "I'll find you."

Epilogue

The following week, I spoke to the curator of the New York Museum of African Art and set up an appointment to meet with him. I told Roy I needed an afternoon off, and spent it at my apartment carefully wrapping the pieces of art I'd acquired during my travels in Africa. Some, of course, I kept. But I wrapped those, too, knowing I would want to see them, hold them again someday. The curator, a middle aged man with a slight build, looked at each object with a circular magnifying eyepiece he kept in his coat pocket. He was pleased, and accepted several items. I was packing to leave, when a beautifully carved elephant, an old piece, started to tip off the table. I reached over and grabbed it before it fell. The curator's hand also shot out, and I thought he meant to help me catch it, but instead he pointed at my necklace. It had slipped out of my blouse when I reached for the elephant.

"May I?" he asked. At my nod, he cupped his hand around the stone that Will had encased in silver for me. I still rarely took it off. The curator stared at the unusual markings, turning them this way and that. "Where did you get this?" he asked, peering so closely that his hair tickled my face.

"In another world and another time," I whispered. He glanced up at me questioningly, but the stone called him back.

"I'm not positive…" He frowned and pulled his magnifying glass out of his pocket again. He studied the markings for so long that my back began to ache from trying to keep my nose out of his hair. He pursed his lips, rocking the stone in his palm, "Very powerful in the right hands," he murmured, and then in the voice of epiphany, exclaimed, "Of course!" His head popped up, and with eyes full of excitement, he told me, "It's a power stone. They were worn by African priestesses and used for healing and spells. I've only seen one other. This one is quite old." He smiled at me. "Do you have any idea what it's worth?"

When the museum and a collector both offered me impressive amounts for the necklace, I thought at first I couldn't part with it. But I changed my mind. Will had given me the stone, and it had protected me when he couldn't be there. Its job was done now, and I knew I needed to let it go. Masuwra had said that we must return what we never owned in the first place. I accepted the museum's offer, even though it had not quite been able to match the collector's. The stone, and all it was, needed to be shared, not locked away in someone's private collection. I had only one stipulation – if for any reason the museum closed or no longer wanted the stone, it was to be given to the Africana Museum in Johannesburg.

The money from the necklace was donated in the name of Dr. William Kincaid for vaccines and medical aid in South Africa. I kept a little aside to send to Amzie and his family, and to the family who had saved me that night in the ghetto. I wanted them to know they would always have a home.

Home – it had been an elusive phantom for me, one I had looked for, but never found during those years I lived between two continents. Africa's boundlessness and crying torment had stretched me and taught me that we are all brothers and sisters of the world. But while our real home is the connection we share with each other, we still need somewhere and someone waiting for us at the end of the day.

After that Christmas Eve, Roy reassigned me to another

division. "Conflict of interest," was all he said. When I went after a story, he gritted his teeth and kept silent, except for an occasional bit of eye rolling or head shaking. But I think he knew I chose the safer path more often. I found myself looking for him when some bit of unlikely news hit the air or something funny happened at work. If I didn't run into him in the hallways, or if I was out of town for a day or two, I could count on a phone call or open my hotel room door and find flowers. Roy was never more than a step away.

One afternoon when the memories came crashing back, Roy was there. When I saw my grief reflected in his eyes, I knew how desperately I needed to let go. We bundled ourselves in coats and scarves against the late autumn breeze. Roy tucked my arm in his and laced our gloved fingers together. We walked in silence until I suddenly came to a dead stop, and a sigh that had been imprisoned deep inside freed itself. It washed through me like a flood, and took with it the phantoms of the past that had clung to me with fingers of inescapable memory.

My love for Will had been the molten rock at my core. When we came together again, it erupted in burning brilliance and threw itself upon the hungry land. Lost in my grief, I had not realized that the rock had hardened and cooled and no longer burned me. But I was not left alone. I carried not only my own genetic story, but also the imprint Will had left within me. Like the mother giraffe that lost her child to feed the hungry cheetah, I knew that the love we shared would be born again, perhaps not in this lifetime, but in an endless tomorrow. I could breathe at last, and my lungs were filled with the sweetness of the air. My goodbye was no longer a farewell, but instead, a timeless journey.

Roy held onto me, his eyes reading the kaleidoscope of

thoughts and feelings swirling around and through me like a spinning carousel. I turned at last to look at him with the end of a long wandering in my eyes. His face was expressionless, but the question was there. Unable to speak, I nodded. My pain had eased with each footstep, gently dissipating on the path behind us. The constant buzzing in my mind quieted, and the recollections of the years with Will gently tucked themselves behind the unlocked doors of memory, settling into a peaceful rest. I was content now to leave them to their repose.

Startled by the small pieces of frozen lace floating down, we glanced up at the spiraling snow flurries. Roy tucked the ends of my scarf around my neck just as a warning gust of winter wind blew me against him and swept my hair across my face. Roy slid an arm around me before I could move away, and then gently ran the fingers of his other hand across my lips to remove the errant locks. The snow was increasing, whipping through the wind in heavy drifts, and I buried my face in his "something nice like this" wool coat. Roy turned to block the stinging wetness and tilted up my chin.

"You're home now, Jackie."

"And you're still here?" I asked. Roy smiled and brushed an errant flake of snow from my cheek with his thumb. He looked into my eyes for a long moment.

"There was never a time my arms weren't around you." The smile disappeared and a steely gaze that wasn't asking permission replaced it. "It's going to be a cold, snowy winter, Jackie. It's time we went in and kept each other warm." And then he lowered his lips to mine.

That was the night that changed everything. I understood now what Masuwara meant when he told me that love is like rice, and that transplanted, it grows again.

The day Roy and I stood inside our first home, I glanced

down the hallways. I didn't see the future and the past anymore. I saw only the present, offering me infinite possibilities. I turned to smile at Roy, but he had knelt down with arms outstretched to catch the small brown haired boy with honey gold eyes, who flew into his arms.